low
expectations

D0948016

Elizabeth Aaron is a fashion design graduate who has worked for Alexander McQueen, Jonathan Saunders and Givenchy. She moved to Paris in 2012 to write *Low Expectations* while working as a nanny. She is currently writing her second novel and first screenplay. She lives in Paris.

low expectations

ELIZABETH AARON

Quercus

First published in Great Britain in 2014 by

Quercus Editions Ltd
55 Baker Street
7th Floor, South Block
London W1U 8EW

A CIP catalogue record for this book is available
from the British Library

PBO ISBN 978 1 84866 699 3
EBOOK 978 1 84866 700 6

10 9 8 7 6 5 4 3 2 1

Printed and bound in Great Britain by Clays Ltd, St Ives plc

Typeset by Ellipsis Books Limited, Glasgow

For my darling sisters

The Deformed Lovechild of Kurosawa's Subconscious

October, Kingsland Road

People think that fashion types are a bunch of semi-articulate, cuttingly judgemental, oddly frocked, stiletto-wielding bitches that haven't eaten a potato since 2003 and think the Gaza Strip is a form of pubic topiary. Which is only half true. Loath though I am to admit I conform to stereotype, there is an element of perfectionism in my character. It is a necessary personality trait for anyone trying to make it in an industry where you must seriously weigh the relative merit of nearly identical buttons.

It is also the reason why I get on so well with Julian, quite possibly the poofiest poof ever to poof. He would take umbrage at this assessment. He has been known to turn down certain cocktails and clothing as 'too gay'. This, from a man who has the restraining order sent from Britney's people framed in his living room.

He waltzes into The Diana, a dingy pub on Kingsland Road whose walls are covered with an enormous collection of royal tat, looking like an Austrian prince – all slicked back auburn hair, thick moustache and waxed trench coat. Scanning the surroundings with an expression somewhere between bemusement and disdain, he catches sight of Rose and me squeezed into a corner table underneath a portrait of Prince Charles.

The crowd at The Diana usually consists of art students, a few confused foreigners and the taxi drivers whose depot is situated around the corner. Depressingly, from some of the conversations I've overheard at the bar, it seems a fair number of the taxi drivers started out as art students. There are times I distinctly regret not pursuing a more academic degree, as per my parents' wishes. Though I'm not certain how feasible a glittering career in science or law would be considering I never mastered long division and my spelling becomes more creative every year.

Julian has a low tolerance for people who don't conform to certain aesthetic standards. When he is not 'nesting' (his words) with his boyfriend Theo, he prefers to stay in the more reliably trendy enclave of Shoreditch House, which he never invites me to. When you reach the age where friends start to join members' bars, you quickly learn where you fall in their social structure. Luckily my taste runs to cheap, cheerful, dimly lit dive bars. Places where you can humiliate yourself safe in the knowledge that no one else will notice.

'Hey babe!' Air-kisses all around. As a teenager I used to mock people who did this; now it is second nature. If someone proffers me a hand I am momentarily destabilized, staring at it like a foreign currency. What to do with the hand? Lick it?

'Sweet Skinny Jesus, has the straight scene always been so . . . rotund?' Julian stage-whispers in horror, his eyes fixed on a man whose swollen belly struggles to break free of its nylon Manchester United prison.

'Julian, when was the last time you left the house? Rationing ended in 1954. This is the price we pay for an abundance of delicious transfats. Be grateful!' says Rose.

Rose is reading Bioengineering at Imperial, has logical and informed opinions on most topics and is able to support them with bafflingly accurate historical dates. In contrast, I have been known to second-guess myself about the current year on application forms. I also misspelt my middle name on my provisional licence.

'This is why I never go out! The shock gets worse every time. I have Permanent Traumatic Stress Disorder. I think it's the underlying cause of my eczema.'

He pushes up the sleeve of his coat and his eyes dart from his skinny arm, its bony elegance marred by a few reddish patches, to a man who could charitably be described as hideous, back to his arm again. Giving a little mock-shriek he cries, 'Look! I swear that one just appeared!'

'Julian, that's awful! Stop!' Rose laughs, throwing back her mane of untamed carroty hair.

Rose is a primary school friend I reconnected with during A-levels when begging for help (if plagiarism can be called that) on a Design Technology project. It was a subject I had chosen with design, not technology, in mind. She unexpectedly accepted my offer to pay her for her troubles with a box of my old shoes, which at the time I thought a sign of fashion desperation. I later found out they were accepted out of pity and donated to Oxfam.

I am less embarrassed about this reunion story than I should be and sometimes tell it to strangers at parties. Putting my best foot forward is something I can be counted on almost never to do, usually because said foot is rammed into my mouth. I figure if you present yourself as lazy and mildly sociopathic from the beginning, you can only improve with time. It's like being impressed by a film you thought would be awful but is unexpectedly amusing, versus the disappointment that can follow a critically acclaimed masterpiece of cinema. I call this 'stealth charming'.

Julian's lack of filter is mitigated by his jovial tone and self-mocking demeanour. He still gets told off for misbehaving a lot. As a fellow sufferer of taking the joke too far, I sympathize. The thing is, he doesn't mean it. Well, he does, but his intention is not malicious. Luckily, for the most part the people who chide him are laughing. He is a little bit too proud of having been slapped twice, though.

'But I think it might be true! My skin is very sensitive, darling, very discerning. At this rate if I ever want a beautiful complexion I'll have to move someplace Scandinavian. It's that or become a hermit. It will take an hour-long wank over Andrej Pejić to get over this exposure.'

'You say that as if it's not already part of your daily routine,' Rose says.

'An orgasm a day keeps the doctor away!' I add cheerfully.

I suspect this to be true, having not suffered a cold in some time. The late, great Mae West is a surprisingly good source of advice on health and love. It boils down to speaking your mind, wearing seven-inch platforms at all times, slathering yourself in baby oil and having as much hot sex as you can. How can you not admire a woman who inspired Dalí to design a soft furnishing in honour of her lips? I would personally hope for my legs to be immortalized in a giant coat hanger by Sarah Lucas. But I digress.

'Darling, as if I have the time! My life is work, work, work. The halcyon days of university when I could wank, let alone have sex, with impunity are but a distant memory. I barely see Theo these days. He thinks he's in love with a vampire. I only see him in the twilight hours looking like some sort of undead creature. I'm so pale and gaunt. Look at these shadows! It's lucky purple brings out the green in my eyes.'

Julian may speak with the air of an extreme narcissist, but he is actually very kind. An incurable romantic, hopelessly in love with his first and last boyfriend, he thinks Rose and I are terrible sluts. If I were a young gay man, I would be haunting the latrines of G-A-Y in a tiny mesh vest right now.

Have I mentioned that I'm single? The initial liberation of being footloose and fancy-free begins to pale after a while. Six months on from my break up and I still haven't met a single man who fits my criteria. Some women have endless lists of the qualities they are searching for in a man. He must be intelligent and funny, a bit cocky but not too arrogant. He will be tall and handsome, but not generically handsome. (Generically tall is allowed.) He should be available and loyal, but never clingy. He must like dogs and scorn fish. He will be employed but not a workaholic; sexual dynamite but not a player; he will read the same Sunday paper and be geographically convenient.

My list is as follows: he must be bearded and love giving head.

Only two requirements and I still haven't ticked them off! Even the beard is negotiable if he gives good stubble. Granted, I have been working crazy hours interning over the past nine months. Fashion spinsterhood is a common complaint amongst my peer group. Over the summer, I met exactly two new heterosexual men, one-hundred percent of whom I slept with. Hopefully now that I am studying again the situation will improve. The final year of university is not an ideal time for a manhunt, but you need to live life holistically. Regular sex is a vital component of spiritual nourishment.

'Sometimes I think about getting out of fashion entirely. I could become an actor or painter or something. I love my job but it's just so tiring,' Julian says dramatically.

Julian is the Assistant Womenswear Designer at Schrödinger's Cat. It's a relatively new brand built by Trigger Hunt, a Trustafarian of undeniable talent and fearsome pretentions. Trigger once had a thing with a hot young physicist and now feels that he holds deep insight into the mysteries of the universe. He uses this knowledge to great effect by running up expensive frocks and giving enlightened quotes on 'How Much Knitwear Is Too Much Knitwear?' to *Vogue*. No one working there, including 'Call-Me-Trigger-But-Don't-Look-Me-In-The-Eye Hunt', really understands the principles behind the name. Nevertheless, pseudo-scientific inspiration is drafted into the press release of each collection with increasingly tenuous connections.

An example: Spring/Summer 2013, which I assisted Julian and Trigger with, grew from a mood board of outer space into images of what Trigger imagined String Theory might look like. This process was achieved by an intern pinning and taping a ball of twine in different formations. These were then photographed and edited so thoroughly on Photoshop that they emerged as something else entirely. This synthetic web became the basis of some of the best prints in the collection as well as a silhouette story involving Samurai Warrior Shoulders and Crinolines (made modern by a clever use of Neoprene). This all sounds like the deformed lovechild of Kurosawa's subconscious and a wetsuit but was actually quite beautiful. It was heralded as a 'postmodern triumph of historical revisionism' by Style.com.

One of the benefits of working for a boss who is brilliant enough to put up with, but is also a crazed, entitled psycho-maniac is that you form extremely firm friendships with your comrades. In fact, I have found the belief that everyone is at one another's throats to be an unjust prejudice against the fashion industry. Certainly, a degree of hatred is inevitable during twelve to fourteen hour days, often including the weekends, in a hothouse environment of gay men, single women and the unpaid slave-children known as interns. But a mixture of hard work, team spirit, humour, hysteria and despair bonds people together effectively, for better or for worse, till burn-out or a better job does them part.

Our social dynamic has shifted when discussing work-related issues now that I've left to finish my degree. Julian is still there, toiling away, and I have defected back to the lifestyle of the carefree, petit-bourgeois student degenerate. I sense he now views me with a mixture of jealousy and suspicion.

'How is the new collection going then? I can't believe you made it out so early!'

It is 10 p.m. on a Thursday, early indeed.

'Oh you know babe, the usual. My day goes from boring to joyful to hellish and back again, sometimes all within the hour. Trigger went ballistic over a missing measuring tape in the fitting room today; I thought I might lose my job over it. The interns always fuck up the most menial tasks! I spend half my time looking after the daily grind of administrative and organizational shit, which I should be able to delegate. But I know from experience it will end up being so cock-eyed I'll have to redo it myself.'

Julian takes a pause in his rant to mutter, 'Not that you were like that,' before continuing.

'I can't wrap my head around some of the mistakes they make. Maybe they pretend not to understand because they feel it's beneath them. They all think they're the second coming of Gaultier and that they should be immediately promoted to doing design work. It's like, I've paid my dues to get where I am and so shall you! If I ask you to sweep the floor, sweep the floor!'

Rose gives me a look as if to say, 'They have to sweep the

floor?' I nod in a way that will dissuade her from voicing the question.

'At this rate my nerves will be shot by the time I'm twenty-six years old!' Julian continues. 'I'm probably going to join that list of famous people who die at twenty-seven.'

'Julian, the Twenty-Seven Club is for rock stars. You're not even famous.'

'I'm twenty-five, babe, give me time. Anyway, enough about work – let's talk about something else. Any men on the go?'

Rose launches into the post-mortem of a date with the unfortunately monikered Phil. It is a name that should be reserved for middle-aged accountants in Surrey, though he is a twenty-eight-year-old sound engineer squatting in Peckham. They met last Saturday in Camden. Rose was dancing on tables, which gives you an indication of how pissed she was; usually her moves are limited to swaying in a darkened corner. I lost her halfway through the night but she reappeared at closing time – that terrible moment when the lights come on and the filmy veil of hopeful delusion lifts to reveal a sea of heavily perspiring cretins.

Rose was being dry-humped on stage by a tall man whose face was entirely obscured by his sweat-licked hair. They exchanged numbers before I packed her off home in a taxi. In an act of sweet hope, sexual frustration or desperation (possibly all three) their initial drunken attraction met the sober light of Wednesday. It was essentially a blind date, as all she could remember about him was that he was probably white and had been wearing a trilby.

'. . . So, I was pleasantly surprised! I thought he'd be a minger, as that seems to be the only factor uniting men I've pulled lately, but he actually had a decent face and really nice eyes. He came on his Vespa though, so we didn't really drink, just had dinner and talked.'

Ick. There has always seemed to me an inherent lameness to a man driving a Vespa outside of the Continent. They require sun, café-culture and Italian sunglasses to be chic. In wet, grey England, a scooter is the clinging and tragic ghost of Cool Britannia. Vespa drivers make this vain stab at bad-boy mystique, all the while unwittingly driving the tricycle of the motorcycling world. I refrain from saying this. If a willingness to look like a reject from *Quadrophenia* is Phil's only character defect he is leagues better than her last boyfriend, Scrotum Mark. So-called because his name is Mark and he is a scrotum.

'Did you have good banter? Did he pay?' I ask.

To me, these are the two vital components of a good date. If a man is incapable of witty flirtation and generosity on the first date, these qualities will never bloom. I have had several flings with boring cheapskates who I managed to convince myself were the strong, silent, fiscally sound types. These men are also rarely good in bed. There must be a direct correlation between the number of pints a man is willing to buy you and his working knowledge of the clitoris.

But maybe the problem lies with me. I am apparently not an inspirer of impetuous, romantic purchases. My mother frequently reminds me of the wonderful holidays and presents she received from devoted lovers in her youth. My sparkling conversation has led to a grand haul of: three DVDs (two of them burnt). It should be said that these were not spontaneous gifts, but for my birthday. Nothing says, 'My feelings for you are tepid and cheap' like a copied disk in a genre of film you never had any interest in. At this point, a Groupon voucher would seem the height of decadence.

'Yeah . . . well, he paid. He was all right. He was wearing "Gap Yah" beads, though. At his age he should really know better. Plus he said he stole them from a Buddhist Temple in Cambodia. Bit of a twat in most ways really, but he was a good kisser. I'm hardly beating men off with a stick at the moment so I'll probably see him again,' Rose says with an air of mild depression, leaning her head in her hands.

'Don't bother, sweetie. You lost me at Vespa. He probably has a mod target tattooed on his chest. It's better to end it before you get attached. If he's good in bed you'll start to think his temple-thieving ways make him the next Indiana Jones. Look at Georgie, she's always giving things a second and third chance and then ends up in relationships with people who treat her like shit,' Julian says, his cocked eyebrow daring me to contradict him.

I wish I could dispute this, but that pretty much sums me up. Moral of my story: don't date out of boredom and never sleep with men out of mild curiosity (especially if they are known to their friends as 'Two-Minute-Michael'). The biochemistry of the orgasm is a cosmic joke whose purpose is to blind you and bind you. Usually to people whom, if they were your co-workers, you would avoid on public transport.

'It's not like I deliberately overlook bad behaviour!' I protest feebly, 'It's just that sometimes it's hard to know if someone is cruel or if they just suffer from severe honesty.' That sounded less pathetic in my head. 'Am I supposed to stay alone indefinitely? The last time I tried waiting for someone amazing all it led to was eighteen months of celibacy. I started calling my vagina the Batcave.'

Rose chuckles at this, while Julian looks repulsed.

'I really liked He Who Shall Not Be Named and I was miserable. Who else have I really been emotionally invested in? Alexi, maybe. God, that was a long time ago.'

'Is he the one who stole your gap year fund?' Rose asks.

'Yeah.'

I met Alexi when I was seventeen. He was my first love, though due to my subsequent betrayal at his hands I rarely voice that aloud. Older, French, sophisticated, he was a compulsive liar and cokehead whom I trusted implicitly for eight months due to mind-boggling naivety and the mistaken belief that I am a good judge of character. I have since learnt to be wary of men who wear wraparound cardigans. It is not a sign of '*je ne sais quoi*', but of sociopathy.

'Well, I'm with you on choosing bastards over cobwebs. Every girl needs to experience one douchebag as a rite of passage into womanhood. But you should limit yourself to one, Georgie! You need more faith that men aren't divided into idiots versus dickheads. Even at my lowest points with Mark, I never thought that. If anything, it made me realize that things can only improve. There are good, funny, kind, hot men out there. I'm sure of it.'

Rose, a serial monogamist, hasn't casually dated nearly as much as I have. I imagine that in a few years' time this refrain will have been beaten out of her by the vagaries of life, but maybe it is a simple matter of choosing quality over quantity. In matters of the heart, that has never been my speciality.

'I'm sure that's true, but they seem to scatter like cock-roaches in a lit room when I'm around. No matter. Positive thinking! It's October so to all commercial intents and pur-poses Christmas. People turn into complete sluts around the holidays. I have high hopes!' I lift my glass in a toast to antici-pated vaginal victories. 'To sluts!'

'To sluts!' they chorus loudly.

A stern, bug-eyed woman in her late thirties, clad in a hideous furry yellow jumper, Russian army hat and skinny jeans, turns around from across the room to give us evils. I smile and wink. Impervious to my charms, she rolls her eyes before turning back to her stony-faced companion. It must be irritating trying to have a decent conversation with drunken twenty-somethings cackling and swearing in the vicinity. However, she is what I most fear becoming. Humourless, bitter and freshly abandoned by the feckless dole-rat, last-chance-before-sperm-bank boyfriend who has been cheating on her for years, with only her bar work to support the acting career she secretly knows will never take off. In short, the withered husk of scenester dreams, in ironic mohair. But maybe I'm projecting a little.

From now on, things are going to be different, I swear to myself. The first term of my last year of university has just begun. It is time to put my annual resolution to develop a super-strong work ethic, by finally developing it. This year I will be productive, in work and in love, though if I have to choose between the two, I will of course choose work. A man might keep you warm at night, but so does a radiator. It seems a more reliable solution than some handsome poet. However, I'll stay open to meeting someone fantastic who I genuinely fancy. This year will be different.

Thus far, this year is not shaping up to be different. I work as a waitress a few times a week for different events around London, at a company that may as well be called 'PoshSlaves4You'. They mostly cater to well-bred people who don't like to be served by those ghastly commoners who drop their h's, or worse, by Poles.

It's poorly paid grunt work, but the odd art opening makes it more bearable. I generally entertain myself by eye-fucking the hot clients and eating as many canapés as is humanly possible. This is a subtle art form that requires lurking behind potted plants and the ability to masticate with minimal jaw movement.

The one I'm working at now, however, has a number of drunken men misbehaving as if at a Dionysian feast, rather than a Savile Row shop opening. As I tour the room with my precariously balanced champagne flutes, it is immediately evident who 'The Savile Row Man' is. The party overflows with minted banker types fulfilling every cliché one can apply to the financial sector. It seems not only has the crisis been forgotten, but so has self-awareness, good manners and the realization that a large number of people still hate them. I assume this blissful state of self-satisfaction was achieved by imbibing gallons of Cristal and rocking out to Chris Brown in Boujis.

The company they keep are even worse. Faux-nymphomaniac gold diggers hang on their every word. Their collagen blowjob lips pout in supplication, silently confirming that these men are God's gift to women. Nods and smiles and titters and tits are all that is required of their better halves.

As a result, these hapless men believe that sexual harassment is a hilarious, panty-dropping tool of seduction.

Unfortunately, our outfits leave us vulnerable to vulgar comments. We girls have been made to wear Santa's Little Slut baby-doll slips and simper when someone asks us for the tenth time if we'd like to sit on their lap to see what our gift will be. Why Father Christmas would expand his empire into Biro-sized erections is a mystery.

At any rate, the champagne flows; the testosterone rages; and sometimes, as now, someone's dick is whipped out. I don't know if any of you have experienced the joy of a portly five-foot-three man-child in a £3,000 suit, skipping like a cracked-out leprechaun, his cock and balls on full display. It is not an impressive sight. I stare in morbid fascination at the tiny, shrivelled ballsack adorned with a button mushroom, utterly perplexed. Why would you do this? Why, when mystery is the only conceivable advantage that your genitals possess?

'Ooh, she's not impressed! Are you a lesbian? Are you a dyke?' The expression of open revulsion on my face has antagonized Merry Micro-Peen. He attempts to stare me down, rather ineffectually as I tower over him in my heels.

'Does my dick offend you, dyke?'

At moments like this, I wish I were a dyke. He has one hand behind his head in a pin-up pose, the other pretending to tweak his nipple through his suit while thrusting his zip-throttled todger arrhythmically to the laughter of his friends.

'I'm not impressed. But that isn't. Because. I'm a dyke.'

I bite out witheringly, while forcing myself to stare at his deformed, impertinent third thumb.

I'm tempted to lose control of the champagne glasses I'm carrying, showering his exposed genitals in Veuve. I seem to do this regularly enough by accident. Somehow I refrain, paste a smile on my face and walk with slow and furious dignity through the crowd.

Am I a beacon for twats? My mother is always going on about our personal auras interacting with other people's auras, attracting or repelling them energetically. I usually don't subscribe to this theory as it implies some responsibility on my part but my mood has been foul tonight so maybe there is some truth to it.

'Bloody motherfucking shitfaced cockhead!'

'Hey . . . are you all right?'

I look up into laughing hazel eyes, framed by sooty lashes. Strong nose. Tall. Longish, golden-brown hair, the colour of toast – my favourite foodstuff. Even in my burning fury the pervert in me is aware that this is one hot toddy, but I'm too irritated to care.

'I'm great, just surrounded by men who think that because I'm carrying a tray I'm fair game for visual assault!' I'm aware that my face is screwed up in an expression of demented hate. 'Champagne, sir?' I spit out with an edge of hysteria.

'Yes please, mademoiselle,' he drawls teasingly as he takes a flute from my tray. 'I heard you muttering something. Seems you're not too keen on Benjo.'

Despite my best intentions, it is difficult not to notice how very attractive he is. If you like an appealingly crooked smile or a light Scottish brogue. Luckily I am resistant to the charms of conventionally good-looking men. By some strange whim of fate, I prefer to date people shorter, fatter, uglier, older, weirder or who are emotionally disabled, with the occasional borderline-psychotic combination of the above. Maybe those are just the only ones who have asked me out.

'You associate with that misogynist?'

'Hey,' He's looking at me more seriously now. 'I apologize for my friend. He's being a prick but he's just very drunk, his girlfriend broke up with him last night.'

'Yes, well.' I say curtly.

It's hard to direct your anger at something so pretty. I'm not usually such a humourless bitch, what's wrong with me?

'Can't say I blame her,' I add in bitter afterthought.

Though the man is handsome, his taste in mates is seriously questionable. Why do some men think that if a girl dumps them (probably for excellent reasons), it excuses their subsequent appalling behaviour? They go one of two ways, becoming either aggressively bitter or unbearably whiney. Though women bear the stigma of the bunny boiler, we deal with the demise of relationships with far more emotional maturity, as was demonstrated in that book *Get Fat, Get Spiritual, Get Fucked* or whatever it was called.

'You're right, of course. I'm sure you've never done something stupid drunk,' he says with a wry grin. 'Though I admit his is an extreme case.'

'I am the soul of class and restraint, actually.'

To be fair, I am usually doing some*one* stupid drunk, rather than some*thing*. But technicalities are always best left unexpressed.

'Yes, class and restraint always come to mind when I hear someone swearing like a sailor,' he laughs and runs his hand through his shaggy hair. 'I'm Scott Montgomery.'

Good name. I hate this cocky bastard. How dare he throw that in my face? If men would learn not to highlight a woman's rational inconsistencies, the world would be a far better place.

'And I'm leaving. I can't respect a man with such poor taste in mates.'

Spinning on my heel, I catch sight of his startled expression before I march off into the crowd with the fake purpose of the directionless.

I had meant my tone to be more jocular, but residual anger hardened my words, making me sound like a bitter, humourless old hag. The kind of person I fear becoming most, but at this point I have no option but to go with it. 'Never surrender! Never apologize!' is my motto and also the reason why I am a terrible waitress.

I'm going to regret this in the morning, I think.

Grace Kelly Lounging in a Boudoir in Shanghai

I awake, in some pain, having bled onto my sheets. Fantastic. That does go some way towards explaining my temper last night. I never have PMT; the week before I am largely unaffected. I am far more likely to bite someone's head off when my innards are twisting, my knickers are stained and my breasts may explode. There's no fighting the insanity of oestrogen. The womb is more powerful than the will, as I believe they say in *Star Wars*. Something to that effect, anyway.

Oh well, I only acted like a massive bitch to that rarest of birds – a very attractive man hitting on me. He might only have been trying to mollify me but I prefer to think the glimmer of chemistry between us wasn't imaginary. Though even if he was chatting me up, he probably didn't really fancy me; there was an extremely favourable ratio of men to women, the likes of which I will probably never see again. I am twenty-four years old and I've been dating since I was sixteen. Only three really good-looking men have ever actively sought me out, so if this trend continues, in a few years it will happen again – barring dramatic weight gain, resurgence of teenage acne, et cetera.

It shouldn't be this difficult, I think, as I drag my aching carcass to the bathroom. Dating the type of boys you meet drunk in pubs and clubs hasn't worked out for me terribly well. And though there are packs of hipsters, they have the off-putting attitude that if you were worth knowing, they would have slept with you by now. These types limit themselves to incestuous partner-swapping within a circle of highly individual friends who all look like they were spat out of Urban Outfitters, though they never shop there.

It doesn't help that I went to an all girls' school followed by a Womenswear degree where most of the men are otherwise inclined. There are, of course, straight guys in fashion, but they are highly in demand. They may not realize it at first, but within a month it becomes apparent that many of the well-dressed women around them are rarely approached. I am always surprised that more heterosexual men don't go into fashion. Seducing the girls is as easy as shooting koi in an ornamental pond.

If your peer group has failed you it is hard to meet new

men in London. People are less confident in approaching others unless they are formally introduced by a third party or are totally wasted. And call me old-fashioned but I take exception to someone grinding up against me in a club before saying hello, often before having a clear view of my face. When you discount the perverts, drunkards and those good eggs not cheating on their girlfriends, it leaves you with a very narrow pool to choose from on a Saturday night.

Sarah, a friend of mine who has been coupled up with a lovely man for some time, suggested I take a crack at Internet dating. As she described it, 'If I could, I would be all over that shit . . . You can have total control! It's like window shopping for dick!' She is the only person I know who sees the grim meat-market reality of OKCupid as exciting.

I pretended I might give it a go, though I've secretly already tried it. Let's face it. Failing at finding love online is not something anyone wants to broadcast. I probably didn't help matters by saying on my profile: 'Willing to lie about how we met,' in the 'About Me' section and posting a funny-not-sexy picture with my face obscured. It is hard to advertise yourself effectively when consumed with residual shame. A few dates later, I deleted my account. They were not in-and-of-themselves catastrophic, just wasted hours of polite tedium and a scramble during awkward silences for the kind of lame conversation I last used while babysitting.

In any case, it seems I am just as cowardly behind a

computer screen as I am in real life. I fall into the same pattern – throwing out my net, being passive, waiting to see what hapless creature stumbles into it and then being totally underwhelmed by my catch. Like a fisherman who catches only anchovies, I am desperate for a cod. Or a salmon. Or a Scotty McWhatever he was called. With his hair of toast.

My stomach grumbles and I dismiss these thoughts as the crazed unrest of a hungry mind. The blues can always be alleviated by something involving cheese, or if the hour permits, booze. If there is one upside to the first day of your period, it is the guilt-free consumption of fat in all its glorious varieties. When someone invents boozy cheese, my life will be complete.

Weekends being life's greatest pleasure, it is particularly maddening that mine is to be ruined not only by The Curse, but also by my flatmate. I can hear noises in the kitchen; I hesitate on the stairway, hoping that she will return to her room before I die of hunger.

Anastasia is one of those people who is superficially normal, but if you were to talk with her for, say, the length of a dinner party, you would soon realize there are cracks in her sanity. And if you were to live with her, you would soon realize that she is in fact totally unhinged. However, I was desperate for a place to stay when my previous housing fell through and I thought, how bad can an acquaintance-of-a-friend-of-a-friend be? The answer is very fucking bad.

Stacy, as she prefers to be known (an early warning sign: Stacy is a name for a child's doll circa 1994, not an adult human woman) is twenty-seven and one of those perpetually out-of-work actors subsisting on, I presume, family money. She claims to be from White Russian stock originally – hinting, but not outright inferring, that she might be related to *the* Anastasia, of Disney and historical fame. She does not believe in banks, cash-points, Eastern Europe, personal space, laughter, starchy root vegetables, the rights of the poor, council tax or central heating.

She does believe in Epigenetics, something I had previously never heard of. From my Google research, I have found it to be rather different from the theories she has subjected me to. In essence, she thinks she can exercise the power of the mind to control her physical sensations. Stacy insists she can regulate her body temperature as though she were a Tibetan monk, even when her lips are blue and the downy pelt on her arms is standing on end like a field of wheat. All this would be harmless New Age quackery I would have no problem indulging, except that the flat is always freezing. She refuses to admit she feels the arctic chill seeping through the Victorian windows of our little terraced house near London Fields. We are currently engaged in a silent Cold War, where I run around turning on all the radiators as soon as I notice she is out, which she promptly switches off again as soon as she returns.

She also believes in water fasts, which apparently 'can heal all ailments the body can experience'. These fasts consist of temporary bouts of starvation, lasting anywhere from seven to fourteen days. Unprompted, she informed me that if I would only follow a water fast for six weeks, I could have the body I have always dreamed of. This was the turning point where I mentally shifted her from 'Annoying' to 'Evil'.

What irritated me the most was her presumption that my dream body must be her dream body – that of Doutzen Kroes. Aside from the fact that if I lost that much weight my breasts would look like punctured piñatas, you can get really creative with a 'dream body'. Maybe a thigh gap is not that important to me. Maybe swimming underwater for prolonged periods of time is. Maybe what I really want is gills.

During her fasting periods, if I come near her with food or liquids other than water, she will glare and find a corner in which to purify her energy, which I have selfishly polluted. Smoking cigarettes inside is obviously against the rules. Smoking blunts, though, is always allowed. I've never been that into 'The Devil's Weed', to use my Mum's terminology. People who claim it is equivalent to alcohol are kidding themselves. Even if I share one joint, there will always be a moment where I wish I wasn't high. It takes a lot for me to wish I wasn't drunk. Anyway, since living with Stacy I've lost interest in it entirely, in case her crazy is somehow catching. I don't know why she bothers – I've never met such an uptight stoner.

'All right, Stacy?' I say. I have relented my pathetic stake-out and stumble into our little kitchenette. It is spotlessly clean, as usual.

It is one of Stacy's stipulations that the dishes be washed immediately after usage. As she does not often eat, this is supremely convenient for her, rather less so for me. She does spend a lot of time in here, standing by the kettle with a mug of hot water and lemon (plus a tiny squirt of agave syrup if she is feeling indulgent) watching my meal preparations with an air of vague superiority. I am convinced she is thinking that if she ever deigned to cook, she would do a much better job of it.

I am currently wrapped up in a sexy ensemble of stripy long johns, a cashmere scarf I found on a bus, a thick jumper, a giant woolly cardigan and knee-high clashing ski socks. Last night's MAC eyeliner has migrated under my eyes. I look like the result of a passionate encounter between Alice Cooper and Pippi Longstocking, raised by 'Stitch and Bitch' enthusiasts.

Stacy is wearing a silky Chinese robe, loosely belted to reveal her sternum and coltish legs, holding a glass full of what looks like pondscum. She looks like Grace Kelly lounging in a boudoir in Shanghai, holding pondscum. She is forever attempting to make me try her algae-vitamin concoctions but I refuse on the grounds that I want to nourish the taste buds I've not yet killed through smoking and anyway we are not living in L.A.

'I'm perfectly well, thank you, Georgina.'

Stacy always calls me Georgina, though she knows full well I hate it.

'Oh dear, you're not looking very well this morning. Late night? There's some more barley-cayenne-asparagus in the fridge if you want. It's good for spots, puffiness and dark circles. I've never suffered from those symptoms, as they are usually related to liver strain and as you know I rarely drink. It would do you a world of good if you took a shot every morning and made some lifestyle changes.' Stacy smiles tightly and looks at my face as if she is concerned.

'Yeah, I was working late. I've got hideous cramps. I think I need a bit more sustenance this morning. Thanks though.' I crack open some eggs and resist the urge to smear yolk on her perfect complexion. The fresh spots on my forehead have elected to co-ordinate themselves with the bobbles on my red scarf.

'I never get cramps. It's one of the benefits of fasting.'

Even her uterus is perfect, damn her. She probably sheds three drops of blood on a super-slim tampon and is done for the month.

'Yes, you've mentioned that. Do you want some omelette?'

'No, I want to keep myself fresh for my date with Cosmo.' Stacy wrinkles her nose in delicate disgust.

She is the only person I know who speaks about food as if it sullies her. I cannot understand this mentality. I have felt genuine angst in debates over the great, imperative, eternal question that wakes truth-seekers up in a cold sweat in the middle of the night: Food or Sex. Gun to your head; no caveats. For ever.

Would you choose a constant supply of fantastic sex with only flavourless gruel for sustenance? Or three-Michelin-star-worthy feasts and eternal celibacy, no masturbation allowed? The additional variable of weight gain or loss might influence your decision. Heart disease is no joke, while sexathons would keep you spry well into your nineties. Though being so well fed, would you cease to care? The smell of scrambled eggs with cheddar, mushrooms and chives wafts up at me. At the moment, I would choose food.

However, if Michael Fassbender suddenly appeared in the kitchen half naked and tried to ravish me, I'd be back to square one. It's an insolvable quandary, you see, best tackled while impassioned and drunk.

Stacy's persistent whining about her date's choice of venue interrupts my reverie. Apparently, though it is super-expensive, it lacks the panache necessary to impress someone of her calibre. I was once taken for a Valentine's Day meal at McDonald's, bitter disappointment flavouring an otherwise tasteless fish burger, while I reflected gratefully that at least I didn't know anyone in Kilburn. So I can at least admire her for having standards.

'I don't think I've met Cosmo, what's he like?'

Stacy has shown no sign of leaving, so I resign myself to the verbal one-upmanship that her conversations usually consist of. Luckily, she rarely wants to speak to me, preferring instead to float about, wandering in and out of various classes. She takes ballet, spinning, yoga and Pilates. I've yet to see her leave for an audition and suspect that 'acting' is something she pretends to do until she finds a husband.

'He's new. An investment banker, very tall and dashing. He stopped me as I was getting out of a taxi and insisted on taking my number. He said I look just like Julie Christie in *Doctor Zhivago* and that if he didn't find out my name, he would regret it for the rest of his life. So attractive when men are confident, don't you think? Gianpiero is still in Milan, but I'm visiting him next weekend. I've chucked Lucas. He was trying my patience – always wanting reassurance that I would stop seeing other men. And you know how I can't stand lying.'

No one likes a needy man, but as a general rule, I think it's rude to complain about how hard it is to juggle three boyfriends to someone who struggles to pin down one.

'Poor Lucas. Oh well, clingy is never a good quality,' I finally say, impressing myself with my self-restraint, as I scrape my omelette onto a plate.

Sometimes, when Stacy isn't around, I simply take a fork and pick at the hot pan standing up, often burning my tongue in the process. It is one of the lazier customs I've developed in an effort to minimize the washing up, but it leaves me with a feeling of contentment. I feel like a caveman by the fire, savouring my kill. It's probably for the best that I have a flatmate, if only to protect me from developing stranger behaviours. My father has a habit of trimming his toenails and then flushing them down the toilet, which never entirely works, so there are always a few yellowish shards stranded at the bottom of the bowl. At least I have a genetic deficiency to blame.

I would like to think Stacy is exaggerating about all these men, but they do fall prostrate before her. She has a complicated, high-maintenance-bitch thing that they find irresistible. Her vague manner translates into a certain mystique and she plays hard to get effortlessly, as her disinterest in the rest of humanity is quite genuine. It also doesn't hurt that she is whippet-thin, with caramel blonde locks down to here, legs up to there and penchant for going braless.

'Clingy is the one character defect I cannot abide. Yet all the men I date turn into absolute octopuses. I encounter it all the time.' She sighs dramatically, inspecting her manicured nails. 'I'm off to Bikram now. They also have a 5 p.m. if you care to sweat out those toxins later.'

Stacy sashays languorously off and I continue stuffing my face, a mustard trail running down my chin. You would think that living with someone so skinny would be a constant source of thinspiration. You would be wrong. If anything, looking at her makes me hungrier.

I do, however, resolve to start a protein diet. Tomorrow. Never start a diet on the first day of your period, or, for that matter, with a hangover. You are not only guaranteed to fail, you will do so with glorious abandon. No gluttony can compare with that of a woman who really believes that, starting tomorrow, she will never allow herself sugar again.

Protein diets are the only ones I've been able to follow for more than two days, as I love meat of all varieties and on those you can supposedly eat it in unlimited quantities. They are best started either before or after a relationship, as the resulting halitosis, constipation and pungent urine can be off-putting for even the most ardent of suitors. I mentally check my diary. Alone last month, alone today, alone for the foreseeable future. Perfect timing.

Produce-Related Prostitution

I am multitasking while at Sainsbury's, chatting to my mother on the phone. I like to tick her off my to-do list along with discount chicken fillets. The conversation, like all post-weekend run downs of the last few months, begins something like this:

'So, have you met any interesting people recently?' she asks, by which she means men.

'No, Mum, still no,' by which I also mean men. I had a great night dancing with some friends from university at a small bar with great disco that is a haven for queers. She will not be interested to hear that I've spent my weekend consorting with drag queens, however fabulous, rather than marriage prospects. In her eyes, if I don't have a rock by twenty-six at the very latest, she will have failed me as a mother. That leaves me a year and a half to find and master-manipulate an appropriate victim into thinking I will make a good wife.

I have repeatedly attempted to explain to her that in this day and age many girls are encouraged in their career aspirations and that, furthermore, I don't know if I want to get married, but this is of no consequence to her. Having never really worked, she is convinced that it is a miserable state and if at all possible it is better to have a husband, an allowance and good friends in a similar position to spend it with.

Wandering aimlessly into the organic section, I subtly eye up a boy in his mid-twenties with a Roman nose, floppy blond hair and punkish army boots just the right side of white supremacist. His basket is demonstrably short of meat and dairy products, so I deduce he might be vegan, but I consider it something that we can work through. I rearrange a bag of onions over my hamburger patties.

'But who knows, maybe I'll meet my future husband reaching for the same pepper in the next ten minutes,' I say, just before his cute, dreadlocked girlfriend catches him up, slipping her hand into his. They grin at each other, skin a-glow from love and all the vegetables and pulses they have doubtless consumed.

Mum snorts down the phone, this single noise conveying both the depth of her exasperation and her diminishing hopes of ever having grandchildren.

ELIZABETH AARON

'What sort of people will you meet at 2 p.m. on a Monday in Hackney? Stay-At-Home Dads and The Unemployed, that's who.' She enjoys answering her own questions.

'That or an off-duty rock star. It's within the realm of possibility!'

And that's when I see him. A man who, indeed, looks very much like an off-duty rock star, political poet, fringe-theatre actor or similar.

Have I ever mentioned my weakness for older men with curly locks and facial hair? It could be due to my childhood obsession with Inigo 'You killed my father. Prepare to Die!' Montoya. Or the result of the Pavlovian association: Santa Claus = bearded older man = cadeaux. Julian thinks I'll end up with a Captain Birdseye doppelgänger. I really do get weak at the knees for just about anyone sporting the requisite level of hirsuteness.

This one is wearing an expensively distressed leather jacket. Black curls swing just below his ears. His luscious beard protrudes a few inches from his face like shrubbery. This is my kryptonite. Beneath the beard, his face is quite handsome. He has chosen to disguise his chiselled features with the only thing marring this vision of absolute deliciousness: heinous plastic-rimmed aviator-style bifocal glasses favoured by rapists, paedophiles and hipsters.

If this is his fatal flaw, it's one I can overlook. The second our eyes meet I am overwhelmed with a heady mixture of lust, insecurity and fear. It's that rare, sledgehammer-to-the-solar-plexus, desire-panic hybrid that has struck me only a few times before.

The last time I experienced it was a *Sliding Doors*-type moment with Elvis-With-An-Afro; an improbable-sounding combination but trust me, it worked. It was a few years ago on the Tube. Our eyes locked and we both involuntarily put out a hand towards each other as the doors closed. The train sped away from him, forever dashing any hope of true love accompanied by a life-affirming pageboy haircut. Which is just as well; I really do not have the jaw line for that.

Those three seconds were enough to make his beautiful face clearer in my mind than that of my most recent ex-lover, Joe, who I would struggle to pick out of a police line-up. But back to The Beard of Glory.

'Mum, I'll bell you later, bye!'

I hang up quickly. He catches me staring at him and smirks. Was that a smirk or a smile? The difference seems vital. Ducking into the freezer aisle in embarrassment, I pretend to be torn over the fish fingers while surreptitiously inspecting my appearance in the glass.

My long wavy dark brown hair is unkempt as usual, raked into a loose bouffant bun. My eyes are very blue, my skin very pale, my lips rouged with NARS Red Square lip pencil. I look like Snow White if she entered her mid-twenties half a stone too heavy, having broken free of her indentured servitude and escaped to the city. Which is as good as I ever look, really.

Thank God I haven't left the house without my face on since the age of fifteen, in case just such a moment should arrive. Though it is a waste of makeup, piling on the slap to go down the shop, at moments like this it's a definite boost to my ever-precarious self-worth.

Moments like what, you ask? Seeing an attractive man and promptly running away to feign an interest in frozen food? I should be bold, daring. I have never overtly hit on a man before, but faint heart never won fair Beardy. I glance around the empty aisle and re-adjust my tits for maximum impact before casually taking a tour back towards the fruit and veg. He's still there, holding a melon. I pretend to be fascinated by the aubergine selection.

The stalking has gone well thus far; if another world war breaks out, perhaps espionage will be in my future. I even have a leather trench coat with a Gestapo vibe that is chicer than it sounds. Say what you will about Fascism – ideological ugliness does not impede you from working dashing outerwear. Now, the more pressing matter is how to strike up a conversation. What would Mae do? Swagger up, eye-fuck him and drawl suggestively, 'Is that a pistol in your pocket, or are you just happy to see me?' I rack my brain for a classic film quote that isn't as desperate. 'You should be kissed, and often – and by someone who knows how.' Bit rapey. 'I am Dracula. I bid you welcome.' Obviously not. How do men do this?

I'm at the point of working up the courage to go down on one knee and break into a passionate rendition of 'We Can Be Loovers!' – because what man doesn't dream of being publicly serenaded with the *Moulin Rouge* soundtrack? – when fate intervenes and he speaks to me.

'Sorry, I'm having some trouble here. How do I tell if this is ripe?' The Beard asks with a lopsided grin. His eyes are disturbingly green. My nervously clenching stomach makes me worry I have trapped wind.

'If you don't know that by your age, I'm not sure you deserve to,' I say flirtatiously. I fear my smile is more silly than sexy, but try to ignore this and concentrate on being as witty as one can on the topic of unripe fruit. 'Word on the street is that you give it a good squeeze.'

Oh God, too much innuendo. Beardy smiles wolfishly.

'You've done this before, haven't you? Could you show me your technique?'

'My services are highly in demand. I don't take on novice fruit wranglers without remuneration . . . I don't know that you can afford me.' Novice fruit wranglers? What does that even mean? I've also implicated myself in some sort of weird produce-related prostitution. Fuck.

'Is that so . . . What if I took you for a drink? Or would you prefer hard cash? I've got £4 on me. That should cover it.'

I giggle in response. Damn his beard, it unmans me.

'That seems like a reasonable exchange. I'm Georgie.'

'I'm Leo . . . What's your number?'

He takes out his iPhone. I appear to be the only person in London without one. I am fond of my archaic Nokia, even though there are impoverished children in Africa who would probably reject it. Duly giving him my details, I'm relieved that he doesn't miss-call me. If he never gets in contact, at least I will be saved the shame of ringing him in a fit of booze-inflicted overconfidence and leaving some appalling message. The advent of video recording apps have laid to rest any lingering hopes I had that I am charming and intelligent when drunk as a skunk. I would probably say something along the lines of 'Uh . . . This is Georgie? The Ripe Melon girl? We should go out sometime! I'm free always. You can show me some other fruit you want to get to grips with. Bananas and cucumbers are my speciality. Bye! I love you!' Yikes.

'Well, we'll discuss the finer points later then, Georgie.' He tosses the melon back on the pile, shifting as if to leave.

'Don't you want to take it home and practise?'

I point to the abandoned fruit and toss my head back with what I hope is cocky flirtatiousness. I believe this is what is commonly known as fronting, as inside I am still buzzing with anxiety and the paranoid conviction that I might actually fart.

'It's served its purpose,' he grins and saunters slowly to the checkout, not turning to look back.

Jeremy Kyle LOVE RAT SUICIDE PACT

More Jeremy Kyle Than Jacobean Tragedy

'"It's served its purpose"? Crikey. That's really hot, but don't you think it's veering towards douche-bag levels of self-confidence?' Rose asks at our usual Vietnamese on Kingsland Road, favoured due to its low prices and BYOB policy. Though we have plans to go out later, I have over-ordered to such an extent that I may only be capable of rolling like a rogue sausage-link on the dance floor.

'That did occur to me. He's definitely a smooth operator, but I'm not in a position to be picky, to be honest. Plus, douche comes in all shapes and sizes; at least I fancy him. Nothing worse than dating someone because you mistake non-threatening for honourable and then find out he's been hitting on all your friends.'

This has happened to me several times.

'Oh God, I've done that to Henry's mate Steve . . . not out-and-out propositioning him but flirting outrageously, talking about how we should have a threesome – jokingly. Last time I smelt his hair. Thank fuck Henry's taken it so well,' Sarah says in between bites of her giant spring roll.

Rose and I met Sarah four years ago at some god-awful club and we bonded in the loos over the usual clichés, makeup and bad men. We were all coked-up out of our minds. For reasons unknown, we actually kept in contact instead of waking up the next day wondering what the hell we were talking about with that random girl and why, having forked out £100 for a night out, we always spend it within a dirty cramped toilet.

'Do you think he might want it to happen one day?' I can't help but ask.

I wonder how such an arrangement would work between friends. Would it be a one-time porno spit-roasting extrava-ganza or would it turn into a tragic love triangle in the style of Truffaut's *Jules et Jim*? It's interesting that it is mostly these extremes that are represented in our popular culture, when stories of men and their harems are so far ranging. Of course, the reality of managing a polyamorous relationship would be a hugely stressful emotional drain and require a tiresome amount of earnest conversations. Which is why I assume most people stick to the tried-and-tested, traditional social mores of monogamy and lies.

'Nah, it's not because of that – Henry's very laid back. He wouldn't want to share though; he thinks a threesome with two men is gay. Which is completely absurd!'

Sarah sloshes more white wine into our glasses, finishing off the first bottle. By the time we have drained the second our laughter will have turned into cackles better suited to an amateur production of *Macbeth*.

'But, just hypothetically speaking, if the moment did arise, I'd go for it. Steve is fit. Obviously, I love Henry, but I have the forbidden-fruit lust thing going on for Steve. And he's just a bit more naughty. I mean, Henry and I have been together for eighteen months so it's normal, but sex with him . . . well, recently it's been third-person sex.'

I laugh knowingly. Rose looks confused.

'Wait, what? I thought you said you hadn't had a three-some?'

'No, not a threesome. Third-person sex. Having sex in the third person. Like, he's pounding away, my body is lying there making appropriate noises and my mind is floating over in the corner watching telly, composing emails and occasion-ally critiquing his technique.'

'Oh God. Is that normal, do you think? I only ever had first-person sex with Scrotum Mark.' Rose looks anxious and fiddles with her long Pre-Raphaelite hair.

She has such a wide, innocent face that it is difficult to imagine how you could lie to her, let alone wreak the trail of psychological warfare that SM did. Towards the end, he had her convinced that she was a jealous paranoid who was lucky to have found a forgiving man willing to put up with her pathological insecurity. This was after giving her herpes, strenuously insisting that it must have been her who cheated on him. After she had shed enough tears, he magnanimously forgave her.

There is a thin line between being naive and incredibly stupid and some might think that at that point, she had crossed it. I had taken an immediate dislike to him from the night we first met. The four of us had gone to a Thai restaurant and in SM's opinion, we girls had lingered too long after dinner with our wine. His friends were already inside a club down the road and he became increasingly impatient with our 'chitchat'. When snide comments about women and their poor time-keeping were ineffective in hurrying us up, he stood abruptly, grabbed the half-full bottle of vino and turned it on its head, decanting it all over the floor. When nothing remained, he set it down on the table and sneered, 'Now can we go?'

We took this in with the same paralysed horror we would have shown had he hurled a sack of squirming kittens into the Thames. Needless to say, it was not the kind of behaviour you hope for from your boyfriend the first time he meets your mates. It took us an hour to persuade a thoroughly humili-ated Rose out of the toilets and into the club to confront him. SM seemed surprised to see us, quickly removing his arms from the shoulders of two blonde girls. The speech we had angrily but elegantly scripted for Rose on the walk over did not go as planned. Within half an hour, all was forgiven.

Rose ignored our misgivings, suspicions and advice. There was a lovable optimism to her blindness that, though frus-trating, I could never totally disapprove of. Always wanting to see the best in him, it wasn't until she caught him shag-ging her cousin in a wardrobe at a family wedding that she came to her senses. The man wasn't even that good looking, though he had a certain hollow magnetism common to master-manipulators. It's shocking how a little charm and a dash of illusion can wrap a tight spell around the mind of an otherwise rational woman.

'Uh, SM, don't mention him! Don't worry, doll, it's not because he was the best you'll ever have, it's because you were always either fighting or fucking. I've been there – it heightens all the senses. You can't sustain it very long before it turns into an out-and-out feud but in those few months before you full-on despise them, God it's good.'

Sarah sighs and looks wistfully into the distance, twiddling with the ends of her curly bob, her big brown eyes softening. After a pause, she says with halting nostalgia:

'One time, in the middle of an argument, my ex ripped

out my tampon, threw it at the wall and just started fucking me. I know it sounds disgusting but it was the sexiest thing ever.'

Rose makes a face. I raise my eyebrows but nod. Women as a whole are far more up for dirty sexual antics than most men have been led to believe, they just need the right person to release their inhibitions. You can be an entirely changed person from one day to the next in bed with different people, depending on how they make you feel.

It is hard to find someone with whom you are free to be yourself, sexually and emotionally. Furthermore, we act as our own harshest critics. Encouraged from birth to modify ourselves to the company we keep, we chip off bits of our noses, our true opinions and our sense of humour. It is a confusing time in which to grow up, in terms of what constitutes inner strength and what constitutes emasculation, what will empower you and what will demean you, what is real and what is fake. It is all largely dependent upon our insecurities of image, manner and presentation, around which a huge industry feeds. An industry I intend on joining; there is nothing so soothing to one's inner doubts as the satisfaction of knowing one's outer shell disguises them completely.

That is why it's liberating to have close female friends with whom we can be unashamed of the moral ambiguity that informs most of our decisions as we stumble confusedly into adulthood. No topic is off limits with us and brutal honesty is the conversational goal, the more grotesque the better. Granted, this honesty is often limited to a supremely superficial range of topics, but who wants to discuss Darfur on a Friday night? To which end, back to ripping out tampons.

'Yeah, I can see what you mean. Extreme passion and that feeling that they have to have you now is such a turn on. If someone asks if they can kiss you or something it just feels so . . . anaemic,' I say, Rose nodding in sage agreement beside me.

'God I hate that! Kiss me or don't but for fuck's sake don't wait on my permission, I'm not your mother!' Sarah shouts, banging the table angrily for emphasis.

Sarah works in advertising and has to assert herself in a largely male team, which is the excuse she gives to anyone who tells her off for being brash; a rare occurrence, as to the untrained eye, she is scary. A sensibly dressed couple in their early thirties have been looking over at us askance, but say nothing. The woman is cross and the man looks house trained. They are definitely having third-person sex.

Rose, ever the voice of reason, interjects calmly.

'Yeah, but men can't really win, can they? For every guy who hasn't kissed me when I want him to, there are ten more who try it on when I think it's perfectly clear I'm not interested. If I don't fancy someone, I'll still be polite. They assume I must like them and then lunge at my mouth. When you prise them off, there's always that ten percent who get even more persistent. There is a complete disconnect between what I want and what they want but they delude themselves that if they want something, I must want it too.'

'Yes, but women also need to be brought up to say no! My mother taught me never to be afraid to say "No". I love it. Say it all the damn time and it never fails to gladden my heart.' Sarah's mother is the sort of resilient Afro-Caribbean woman who brooks no shit. She once chased a burglar out of her flat armed only with a frying pan.

'So true! We are taught to be malleable and play nice. Then when we don't speak up somehow we are the ones at fault. I have had to say, "Take your hand off my breast, don't touch me, don't follow me, don't speak to me," over and over. Do they want it in writing?' I wonder.

When I was fourteen, a man started wanking off next to me on an empty bus in broad daylight. I was too scared to do anything but leap over him and get off at the next stop. I called the police afterwards, but they said it was unlikely they would ever find him and then patronizingly started asking the details of my attire.

Gradually you develop armour. You cease to hear catcalls and are only afraid alone late at night. There is always a moment when your heart jumps into your throat, though. When you don't know if increasing your pace will deliver you from a sticky situation or antagonize the man into pursuing you. 'Ah, look – you're scared! It's so cute that you're scared!

What's your name?' For the record, if in hitting on someone you need to mention their obvious terror in your presence, it is probably not the moment to strike.

'Well, perverts are perverts, that's a lost cause. It's the coming generation of as-yet-unformed perverts that concerns me. Kids are practically brought up by porn and misogynistic music videos. They should teach them how to read and respect body language at school, there are a million ways to say no without ever opening your mouth,' Rose says firmly.

'Add to that, lessons in how to actually touch a woman. Half the time when you finally get the golden ticket of a guy you like, who likes you, the sex is still mystifyingly terrible,' I sigh, thinking of Joe. He thought the G spot was located near the cervix. I left his house feeling like I had just had a smear test.

I have a 'Three Strikes and You're Out' bad-sex policy. You can't expect miracles the first time but if by the third it is still regrettable, you either need to move on or gird your loins for what is bound to be a cringe-making conversation. No man takes 'You're shit in bed' very well, however diplomatically you've managed to phrase it. How are you supposed to politely dilute 'You use your penis like a very small saw' and still get your point across? *Cosmo*'s Rent-A-Sex-Therapist approach seems to advise training up a man as if you were Siegfried or Roy, using illusionist mind games to guide them in the right direction, all the while trussed up in sequins, spandex or leather.

If clear but non-verbal communication is indeed the key, perhaps mimes make the best lovers. I make a mental note to investigate this untapped sexual resource.

'My theory is that some men are unteachable,' Sarah opines, 'you either have it or you don't. It's like academic intelligence – with tutoring you can improve but it all depends on the baseline you're born with. I've slept with super-experienced thirty-something guys who were unbelievably shit, but remember The Virgin?'

We nod. She had been seriously concerned about being his first but said he was 'a revelation'.

'Some men just have an affinity for pussy in the way that others are good at maths,' Sarah says loudly. 'It's genetic.'

As our waiter arrives with a plate of spicy eels, he does a double take, as if afraid that he heard her correctly. She ignores him. My embarrassment threshold being a touch lower than Sarah's, I wait until he has left before chiming in.

'Obviously some people are just crap in bed, but I think it's just about finding that magic person with the same sexual peccadilloes. I saw a couple kissing on the tube escalators who were licking each other's tongues. They were lapping at each other like dogs.'

As I give an enthusiastic and sloppy impression of this meeting of mouths, our waiter passes by and flinches, revealing a micro-expression of pure horror. So much for being discreet. He is clearly unused to the charms of the English Rose.

'That's revolting. What is it about being on an escalator that makes couples go all lovey-dovey?' Sarah has a well-documented hatred of anything romantic. She once drunkenly admitted that in her first relationship she shared sickening bird-themed pet names with her lover. Months after they broke up, she hacked into his email account and found that he was calling his new girlfriend 'My Cocka-Tootle-Poo'. Enormously betrayed, she rejected sentimentality with the fervour with which Linda Lovelace rejected porn.

'Presumably every time they are stationary the enormity of their love overwhelms them,' I say in their defence, though it is met with sour faces. I secretly love PDAs, but it's not disgusting when I do it, obviously.

'I don't get that. I love Henry but I've never felt like he completes me. I've always assumed I'd get married for the same reason my Mum did – become emotionally exhausted searching for some perfect guy, hit thirty and think "You'll do".'

'How depressing! She admits that?'

'They are happy together so maybe that's the way it should be done. A shared love of *Crimewatch* and antiquing keeps them strong. So, Rose, have you seen any more of Scooter Man?'

'Meh. I can't be arsed, to be honest. I cancelled on him

twice and yesterday he left me several drunken voicemails which were practically incomprehensible.'

Not texting back is one of those things that, when done to someone else by you, seems like no more than they could reasonably expect. It is a swift, clear and satisfactory end to an over-long, muddy and unsatisfactory meeting of minds/genitals. When it is done to you, however, it leaves you torn between bewildered hurt and a secret conviction that they have been mugged, sustained a head injury and are suffering from amnesia in hospital. Unable even to identify themselves, they are still, on a subconscious level, obsessing about you.

'Voicemail is the devil. He'll probably redouble his efforts if you don't reply though, blanking is a well-known male aphrodisiac,' Sarah says.

'Yeah, but what do I say? It seems a bit serious to have some stilted conversation to end a relationship that never began. I wish you could just be like, "Look, you seem like a decent enough fellow, but you leave my vagina drier than a drought in the Sahara. Please never contact me again!"' Rose sings, a bit tipsily.

'Er, I believe that's exactly what "It's not you, it's me" and "We don't have chemistry" mean,' I say.

My phone beeps. I've had it on the table so I don't have to go through the tragic rigmarole of checking in my bag every ten minutes in case Beardy has texted me.

It's been four days since our fateful melon encounter and I

am starting to lose hope. Knowing my luck, he will never call and I'll be doomed to run into him in Sainsbury's while he's using his melon line on some other girl. She will be thinner, cooler and less eager to please than myself. They will live happily ever after in Victoria Park and have a brood of kids with their own mini-pairs of hipster glasses.

I unlock my phone, mentally preparing myself to see a message from my mum, but lo and behold! An unknown number. Oh Beardy! I knew it was written in the stars!

'Yay! He's texted me! He says . . . "Yo. Drink later?" Hmm. That's quite abrupt, isn't it?' What happened to the wit and charm? How did wooing a lady with fruit turn into 'Yo'?

'Oh don't worry, it's quite rare to find a man who's good at text-speak. Henry never realizes when I'm taking the piss, gets offended and sulks. It's pretty pathetic.'

'Still, imagine if Romeo had gone to Juliet's window and said, "Yo, fancy a fuck?" Which is essentially what this is. I mean – it's nearly 11 p.m. Texting someone directly at pub closing time is pretty much an out-and-out shameless booty call.'

'I think you're reading too much into it. And if he were alive today, Romeo would totally do that; he was a right shagger! Rosaline didn't let him in her pants, whereas Juliet did and they both died of an acute case of the melodramas before someone else could catch his eye. Otherwise, I assure you, he would have eventually chucked her. The ending would have been more *Jeremy Kyle* than Jacobean tragedy.' Rose concludes this depressing evaluation of the star-crossed lovers with a professorial air, convincing us all in spite of her occasional slurring.

'Just text this dude tomorrow evening and say you were busy doing something vague and cool,' Sarah advises. 'Actually don't even give him an explanation, just say hey and suggest another night. And don't send one of your funny texts, they never work on men.'

'Are you saying my texts aren't funny?' I cry in mock-indignation.

'They are to me, because I know you, but if I didn't they'd just be weird. Men don't care about humour initially; don't bother trying to impress him. It will only confuse him. Don't flirt either, you can sometimes come across as kind of mean. I think mysterious is definitely the way to play this one.'

I decide to follow her instructions to the letter and try out a new Mute, Mysterious Me on Beardy, as the Real Me has otherwise been a crashing disappointment. Everyone knows trusting your instincts in love leads to a slow suicide via industrial quantities of carbohydrates when even your most pathetic of relationships finally peters out. Then you must confront the grim reality that you are Not Special Enough and will grow old alone. Which is much worse than dying alone, if you think about it. In fact, a cramped retirement home might be the social highlight of my twilight years.

In the meantime, hope is not lost – the night is young and London is full of beautiful people trying to find love, or get laid. To that end, we double up on our drinking efforts in preparation to go dancing. I have it under good authority that whiskey has excellent digestive properties and will hopefully terminate my food baby by the time we get to the club.

When I awaken hours later, my supine form is sprawled on the living room floor. My face is nestled into the saucy remains of a kebab. I can't believe I had a second dinner. How the hell did I get home? And why can't I ever time-travel to my bed? I hope Stacy hasn't seen me; I may hate her but I also hate living up to her expectation of me as a disgusting slob. Even my hair feels polluted, to say nothing of my soul.

Why is my alarm going off on a Saturday? I scrabble blindly for the source of the noise, ready to turn it off and throw it across the room. Annoyingly, it's Rose phoning. She's already called twice. I debate whether or not to ignore it and continue the epic dream in which I, an alien prince, saved the world from imminent disaster. Though tempted, I pick up on the off-chance that she's done something terrible and has wound up in jail.

'Hello? Rose, it's 10 a.m. This had better be worth it.'

'Georgie, quickly, do you remember the name of the guy I got off with last night?' Rose whispers feverishly. I cast what's left of my mind back. We were all dancing drunkenly to bad techno; Rose was pressed up against a wall with some handsome Mediterranean type.

'Rose, I can barely remember my own name. You mean that swarthy-looking bloke? I have no idea. Did you shag him or something?'

'Yeah, I'm at his now, he's just gone to make coffee. What should I do?'

'Just style it out, man. Call him darling until you can figure out his name. Go through his mail when he's in the toilet or something.'

'The toilet's down the corridor; I already tried that. His flatmate has a weird foreign name as well, I can't very well do a fifty-fifty guess!' Rose hisses. I start laughing; this is so unlike her.

'Well, just say he has a very unusual name and ask him how to spell it—' The phone cuts out. Presumably the Italian Stallion has returned.

Ten minutes later, I'm cleaning up last night's sticky detritus from my coat when Rose rings me back.

'He has two flatmates and his name is Steve. Thanks.'

She hangs up again, leaving me to slog through as much work as I can manage with a dreadful hangover, all the while suspecting that there is no point as I may, actually, be dying.

The Pubic Spring

Procrastination, or 'the creative process', as it is also known, is around one-third masturbation. Another third is spent reading the *Daily Mail* online, whose celebrity titbits are unrivalled in their profound vapidity and addictively frequent updates. The remaining period is devoted to productive activities such as plucking whiskers from moles, trying on experimental eye-makeup ideas from *i-D* and stalking future lovers on Facebook. When I have finally tired of these ventures, or run out of rogue hairs, deadline panic sets in and I find myself at three in the morning wondering what in God's name is wrong with me. Why I am unable to complete the simplest tasks until I have bored myself so completely?

All this is by way of saying that I am meant to be working

and have achieved very little. It is the horrible conundrum faced by many middle-class students who have chosen a creative degree; I am used to talking about work, thinking about work and mostly convincing myself and others of my own bullshit while rarely sitting down to complete any of it.

Guided by a conviction, born of years of being told I am special and talented by my parents and teachers, of my vast (largely untapped) potential, I feel sure that I am utterly capable – of something – despite the fact that I have rarely brought any self-directed project to pleasing fruition. My internships have been a baptism of fire into the world of design and taught me innumerable new skills. However, it is far easier to use your talents to construct someone else's vision under their direction, to act as a conduit rather than a creator.

I am sitting in the makeshift studio in my blessedly large closet, surrounded by fabric, paper, pins, a dummy, research material and miscellaneous craft utensils. Sitting here staring at a blank piece of paper is the easy part; having the self-discipline to construct something beautiful out of nothing is trickier. I comfort myself with the thought that my imagination is probably gestating a grand idea for my final collection that will spring fully formed from my forehead at any given moment.

It is early November and, being only three weeks into the final year of my degree, I should have plenty of time to research for my first meeting with Zelda, my tutor, next Tuesday. A passionate and charmingly bat-shit-crazy woman in her early sixties, her intense love for fashion after all these years should be energizing but sometimes has the opposite effect of making me feel flat in comparison. I don't obsess about or feel compelled by this industry in the same way – perhaps, I simply don't want it enough to succeed.

Eventually I will need to present my collection of six looks. But first, baby steps. Collating research, fabric and mood boards, defining the clientele, comparative shopping, market research, consumer buying trends, economic trends and of course aesthetic trends are all a necessary background to a concept. What goes on after all that is where the magic happens. Or not. The moment of truth occurs when, having put pen to paper and turned paper to fabric, finally a body transforms it – into a visual delight or a dog's dinner.

Right. My date with Beardy is scheduled for this evening – I have four hours in which to produce something fantastic before I need to get ready. I start by getting out some swathes of fabric and draping and pinning them on the stand in an elaborate fashion, taking billions of pictures, drawing and making notes as I go. Images that 'inspire' ideas are tacked up on every available surface, with others scattered across the floor. During term time, my room looks like John Nash's bunker in *A Beautiful Mind*, if he was into frocks.

By late afternoon I feel calmer now that I have actually achieved something. I turn myself over to the more immediate task at hand. That is, grooming, painting, plucking, buffing, fluffing and otherwise disguising my natural state as far as is humanly possible for my date with Beardy. I hop in the shower, shaving my legs and underarms for inner confidence even though it is too cold for bare limbs. I hesitate over my minge.

If I am groomed to porn star levels it will be extremely tempting to sleep with him immediately, if only to avoid wasting the precious twenty-four hours before my skin breaks out with ingrown hairs and bumps that will take a whole week to disperse. The prudish, Victorian part of me – it is, admittedly, a slender sliver – cries out weakly that I should leave a chastity hedgerow. Vanity is the only defence my weak virtue possesses.

However, as my self-control is tenuous at best, if I do get carried away in the heat of the moment it will be extremely embarrassing if he discovers what looks like a Muppet toupee stolen from Bert or Ernie trapped in my pants. Unless Beardy likes that sort of thing, which from what I have gathered would make him an anomaly.

When did this idea that a pussy needs to be bald totally permeate popular culture? When did pubes undergo the transformation from erotic and sensual to grotesque? If I were a superhero, I would be BushGirl and fly around the world inciting vaginal hair to sprout in constant unruly rebellion until everyone bloody well gave in and stopped oppressing them. The 'Pubic Spring', if you will.

Though I am well groomed, I am determined not to sleep with Beardy until we've had a few dates. Men think that they are irresistible players if a woman hops into bed with them immediately, but that couldn't be further from the truth. Enough social pressures persist that the fear of looking like 'That Kind Of Girl' exerts its force amongst even those fundamentally inclined to sluttiness (i.e. impulsive females with active libidos who are, despite these grave hindrances, still capable of fidelity and loving relationships). The men you roll over for are the ones you aren't that bothered about seeing again. It's the ones you really like you wait for. Or so I'm told.

As with any rule of thumb, there are exceptions. If you get carried away by lust for someone you want with every fibre of your being, you may have to give in to voluptuous abandon. Then, you wait, and hope he's not the type to consign you to a mental bin labelled 'Random Whore' the moment he reaches orgasm.

I hate that I am reduced to this kind of tragic forethought, but it is impossible to escape. Sex requires far too much effort to ever really be casual. Though having said that, I want badly to sleep with Beardy. Between two people who really fancy each other, why shouldn't first-date sex have the simple significance of an intimate handshake, a respectful but way more fun method of saying I acknowledge your existence, am happy to know you and delight in your body?

I reflect on this unlikely scenario while blow-drying my hair. It is a tedious hassle and I never usually bother, but tonight I feel it's necessary to use every beautifying technique in the book. I leave it down for once, forgoing hairspray so it remains in touchable waves. I'm now ready for the real artistry of the evening. I put on my 'natural' makeup face, which involves concealer, foundation, powder, blusher, bronzer, highlighter, eyebrow pencil, soft eyelid pencil, eye shadow, liquid eyeliner, mascara and lipstick. These are exactly the same components as for my 'nightclub' makeup face, but the level of application makes all the difference.

Deciding what to wear on a first date with someone you suspect is out of your league must exist as a circle of hell overlooked by Dante. I'm drawn to excess, but being obviously try-hard is the kiss of death. Whatever I put on is variously too sexy, too dull, too wacky or just unflattering and I regurgitate the contents of my wardrobe onto the floor in the process. I finally choose a clingy-but-grungy grey knit jumper that's a bit old-school Marc Jacobs, covered by a beat-up, fitted leather bomber. I pair this with a long black skirt, huge wooden platform ankle boots and gold hoop earrings. It's a little bit sexy, a little bit rock, a little bit chav and a lot Amish. But, you know, in a cool way.

I leave the house with a spring in my step, feeling chipper, excited and only slightly nervous. You know how women are supposed to have some mysterious feminine intuition? Well, that's a load of balls, otherwise I would have anticipated the humiliation to come and stayed in with a bottle of vino and *Apocalypse Now*.

We met in Dalston. It started well, with no uninterested silences on his part or inane babbling on mine. I was remarkably relaxed considering how much I fancied him and felt I was on good form – a bit more argumentative than is usual for me, but I blame that on the tequila shots.

Perhaps I should preface this by mentioning how very bad some of my dates have been. I have managed to give myself a black eye and concussion by tripping down a stairwell into a railing (A&E is a shit venue) and once had to leave a bloody tampon that wouldn't flush in the toilet cistern of a man's bathroom left thoughtlessly devoid of loo roll and bins. I can only pray that if discovered, it was never spoken of, but silently blamed on his flatmate's girlfriend. I also once cut a date short when it slowly dawned on me that I had slept with his brother a few months previously. Even I have certain standards to uphold. But the worst date by far – until now – still brings on fresh waves of shame.

Being a smoker is now much like being a heretic. Unless you are in the company of other sinners you must publicly hide your sickness in the knowledge that large swathes of the population consider you to be a worthless pariah. However, safe haven from this persecution can still be found in France and Italy, where respect for one's lungs has largely failed to catch on.

You may have heard that there are some negative aspects to smoking: being the recipient of whingey comments from overbearing tourists, contracting frostbite in winter and a few health risks that I like to think of as Bolshevik propaganda. But the worst aspect – well, I say it is the worst, but it is the most embarrassing thing, really. The *worst* thing is premature ageing. The most *embarrassing* thing is the unintended consequences of the smoker's cough.

The resulting phlegmy vowels can on occasion, after a late night, sound quite sexy. You feel as if you're some fifties temptress that's spent a night drinking whiskey with Sinatra. 'Oh Sinatra! You charming cad . . . Put down that cigar and take me on the billiards table.' At other times, invariably in public, this phlegm winnows its way up through your throat to gather sinisterly, waiting for the right moment to strike. You find yourself, mid conversation, coughing up and flinging this congealed goo into mid-air.

My worst date ever had the dubious honour of one of these projectiles landing in his pint. It's hard to recover from that, really. He didn't call, but he had an early tennis game the next morning and you know what that's like. Dangerous sport, tennis. Any number of fatal accidents might have befallen him.

What could possibly trump that, you ask? Perhaps these dates deserve equal billing in the mortification stakes but, as I like Beardy more, he wins by a narrow margin.

It was all going smoothly – too smoothly. He was fairly witty and very beardy; I was charming and light-hearted. I laughed at all his jokes, which were funny seventy-five percent of the time. Things got a bit frosty on his part after a drunken debate over whether the Western empire was in decline and China would instigate and win World War Three within the next twenty years. I put up a good fight, as one of my more useful life skills is being able to sustain cohesive, convincing arguments on topics I am minimally informed on.

However, I realized that things needed to get more sexy to revive the date and resolved, as per my mother's passive-aggressive dating advice, to 'Let the man win, then disrespect him to your friends'. Her other gems include 'Hate the man, not the gifts' and 'Marrying down will always lead to misery – and, far worse, penury'.

So, I flattered his ego and amped up the flirting. At this point, we were in a dark, dingy basement bar with incongruously expensive leather furnishings and large white candles on gothic stands. Though extremely humid, the flattering lighting and excellent cocktails were worth a mild film of perspiration. He leaned in for a snog.

It was everything you hope from a first kiss: soft, insistent, building up pressure slowly, getting gradually passionate and heated as our tongues and bodies intertwined. Disturbingly hot. Burning in fact. What was that shouting? Beardy pulled back and was staring at me in alarm. Time passed slowly. Bizarrely, someone kept shouting 'Fire! Fire! Fire!' Still a bit dazed from the heat of our embrace, I looked around for the potential source of this calamity, only to see an enormous bouncer running straight at me. He was waving his arms like a madman, repeating 'Fire!'

It dawned on me that I was on fire.

Beardy later said it looked like I had a halo of flames but that he could only stand and stare. The bouncer, bless his rapid-reflexed soul, smothered my head with his leather jacket, putting out the blaze and saving me from a wig-filled future. Thank God I had forgone hairspray that night. If someone, in a misguided attempt to put out the inferno, had tossed a cocktail in my direction, the night could well have been even worse.

The pretentious clientele were all staring at me with a mixture of shock and amusement. I ran to the toilets, not having fully processed what had happened but filled with dread. I pulled out clump after clump of what looked like balls of charcoal with hair strands sprouting out of them. The smell was atrocious.

After that debacle, the evening rapidly deteriorated. Grateful though I was to have been merely humiliated in front of the sexiest man I had ever dated and not gravely wounded, this sort of thankfulness cannot restore a mood. I tried to laugh it off, but the pressure was too much. After a restorative whiskey and both inane babbling (on his part) and shocked silence (on mine) I opted to bolt for a taxi. I could barely mumble goodbye. Oh God. I will be forever known as The Girl Who Set Her Hair On Fire. I am a budget dating-disaster version of Lisbeth Salander.

Oh well, I have to look on the bright side. I had a smouldering – ha – kiss with a very beautiful, very hairy man, who might conceivably call me again, if only out of pity. I am not burnt or bald. I am memorable. I did not cry publicly. I have an excuse for an expensive haircut. I did not projectile phlegm.

It Was A Musical Vibrator

It is with astonishment and tentative delight that I receive a text from Beardy the following Saturday, inviting me round for dinner. After my fiery performance, I suspect it can only be a booty call wrapped in the pretence of romance. He will most likely pounce after the first course – assuming that he provides a starter, main and dessert. If he serves a plate of fish fingers I will immediately know where I stand.

A full week of silence is usually the death-knell for any budding romance, so I think it best to proceed with caution and guard the lowest possible expectations for the night to come. It is possible that he has had a last-minute cancellation from one of his many hipster concubines. English boys can be so relentlessly ugly that it's safer and less painful to assume from the beginning that the good-looking ones have a longstanding harem in place. If after several months of dating you have been suitably fabulous and undemanding, he will with any luck have become sufficiently lazy or fond of you to consider your installation as The Official Girlfriend.

Impulses to voice insecurity must be quashed with the swift annihilation usually reserved by American armed forces for insurgents in the Middle East. A serene, Stepford-girlfriend mask will be carefully held in place until the moment that you actually catch him *in flagrante delicto* with some tattooed seventeen-year-old in a Hervé-for-Topshop bandage dress.

This can't of course be true of every good-looking man in London, but from my personal and vicarious experiences it often proves accurate. What the less fortunate boys might lack in good looks, they often make up in wit and charm; there are certainly plenty of men in London capable of panty-dropping prowess armed only with their intellect and a wonky smile. However, that is also no guarantee of integrity or fidelity, so why not risk being heartbroken by someone who looks like a heartbreaker rather than someone who looks like the back end of a bus? It's less of a slap in the face when they cheat on you if you've felt all along that you probably don't deserve them.

So, with these thoughts in mind, feeling rather depressed about the whole venture, I accepted his offer of dinner. It is sure to be some simple Italian dish that he will insist is his speciality but will taste as if he got it out of a tin, as that is the origin of everything save pasta. Why English men think that the ability to wield a can-opener and boil linguini mystically transmogrifies them into a chef is best left unquestioned. According to my mother, any effort a man makes on your behalf should be fawned over. She believes it is possible to train men, like dogs, to do your bidding with the power of positive reinforcement. This can take the form of excessive praise, cow eyes, feigned personal incompetence for whatever task they are currently engaged in, applause for simple feats and blowjobs for difficult ones.

This didn't prevent my father from descending into a middle-aged stereotype when he ran off with Vitoria, a twenty-six-year-old Brazilian acting as nanny to our neighbour's children. Presumably she was even more experienced at slyly controlling tactics, having been surrounded by small boys. At any rate, I resolve to be flattered and impressed by whatever watery disaster awaits me.

I carry on with the task at hand, namely, updating my CV. I've decided to get some shifts at a pub rather than continue being a freelance waitress at random events. The whole appeal of working for these high-profile parties was that you could supposedly fit them around your schedule, working as little or as often as you like. In practice, it means that the managers ring you every day you are not already booked to guilt-trip you. They are permanently understaffed due to their own idiotic policies.

There is nothing worse than being woken regularly at 9.02 a.m. by Harried Henrietta snapping, 'Yes, well, we'd all rather be doing something else wouldn't we, but we can't, that's what responsibility and commitment to good service is all about. We need at least ten more people for this wedding, you should be honoured that you have been called; it's a chic celebrity affair at a secret location. And also, you actually owe us now – this is your second non-standard attire fine. For each offence, there is a £5 standing fee. Black ballet flats are not black pumps and thus fall short of our uniform requirements.'

Just from her voice, you can tell she is somewhere in Fulham wearing a gilet and Hunter wellies, daydreaming of her horse as she twiddles blonde extensions paid for by her wealthy boyfriend Tibur.

Tempting reluctant staff into extra hours by dangling the dubious carrot of proximity to fame is at best uninspired. The only way I could possibly be swayed is by the presence of one man (Nicolas Cage). At any rate, it is more likely to be someone entirely irrelevant to the whole of humanity, like Gordon Brown. However, I'm afraid this morning after fielding three such calls, irate and nursing a hangover, I finally told her to take my promising career as a waitress and fuck herself with it. I will miss the canapés.

I march into the fresh autumn air, free of my burdens. My plan is to hand out CVs to every pub imaginable before meeting

Beardy at his flat in Bethnal Green. I'm wearing a simple outfit appropriate for both job- and man-hunting: sheepskin coat, white vest, deconstructed Vivienne cardi, skinny jeans and five-inch lace-up boots. My hair, after the disaster last week, has been freshly layered and, though shorter than I prefer, has a certain Joan Jett After-The-Mullet-Years quality. Today, I will charm bar staff and Beardy alike into swooning submission.

This feeling is difficult to sustain after going into twenty bars, all of which are fully staffed, to be fobbed off by managers who nod robotically before, I'm sure, chucking my CV straight in the bin. I soldier on, taking circuitous routes on side roads in the hopes of finding someplace so mystifyingly located that I will have minimal competition.

Finally, I come across a pub in Haggerston that appears to be finishing a recent renovation. There's some scaffolding on one side and it is just the chicer side of shabby. The traditional Victorian brick façade appeals to me, as does its name, The Pissed Newt. Besides being a state I find myself in on a tri-weekly basis, 'newt' is a humorous word to say, though there is not much opportunity to do so outside of medieval apothecaries.

'Hello! I'm Georgie . . . it looks like you're just opening – I was wondering if you need any staff at the moment? I'm looking to work part-time and to start immediately,' I smile at the man behind the bar, a weather-beaten type with kind eyes, a wide grin and 'MUM' tattooed in giant gothic typeface on his upper arm.

'We've been open for over a year, love, but we've only just found the dollar to do the place up . . . and there's always work here for a pretty lady,' he smiles, eyes twinkling in a friendly manner.

I laugh and twirl a lock of my hair excessively, which I immediately regret, but am forced to work to comic effect once I've started. Nothing is weirder than suddenly abandoning a faux-flirtation. He laughs at my lameness and I feel at ease. An hour previously in a different bar, a leery bloke had said the same thing with an entirely different effect. It's funny how two people can read from the same script and from one person it will be charming, from another creepily inappropriate.

'In that case, can I speak to the manager?'

'The owner manages the pub but he's got a few other places he takes care of. I'm the assistant manager, Gary. How much experience have you got?'

'Well, I've done waitressing and bar jobs at festivals so I think I'd pick it up quickly. I'm a student so I'm looking for something three nights a week, I'm flexible on days,' I say, getting out my CV and placing it on the bar.

'Okay, just a few more questions then.' Gary hums while getting out a pen, inspecting my CV and scribbling some notes on it. I wait, hoping his queries don't run to the dreaded quirky variety. I'm not talented at sounding spontaneously cool, probably because I am not spontaneous or cool. It would take at least a week's preparation for me to be reliably down with the kids. Is the recession so bad that to get a job pulling pints you have to have model looks, a winning personality and a solid knowledge of underground music?

'How old are you?' Phew. That I can answer.

'Twenty-five. Well, I'm twenty-five in April. That's ages away. But now I'm twenty-four. Evidently.' For God's sake, woman, I scold myself, have you learnt nothing from Two-Minute-Michael? Brevity is the soul of valour.

'Favourite film?'

'Oh, um . . . *Bitter Moon* has great, amazingly terrible dialogue. And *Showgirls*! I love really tacky excessive films. But also, you know, good ones . . . like . . . uh . . .'

Don't say *Samurai Cop*. Or *Birdemic: Shock and Terror*. What have you seen that's good? You've watched loads of good films – you can just never remember the titles, directors or plots. What about that Werner Herzog documentary that you found inappropriately amusing?

'*Grizzly Man*,' I finish breathlessly.

'Ah, that one about that guy who was eaten by bears? That was rough.'

'Yeah, pretty gruesome.'

'If you were on a pirate ship, what would you be?'

'What, you mean, first mate or skipper or something? Uhh

. . . I'd be . . . probably pregnant!' Great, I am a slag with poor taste in films.

'What's the most humiliating thing you've ever experienced?' Now, that question gives me a wealth to choose from.

The truth, which I will not share with Gary, is that when I was fourteen years old I explosively shat myself in the Harrods Food Hall. I had terrible food poisoning after eating a bad oyster with my mum and I was wearing a white sundress. I left a trail of runny defecation as I ran through the labyrinthine corridors, from the Fragrance Rooms to the Egyptian escalators, searching for the exit. Ten minutes of intermittent yet unstoppable diarrhoea feels like a lifetime. However, I sense I should avoid telling this story or his impression of me will forever be: Twenty-four/B-Films/Knocked-Up/Shitter. So I say,

'Well, this charming new haircut I'm sporting is the result of setting my head alight on a date last week.' I swish my hair and laugh. 'Is that bad enough?'

'I'll pass on your CV.'

I try to subtly lean over to work out what he's scribbled on it. I think I catch: 'Student. Twenty-four. Some Experience. Friendly. Bit weird'. I'll take that!

Beardy answers the door barefoot, in a tight white T-shirt and low slung ripped jeans that show off an inch of his toned stomach. I have to swallow and avert my eyes from those

74

glorious hipbones, reminding myself not to slobber like a dog on heat. Lord, give me strength to comport myself like a lady, not a desperate slapper. Though I am agnostic verging on atheist, like all sensible people I turn to prayer in times of dire financial or sexual need. Just in case.

'Hey there,' Beardy grins. He's not wearing the heinous glasses. His eyes are a deep green, the colour of moss on a rock. Which doesn't sound as sexy as 'With eyes like the sea after a storm,' but totally is. His hand reaches out and lightly runs through a lock of hair that's fallen over one of my eyes. 'Like what you've done with the barnet.'

'Haha, thanks, sorry for rushing off like that before, I was a bit shell-shocked I think, but I was overdue for a haircut anyway, really, they nearly gave me a mullet-shag though, it was a close shave. Have you had a good week?' I prattle as I step inside. Slow down. Shut up. Mysterious. Remember: your flirting sounds mean and you are not funny.

'Hey no worries, that's cool . . . I'm all right. I've had a lot of work on and been rehearsing with my band and stuff. I would have texted you to ask how you were but I had phone trouble.'

Ah. Non-specific phone trouble. I used to give more credence to this type of excuse but have had difficulty ignoring my suspicions after running into an old one-night-stand. In a fit of embarrassment, he said the reason he never called was that he'd thrown his mobile into the Thames after a fight with his best friend. I believed him, too, until his pocket started shaking wildly, emitting a 'Smack My Bitch Up' ringtone. When I asked, quite mildly considering, 'Then what's that then?' he had the gall to respond that it was a musical vibrator.

These days, I'm a firm believer in the old adage that if he wants to find you, he will find a way; if he hasn't, move swiftly onwards. And Beardy did find me, even if it was a week late. It's kinder that he's offering up an excuse. Now we can both pretend that I gave him the benefit of the doubt, having more self-respect than someone who leaps at a last-minute Saturday night probable sex-date.

'So that freelance project you mentioned is going well then?' I ask.

Beardy, like every third person in the East End, is a graphic designer. As I am a womenswear student, soon to be swelling the ranks of unemployed fashion designers, I can't really fault him for being a cliché. He also plays lead guitar in a band called Tinny Wake Up Call or something equally odd. From what I remember it's some sort of rock/minimal-electro/grime mélange that I pray I won't be subjected to.

'Yeah, it's very commercial but it pays the bills. Once Tin Can Bang takes off I won't need to bother with that shit any more.'

He leans against the wall with his arms crossed. One of his biceps is covered in tattoos; I hadn't noticed that before. He looks like a walking Levi's commercial. The kind of man that men want to punch and women want to go down on in alleyways. Suddenly, I don't care if his music includes the cries of abandoned puppies.

'You sound quite confident . . . cocky even . . .' I smile, one eyebrow raised flirtatiously. I try to lean back against the wall sexily, mimicking his pose, but fall over my left foot in the process before righting myself. Luckily, he appears not to notice.

'It's not cocky if you're really fucking good, which we are.' God, what is it about grown men still utterly convinced they are going to be rock stars that is so damn attractive? I do love a textbook man-child.

I have dated musicians at various stages of failure before. It's definitely time to leave when the realization dawns on them that they are going to be living in a bedsit in Willesden for the rest of their lives, teaching guitar to spoilt posh kids in W11 and having the landline periodically cut off. Even if you don't care how much he earns initially, the depression that results from his unfulfilled egomania will get to you. You will start to see his future. He will spend his late thirties exaggerating his past accomplishments to impressionable but increasingly bored young girls. He will convince himself this is a sign that he's still got it, rather than the reality, which is that than no woman his own age is willing to put up with his bullshit. By the time he is sixty, he will be one of those alcoholic perverts you once mocked in Sixth Form.

I say none of this, as it would be unbearably rude and the key to a successful love life is to ruthlessly repress any thoughts or opinions that might cause offence for at least the first six months.

'I'd say good luck, but clearly you don't need it. You play what . . . ? Keyboard? Tambourine?' I let the question dangle in the air coyly, as if far wittier than it is.

'Lead guitar, I sing a bit too.' He leans over me, with his hand pressed against the wall at my head. 'But you knew that.' He leans his leg between mine and starts nuzzling my neck before we start kissing passionately. This is why I like cocky wankers.

I come up for air, breathless.

'Lead guitarists and singers are the worst. Narcissists. Girls really like drummers. They're not so desperate for the spotlight. Or a bass player, someone able to share the stage a bit.'

'You've got me there. When I want something, I don't like sharing.' He pushes me up against the wall. Oh my days.

We never do get round to making dinner.

The Repulsion

'Oh ho! Don't you just look happy as a clam!' Rose says, as she spots me walking towards their table in The Queen Vic Tavern.

There's nothing like a beer garden on an unusually sunny, crisp November day to bring a smile to my face, but there is a bit more to it than that. I take my seat on the bench, taking care to swirl the fabric of my full, knee-length skirt over my thigh-high easy access stockings. I am wearing them on the off-chance that Beardy rings me later tonight after my trial shift at the Newt. Only true lust would make me behave thusly with winter around the corner.

'Yeah, a clam who's been fucked repeatedly,' Sarah adds dryly. Bingo!

'What a beautiful day, what a beautiful world!' I put down my pint of organic cider and inhale the midday air dramatically.

'Christ, it's amazing what a good rogering can do for a cynical soul. I've forgotten what that's like.' Sarah manages to sound happy for me and completely morose at the same time. 'So, details, woman!'

'Well, as you know from my ranting over the hair incident, I was expecting things with Beardy to fizzle out, but Saturday I went round to his and it was just . . . so hot. We were messing around and drinking wine. I managed to restrain myself and not just full-on go for it . . . it was really hard as part of me was thinking, "If this is my only opportunity to shag him I want to know what I'll be missing for the rest of my life!" At about three in the morning I was drunk and starving, so I made my excuses and went home and had a fry up.'

'What! Why! You chose food over sex? Georgie, I thought we were on the same page on this one.' Sarah looks betrayed.

'I was really fucking hungry, okay? I hadn't eaten since lunch! I wanted to keep the sexual tension going and didn't want to eat some massive meal then start kissing him again feeling all bloated.'

'Yeah, but you wouldn't have to necessarily eat a massive meal . . .' Rose is one of those people who likes her food well enough, but doesn't, unlike me, spend a good deal of the time she's not eating planning her next meal.

'No, it's so dissatisfying picking at something when you want to gorge to your heart's content. The point is – I made the right call because the next day he rang me up and we ended up spending all day in the pub, talking and playing Scrabble. Really nice relaxing Sunday. And then I saw him Tuesday night and pounced . . . I didn't have class and he sacked off work so we just stayed in bed shagging, watching telly and ordering takeaways until Thursday afternoon. It was amazing.'

'God, that does sound amazing. I wish I were still at uni. And had a hot new love interest. So, what was the sex like?' Sarah waggles her eyebrows.

'Pretty drunken and messy at first. We were basically just ripping each other's clothes off. It was really good though, he definitely knows what he's about . . . no awkward moments.'

'Gosh, sounds perfect! Are you seeing each other again soon?' Rose asks. Sarah looks at her with mild perplexity. I don't think the word 'gosh' has been included in her vocabulary since primary school.

'Yeah, we're having a Scrabble rematch on Sunday. He tried not to be a sore loser but it was pretty clear my winning didn't sit well with him.'

'Fucking hell, you've gone from a lovelorn single to properly coupled up in a week! When are we going to meet this hairy paragon?' Sarah says with an interrogative edge.

'Oh, I don't know about that, I'm going to take things as

they come . . . but I also had a really productive tutorial today and I've got a trial at that pub I mentioned tonight, so life is going unexpectedly well! I'll have to leave soon to get there, though.'

'Humph. That's so unfair. Tell me something bad about him. There must be something. Tiny dick? Granny fetish? Throw me a bone here.'

Oh dear. Things must not be going very well with Henry. When Sarah is content, she has an air of oneness with the whole of mankind; when she is dissatisfied, she likes to rip them all to shreds, starting with their penises. Lately, it's been rather more the latter.

'Oh, come on Sarah, allow her infatuation to remain pure for the first week at least.'

Rose rolls her eyes while twisting a long lock of hair in her fingers, watching the gingery gold of it catch the light. It's something I've observed her doing when she has her eye on someone. Sure enough, there is a tall, geek-chic Lothario standing opposite us, smoking a fag, pretending not to be entranced.

'I am totally infatuated . . . but I'm not blind. Okay, bad things: a) He wears those hipster glasses I mentioned not only by choice, but unnecessarily. The lenses are clear; I checked when he was in the loo. As a visually impaired person I find this offensive; b) He's a grower not a shower, that doesn't matter in any real sense but it might make you feel better.'

'True, it does. Henry has a glorious cock, even totally flaccid.' Sarah is something of a penis connoisseur.

'And c) He is a bit pretentious. I mean, confidence is hugely attractive, but he's a bit dismissive with it. I get the feeling that he's used to groupie-type women who don't necessarily have that much to say, so when I occasionally challenge him – in a jokey way – he gets annoyed.'

'That's no good! Well, bitch, he'll just have to get used to a strong independent woman!' Rose purses her lips and clicks her fingers.

I nod my assent, but have decided to merely bite my tongue next time like a good Stepford Wifey. Good beards are hard to come by. Also, I've always secretly suspected that if you find someone you really like, it's wise to alter yourself to their desires to keep them.

The whole concept that you are special just the way you are and you should be unfailingly proud of your personality and beliefs with no regard for others is at best vastly overrated advice, and at worst detrimental to the human race. Well-intentioned, rather American in sentiment, it wants the best for everyone and inadvertently brings out the worst. Maybe traditions of shame and public self-restraint are more bene-ficial to society in the long run. Don't you think the world would be so much more elegant if people stopped inflicting even ten percent of their worst character flaws on each other? If rational criticism wasn't met with 'Haters gonna hate' swiftly followed by an Instagrammed photo of a raised middle finger?

'I'm sick of being a strong, independent woman,' Sarah says. 'Sometimes I just want a caveman who will tell me what to do with my life, has throwdown in the bedroom and falls asleep immediately after coming, not some pussy who curls up in my arms like a child and says he feels neglected and can we talk about it. All we do is talk! We barely fuck! I can't take it.'

'Oh . . . dear. So things have come to a head with Henry, I take it?' Rose asks gently.

'I just feel that, because I'm a confident woman who knows what I want, I somehow scare away confident men who know what *they* want – because what they want is an easy life with some bimbo. So I get the nice guy who is perfectly decent in every way and very good to me, but miss out on the thrill of someone with some sort of . . . personal power. I feel like I'm his mother half the time.'

'Henry's lovely, but just because he's decent doesn't mean feeling like his mother is healthy! Maybe you should take a break?' I try to look concerned while concentrating on rolling my cigarette, a feat that after two years I have yet to master.

'I know. But I want to be totally sure before I do, it's not fair of me to have one foot out the door, but it would be worse to realize I still want him after chucking him and mess him around like that.'

'Do you think he'd definitely take you back if you dumped him, then?'

Rose takes a long, slow sip from her vodka and tonic, keeping eye contact with the Casanova across the room. It's pretty ballsy of her, but he doesn't approach.

'I know he would, absolutely. Which is the problem. Who wants someone whom you're one-hundred percent sure of? Where's the challenge in that?'

'So are you just waiting for the repulsion at this point?'

You all know of what I speak. It can strike after a betrayal, the passage of time, or even one too many bad jokes. The moment when after days, weeks, months or years, you turn to your erstwhile lover, the scales fall from your eyes and they fill you with, well, The Repulsion. This is something from which you can never recover.

'Basically. I think I'm nearly there, to be honest. Every little thing he does fills me with irrational rage, and because he's so goddamn nice I hate him even more. The other day I mistook one of his socks for my own and even just putting it on halfway made me shudder with disgust. It wasn't even dirty. So you can imagine how I feel about his dick.'

'That's not ideal.'

'Excuse me, ladies, I'm sorry to interrupt you . . . Do you by any chance have a lighter?'

Rose's seduction technique has finally paid off. I approve of his approach; nicotine-related icebreakers are classic, the Bogart of come-ons. They have just the right amount of smoothness while, crucially, providing a dignified escape if met with cold impartiality. If they then light your next cigarette while holding steady eye contact at that sweet spot between flirtatious and creepy, you're golden. I shall dearly miss them should I ever give up.

'Has anyone ever told you that you look like a painting by Rubens?'

Aaand he had to ruin it by conflating his artists. Rose has a lovely figure but like every woman is highly sensitive to any 'fat' connotation. She blanches.

'Do you mean the Pre-Raphaelites?' Sarah says, trying to save him.

'No, no, Rubens.' He grins widely at his cheek. 'Definitely Rubens.'

'Are you negging me, cause I warn you right now that shit only works on girls with very low self-esteem,' Rose ripostes with a steely glint in her eye.

'Kiddos, I've got to go. Can't get too pissed before I go to work.' Winking at Rose, I leave them to it.

The Pissed Newt attracts a mixed crowd typical of East London. There are a few disgruntled old Cockney men sitting in a corner downing pints of bitter and reminiscing about the good old days before gastro pubs changed their corner of the world for ever. Students talk loudly about last night's sexual adventures, vainly trying to distract themselves from the likelihood that student loans will be the financial highlight of their lives. A few artfully unwashed types lounge about debating whether or not Leipzig is the new Berlin, looking from their threadbare but chic accoutrements as if they are either destitute or absolutely loaded. It's possible they are both; squatting in an old factory in Bow doesn't mean you can't also weekend in Surrey with the family. But it does mean that when you tire of running from the money you come from, you will eventually die of asbestos poisoning.

With Gary showing me the ropes, I settle into a rhythm working the bar, trying to present my most confident and shiny self. I am certainly shining with a sweat beard if nothing else – nervousness has made me flustered and I find it impossible to pull a pint without a huge head. This would make me an instant success in Belgium but in England my efforts receive barely concealed disgust. I try to keep up a stream of friendly chat with the customers and my fellow barmaid, Joy, who has been given a terribly misleading name. A sullen girl in her early twenties, she manages to be nearly mute, yet shout her displeasure at my presence through a series of rolled eyes, sighs and muttered asides that drip with disdain.

Although a strong profile on a lady can be very striking, I can't help but think uncharitably that her face would benefit from a nose job. She has that slightly inbred look typical of English aristocrats, with sloping eyes too far apart and a weak chin. Though her azure-blue irises and strong cheekbones give shades of beauty to her features, her conker obscures them to any but the most determined observer. It leers menacingly out of her forehead, casting its malevolent shadow over her other more attractive characteristics like a tiny Voldemort.

Despite this, she has clearly never been short of male attention, as her body is quite frankly one of the most magnificent and undeserved I have ever seen. She leans back against the counter eating a packet of pork scratchings; her low slung jeans reveal an expanse of concave stomach; the thin fabric of her shrunken Iron Maiden T-shirt clearly shows the outline of her large, perky, braless breasts. I think of my own sunken torpedoes with despair. Sometimes it seems like everyone has aggressively lofty nipples, while I've been tempted to staple pencil rubbers to the uppermost point of my bra and swan around in a wife beater just to see what that would feel like.

By closing time, we have firmly established a dynamic whereby I try valiantly to remain pleasant and she pretends I don't exist. At least she hasn't singled me out for her hatred – in that respect she is quite democratic. When a forty-something Phil Collins doppelgänger in a bad suit leers a little too close to her while she pours his Carling, she snaps loudly, 'Do you mind? I have an irrational fear of bald skin.'

Joy is such a pill that I am tempted to refuse a position if they offer one to me, but as that is doubtless her aim I don't want to give her the satisfaction. In any case, Gary makes up for Joy's presence. A burly late thirty-something with an array of fairly hideous tattoos that he got under the influence of faux-heterosexuality in the nineties, Gary is full of stories that become increasingly implausible as the night wears on and is not averse to slipping me a G&T every so often.

After we have finally wrangled the drunken punters out the door at 1 a.m. and Joy has stalked off home, Gary puts on some Eartha Kitt and we sing along gustily while clearing up.

I have just finished putting up the stools and turning out most of the lights. Lost in a rather good rendition of *C'est Si Bon*, I am romancing the last remaining chair with a waltz while singing '*Ou peut-être quelqu'un avec un petit yacht, non?*' when a bang from a darkened corner makes me whirl around in shock.

I wield the chair in front of me in defence as I peer vainly into the dim corners of the pub. Quieting my breathing, I step lightly away from the centre of the room towards the wall. I stay absolutely still and silent, my irregularly beating heart pounding in my ears with a volume I'm afraid can be heard from miles off. A hulking, misshapen figure is emerging from the darkness. Gary is in the storeroom, unaware of the intruder. My mouth dry, my throat constricted, I try to emit a scream, but when none is forthcoming I settle on hurling my wooden makeshift weapon at the shadowy form. It falls back with a crash.

'Argh – what the – what the fuck!' The intruder is evidently Scottish. Emerging into the light with one hand over his eye and the other clutching a bleeding knee is a hunched figure. 'What the bloody fuck!'

'Er . . . Er . . . We're closed! What do you want?' I shout, my body still trembling though I am starting to doubt he poses a threat. The man has rumpled hair sticking out in all directions and is wearing a white T-shirt, Snoopy boxers and one sock. Not the sort of apparel I would expect from a thief, rapist or murderer.

'I own the bloody pub! And who the fuck are you?' He has dropped his hand from his eye and is moving towards the wall. Flipping a switch, he swears as the lights come harshly on and again, more loudly, as he inspects the gash on his knee. As I process his words, the physical manifestation of 'Shiiiit' spreads through my chest, in a sort of rigid seizure of regret.

'I – I'm new! You should thank me; I was defending your pub! You shouldn't sneak up on helpless females!' I still feel caught between an impulse to fight or flee. Currently, fight is winning and I seemed to have summoned all of my outrage.

The man snorts, straightening up and leaning back against a table to gingerly rub at his bruised eye.

'Helpless females. I don't think I've ever met a less helpless female in my life. I count myself lucky you were holding a chair not a bottle. See who's there before you throw something next time. Where the hell is Gary?'

'What was I supposed to do? It's dark and you looked like Quasimodo!' I am dimly aware that my tone should change from outrage to supplication at some point but I am still too taken aback to control myself.

'So your standard reaction when confronted with a cripple is to attack them. I see,' he says dryly, brushing his hair off his forehead. 'Fantastic customer service, very P.C.'

'At least I know that referring to the disabled as cripples is frowned upon these days . . .'

Oh dear. Must stop insulting the owner. He takes a few steps towards me and peers at my face searchingly, as it dawns on me that I know him from somewhere.

'Scott, Scott, whoa . . . What happened? Are you okay?' Gary flicks on the main light and rushes over. 'Ouch. That's gonna be a bruiser. Did you run into a door or something? And what happened to your knee?'

Scott? Scott? Oh, *Scott*. Oh, *shit*.

'I appear to be the victim of domestic violence.' A trace of humour inflects his voice, I notice with relief. 'I was just coming down to tell you queens to stop your bloody caterwauling when I met . . .'

'Georgie,' I mumble, looking down and trying to hide my face in my hand.

'Georgie. I suspect if she'd been better prepared I would have met a sticky end.' Scott Montgomery gives me a lop-sided smile. I am torn between hoping against hope that he does not remember our first encounter and hoping that he does.

'It's lucky I left my nunchucks at home . . .' I say with a weak grin, which is met with an unimpressed silence. 'I really am sorry. I was just – you took me by surprise.'

Scott stares at me inscrutably for an uncomfortably long time, then says shortly:

'That's not a mistake I'll be making again, I assure you. I live upstairs. You should be aware that I come down from time to time.'

'You mean . . . you're still going to take me on?'

'Well, we could use a guard dog.' A smile plays on his lips. I feel hysterically relieved.

'Hey careful! If you call me a dog again you might find me pissing on a wall to spite you.' I can't believe I've just threatened to piss on his walls. What is *wrong* with me?

Gary looks between us, faintly bemused.

'Do you two know each other from somewhere?'

'N-no . . .' I stutter, as Scott raises an eyebrow.

'I have had the pleasure of her acquaintance before, though then I emerged unscathed . . . physically at any rate. Perhaps my injuries are so disfiguring that you don't recognize me?'

'I really don't know what you're talking about.' I feign ignorance. 'And that barely qualifies as a flesh wound. Though you should probably put something on that eye.'

I walk over to inspect it more closely. He brushes back a

thick lock of his soft hair. I am struck again by how golden-brown it is, like Lucky Strike tobacco. Disturbed by this line of thought, I lean in to squint at the bloodshot eye beneath his purpling lids.

'Everything looks perfectly in order. You should be fine.'

'I think I'll go elsewhere for medical advice, thank you. You don't seem a likely nurse. What do you do anyway? Aside from accosting your employers.'

'Fashion design – so I'm handy with a needle and thread. I am also a hypochondriac so am familiar with pretty much any diagnosis available on Google. That's practically a medical degree in and of itself.'

'I'm just going to close the till and then we're finished here . . .' Gary says, moving off behind the counter.

'I really am sorry,' I whisper, feeling strangely intimate with him as we are left alone. He shakes his head as if to say it was nothing.

'You'll be thanking me in the end; it'll look like you've been in a proper fight with a scary man. Men, even. You can pretend you did something heroic.' In awkward moments I always reach for a humorous take on the situation. It is usually inappropriate.

'There's no need to pretend . . . I think you'll find I do heroic things on a daily basis,' Scott grins. My stomach flips slightly.

'I . . .' I have no idea what I was about to say, but am interrupted by my phone suddenly going off in my pocket. I silently curse the fact that I haven't changed it from 'Call On Me', which wasn't particularly clever five years ago and is definitely cringe-making now.

'Excuse me one second . . . Hello?'

'It's me. I'm drunk and I want you. Come over, I'll bring the wine if you bring the cigarettes.'

Ah, Beardy. There's something so thrilling about a man who knows how to tread the thin line between sexy-demanding and controlling-demanding. Though I love the company of women and am as aggressively feminist as a lazy and apolitical person can be, if I'm honest I think that most women want to be led with a firm hand – as long as it's kept to the bedroom. However, tonight I feel a pull of resistance.

Moving away from Scott, I hem and haw on the phone while Beardy tries to persuade me. Why do I put myself in situations in which men with minimal interest in my wellbeing feel justified in ringing me up in the midnight hours to propose drunken sex? Shouldn't I be saving myself? But saving myself for what? Something special? Special has been thin on the ground in my limited experience. If I had waited all this time for whatever Special is, I'd probably ruin things. Better to be practised enough with varying degrees of Not-Special, Decidedly-Average, Quite-Shit and Out-And-Out-Horrific so that when Special comes along you have the gaming where-withal not to scare it away. Really, Beardy is exactly what I've been looking for. Sexy, fun, easy and non-complicated.

There are worse ways to pass an evening. Making my excuses to Gary and adding a final profuse apology to Scott, I leave the bar to go and find pleasure in a cold bottle and a warm body. In the words of the inimitable Janis Joplin: 'Get It While You Can.'

Post-Apocalyptic David Lynch Zombies

I awake to the sound of my ringtone blaring somewhere in Beardy's room. I struggle out of bed naked to search for it amidst the jumbled mass of our clothing, eventually upending my bag all over the floor in the process. Filter tips, tampons, pieces of gum, tobacco, small change, a leaky biro pen and grotty lipsticks fly in every direction. Finally I find my phone in the pocket of my coat.

It is my mother, of course. No one else would call repeatedly at 9 a.m. on a Sunday. Wrapping a manky old towel around myself, I sneak into the corridor to take her call, knowing that if I don't answer immediately she will assume I have died in a tragic accident and contact half my friends to determine the whereabouts of my mutilated body.

'Yes, what is it?' I answer grumpily.

'Hello, darling. I was just calling to make sure you are alive and well. Have you done something productive this weekend or are you wasting your life as usual?'

'Yes, yes, I'm alive.' A good seventy-five percent of my ever-reluctant telephone conversations with her begin like this; hopefully by the time I reach thirty she will have more faith in my ability to survive the weekend. 'I won't be well until I've had more sleep. I'm just at Beard— at Leo's.'

I pick at the formerly white, now yellowing and coffee-stained terrycloth fabric wrapped around me. I would be tempted to marry a man who replaced his towels occasionally, though I suppose it is a blessing that Beardy even has sheets. It's shocking how many grown men think it's acceptable not to own them. Regrettable one-night stands and the feel of a bare mattress against my skin are indelibly linked in my mind.

'Leo! Who is that? You didn't tell me you have a new boyfriend!' My mother manages to sound accusatory, worried and elated all at once. Shit. I had forgotten about my resolution not to tell her anything about my love life until an unavoidable occasion such as a wedding or childbirth. I always live to regret passing on any gossip to her, as she is both extremely judgemental and irritatingly accurate in her character assessments.

'Erm, well, it's early days . . . I wouldn't say that exactly.'

'Oh, darling. You haven't slept with him, have you? Why buy a cow when you can get the milk for free? I kept your father waiting until our wedding night.'

And the over-sharing guilt trips commence. I know far more about my parents' former sex life than can possibly be healthy, especially coming from someone who believes that vibrators are a feminist myth propagated by 'The Media'. In her mind, 'The Media' is run by gay men and radical feminazis. No amount of high street sex shops will ever be able to convince her otherwise.

'And why buy a pig for a sausage link? Mum, you sound Victorian, it's like the women's movement never happened. Only crazy ring-obsessed ladies who think they can use a man's sexual frustration to blind him to their flawed personalities do that these days. And I'm only twenty-four, Christ.'

'What are you saying, you're nearly twenty-seven!'

'Seriously? Mum, I'm twenty-four.' You would think that your only child emerging from your genitals would constitute a memorable occasion, but apparently not. Lying about her own age has apparently scrambled mine.

'What? Oh. Well, it is your birthday come April. Twenty-five is nearly twenty-seven, which is nearly thirty. You really need to start thinking that your next boyfriend might be your husband and practise pretending to be wife material, you know. Where is this boy from? He doesn't have a speech impediment like that last one does he?'

'He didn't have a speech impediment. He was Northern.'

'Oh darling, it amounts to the same thing.'

'Did you call just to hassle me?'

'What does this Leo do then?'

'Uh . . . he's a graphic designer. And a musician.'

There is a pause. I hear a deep whistling sigh on the other end of the line. And then it comes, as I knew it would come:

'Darling, do try to meet a man who can afford you. I really don't want to see you ending up divorced, or living on a council estate with some wastrel husband who's lost his good looks to drugs. He is at least good looking isn't he? Please don't give me ugly grandchildren; I have enough crosses to bear as it is. You know, you give birth, children are so expensive and then they go off and waste all the money you've invested in them designing clothes and sleeping with swarms of unsuitable men who only want One Thing.'

I wish. Going through swarms of unsuitable men is a long-cherished dream.

'Well, maybe you should have aborted me and invested your money in something with better returns. I'm your only child, not some vanity project gone carelessly awry,' I say dryly. We've had this conversation many times before and it has long since failed to register emotionally. In our household, saying something like 'You should have aborted me' carries no more weight than 'You forgot to buy the milk'.

'Darling, you know I love you; it's just hard for me to see

you wasting your looks, youth – what's left of it – and your talents. You could have been a barrister!' This comes up frequently, despite my having never shown any interest in or affinity for Law. I can only assume the fact that I don't break down and weep during our heated arguments qualifies me. 'And why shouldn't I get some sort of return from you? People originally had children because they worked the farm and cleaned the house, not because they brought them joy. The only thing you can do for me these days is to reflect well on me, is that so much to ask?'

As irritating as this little chat is, I do understand her perspective on things. What is the point of having children? Likely as not, they will drain your finances in their youth, remain adolescently dependent well into adulthood and then totally ignore you in your dotage. If you're lucky they might spring for a half-decent hospice, but more likely death will be a sweet relief from whatever poorly funded NHS pit you are thrown into.

'Well, sorry, I'll try harder in future. Was there something else?'

'Yes. Your father is in town and wants to have supper to discuss something, he won't tell me what, of course. You need to be there. I would like some moral support please. That Woman will be with him. I'd like you to be on my side this time.'

'Oh, right. Okay. Are you all right? When?'

Dad lives in Rickmansworth in Hertfordshire. To Mum, this is is so far outside Greater London he might as well have moved to the Gobi desert. They've been divorced for years, but they are still fiercely opposed. In my mother's words, 'How can the greatest betrayal a wife can face ever be amicable?' I do try to be on her side, but it's difficult when the battle lines have been drawn over decades and you are never quite sure where they might lie.

If my father had been discreet, I'm not entirely sure she would have been too concerned. She frequently opined that polygamy is a practical solution to the difficulties that modern longevity have added to marriage. In her romanticized fantasy, however, she as the First Wife would act as Empress with the Second Wife as a Concubine who would not only take over her unwanted sexual duties but also act as her personal slave. If Dad had just taken a mistress, Mum might have felt a certain relief in sharing him with someone else and even fooled herself that it was a rather Continental arrangement. Walking in on him cheating in their marital bed shattered that illusion. The combination of betrayal and abandonment scarred her deeply.

'Of course I'm perfectly fine darling, I'm so much happier without that old blowhard. He can have his floozy – I know deep down he must be miserable without me. She's as dull as dishwater and has probably been more thoroughly used. We're having supper at The Brompton Bar and Grill on Thursday at 8 p.m. Wear something appropriate please.'

'Yeah okay, cool. I'll see you then. Have a good week!'

'Yes, of course, darling. Bye, dear.'

Yikes. Is the sacrament of marriage really worth all the wounds you'll inevitably inflict on each other long-term, let alone the initial bureaucracy and paperwork? There are times when it is inconceivable to me that I might ever be so in love that I could delude myself that marital vows are anything more than conditional promises no one really intends to keep.

'Hey, what are you doing out there? Come back to bed.' Beardy's deep voice nudges me out of my reverie. His head pokes out of the doorframe and one arm snakes out to tug at my messy hair affectionately. God I love the look of a man who has just rolled out of bed, still sleep-rumpled, smelling of night sweats and duvet. There's nothing like the whiff of light perspiration on someone you really fancy.

'Just gonna nip to the toilet first,' I say, suddenly aware that while a man can look rugged and effortlessly hot in the morning, my streaked makeup and puffy cheeks bear more than a passing resemblance to one of Lindsay Lohan's mug-shots.

I repair my face and hair as much as is possible with the limited repertoire of products in Beardy's bathroom. It is a depressing struggle which leaves me seriously considering having my patchy eyebrows tattooed into uniformity with semi-permanent makeup. I slink back into his room and pray for low lighting.

'Come here, you.' Beardy wraps an arm around me as I slide under the blanket. I usually love having a lie-in the arms of a warm man, but after my conversation with my mother I feel restless.

I toy with launching into a confessional about my family situation to explain my weird mood, but decide it's too early into our – whatever this is – to have a deep and meaningful conversation. I can see how it would pan out. I would feel uncomfortable and over-share, he would pretend to be sympathetic and try to console me with sex, which would annoy me because why can't men understand that sometimes you just want to be listened to for ten minutes without having a penis inside you? I would get upset and reject him sexually, neither of us would get what we wanted from the situation and we would both end up frustrated. I decide to stick to mysterious silence. He probably hasn't even noticed I'm upset.

I stare up at the ceiling, tracing the cracks and wondering when I can reasonably get up and leave. The artificial closeness from the night before has dissipated, leaving me with a dull hangover and a desire to be free of the entwining limbs and demands of the body next to me. He pulls me closer, running his hands over my breasts, stranding me somewhere between desire and irritation.

I wonder what it is I want from him, if anything. Most of the relationships I've had have been less a matter of falling in love with a person and more a slow, inexorable movement towards exclusivity based on the passage of time and a lack of other contenders. They have left me feeling not secure, but trapped.

I hate to say it, but the exceptions have been the bad boys. With He Who Shall Not Be Named (oh, fine – Anthony), I felt relentlessly insecure but wild enough to forfeit my freedom. He led me to believe a litany of lies so absurd that, really, he deserved credit for his creativity. My personal favourite was his fervent contention that the hickeys on his neck were the result of falling onto gravel. After we broke up, the full extent of his psychopathic tendencies was revealed. In a misguided attempt to guilt-trip me into speaking to him, he pretended he had committed GBH and was going to prison. Why he thought this would garner my sympathies is still a mystery.

Before that, of course, there was my first love Alexi. His French accent and spaniel eyes were so soulful that I abandoned all rational thought completely, only to be left behind when he stole my money and took the flight to Colombia without me. People often remark that love is blind, but far more worrying is its ability to make you deaf and dumb.

Clearly, the lesson here is that I should avoid men whose names start with 'A'.

'I'm playing a gig tonight with the boys . . . wanna come?' Beardy's low voice draws me out of my brooding.

'Uh, yeah, I guess so . . . I'm not sure. I should really get some work done. Where are you playing?'

'The Bomb Shelter, at ten. We're shooting a new video for a single this week you know, it's gonna be great, we have a sort of apocalypse zombie from outer space theme but sort of with a David Lynch vibe. It's really low budget, just us in it but we've managed to scrape together some friends who can help with the set and makeup and stuff so it should be really cool.'

'You're putting out a single?'

'Yeah, I mean, we're unsigned but who knows . . . it's all about building support from the ground up, we'll put things online and see how it goes, generate some interest . . . next stop, Glastonbury!'

We both laugh, but I can tell he's partly serious. I can't decide whether it's charming or incredibly naive that he believes that one day he's going to be headlining major festivals. Maybe it's because I've never had the combination of relentless ambition, dazzling ego and singular focus that is the mark of superstars and delusional failures alike. Who knows, perhaps he's the next Mick Jagger. I've avoided listening to any of his music in case it's terrible.

My ambitions have been rather more prosaic – don't fuck up or get fucked up too much, find a job that's satisfying enough, enjoy the company of good friends, find a man who treats me well, and hope for a window of a few years between spots and wrinkles where I have really good skin. It's not asking for the world, is it? So why do the people with the grandiose dreams seem, somehow, happier?

'The video sounds really good, if you can pull it off . . . post-apocalyptic David Lynch zombies sounds like it might take more than a couple of hundred quid and a few days' shooting,' I say in a reasonable tone.

'Nah, you don't understand. It's a gift I have – I pull things off. It's a combination of talent and bullshit. I've always been that way; things just seem to come together for me.' Beardy smiles, more to himself than to me, with supreme self-satisfaction. I am both very attracted to and supremely jealous of this smug cocoon.

'Do you think that's maybe because you're really, really, good looking?' I ask, doing my best Blue Steel impression.

'Probably . . . and you haven't even heard me with a guitar.' Beardy walks naked to pluck his beloved instrument from its case across the room. It was too much to hope that he wouldn't start serenading himself (ostensibly me), at some point. Trying to sustain an expression of polite but not-too-encouraging interest while a man masturbates for what feels like hours on your fiddly inanimate replacement is torturous. Worse still is the frequent assumption that it makes up for actual foreplay.

Why is it men think that because women get their panties in a twist caught up in the mass hysteria of watching a famously talented musician at a gig, they will be equally floored by an unrequested, substandard version of 'Little Wing'? After about two minutes I'm usually fantasizing about a tone-deaf accountant who, though he may have a tiddly-winks hobby, will at least never force me to watch him play and think he's doing me a favour.

In fact, oftentimes the only way to get them to shut up without hurting their feelings is to seduce them. So I suppose I've answered my own question.

'Babe . . . you're so good at that. Come back to bed,' I try to purr, laughing to myself, while lounging in what I hope is a seductive manner, my legs bent at the knee. I swing them back and forth in a peepshow effect.

Beardy grins at me appreciatively, but keeps on strumming. Staring around his room, which is bare but for a few biographies of football players, a giant stereo and a truly hideous ethnic wall hanging, I wonder why it is that his room expresses so little of his personality. I've seen more effort in prison cells on the telly. There's a certain thrill to being in another person's home, inspecting how they choose to decorate and display their taste. It is like seeing a little part of their soul. When so little effort is put into it, I feel strangely affronted that my nosiness has not been catered to, as well as a suspicion that not much lies beneath.

Beardy's head has begun to shake in time to the music and he's beginning to croon. I make my way to the toilet, not out of particular necessity but in order to pass the time. I try to walk past him with a seductive wiggle but he is oblivious, eyes closed in a trance. Strangely, though I have as many body hang-ups as the next girl, I feel much more comfortable naked in front of a man than I do in a bikini on the beach. I suppose my logic goes that if they're fucking me, I must not be that repulsive to them, whereas on the beach I'm a visual imposition that may or may not be appreciated.

Sitting on the toilet, I feel something strange. Looking down, I see the gnarled plastic of last night's condom hanging between my legs. We weren't completely wasted last night; surely he would have noticed the condom coming off? I curse under my breath. So rude. Was he intending on ever mentioning this? I pull out the offending article and flush.

'Um . . . did you realize the condom came off last night?' I lean on the doorframe, arms crossed, trying not to appear too irritated.

'What? Oh, I don't know . . . ah, did it?' Beardy looks up at me with wide eyes, a little too innocent to be completely believable.

'Yeah, it did. Were you planning on telling me?'

'Hey, what are you accusing me for? I didn't know . . . you'll be fine. There's a clinic not far from here, you can get the morning after pill.'

'Because that's just how I want to spend my Sunday, hungover in the clinic hoping they have a free appointment. You aren't just guaranteed a space, you know. I'll probably end up buying it at the chemist.'

I've had to buy the pill often enough over the years, at times back in the day for friends who were too embarrassed to do it for themselves. In my opinion if you can't walk into Boots to get the magic baby-eraser shame-free, you probably shouldn't be having sex in the first place. However, the statistical probability of being served by a disapproving woman combined with the interminable wait in a chair directly facing both the condom and pregnancy test aisles leads me to believe the chain is waging psychological warfare with young women.

'Fine, I'll give you the money so you can buy it from Boots then.'

His tone suggests he is the soul of generosity. Finally putting down the guitar he comes over to me, still naked, sporting an impressive hard-on. As he starts kissing my neck and ear, I start to unwind a little.

'You know . . . since you're going to take the pill anyway . . . we could just not use one . . .' he whispers in my ear.

For fuck's sake. Condoms are obviously not the sexiest things in the world, but being a hypochondriac of the highest order, the thought of spending the next few weeks thinking

I've caught a disease every time I have an itch is really not worth the ten minutes of plastic-free pleasure.

'Er . . . I don't think that's really a great idea . . .'

'C'mon, I'll pull out too, it'll be fine. I pulled out all the time with my ex, she wasn't on the Pill and it was fine.'

Ah, the prayer method, so effective the world over. With all the options available to women today, it's surprising how many of us go along with a blind faith that you can will your ovaries into inactive submission even if it means being convinced you are knocked up ninety-five percent of the time you are not actually bleeding. Of course, it isn't even pregnancy that particularly worries me, though an abortion would be seriously traumatic. At least an embryo can be removed. Genital warts are for ever.

'Er, definitely not. Actually I should really go.'

'What, now?' Beardy looks down at his dick comically. 'Don't leave me this way . . . c'mon baby.'

I sigh and let him kiss me, feeling my resentments slowly melt away as he lifts me onto a desk and does something delicious to my neck.

'Fine, fine, just make sure you use a condom,' I mutter before we get too involved. I suspect he might attempt to just stick it in and hope I won't notice.

I dimly wonder when I'll be a proper grown-up woman in a proper grown-up relationship. The type in which both parties have had sexual health screenings, she's on birth control and they both genuinely trust each other not to stray, like you see in the talkies. I'm beginning to think that Beardy is the sort of man who sees one of the perks of being in a relationship as being able to fuck someone while they're asleep and have an unspoken understanding that it's consensual.

In the meantime, however, he's naked, I'm naked, we're together and any further reflections seem, under the circumstances, rather pointless.

Hamster Mouth More Lethal Than Listerine

After an interminable conversation with Javier the pharmacist about the risks of the morning after pill, that ended only after I waved my debit card under his nose, saying repeatedly 'I know, I need to go,' I left Boots with my purchase. I am now armed with a host of possible complications for my paranoid mind to ruminate on.

How is it possible that I never knew that the morning after pill could cause ectopic pregnancies that, left untreated, can be fatal? I had always thought that the worst aspect of it was simply the annoyance that your period can arrive sooner, later or at exactly the same time. Of course, Google has also revealed that severe gingivitis can lead to stroke, heart disease and death, so I try to focus instead on the reassuring improbability of all these statistics.

Trudging back to our little Victorian terrace house, I see that Stacy has strung up red heart-shaped fairy lights in the living room. This addition against the black velvet curtains gives it a look somewhere between a vampiric den and a brothel.

As it is her place, I've little right to complain about the décor, but her taste does represent a schizophrenic divide in her psyche. Half aggressively minimalist, with hard angles, simplicity and bare functionality, half gothic froth, as if she can't quite decide whether she wants to project clean perfectionism or messy seduction. I do lust after her free-standing wrought iron and white porcelain bath with skull feet, but it is in her bedroom and purely decorative. When I once suggested we fill it with ice and use it to cool booze at house parties, she looked as if she might have a heart attack. This was before I realized there were to be no house parties chez nous.

'Hello?' I call out, as I walk into the narrow hallway and hook the collar of my coat on the silver row of metal spikes that serve as the most dangerous clothing hangers ever designed. I am convinced I will be blinded before the year is out.

'Georgina? We're in the living room if you care to join us,' Stacy calls out. I wonder which of her lovers she is entertaining. I don't think I've ever seen her just relax at home with a mate; though she seems to have a wide variety of female acquaintances, I suspect they are most important to her as contacts and that she considers the whole idea of friendship rather childish.

I walk in feeling awkward and grimy, wearing ripped jeans that haven't seen the inside of a washing machine in months and one of Beardy's old Radiohead T-shirts. I like the idea of wearing a man's baggy shirt, but in practice my breasts are too large to make it look sexy and I end up looking like a dumpy roadie.

'You must be Georgina. Lovely to meet you,' says a man I presume to be Cosmo, though the rotation of men in Stacy's life is too rapid for me to risk saying his name aloud.

He is very good looking, with one of those perfectly symmetrical faces typical of her men friends. Though flawlessly handsome, to my eyes they all look rather bland, like a carousel of revolving 'I'm-In-Finance' Ken dolls. Lean and athletic, he sports the off-duty investment banker's uniform of crisp white button down shirt with contrasting collar and cuffs, perfectly tailored Ozwald Boateng cobalt suit jacket with dark fitted jeans, completed by a black Hermès belt and Italian loafers on bare feet. I wonder how cold it needs to become before he gives in to cashmere socks. Does he think it sexy, the wealthy urban male equivalent to Northern girls going out half naked in the winter, or is it a status symbol, signifying that his feet will remain permanently toasty as he is never far from his chauffeur? One of my most granny-ish pet peeves (and I have many) is weather inappropriateness.

'Yes, thanks, lovely to meet you too.' I try to smile in a confident manner, while aiming my face to the side. I am concerned that I have dragon breath. Why is it with certain hangovers you can brush your teeth multiple times yet still feel like a furry hamster is rotting in your mouth?

Stacy stays seated, elegantly draped along the couch, smoking a joint. All of the furniture in this room is so poker straight and unforgiving it seems to have been lifted from a medieval church. I have wondered if this is a clever tactic to put flatmates off lingering there, thus allowing her to keep a private salon.

'Do you want some? It's Nepalese hash, very smooth.' Wearing only a thin silk jersey dress, her blonde hair loose and golden, Stacy looks very relaxed, with a warm glow about her. I hope this is due to the drugs and fairy lights rather than rampant sex in communal spaces.

'Ah, well, maybe a few tokes, I'm not the best company stoned.' I have no particular desire for it, but there is a part of me that still thinks that a free high is always a good high. This has led me into many questionable situations over the years, but none I've regretted enough to reform my character.

'Cosmo brought it for me – it's the best I've had in London. He refuses to reveal his sources, though, the tease.' Stacy looks up at him coyly through dark lashes that she has tinted bi-monthly.

'I need something to keep you coming back to me, beautiful.' Cosmo walks over and strokes her hair before kissing her tenderly.

'I'd always find an excuse to come back to you, darling!' Stacy giggles girlishly, a noise I would previously have thought so out of character as to be impossible.

Jesu Christi, I think incredulously as I take a deep hit, girl's got it bad. I have only seen her behave with indifference or outright contempt around her other men, to the extent that I thought she was incapable of emotional attachment.

'I'm not much of a smoker, I hope it won't be wasted on me . . .' I trail off as they carry on, looking like two turtledoves batting their heads together in a frenzy of desire. I haven't seen Stacy around much in the last two weeks and feel rather like a Who down in Whoville after the miraculous transformation of the Grinch. What could have effected this metamorphosis, that her heart is no longer two sizes too small?

'So, Cosmo,' I say, searching for a topic of conversation to distract them from each other's tongues, 'any special plans for Christmas?'

Drawing away from Stacy with obvious regret, Cosmo sits on the floor opposite us. He must have already experienced the inhospitable nature of the chair next to him.

'Yah, well, some of my best mates and I are going to Verbier for the week, who knows what I'll do for New Year's . . . I'll probably have to come back for this little beauty, if she won't join us skiing.' Cosmo looks fondly at Stacy, while I try not to cringe at the 'little beauty' remark. It seems the sort of compliment a man might pay a horse.

'Hmm, how fantastic.' I am envious. Christmas over the past few years has become a terrible emotional tussle in which I, the only child, have become the prize. It is supposed to be Christmas Eve and Day with Mum, Boxing Day with Dad and Vitoria, but oftentimes I am emotionally blackmailed into staying with her longer. Mum's hyperbolic tendencies are extreme when describing their age-gap relationship. My tolerance for hearing things like 'Your father already has a child with him', 'They are probably playing Hide-The-Candy-Cane right now' and, even worse, 'I bet her presents cost more than yours' is low. Thus masterfully manipulated into feeling disturbed at the thought of seeing them together, the thought of the trek to Rickmansworth combined with a relentless December hangover is too stressful to bear.

'It would be even more fantastic if my little beauty here would accept my invitation and join us, but she's been so resistant!'

Is 'My Little Beauty' his actual pet name for her? That may trump Cocka-Tootle-Poo in awfulness.

'Oh, Cosmo, I can't just cancel my plans at the drop of a hat, you know that,' Stacy evades.

'You seemed keen before! I even bought you that Stella ski jacket.'

'Darling, it isn't an act of generosity if you then try to bribe me with it. There will be other ski trips. I just realized how rude it would be to Tarquin and Cordelia to cancel on them all of a sudden.' A note of irritation creeps into her voice and she pulls away, tucking her long body into the couch and turning her face to the wall.

Slightly stoned, I try to make a mental note of this inter-action in case I ever date a rich man whose plans I want to refuse but gifts I want to keep. I rather doubt this is in my future what with my general tendency to date men whose most expensive possession is a Zippo, but here's hoping.

'Well, is it bribery if I offer the matching suit to go with the jacket if you change your mind?' Cosmo cheekily inquires. How a man can manage to be cheeky while offering to pur-chase a £600-plus designer item that can be worn at maximum a few times a year is baffling to me, but evidently in Stacy's world this is the norm. She swats at his broad shoulder in mock-irritation and quickly changes the subject.

'Did you enjoy your weekend, Georgina? You look a bit out of sorts.'

'Out of sorts?' I parrot idiotically.

'You know. Rather . . . grungy. And spacey.'

'Just unwashed as usual and now a little bit stoned, Stace.' She hates it when I call her this, thinking it sounds common, though I think Stacy is much more chavvy and am always surprised she ever shortened it from Anastasia. Failing that, 'Stasia' would fit in better with the Tarquins, Cosmos, Cordelias and Lentils that make up the majority of her acquaintance.

'No need to get snitty, dear.' Stacy inspects her perfect nails before glancing down at my grubby ones. I wonder, not for the first time, what she's like when she's not smoking – is it possible she's actually less uptight? I also start to wonder if maybe I smell, though I remind myself I've taken a shower and brushed my teeth. Could it be my alcoholic pores are stronger than any power-shower? My hamster mouth more lethal than Listerine? Or was wearing Beardy's shirt a mistake? I am about to furtively sniff my armpit before deciding I'm a fixating paranoid and should really just stop smoking and make a speedy exit.

'Ah, on that note, I think I'd better leave you two lovebirds . . . I might go out later so I should probably shower. Thanks for the warning, Stace.'

'I think you look great! Grunge is in, isn't it, Stacy? Where are you off to?' Bless Cosmo and his well-brought-up little heart.

'I'm not sure if I'll definitely go, this guy I'm seeing is playing a gig at Shelter. I'm not sure if I'm up for it, I'll see how I feel in a bit.' Doing any uni work, as I had originally intended, is out of the window at this point. I need a full, unbroken day to really start, so I have sufficient time to waste in the interim to build up my motivation to the point of blind panic.

'Shelter? Sounds hip. Is it a wine bar? Well, enjoy your night, we'll be out having a drink at Boundary later if you fancy stopping by.'

Cosmo is far and away one of the nicer men Stacy has brought home. I strongly suspect that if they stay together for any length of time, she will make him miserable. I hope he makes a lucky escape.

A Hint Of Insanity Is Sexy

Stepping out of the shower, I check my phone to see if anyone is about tonight. The evening hinges on this – I refuse to go on my own to watch Beardy for fear of looking like a love-sick groupie.

Actually, I don't think I've ever gone to any social event alone and prefer to walk around aimlessly than sit in a pub by myself if my friends are late; a frequent occurrence. The longest I've ever waited alone in public was when I languished on a park bench in Mornington Crescent drinking cheap vodka and cranberry from an Evian bottle on my eighteenth birthday. All fifteen guests managed to be at least an hour late. After forty-five minutes or so, I started to cry, which was actually quite restrained, considering a group of rude boys had started chanting 'Tranny' at me thirty minutes in. I haven't worn stripper shoes since.

My phone buzzes and I feel a moment of hope. Maybe I do want to go to this gig after all. It's hard to know the true state of your emotions when you spend all your free time drinking or hungover. 'Soz doll, having din-dins with Jake and Caro tonight xx' reads Rose's text rejection.

Jake and Caro are an old married couple in their early twenties who are both very nice but seem to have stepped out of an alternative dimension in which everyone is kind and punctual, wine is sipped parsimoniously throughout dinner, swearing is vulgar and jokes are socially appropriate. The first time I met them they were throwing a vegan dinner party, to which I arrived late, tipsy and bearing a charcuterie platter. I also made the hideous faux pas of wearing a beautiful white fur coat.

Caro had looked me up and down slowly before grimacing with disapproval. Meanwhile, Jake asked in an unnaturally sonorous tone that sounded like a bad impersonation of Brian Blessed, 'And What Was That While It Lived?'

I drunkenly tried to make light of the situation by declaring, 'Peter Rabbit and aaall his little friends!' while maniacally stroking my fluffy collar like a cracked-out Cruella De Vil. Rose tried to defend my honour by explaining I hadn't known they were vegan (true) and the coat was vintage (false) but when I rooted around in the hall and waved

Jake's leather shoes under his nose, asking why cows don't have equal rights, the evening took a decided turn for the worse. I haven't been invited back since, to everyone's collective relief.

'No problem my love, send my regards and spike the Quorn with some bacon for me xxx', I respond. I still haven't heard from Sarah, Julian or Annabelle, who is a definitely a long shot, being a hippy-ish childhood friend who drops off the radar only to text me back weeks or months later. She's always been flighty, but since returning from six months travelling in India she despairs of the isolation of city life and walks around swaddled in scarves, like Moses. I fear she will soon disappear back into the bowels of the Third World, never to return again.

I slip into a bathrobe from Primark, which gives me more pangs of conscience than fur ever has, though visions of slave-labour magically never assault me when I am actually at the till. I tiptoe down the narrow stairway to the kitchen hoping that Stacy and Cosmo won't join me and witness my very fetching drowned rat 'do as I help myself to a large glass of white wine, thus completing what I suspect is my reputation as a minging pisshead.

I have a separate collection of glasses to Stacy, the '4 for £4' set from Sainsbury's, purchased after I broke one of her black goblets doing the washing up. She nearly had my head, complaining that they had been £40 each. Of my eight Sainsbury's glasses only two remain, cowering survivors lurking in the back of the cupboard, their comrades having met oblivion in the hands of careless drunk people, mainly me. It might be worth investing in something that doesn't shatter as soon as you look at it, but I don't feel quite ready for that level of adult responsibility.

I take a few swigs and then fill my glass up again, enjoying the warmth spreading through my veins before creeping back up the stairs to my room. If I am to go to this gig alone, as looks increasingly likely, I am going to need some Dutch courage.

My room is fairly spacious, the walls covered with inspirational research. It has good storage space, a must for the ludicrous amount of clothing I've accumulated over the years. I do a thorough pruning every year but somehow seem to end up with more unnecessary shit than ever. My new policy is to wear something down into the ground before I replace it, but it's difficult to restrain myself when window-shopping is a vital part of my degree. Luckily the majority of the things I love are too expensive to induce real temptation.

My favourite part of the room is on the far side, and the piece of furniture that sits underneath a large bay window. It is a twenties Art Deco dressing table I bought last year on eBay, at a reasonable enough price that I feel I can lie and pretend it was a steal. Not only does it provide natural lighting for putting my face on of a morning; it allows me to display all the pretty products I rarely use but end up buying because I am a whore for packaging. I have at least ten perfume bottles. I almost never wear perfume. Considering my paranoia earlier tonight, however, maybe I should start.

I put on some Josephine Baker and buff a layer of powder on my face while I smoke a secret cigarette and drink my wine – the best and most classic of all stimulant combinations. People can talk smack about smoking all they want but I am convinced that if it weren't for all the paltry health concerns, everyone would be doing it.

Why is it the things I most enjoy in life seem to have the threat of eventual disease and death marching alongside them? Alcohol, tobacco, sex, transfat-laden food, walking in vertiginous heels . . . For even seemingly innocuous pleasures, like wearing non-organic cotton, there is a price being paid by some poor farmer being gassed by toxic pesticides. Of course, even if you do buy organic, cotton itself is environmentally questionable due to the huge reservoirs of water required to grow it. Yet synthetics are equally damaging in other ways. It's easier not to think about it and instead spend life in a cycle of mindless consumption: bad men, chemical highs and unnecessary shoes.

I belatedly remember to take the morning after pill, gulping it with my wine, which, according to Javier, is fine as long as I don't throw up in the next twenty-four hours. My phone beeps. It's Sarah – she's with Henry at The Eagle Rests, a shitty old-man pub in Shoreditch. We originally started going there when the crowds got too much to have a conversation in the better options nearby, but have become strangely fond of its coarseness.

It can be refreshing to go to a bar that looks as if it has travelled through a time warp from the non-glamorous side of the fifties, when everywhere else you go you are inundated by the carefully curated nostalgia that seems to have gripped interior design recently. It is now 8 p.m. They are probably not going to be up for Shelter but I will do my level best to persuade them.

I teeter down the road to the pub, mildly buzzing, in some beautiful Miu Miu burgundy heels that make my ankles look like heaven and feel like hell. However, I am confident that the anaesthetizing powers of alcohol will keep me upright. I still haven't replied to Beardy, as my confidence in convincing Sarah and Henry to give up their quiet Sunday night drinks to rock along to Tin Can Bang's finest is minimal. But according to *Cosmo* (the mag not the man), men love a bit of mystery, an unattainable woman with her own life to live, right? We all know that a woman's magazine written as if its audience consists of lovelorn nymphomaniacs with a mental age of twelve would never tell a lie.

It's easy to spot them in The Eagle, which is otherwise entirely empty of customers. A bartender glares menacingly at my arrival. One of the most charming features here is that they never fail to make you feel unwelcome. The chips are also inedible. You know you're getting older, poorer and more pathetic when this is your chosen option if you want to have drinks and a conversation for less than a tenner on a Sunday. At least there is no chance of running into Stacy. She'd rather self-immolate than put one shoe on its scuzzy old carpet.

'Lover! My darling, come here!' Sarah looks drunk and incredibly happy to see me, almost maniacally so, while Henry is a bit pained. 'You look fab! Very tits out tonight I see; you aren't out to seduce the barman are you!? This is my favourite desperado joint and I refuse to avoid another pub cause all my friends are slaags!'

'Excuse me! One barman two years ago and I never live it down. He was too fit to resist . . . and we barely go out in Soho these days in any case.'

'You found a fit, straight barman in Soho?' Henry feigns incredulity, his bright blue eyes crinkling in a sad, but amused, smile.

'I know, I thought it was quite an accomplishment too, but he was Aussie, they're usually fairly reliable skirt-chasers.'

'You sound disappointed,'

'I was, I hate Australian accents on men. But he looked just like someone I used to fancy on *Home and Away* years ago, so it wasn't a total loss.'

'The Dog And Three Bowls was a terrible loss to me, that

was when it was at its peak! Remember, darling, that's where we met.' Sarah plants a drunken kiss on Henry's face, running a hand through his curly brown locks. He looks away, wincing slightly. 'Oh don't be such a wet blanket, are you still upset?'

'Is something wrong?' I take a seat warily, suddenly sure that I am intruding. As usual, it is some painful discussion that Sarah wants to avoid and Henry wants to deal with. I've been a bystander/pawn to their arguments before and it is rarely pretty.

'Oh, Henry's brother's wedding is in six months in Ireland and he wants me to book tickets and a hotel and buy a dress and all that bloody bollocks now. I don't see why I have to agree to go to an expensive foreign wedding anyway, it's so selfish. It's not like they live in Dublin, you know, they live in Wandsworth.'

'Fiona's whole family live there and her mum's disabled, you can't expect them to trek over to Wandsworth just for your convenience! It's my only brother and it's one weekend, I fail to see how you can't afford it.' I have never seen Henry quite so heated. My spidey sense tells me that Tin Can Bang will have to wait.

'For God's sake! Can we talk about this later? Stop pressurizing me, it's months away! We can decide later.' Sarah glares at him and then with a rapid about face turns to me, smiling. 'Do you want some vino? I'll go get an extra glass.'

As she marches to the bar, Henry necks the last of his drink and hurriedly puts on a big lumberjack coat, his jerky movements as he does so pulling up his sweater, showing a length of tanned stomach. Sarah has started speaking of him in such disparaging tones of late that it's easy to forget that he's very attractive, as well as very nice. I hope she won't regret whatever trouble she's started brewing.

'Try to talk some sense into her, if you can. She's so fucking stubborn.' Henry shakes his head, looks as if he's about to speak again, then shuts his mouth. 'Take care, Georgie. See you later.'

Sarah comes back just as the door swings shut behind him, both relieved and frustrated to find him gone. Sitting down with a thump, she pours both our glasses up to the brim.

'Argh! That man! It's killing me. I still love him, I think, but I just can't see six months ahead! I'm not a fucking clairvoyant! If I were I wouldn't be in fucking advertising – I'd be in fucking finance! And we'd all be fucking rich and not drinking in this shithole.'

I take a gulp of wine with some trepidation, but she deflates.

'So, you really think it might end? He still seems to adore you, you know.'

'I know, I know. God knows why, I've been such a bitch to him lately. It's just . . . six months! I can afford to go if we do go but I can't afford a write-off on that scale, you know? And his brother hates me anyway, it's not like I'll be missed if we are still together.'

'His brother hates you? Why?' I say, trying to sound surprised, though I have an inkling as to why that might be.

'He thinks Henry can do better. Or if not better, kinder, probably. Their mum is a bloody saint, and so is Fiona and I'm the loud, odd one out, who doesn't cook or iron his pants or wait up for Henry with a glass of bloody Horlicks or whatever it is they expect me to do.' She laughs hard, presumably at the thought of ironing.

'Do you think he realizes what the real issue is?' Poor Henry. It's always sad to see a relationship in its death throes when you genuinely like the other person involved. Still, I'm Sarah's friend first. Although I can express my perspective on the situation, it is ultimately my duty to support her in her choices. Who ever really acts on good advice? Generally speaking, the more perspicacious the counsel, the more swiftly it is dismissed.

'What, the countdown to the end? I have no idea. It must have crossed his mind. But I don't even know if I really want to end it myself.' Sarah smiles with a wry self-loathing. 'I think he thinks I'm just a crazy woman and this is one of my fits of pique. I don't know if it'll ever be resolved. He's too nice and I'm too scared.'

'Too scared to break up with him?'

'Too scared to break up with him, or to really be with him.

Either way I'll feel I'm missing out. I hope this is just the horrible indecision of youth and I grow out of it . . . or I'll never be happy.' Sarah looks at the table miserably. I've never considered her as someone fearful before – if anything, she is rather the opposite. Strong and opinionated, it has always been hard for her to fully give herself to someone else. There is surrender in love that I sometimes wonder if she is incapable of.

'But you've been together for ages now. Don't you feel like you've given it a fair shot?' I ask, sipping my wine at a normal pace. Sarah is drinking hers like it's tap water.

'Yes. No. I've done the bare minimum. I haven't cheated on him, but I've wanted to. We live together, but most of my stuff is still two postcodes away at my mum's. I still stay over there some nights. He jokes about what our kids might be called but I've only met his mother once, under duress.'

'He is five years older, a lot can change in five years.'

'A lot can change in six months.' Sarah shrugs. 'That's the problem. What if I break up with him and play the field and satisfy my curiosity only to find he's what I've been looking for, that I just want too much?'

'That is the risk, I guess. What about if you took a break? Tested out being single again?' I wish I had something more edifying to add, but having never been in a relationship where it's even crossed my mind that there could be something there worth committing to, I'm not the most useful agony aunt.

'He'd probably find someone else in the meantime. Probably that bitch friend of his, Cathy from work, she's always been waiting in the wings for the moment to catch him. The boyfriend-snatching whore.'

'What, Cathy, that mouse-like creature? I doubt you have anything to worry about there, she's so boring and timid, she's totally different from you!' If you can imagine a dormouse transmogrified into human form with a blonde shag wig and oddly prominent collarbones, that's Cathy in a nutshell.

'And you don't think that would be quite attractive after I've steamrolled all over him? She's just like his mother. All men end up with their mothers. And I . . . will end up . . . alone.' Sarah starts laughing, with tears in her eyes.

'Oh Sarah! Don't say that!' I pat her shoulder ineffectually and reach for the blanket statement all women use when reassuring each other their lives won't turn out like shit. 'You're beautiful! Look at you! And you're smart and fun, you're just confused about what you want, which is perfectly normal. None of these things need to be decided today.'

'I know. I just wish I knew what to do now. I'm not the most patient woman. Sorry about this, I've been a mess tonight. What was that thing you thought might be fun to go to?'

'Er, to be honest, I was going to try to charm you into

watching Beardy's band at Shelter. But I think they're on in ten minutes and it doesn't really seem like the moment. It's okay!'

'Beardy! Oh shit, sorry! No, let's go, I want to meet your man! I haven't met any of your love interests since Anthony, you never bring them out!'

'Yeah, cause they're either non-existent or it ends before we reach the stage where you bother with all that. It's all shag, shag, shag, the scales fall from my eyes, I realize they're a troll, time passes, I'm desperate, rinse, repeat.'

'Well, in that case we must go. If we get plastic cups we can be there in fifteen minutes. You wouldn't want to be bang on time, would you? Do I look ok? Mascara in place, insanity hidden?'

'You look gorgeous! Mascara in place, just a hint of insanity.' I get out a compact and quickly reapply my red lippy and adjust my cleavage, thankful I have not dressed like a scarlet harlot for no reason.

'Good, a hint of insanity is sexy I hear. You look wonderful, darling; don't worry. *Vamos, compadre!*'

FREAKS

THE STORY OF THE LOVE LIFE OF THE SIDESHOW

TOXIC LOVE! HUMILIATED BY THEIR MEN! | MY BUTT WON'T STOP GROWING! HE'S GAY! | MONSTER MOM! MARRIED TO A MADWOMAN!

The Freakish Dregs of Society

As we turn down a poky little road to Shelter, a converted warehouse with bare cement interiors, I am disheartened by the long queue snaking its way down the road.

'Fucking hell,' I say, rooting in my bag for my phone. 'Sorry, I won't make you wait in the cold, let me just see if I can get hold of Beardy.'

I am always amazed by how long it takes me to find my Nokia, considering it is the size of a brick. Finally locating it, I open a message from him. As I read it, my lips pucker and my eyebrows raise in an expression my mother always warns makes me look like Groucho Marx.

'Is that your man? What did he say?'

'He said he put my name and a plus one on the guestlist

and hopes I can make it.' I am surprised at his thoughtfulness. Though perhaps my expectations are just extremely low from years of being left out in the cold, sometimes literally.

'Ah, thank fuck, I didn't want to let you down, but there is no way I'm standing behind that mob. They're all about seventeen and look like they've spilled out of a Pearl Jam concert circa 1994.'

'I know, I remember when I was seventeen. I thought any woman who went clubbing after the age of twenty-one must be desperate and looking for someone to marry her. And all because she wasn't puking up snakebite on the street at two in the morning, then arguing with the bouncer to get back inside. I fear I've made very little emotional progress.'

'Uh, I'm twenty-seven in three months; let's not talk about age. Let's get some snakebite!'

Once inside, we make our way to the bar where everyone has congregated. Maybe the crowd is still too sober to break off from the pack for fear of being picked apart by judgemental fashionistas. A few brave teenage girls dance with studied nonchalance to remixed nineties hip hop, drawn like moths to the DJ booth whose magical powers have transformed a skinny, bald nerd into a prince of parties. Some swarthy men are setting up on stage, but I don't see Beardy amongst them.

'Sarah? Oh my gaaawd, I haven't seen you in aaages, what's

the crack?' A lanky Irishman in a fur coat and horn-rimmed spectacles kisses her lingeringly on the cheek.

'Alistair! You look gorgeous! What are you doing here? Aren't you getting on a bit by now, shouldn't you be wrapped up in front of a fire with a hot chocolate or something?'

'Weell, you haven't changed! It's a comfort to me to see you're still the same bitch I knew and loved! Thirty-two is the new twelve, darling, and besides I'm far too beautiful to be hidden away like Mam's best china.'

As they become wrapped up in a flurry of banter, I give up on straining to hear and set myself the task of ordering two snakebites. I am usually too deaf to join in these conversations properly without being intrusive and secretly look forward to the day when the ear trumpet makes its triumphant return. Just as I catch the eye of the barman, I feel a tap on my shoulder and turn around. Irritated to have missed my window, I swivel with a frown to be met by familiar hazel eyes.

'Hello there, you,' Scott grins. 'Not brandishing any chairs this evening I hope?' For a moment, God knows why, I feel like I'm having a mini-seizure in the chest area, but it passes and I maintain an unruffled expression. I hope this isn't a sign of incipient heart disease.

'Oh, hey! No, no chairs, they have a strict no furniture policy here. You're having a night off from the pub then?'

Seeing Scott out of his boxers and white T-shirt and into

a rather dashing suit destabilizes me, particularly as he is sporting a six o'clock shadow. Out of the corner of my eye I see Sarah looking over curiously, mouthing obviously, 'Is that Beardy?' complete with pointy hand gestures. I subtly shake my head no.

'It's not my usual scene, to be honest, but I'm here supporting a friend.'

'You mean you weren't enticed by all the teenage girls?' I ask, as a precocious jailbait blonde sticks out her tits and brushes them against his arm as she walks past. Scott, gratifyingly, appears not to notice.

'I was told this was an establishment of class and restraint, but I seem to have been led astray. I—' Scott turns as someone taps his arm and a woman with the kind of face that has launched a thousand wet dreams appears next to him.

'Oh hello! Sorry to interrupt, I wondered why our drinks were taking so long. I'm Alice.' Alice waves a thin, elegant hand and smiles cheerfully. I love her dress, though I could never wear it. It is the sort of baggy designer swag only the very thin can pull off without looking like they're trying to hide two extra stone.

'Oh! Hi! I'm Georgie. I'm just . . . Scott distracted me, but I can get your drinks too if you want?' I stutter.

'That would be fantastic! Two double G&Ts please.'

I give two thumbs up and wedge myself in at the bar, feeling a bit idiotic having relegated myself to a waitress in the face of her glory. It seems unfair to have someone of her calibre casually walking around in the world as if it is a perfectly normal level of hotness.

In fact, I've noticed a recent pandemic of average men with normal jobs bagging goddess-like women. It's a trend that affects us all, as they have ridiculously high standards afterwards. Not content with that, they infect their circle of friends with the idea that maybe they too have a supermodel waiting for them around the next corner. Of course, the longer she fails to arrive, the more perfect she becomes – a permanently wet Rachel Weisz-alike who will listen rapturously to their Red Dwarf fan fiction and fake her orgasms convincingly. It leaves the average girl capable only of attracting the freakish dregs of society. Why can't the beautiful stick with their own kind? It's unfair on the rest of us.

After I finally receive our order, I turn around to pass them their drinks. Alice and Scott are deep in conversation, her almond eyes sparkling as she flicks back luxurious sable hair. I hope its artful disarray is the result of hours at the hairdresser, but it appears annoyingly natural.

'Oh! Thanks so much, Georgie. Scott was telling me you work at the Newt?' Her bee-stung lips move around her slightly too large teeth exaggeratedly as she speaks, as if trying to make room for them. The effect is captivating.

'Yes, well, I'm quite new, I have my second shift on Tuesday, so here's hoping I don't fuck up too much!' I laugh nervously and lift up my pint to cheers, wishing I hadn't said fuck. However, I suspect that pretty much anything I say in front of Alice will make me feel déclassé.

'Are you drinking snakebite?' Scott peers into my glass, looking amused and slightly horrified, which doesn't exactly assuage my feelings of gross inequality. I move slightly to the side so we aren't both in his line of vision at the same time.

'Oh, you know, when in Rome . . .'

'You whore! There'd better be one of those for me as well!' Sarah shouts, by way of introducing herself.

'Don't worry – I would never drink this alone. It's on the bar. Who's the Irish Adonis you were talking to?'

'Only the campest straight man in East London, which is quite a distinction to have. We went out for a few months, years ago, before I decided it was too threatening to date someone with more male admirers than myself. And who are . . . ?' Sarah smiles at Scott and Alice.

'This is Scott Montgomery, he owns and manages The Pissed Newt, and his . . . Alice, whom I've only just met. Scott, Alice, this is my friend Sarah.' Why am I speaking as if I'm at a smart cocktail party? I suppose it's preferable to saying 'This is Scott, my hot boss who I have verbally and physically attacked and Alice his gorgeous date who I want to stab in a fit of envy. Sarah and I met in a toilet doing hard drugs a few years ago.'

'Ah right, you took on Georgie at the pub? She was a terrible waitress, you know, but maybe she'll be better behind the bar. Wow, I have to say, you guys make a gorgeous couple!'

'Thanks for that ringing endorsement, Sarah,' I say through gritted teeth. I am a bit curious to see if they are a couple though. Even if they aren't together, he must be hopelessly in love with her. Not that it's any of my concern.

Scott starts to say something but is drowned out by a drum roll and I hear Beardy's voice ringing out, 'Ladies! This is Tin Can Bang playing especially for you, tonight. Everyone else can fuck off,' before tearing into a song.

I had momentarily forgotten why we were even here and turn towards the stage. Though their intro was a bit dickish, Beardy is looking good.

'So that's your man? That's quite a beard! That's like, two inches away from Rasputin. But he definitely has a certain charisma,' Sarah says loudly into my ear. I laugh and nod along, swaying to the music.

Their sound is reminiscent of the post-punk, indie-rock, grime-flavoured style employed by countless others, but if they aren't terribly original they are by no means bad. In fact, having seen a fair few original gigs in my time, I have established that at heart I am a bourgeois pig and prefer the derivative to the avant-garde. This no longer bothers me as it did when I was a pretentious sixteen-year-old, searching fruitlessly for the capacity to appreciate obscure dissonant trance to impress a boy. The experience was so painful I vowed never to feign a shared passion again, or at least not without thorough research beforehand to see what exactly I'd be getting myself into.

I look over at Scott and Alice. Scott is nodding along amiably enough as Alice grins, dancing happily and smiling into his face. Alice has probably never had to feign an interest or fake a hobby in her life. The most irritating thing about all this is that she actually seems genuinely very nice. It's probably for the best that I am no great beauty, as I suspect I would be a heartless bitch of the first degree.

'Do you want to go nearer the front?'

'Let's get some tequila in first.' I should probably get over myself, but I still find the idea of being in front of Beardy dancing along to his music pretty cringe. We haven't been seeing each other long enough for it to be natural and I feel it will make the balance of power swing in his favour.

I catch Scott looking at me and use my impressive powers of mime to indicate we are getting shots. The physical tableau involves squinty eyes, a grimace and my cupped hand shooting towards my face, though I belatedly reflect this is also a very accurate impression of tossing someone off. Scott nods and follows us to the bar.

'I'll get these. It doesn't look right to run a pub and let your staff pay for your drinks.' Scott gives a lopsided grin and in an action that never fails to bring a lift to my spirits, takes out his wallet. 'Have you heard this band before? They're quite good; they come to The Chariot, my other place in Angel, quite a bit. Alice's brother is the drummer.'

'No way! Georgie's boyfriend is the guitarist, that's such a funny coincidence!' Sarah giggles and puts her hand on Scott's bicep. 'You should all double date! Wait, that doesn't make any sense, her brother would be the fifth wheel. Well, if he looks anything like Alice, I'll accompany him! I mean . . .'

'You're Leo's girlfriend?' Scott's eyebrows are hovering disarmingly high on his forehead.

'Er, no! No, no. We're sort of seeing each other but nothing like that, nothing serious,' I babble, desperately wishing that for once Sarah had some tact. If this gets back to Beardy it will sound like I'm telling tales and now it will seem to Scott as if I'm just one of many groupies Beardy is shagging around with. Which could be entirely true, but is hardly what I want to broadcast. If my options are to look as if I'm being used or like a man-eater, I'll choose the position of power every time.

'Do you know him well?' I ask, trying to regain control over the situation.

'As well as you can know someone who gets drunk in your bar on a weekly basis. It's not exactly a deep relationship . . . I guess I have been seeing less of him recently; now I know why,' Scott smiles with a rather odd expression on his face. 'Ah! Finally. Three shots of your finest tequila please, with cinnamon and an orange slice.'

'Er, what?'

'It brings out the true taste of the tequila. There was a bad batch of Cuervo in the twenties and they marketed it with salt and lime to disguise the flavour. Try it, and if you don't like it I'll buy you another with salt and lemon,' Scott says, with the smoothness of a long-term bartender.

'Is this a ploy you use to get girls drunk?' I flirt lamely, taking up my shot glass. Scott laughs and winks.

'If it is, I fully intend to abuse it and I give you my hearty thanks in advance,' Sarah says, slurring slightly. 'Cheers!'

We all take the shot and grimace. Biting into the orange makes a welcome change, but I'm afraid I don't have taste buds capable of detecting any difference in the tequila. To me, alcohol tastes like alcohol. Luckily, I like the taste of alcohol.

'Do you want to dance? I think we should dance!' Sarah's eyelids are drooping and it is clear that she is three sheets to the wind. Happy to oblige any impulse that provides conversational damage control in front of Scott, I thank him, wave at Alice and am pulled into the crowd.

'Your boss is fit! F. I. T. And that Alice girl – phwooar!' Sarah shouts in my ear, as she bops along to the music, knocking into everyone around her so much that I fear she will create a mini mosh pit. I haven't seen Sarah this pissed in quite a while. While not a shining example of health and sobriety myself, it is concerning – there is a desperate quality behind her eyes tonight.

Between trying to prevent Sarah's lurching giving someone a black eye and my attempts to spy on Scott and Alice, I have forgotten about Beardy. That is, until I turn to the stage to find that he is staring at me intensely while singing, leading to a long moment of uncomfortable eye contact. I give a small, embarrassed wave. He really is very handsome, I think as he croons into the microphone. Even if he is wearing fringed leather trousers and a red velvet brocade vest. His beard might be nearing Rasputin territory but in the face he is much closer to a young Stalin, who, while a terrible tyrant and murderer of the first degree, was also pretty damn sexy.

Sarah interrupts my reverie by grabbing my upper arm, digging her fingernails into my flesh. Her drunken gyrating has come to an abrupt stop. Her eyes open wide and her cheeks turn an ashy grey. There can only be one of two reasons for this – she has either seen a celebrity or she is about to puke.

'Oh shit, let's get you to the loos!' Luckily my bladder, of pea-sized proportions, has left me with a good working knowledge of pretty much every bog in EC1. I flex my elbows like an angry chicken and use them to batter my way through the crowd, dragging Sarah behind me and hoping she won't projectile on my back.

'Oh God, sorry, dear. So, so sorry. I didn't have dinner. I feel like shit . . .' Sarah moans with her head resting against the porcelain, her legs splayed across the dirty tiles. It's amazing how little it takes before all notions of propriety and hygiene are chucked out the window like so much garbage.

'Hey, don't worry about it! It's fine. As far as I'm concerned, you managed not to puke on me or in front of Scott and Alice, or Beardy: that earns you a massive gold star!'

Sarah gives a weak laugh, which brings on some retching.

'You've had a stressful night, man, it's cool.' I rub her back and smooth back her hair as the snakebite makes its unwelcome return. 'Jesus, snakebite was a terrible idea, let's never order that again. You'll be fine, everything will be fine.'

'I . . . I think I want to break up with Henry. Where's my phone?'

'No, no, no, don't do that. Here, we'll get you cleaned up and smuggle you out. You can stay at mine – don't make any decisions tonight, yeah? We can keep this whole palaver between you, me and the toilet.'

Somehow, I manoeuvre Sarah's crumpled form through the crowd, out the door and onto the night bus home without running into anyone. The moment we are comfortably installed on the 242, Sarah regurgitates purple liquid all over the floor. It sloshes disconsolately back and forth between the aisles, a smelly rebuke for our overindulgence. After enduring the death stares, disgust and pity of the other passengers throughout the painful journey, I bundle her into my bed, where she passes out before she even hits the mattress. I manage to send off a quick text to Beardy explaining our absence – lying, obviously – as I lie down next to her, too exhausted even to take off my makeup, a cardinal sin for the spot-prone.

My last thought before I fall asleep is, 'I hope Scott didn't notice any of that.'

Old Age Is The Revenge Of The Ugly

The week passed in a blur. I tried to juggle catching up with my uni work with shifts at The Newt, where Scott was largely absent. I was surprised at how much I noticed this. On the other hand, I had to screen my calls to avoid Beardy, who acquired an inexplicable, ill-timed surge of affection ever since I was so distant at his gig. While it is refreshing to feel in control of a relationship in which I had anticipated being the insecure one, I'm ashamed to admit it has also made me go off him a bit.

During the past few weeks I have become woefully behind with my sketchbook and fabric boards so I've been getting up early each morning to spend the day drawing and working on the initial pattern cutting for my collection. As with all creative endeavours, unforeseen snags appear and everything takes longer than anticipated. Thursday's crit with my tutor was a depressing experience, as I struggled to defend the marketing figures and consumer research underpinning my designs for a new luxury womenswear brand. I have a general, vague faith that things will come out all right in the end, interspersed with moments of guilty panic and conviction of utter failure.

These anxieties add to my general trepidation as I make my way to South Kensington to have dinner with my estranged parents and Vitoria. My mother calls her The Brazilian In-Need-Of-A-Wax, due to a downy layer of light brown hair on her face that she likes to think of as a full-on beard. Once, at a disastrous dinner party before they instigated an apartheid within their friendship circles, Mum got a bit pissed and loudly suggested it would be polite of her to shave before social engagements. The fact that after this public humiliation, Vitoria has not made any depilatory facial arrangements has earned her some reluctant respect. It takes balls for a woman to own her peach fuzz.

My grudging admiration deepened the other day when, to my horror, I tried to wipe off what I thought to be a brush bristle on the side of my face only to find that it was attached. I've always had one long blonde witch's hair under my chin that pops up overnight every six months and is mysteriously an inch long, but felt a blinding dismay when it occurred to me that they are becoming more numerous and migrating higher.

Walking into the restaurant, a chic French bistro where a bottle of water costs £6, I see that my mother is already sitting down with what I hope is her first glass of wine. Her tall frame is wrapped up in a fox-fur stole and one of her legs, in three-quarter-length black trousers and ballet pumps, jumps up and down underneath the table impatiently. With thick dark hair tied up in a chignon and large expressive brown eyes, she has the air of a latter-day Audrey Hepburn, if Audrey Hepburn was permanently irritable.

As befits a woman who will do anything to counteract the ageing process aside from giving up smoking, drinking or refined sugars, she has had a few minor nips, tucks, peels and injectables along the way. Publicly, she insists to whoever will listen that she would never go under the knife. Privately, she justifies this hypocrisy with the logic that 'It's only cosmetic surgery if you are under general anaesthetic, darling.' Luckily she has managed, through good bone structure and an excellent surgeon, to avoid the deflated-balloon-pulled-over-a-skull appearance that has befallen a few of her friends. She looks like a natural, strikingly well-preserved older woman.

Despite this, she is perpetually dissatisfied with her appearance, due to the fact that she was such a beauty in her youth. As the French proverb goes, 'Old age is the revenge of the ugly ones.' Occasionally she congratulates me that I have made the most of myself with this backhanded compliment: 'You are a pretty girl, but you can't rely on just your looks to get by. In the long run, that is far more useful than stopping traffic'. She then usually bemoans the fact that she no longer stops traffic and recounts for the millionth time the story of how she once rejected David Bowie in the late seventies.

'Hey Mum! You look great,' I say, as she stands to her full height, five foot ten in flats, to peck at my cheeks. I am a few inches taller in my stacked platforms and the good posture that she instilled in me from a young age, for which I must be grateful. She gave me three mantras with which to conquer life: 'Tall and hunched never gets asked to lunch', 'Tall and thin gets the diamond ring' and of course 'Chips are for poor people'. She pulls back, holding my shoulders steady and looking into my face, perturbed.

'Darling, have you been drinking too much recently? Your face is puffy.'

'Er, not since the weekend. I think it's just the curse of the baby face.' I put one hand to my cheek self-consciously and try to comfort myself with the hope that my cheekbones might emerge gloriously in my thirties, if I manage not to drown them under a sea of fat. I fail to understand why ageing celebrities willingly stuff themselves with fillers to create the chipmunk silhouette that is my bête noire.

'Yes, you get that from your father. He is getting rather jowly these days,' she sniffs, sitting back down and taking a sip of wine. 'He's got quite fat since he's taken up with Her, you know, she doesn't take very good care of his diet. She might well be hoping to bring on a heart attack.'

'I fail to see how that would benefit her, seeing as they aren't married,' I say idly, as I take my seat. Mum stiffens and I immediately regret voicing the thought. It had occurred to me that a marriage announcement might be in the works tonight but I've been hoping it will be something with less emotional fallout.

She pauses, then says firmly, 'If he hasn't asked her by now, I very much doubt he will. It would have lent their whole affair some gravitas at the time, but she's still nothing but a live-in girlfriend. It's been six years now – that ship has sailed. If a man doesn't propose after a year of living together, Georgie, darling, just be aware that you are his maid and whore, convenient but nothing more.'

'Mum, that rhymed. How poetic.' I grin weakly to dispel the tension and am rewarded with a smile and a roll of the eyes.

'I know, I know, old Mummy spouting off her antiquated ideas again with only one failed cliché of a marriage behind her to lend her any credence. Just because something isn't fashionable to say these days, darling, doesn't make it any less true. The world has not changed in the last fifty years as much as you think. Men and women have a dynamic that's been worked out over tens of thousands of years. A few women running around sporting underarm hair, claiming to be proud of their sagging bosoms changes nothing.'

'That's a ridiculous way to view feminism! Without those women neither of us would be able to direct our lives autonomously. We'd be dependent upon a man's signature to even get a loan or a mortgage.'

'Yes, but we are both still dependent on your father to pay the bills. And what is a bank loan or a mortgage but begging money off a Big Daddy with no emotional ties and no qualms about throwing you in prison if you are in debt? Furthermore, if you do manage to succeed you need to pay the money back.'

'That is the nature of a loan, Mum. Plus, I'm pretty sure the whole bankruptcy option put an end to debtor's prison; you should read less Dickens. But we are seriously not having this conversation. What about all the other things – like the right to be independent, to work, to vote?' I say, in between munching on a heavenly piece of warm black olive and walnut bread and ordering a glass of white wine.

'I've never voted in my life, darling, really most constituencies are fixed Tory or Labour, there is no point in going to all the bother. But you know I'm not talking about all that. I'm talking about the lies we women tell ourselves in the hopes that we can have a career, then marriage, then babies, all without any help or something falling apart. Trust me, darling, if you want to be happy, find a good man, get married and have some sweet little children. Then you can open a nice shop on his coin when they go to school.'

She finishes her glass of wine and signals to the waiter for another, looking more relaxed and slightly smug. What appears to me to be a tragic indictment of the pervasive inferiority of women, she finds a strange comfort in, possibly because it makes her feel that we are all hurtling towards the same miserable destiny.

These reflections are interrupted by the arrival of my father and Vitoria, who clatters over to the table, a gazelle in Louboutin wedges, wearing a clingy vest that suggests that at least their news isn't pregnancy. With her girlish frame clad in white skinny jeans, set off by poker-straight hair parted down the middle and minimal makeup, the difference in their ages is striking. My father was a very good-looking man in his prime and still sports a mostly full, if grey, head of hair. Though he has retained his dashing dress sense into his late fifties, he is looking more tired and flabby than ever before. It worries me.

'Dad! Lovely to see you. Vitoria, hey. You look well,' I mumble as we all greet each other with two kisses on the cheeks. Mum sits down abruptly afterwards, takes up a roll and bites into it viciously.

'You are wearing a very beautiful fur, Polly,' Vitoria compliments Mum politely, who makes a point of chewing her bread so slowly before answering that it is insulting. She is very talented at taking a simple physical gesture and imbuing it with a subtle malice that is apparent to women but usually invisible to men. She doesn't have many female friends.

'Thank you, Vitoria. Edward bought it for me in Paris. How long ago was that? Seven years now? That was a beautiful holiday, wasn't it? The George V, that lovely evening at the Opera . . .'

'Er, yes, it was. It was. Do you know what you're going to order?' Dad blusters. 'I'm going to get the steak tartare. It's fantastic here, Vitoria, you should try it. No, no thank you, Polly, I'm not drinking tonight.'

Dad gave up drinking quite a few years ago, without much fanfare or drama, but still insists on saying he's 'not drinking tonight' every time someone offers him a glass, which Mum always does. It's one of those irritating ritual charades performed by people who have known each other for far longer than they might have chosen to, that somehow demonstrates that they care.

Though the undercurrent is prickly, the fact that Mum, Dad and I have dozens of these rituals, while Vitoria is involved in none, unconsciously delineates who has more shared experience and history. They create an unpleasant labyrinth of inclusion and exclusion amongst (ex-)families, but I suppose they are inevitable within any group of people who through an accident of love, fate, or simply sperm, are inextricably tied together for formal occasions till death do them part.

'Dad, so, what's going on, are you okay? What do you need to talk to us about?'

'Edward, the Pouilly-Fumé is really quite excellent, I don't know why you won't try some, it's really too boring of you.'

'For God's sake, Polly, will you stop banging on about the bloody wine. I've had quite a day and I'd like to enjoy my supper. I've been thinking about the steak tartare since lunch. After we've ordered I'll tell you why I've asked you to come here today. It's nothing to get too alarmed about.'

'Edward, you should really order seafood or something lighter, too much red meat at your age will be the death of you,' Mum sniffs. 'You aren't looking your best you know, dear, you look positively fat, not to mention grey. Ashen. You are perfectly fat and ashen. You should really consider your health, for your daughter's sake if for no one else.'

'Well, Polly, it may be too late for that already,' Dad says abruptly. There is a pause as this sinks in around the table. My heart skips a beat, recommencing at a startling pace as my insides twist with a leaden dread. 'I probably have cancer. And I'm damn well getting the steak tartare.'

'*Meu amor*, that is not kind.' Vitoria gently places her hand over my father's at the table and turns her limpid eyes on my mother, who is, for once, speechless. 'He found a big lump on his *bolas*.'

'W-when was this?' Mum looks as if she is in a daze and all the blood from her face has drained down to her décolletage, where it forms an angry red rash.

'*Bonsoir*, Mesdames et Monsieur, would you like to hear the specialities of the kitchen?' Our overly enthusiastic young waiter has taken the grave hush at our table for bored silence and has bounded in to save the day. Mum is usually either rudely confrontational or embarrassingly flirtatious with anyone in the service industries, so to see her submit quietly to the long list of specials, never taking her eyes off my father, is disturbing.

'I'll have the steak tartare and a side of spinach.' Dad's voice is jarringly loud and deeper than usual, his tone rebellious, as if he could scare off the threat of death with a ringing baritone in a show of virility.

As the waiter looks at me expectantly, I numbly stare down at the menu, my eyes unfocussed. I can't remember any of the specials he has just recounted, so I respond on autopilot, asking for the pumpkin soup.

'I cannot eat.' Vitoria rubs Dad's hand and looks mournful, though I've rarely seen her eat much of anything. Mum snaps to attention at this and throws back her head, flaring her nostrils as if in challenge.

'Nor can I, I feel absolutely dreadful. How could anyone after such an announcement? Really Edward, did we have to come to a restaurant for this kind of discussion?' Her voice is cold, but there is a panic behind her eyes not evident to the casual observer.

'Can we tempt you with something light, the radishes with mayonnaise are delicious, or a salad perhaps?'

'Oh just fuck off, would you?'

This sort of behaviour makes me cringe. My mother has probably unknowingly ingested more bodily fluids from vengeful restaurant staff than most, but it's also a relief to see her start behaving with her normal awfulness again.

'I'm sorry to spring it on you like this, but I thought it would be better to talk about this calmly and publicly, no scenes or tears,' Dad says, his words immediately causing tears to prick my eyes, as Mum works herself up for a scene. 'But before you start up, we don't know anything for sure yet. Obviously the fear is testicular cancer. I have a lump, it is quite large, but it is a highly treatable cancer and Dr Chase is very capable and respected.'

'Are you having a biopsy then? What happens?' I choke. I try to reassure myself desperately that he will be fine – everything will be fine – it will turn out to be benign, a foolish mistake, a fuss over nothing. But the evidence springing forth from my eyes seems difficult to contradict. He looks, as my mother had cruelly but truthfully stated, fat and ashen. Moreover, he appears so much older than when we saw each other last.

'There's no need for that, yet. I have an ultrasound on

Monday. If it's likely to be cancerous, they will remove the testicle as soon as possible and do further checks to ensure it hasn't spread to the lymph nodes. That's the real fear, but I don't think it is very likely as I think it has only, er, formed recently. We'll find out soon enough. In the meantime, there's really no point worrying.'

'But we will worry, Edward. We are your family. We've been a part of each other's lives for twenty-seven years. I want to go with you.' Mum's voice is quiet. Dad's eyes shine and he looks at her quite tenderly for a minute, before Vitoria draws him in for a kiss and whispers something in his ear. Mum finally looks up, sees them and knocks back half her glass.

'Well at least nothing's certain; it could just be a lump, right? Do you want me to come with you, too? I'd be happy to,' I ask, though I'm fairly sure joining the crowd at an ultrasound of my Dad's testicles is crossing a line.

'That's sweet of you, Georgie. I think you should just concentrate on your studies until we know anything further, it will probably be nothing. But, yes, I'd appreciate that, Polly, thank you. I probably shouldn't have told you girls about this. I should have waited until things are certain. I've just . . . not been feeling my best lately and I felt you ought to know. You are the most important people in my life.'

I reach over to hug him. Though it might appear odd to some – the ex-wife and current squeeze both at a cancer screening – boundaries have historically never been something my parents have respected. Somehow we all manage to talk fairly pleasantly, in circuitous and empty pleasantries, until our plates arrive. It's clearly going to be a short meal, between my pathetically small bowl of soup and Mum and Vitoria's foodless grief-off. I thought I'd never feel hungry again, but misery has awoken my prodigious appetite with an embarrassing rumble, with no regard to the potential tragedy of the situation. If Dad dies, I will probably soon follow, choking to death over a bowl of crisps at the wake.

'Someone's hungry I see! Don't you silly women wish you had got the steak tartare now?'

'Yes, Dad.' I inhale what seems like half my soup while reaching for a bread roll. 'I was in shock. I could barely see the menu.'

'Oh, you're blind as a bat anyway,' Mum says, picking at her nails distractedly in a way that I know means she wants to escape outside for a cigarette. Dad thinks she quit ten years ago but she is able to keep up the pretence of being a social smoker by going to lots of alfresco lunches and boozy parties.

'I cannot eat at times like this.' Vitoria is looking at me with a combination of pity and incomprehension, but she is not unkind. I would have wished more for my father than a partner who seems incapable of anything but the most superficial of remarks, but at least she has a good heart. I suppose he might have thought, as I did, that with the passage of time and the improvement of her English, she would reveal a sparkling wit, or at least share some topics of interest with him. In moments of hardship and illness, however, qualities of character are more vital.

'Hey! I have a joke; I made it up in preparation for Monday. What do you call an insect that you don't want to have picked up on a scan?'

We all stare at Dad blankly. He is grinning with awkward pride, trying to lighten the mood. There is nothing quite so poignantly square as a middle-aged businessman trying to turn his hand to comedy when confronted with his own mortality.

'Edward, what on earth are you talking about? What insects would be picked up on a scan?' Mum has stopped worrying her nails to look at him incredulously.

'Just – work with me, okay? My last request, let me tell a joke. Even if it is terrible, promise to laugh. Promise me.' They tentatively grin at each other and she finally laughs her assent. 'Okay. Let me start again, I'll rephrase it. What do you call insects who have cancer?'

'Creatures so short-lived they'll never see it manifested?' Mum says dryly, as Dad barks out a laugh.

'No . . . Bee-nign and Malign-Ant!'

Whether it's because of Mum's promise, repressed hysteria or merely the image of my father inflicting this terrible pun on an oncologist who has doubtless suffered more than his fair share of unfunny black humour, we fall about laughing, quite genuinely, while Vitoria and the nearby patrons look on, confused.

Glenn Close In David Gandy's Clothing

'Oh God! Babe, I'm so sorry. He's not going to die is he?' Julian wraps me in a big bear hug. I am not usually very tactile with my friends, so this takes me by surprise and I get a bit choked up. I take a few gulps of my cocktail and blink rapidly. The pop-up establishment we are trying out is not the place to make a scene in public. It is one of those places where the bartenders are even more terrifyingly glamorous than the clientele.

'God, I hope not. I'm trying not to think about worst-case scenarios at the moment. He's only in his early sixties, but that isn't a guarantee of anything,'

'When does he get his results back?'

'The day after tomorrow.'

'It's so fucked up, reaching the age when people start to get ill and it's not a shock. Theo's dear Uncle Bunty died recently and one of Trigger's friends passed just a month ago – she had a heart attack while training for a marathon – it's so sad. I'd hate to die doing sports.'

'Ugh, tell me about it. At least that's one thing I don't have to worry about.' With Christmas around the corner and mortality on the brain, it is easy to absolve myself of bingeing guilt and become cocooned in a comforting duvet of fat.

'Death comes in threes, have you heard that? Everyone's been dropping like flies!'

I blanch.

'God, sorry, that was insensitive, even for me,' Julian is genuinely chagrined. 'Levity is my way of dealing with sadness, I promise! Please forgive me.'

'It's fine, I really don't want to go on about it all night, it could very likely be a false alarm. Even if it is serious, it's treatable. Bring on the levity!'

It makes me uncomfortable to think that others are sanitizing their thoughts on my account. Just because my father is having a serious health scare doesn't mean that everything has to be doom and gloom from now on, does it? I'm not one to dwell on the painful possibilities of life, preferring to ignore them until they go away.

'In that case, did I ever tell you about when I first met Uncle

Bunty? I wanted to tell the story at the wake but Theo told me not to.'

'No, go on!'

'Well, let me start by saying that Bunty is one of the most fantastically, fragrantly and flagrantly gay married men I have ever met. He lived a straight life till the day he died but I am pretty sure he was one of the closeted.'

'Why do you say that?'

'A ballroom-dancing, musical-loving, ballet obsessive? Come on; that's like the Holy Trinity for fags. His wife was the spit of Judy Garland in her youth and he named his first son Nijinsky.'

'That is pretty damning.'

'You have no idea. I'll never forget the first time I saw him. Theo and I had just started dating and had gone for a drink in West London. He had a spare set of keys to Bunty's place and thought the family was in the countryside. So, around 3 a.m., we came in through the garden. There was music on from the lower ground floor; we thought they must have left a record on. So, we walk downstairs and there is portly Bunty, in full regalia, dancing along to a recording of *Scheherazade* projected on to the wall.' Julian laughs fondly at the memory.

'That's actually really sweet!'

'I thought so, too!'

'Was he weird about it?'

'No, not at all. He was a man completely unembarrassed

by his passions. He just put a Chinese robe over his belly-baring costume, offered us some cognac and cooked us a brilliant three-course meal from scratch. We ate by candle-light, smoked a joint together and went to bed. He was a real character.'

We both go silent, musing over Bunty's late-night passions. I knew Julian would be just the man to take my mind off the test results tomorrow afternoon.

'God, remembering that makes me sad. I need another stiff drink, I think,' Julian says with a rueful smile.

We order more cocktails from a woman who looks like Shalom Harlow. It is hard to concentrate on speech when admiring such fantastic cheekbones.

'God, what must it be like to go through life so beautiful?' I muse.

'She is stunning. I wonder if she'd surrogate.'

'What?!' I sputter. I am of an age where I have to accept my parent's mortality, but the thought of my friends having babies still has the power to shock. 'Are you and Theo talking about having kids already?'

'On occasion,' Julian smiles. 'We want to be more estab-lished before we start hiring wombs.'

'And you'd definitely want a surrogate then? What about adoption?'

'Obviously that's a possibility, but I'd prefer not to. I mean, one of the reasons you choose a life partner is because they have qualities you admire that you would like to see passed down to your kids. Even if we don't know whose sperm took hold, at least it will be one of ours. Frankly, with adoption . . . well. There are a lot of stupid people in the world. You don't know what you're getting.'

'Julian!'

'What! I was adopted myself! But I recognize that my parents were extremely lucky.'

'I see your point, but that's pretty un-P.C.'

'Come on, wouldn't it be one of your concerns? Anyway, one of the benefits of being marginalized by society is that you get to take liberties with the freedom of expression without any fallout,' Julian laughs.

'I bet you're making brilliant new friends everywhere you go. No wonder you and Theo are such a gruesome twosome. You've scared off everyone else!'

Whether he has always been blasé or it is the result of being in a long-term relationship with Julian, Theo is the most unshockable person I have ever met. Which isn't to say that he is without humour or empathy, but simply that he takes life in with a measured calm, not unlike Mr Miyagi. If Mr Miyagi was a posh, blond interior decorator from Somerset.

'Ah, whatever, I took a gap year darling, I've travelled, I work in fashion, I know people from all over. The more people you meet, the more you realize that wherever in the world you go there is exactly the same proportion of kindness, gormlessness and arseholery as here, there or anywhere.' The humorous twitch to Julian's mouth has disappeared. His face shuttered, he says with unusual gravity, 'I used to think that most people were basically good, but the older I get the more I wonder if it isn't in a descending triangle. That if you scratch the surface, most of us are just shits.'

'Julian, what's going on with you? You sound even more bitter than normal. More bitter than me, even. That's a terrible, terrible low to reach.'

'Ah, babes, I'm not sure I want to talk about it. Even before we met and you told me about your Dad's poor diseased testicles I thought "No, don't mention it, don't rain on her parade" and now that I find that life's already not just rained but shat all over it, I don't want to add to it, you know?'

I am starting to seriously worry about Julian's wellbeing now. This self-restraint is very uncharacteristic.

'Come on, you can hardly start a speech like that and leave me in the lurch!' I go full Nancy Mitford on him. 'I'll positively die of curiosity! You promised that you would distract me and nothing makes me feel better about my own circumstances than talking about other people's problems, yours included. You know that. It's why we're friends.'

'I certainly can't argue with that logic. Oh, Georgie, I'm such a terrible shit. I feel like the lowest of the lowest of the low at the moment, I've done something really terrible.'

'Hey, it can't possibly be as bad as all that! What's going on?' I am torn between dread and anticipation.

Julian hesitates, holding his head in his hands in silence before launching into a low-voiced confessional.

'Things have got a bit strange at work. Between me and Trigger's assistant, Marco. I've always felt – and I know you think that I think everyone wants a piece of me, but that's only because it's true – that there was a bit of a frisson between us. Just a tiny bit. I mean things are great with Theo. First and last love 4eva, totes—'

'Wait, wait, whoa! Are you having an affair? Who is his new assistant? This Marco is the new guy that replaced Churchill?'

Churchill, real name Gaz, bore no physical resemblance to the former prime minister: jowls, fat and baldness being three characteristics Trigger could not have borne in his right-hand man. He was so called because of his propensity to wear bowler hats and dramatically chew on cigars that he never lit, a strange affectation I could never understand.

He had been caught six months ago racking up lines in Trigger's office. A solid gold kit that contained a razor, a spoon, a snuffer in the shape of a hoover and a glass bullet, all monogrammed with a little TH, were spread out neatly on the desk.

This was a normal part of his job description rather than a punishable offence, but this time he was caught by a journalist and photographer who were being given a tour for an interview with the *Sunday Times*. He had dramatically taken all the blame, expecting to be reprieved after the article had gone to press. Evidently, Trigger had been looking for an out and used the opportunity to sack him.

Churchill complained bitterly afterwards that drug prep was probably the least humiliating of the many menial tasks assigned to him and that if he wanted to he could bring down a shit-storm with the salacious gossip he was privy to. He did not voice this so loudly as to earn the wrath of Trigger Hunt and Never Work In Fashion Again. His replacement was, I'd heard, Trigger's usual type: a tall, lithe Mediterranean with a face like a gangster slash altar-boy.

'Yes, that's him, but no, there is no affair! Affair is a terrible word for what this is; it's far too romantic and exciting. This is just an indiscretion! An indiscretion that's gone horribly awry and is making me rip my hair out.' Julian strokes his perfect hair in annoyance. He is far too proud of his thick locks to endanger them in the throes of grief, but the fact that he has even alluded to the possibility is a sign of deep emotional disturbance.

'Oh Julian, what the hell is an indiscretion? Is this one drunken snog or have you gone as far as seeing each other naked?' I ask.

'We've seen each other naked but we've never even kissed, I swear.'

My eyes lock on his in an Oprah-style gaze; hard but engaging.

'What? How does that work? Are you , , , cyber-sexing? That's not so bad. I mean, obviously it's not great, but nothing to freak out about.'

Obviously Oprah never says that, she's too spiritual, but it's what she means.

'No one calls it that these days, you're so noughties. No, at first we just were flirting in the office a bit, very discreetly. I thought it would be kept to that, nothing more, but two weeks ago Theo was at a furniture convention thing in Milano and I was enjoying a rare evening in with *Downton Abbey* and a box of Chianti—'

'A box of wine? Julian, I think maybe you have bigger problems than this indiscretion.'

'It was from Waitrose, what do you take me for!'

'Ah, that's all right then. Sorry, carry on.'

'As I was saying, I was enjoying yelling at that idiot Lady Sybil for falling for the chauffeur who will lower her into Bolshevik poverty – in twentieth-century Ireland of all places – I had drunk a fair amount of wine and I was rather horny. Raging at the telly always enflames my libido. And then just at that moment Marco texted me something suggestive, things got flirty and then pictures were sent. It was just harmless posing, it's not like I taped myself wanking or anything. I ended up passing out about thirty minutes in. To be honest,

I was shattered and when one is too drunk to write "cock", even with predictive text, one knows one should call it a night.'

'Did one find that in *Debrett's Guide to Sexual Etiquette in Modern Times*?' I tease, relieved that things weren't nearly as bad as I'd feared. Really, in this day and age, given the advanced technology available and the myriad temptations to cheat, sexting is almost sweetly old-fashioned.

'These elegant social touches are just a small part of the homosexual élan, my dear. Dating one's own sex is so very much more civil. Except, of course, when your beauty and dare-I-say magnificent penis incite such torrid lust that it endangers your relationship,' Julian says with a deep sigh.

Although deeply concerned about the potential repercussions of his actions, I can tell Julian also enjoys having a personal drama for once. His usual input in relationship discussions is limited to something along the lines of 'No news is good news', or more colourfully, 'We tried to spice things up in the bedroom by renting fetish porn but everyone was so ugly and poorly dressed we just ended up mocking them all.'

It must be killing him not to be able to talk about this at work.

'Have you carried on exchanging pictures?'

'No, of course not. I woke up the next morning with my Helmut jeans around my ankles cradling the empty wine box and totally forgot it even happened. I thought I'd passed out mid-wank. It was only as I was taking a bath an hour later that I had a hideous flashback. I jumped out and charged my iPhone and I had, like, three extra messages from him. Not a freakishly abnormal amount, you know? Just make a joke of it on Monday and I'm in the clear—'

'Wait, first, so, did you keep the photos? Can I see them?' I have never sent or received nude photos. I did try to take some sexy lingerie pictures for an ex once, but it's damn hard to twist your body into flattering positions while trussed up like a chicken and holding a digital camera. I nearly threw my back out and ended up deleting them all. I looked like I was writhing in death throes.

My attempt was a dismal failure, but receiving a hypothetical cock-shot would leave me baffled, if only because of the lack of effort put into it. Women go the extra mile and men won't even put on a garter. Of course, I am also paranoid that such pictures might end up on www.mywhorexgf. com when the romance, such as it is, inevitably fades. Love is ephemeral; evidence lasts forever.

'I deleted anything incriminating obviously; I ain't just a pretty face. I mean, I had a good long look and if he wasn't such a psycho, I'd be tempted to keep them. But! The point is, Monday we ignored each other all morning. Things were super-busy anyway trying to get all the fabric orders in, the fucking French and Italians are barely open the entire month of December, the lazy bastards. Trigger changes his mind constantly and we need the metres sent asap. You remember how hectic it is. Frankly I thought the whole thing might go undiscussed. But in the afternoon he pulled me into the toilet, pressed me up against the wall and started saying all this stuff about how he'd thought about me all weekend and couldn't wait for us to be together, that he'd wanted me for so long – I know! Scary!'

'Oh, poor Marco! He sounds like he just really likes you and finally thought he'd got an in.'

This is exactly why I am always in total denial about my own infatuations unless I am absolutely positive, through verbal and preferably written confirmation, that they are reciprocated. If you want something badly enough it is very easy to convince yourself that the other person feels it too. Being thought of as a bunny boiler is too much for a fragile ego such as my own to take.

'Er, poor Marco? Poor me! I prised him off and let him down as gently as I could. I explained the situation, that I love Theo and that we've been together six years, et cetera. He looked like a petulant five-year-old child and stormed off. Since then I've received dozens of texts, emails, pictures, some romantic, some sexual, some threatening to tell Theo, or Trigger, I don't know what would be worse. My job and my man are my life! He's trying to blackmail me into sleeping with him! Who does that? He's Glenn Close in David Gandy's clothing. I don't know what to do! He has those pictures of me, but it was just a stupid mistake and . . . and . . . I wish this would all just go away.'

Julian's pretty face is crumpled in misery and he is close to tears.

'Well, whatever you do, don't sleep with him! That will make things far worse! You need to tell Theo and accept the consequences, it's not so bad a mistake as all that. I'm sure he'd forgive you. Plus, isn't this sort of indiscretion usually taken a bit more lightly in gay relationships?' I had toyed with not asking the question but as usual, curiosity won over my politesse.

'Really? Georgie. In all the years I've known you, have I ever cheated? Have I ever said I'd condone it? Have I not mentioned if Theo stepped out on me that I'd slice his balls so thinly that they would pass for beef carpaccio? Monogamy is super-important to us both. It's one of the cornerstones of our relationship. I know some gay men are more forgiving, but really, is that sort of question necessary?'

'Sorry! I didn't mean to be rude, but I was, I just thought, that it's one thing to say things like that and another to really mean them. I think I could forgive cheating, but I wouldn't necessarily broadcast that to the world as it sounds weak. I certainly wouldn't tell my partner, in case they thought they had carte blanche to do what they liked. If I was super in love, well, I've been in enough shitty relationships to know how rare that is, so I think I'd try to salvage things.'

'It's easy to forget how rare it is, that's the problem. I did, momentarily. Look where it's got me. I know I should tell him; I just don't want to see him hurt and disappointed. Why is it that if you do things right ninety-nine percent of the time, it's only the one percent that counts towards anything? I would understand if he flipped, of course. If it was the other way around, I would be super-suspicious that they had actually been shagging each other all along and this was damage-control.'

'I don't think Theo is the suspicious type, you know. I think he'd believe what you tell him, as long as you tell him now and he doesn't find out from someone else. That's so humiliating. It's like what happened with Anthony when he was shagging his best friend for months right under my nose. I knew there had to be a reason why she was always so smug. I actually caught her with her hands down his pants while he was cooking for me. I haven't eaten raclette since. Can you imagine how traumatized I was to be put off a dish involving melted cheese, for life?'

'There's certainly no chance of that happening with us. I haven't cooked in years. In all seriousness, though, I will, I'll tell him before everything gets out of hand. Luckily Trigger and Marco are going to the factory in Milan this week. It gives me time to think.'

The last order bells ring for the second time; Julian and I decide to head off home for an early night like the responsible adults we pretend to be. He will spend the evening contemplating how to manage his confession and salvage his relationship. I wonder what I will do with myself in the hours before drowsiness smothers me.

I should do something mindless but productive to try to take my mind off the possibility that my dad has cancer, like scrubbing down the house, a long-overdue task. At moments like this, swamped in an existential trauma with no real belief to fall back on, the likelihood is that I will deal with my worries in the far more reasonable, grown-up manner of drinking myself into a stupor while watching South Park. This is not such a huge departure from my weekly routine.

Unbalanced With A Chance Of Psycho

So, as it happens, my fraught weekend was for naught and my dad's cancer turned out to be, according to him, 'an abnormally large but benign epididymis cyst'. According to my mum, it was, 'perfectly obvious that it was an ingrown hair – really, only a man with no experience of genital landscaping would have put us through all that trauma. Vitoria must be sporting a full bush as well as a sack of rocks for brains'.

I'm relieved I wasn't at the hospital to witness the ensuing conversation. It's probably healthier to have one's first experience of an ultrasound be, 'It's a boy!' or 'It's a girl!' and not 'It's a hardened hairy growth of indeterminate but non-cancerous nature!'

Though Mum's reaction was typically bitchy, she responds

with anger when she's been unduly worried. Apparently she had been in an agony of guilt all weekend, convincing herself that she had cursed Dad and was thus responsible for his incipient demise. All this added stress was because of a voodoo doll she had made in the early stages of their divorce.

As she is just about the least crafty person that I can think of, I sympathized with her – she must have been in a lot of pain to have gone to the trouble of stitching up a mini Dad-shaped pin-cushion and repeatedly striking its genitals. Though she later clarified that she had in fact bought a figurine of The Stig from Harrods and super-glued some of my dad's hair to it before bashing it in with a hammer, scissoring off all its appendages and setting it on fire. Far more her style. She sometimes (rarely) wonders if she's made a mistake by over-sharing these sordid details, but promises to pay for private mental health care if I ever go off the rails. It's quite loving, after a fashion.

Although I am overcome with relief that the situation has resolved itself so painlessly, it does make me wonder what on earth is wrong with Dad that he looks so old these days. As far as I know, he is far healthier than Mum and they are close in age. Can it be that her regime, consisting as it does of smoking, drinking, daily croissants and the occasional Valium, is actually superior? Maybe it's just that age has finally caught up with him and all he needs to keep his spirits up and stress levels down is a trip to a cosmetic surgeon. It's easy to forget what a man in his early sixties looks like when accepting the ravages of time. So many of them are slyly altering bits and moobs on the side.

As usual, my mum has managed to turn someone else's drama into her own. Quite apart from the whole voodoo thing, which I hope goes the way of her brief colon-cleansing phase (i.e., down the toilet), she is now going through what I can only assume is a belated midlife crisis. While she was feeling low this weekend she decided that she was – her words – sick of *looking* like somebody, but not *being* somebody, the unspoken ending to that sentence being important. Why she has come to this conclusion after fifty-odd years of gracing the world with her presence is a mystery; my guess is Narcissistic Personality Disorder or some other borderline behavioural issue. To this end, she has decided to write a tell-all memoir-cum-guide currently entitled *This Lady Left The Tramp: Surviving Betrayal With Impeccable Manners*. I fear it is not satire.

I related this sorry tale to Gary in between clearing pint glasses on Wednesday evening at The Newt. The pub was not particularly busy, with only a few regulars getting pissed by the fake fireplace, including Toothless Jonny, famed in these parts for his gummy smile and proposals of marriage to any female aged between fifteen and eighty-five. He can be annoying, but is generally tolerated as long as he doesn't get rowdy and start his lisp-y rendition of 'I Love You Baby'. The jury's out as to whether he's a fan of *Ten Things I Hate About You* or *The Deer Hunter*. I prefer to think the former. Around 6 p.m. the place starts humming with after-work drinkers profiting from the run up to Christmas by getting silly-drunk, knowing they will not be told off for their hangovers the next day by equally incapacitated superiors.

'Christ on a bike, your mum's a right character. I think I'd like her – she sounds like Bette Davis or Joan Crawford, some fabulous but unhinged old broad. My mum was more like Pat from *EastEnders*. Apart from the prostitution. But she was Miss Butlins in the sixties!' Gary chortles, patting the MUM tattoo on his upper arm affectionately; a habit that he says makes him feel closer to her in the five years since she passed away. I'm pretty sure if I got a commemorative tattoo in honour of my mum she'd rise up from the grave to disinherit me.

'I can see where you get your good looks from then! What a stunner!'

Gary blows me an air-kiss in response and waves like the Queen.

'At least she's gone through the menopause now,' I continue. 'I used to hear her screaming down the phone at the building managers saying they were persecuting her with their choice of wallpaper in the entrance hall. She claimed it was harassment. I actually thought she had gone mental.'

'What, did she start HRT and chill out then?' Gary looks

relieved that he will never have to shack up with an ageing wife.

'No. After a few weeks she realized that the colour – a sort of green-beige, hardly a psychedelic eyesore – was actually weirdly flattering to her complexion and she pretended none of it had ever happened.'

'Wow. Well, I can't say I can totally blame her for that. I too would be antagonized by bad wallpaper. You're okay though? Scott told me I should keep an eye on you, make sure you're all right and everything.' Gary looks at my face intently as I feel a red blush making its way up my neck.

'He . . . he said that? That was kind of him.' In a deeply embarrassing moment the past Saturday, during which my resolution to get on with things came to a grinding halt, Scott had found me crying in the storeroom cupboard. I hadn't wanted to go into details, so I told him that I was having a few personal problems, something I later bitterly regretted. Hysterical women are always assumed to be on the blob.

As he caught me in a bear hug, I appreciated the comforting warmth of his broad chest but it was not so much romantic as super-awkward. Not that it should be romantic – he is my boss. After initially relaxing into him, however, the neurotic paranoia that underpins all my thoughts went into overdrive. Trying desperately to muffle my tears, fearful visions of spraying mucus or spittle on his jumper running through my mind, I went completely rigid.

Mumbling something incoherent, I brushed him off and ran away to the toilet. It was childish, ungrateful and stroppy; I felt like a schoolgirl. He left before I had found a quiet moment to explain things and apologize for my behaviour. I haven't seen him since; though as this is my first shift back, I'm not overly concerned that he's avoiding me. Yet.

'He's a kind guy, our Scott. A really loyal, decent guy. Don't be surprised that he's looking out for you; he's like that. I think he thinks you've got boyfriend troubles or something.' Gary smiles, although his words have had the unintended effect of depressing me. Of course Scott was being kind because he's a nice guy and not because he likes me in some slightly special way. He barely knows me! And what he does know has been mostly unbalanced with a chance of psycho.

'Ha! Hardly. Well, I've been seeing someone for a bit but we haven't known each other long enough for him to make me cry. I don't think I've ever really cried over a man, actually,' I say, pausing to reflect. That isn't true at all. Less than a year ago I was crying myself to sleep on a regular basis. How quickly the mind forgets old wounds. Or maybe I am just lucky to be exceptionally un-nostalgic.

'Really? I have! Buckets. I don't think you've ever really been in love, my dear.'

'Oh, who knows. Is love best gauged by hurt?' I used to think that way, but I am hoping that was a phase and not a pattern.

'Pain, misery, unbearable joy, delusion and rampant sex all as intertwined as the congealed hairs you find languishing in a drain, that's what love is. I'm not sure I'd recommend experiencing it more than once or twice in a lifetime. It is exhausting. Mind you, the first time I thought I was in love I was just really, really hungover.'

'What? How does that work exactly?' I lean back on the counter and eye up the clock. It's a quarter to six; I get off at half past midnight but will soon be joined by Joy, which makes me dread the remainder of the evening. I'm tempted to buy Gary drinks all night so that he stays on the other side of the bar to keep me company, but that would kind of defeat the purpose of working.

'Oh you know . . . he was some guy I liked well enough, one of my first boyfriends. He was a total dick, but he was handsome and I was cockstruck. One morning after a really late night he started screaming at me over some stupid joke I'd made that offended him. Waking to a two-hour bitch fest with a pounding head was just too much for me. I started crying, thinking that no man could make me feel this bad unless I was really in love with him. So I told him as much and he was all chuffed – though the arsehole didn't say he loved me back. Anyway it got him off my back and for a few hours I really thought it might be true. But after I'd arrived home and was sat in bed with a cup of tea and *Corrie*, I realized that all it boiled down to was that I don't take well to being screamed at. And that was that! Finito.'

'What a tool! I don't think I could tell a man I loved him first, though, that's brave of you. Though I suppose if you're both men the rules are less clear,' I muse.

Anthony was the first man ever to tell me he loved me. I never responded in kind, though he began to say it after two months. I guess a part of me always knew there was something false about him. I was particularly grateful I never gave in to that sentimental impulse when I confronted him about his cheating. I asked him, 'Why would you do this, if you love me?' He had looked at me with incredulity and replied without missing a beat, 'Georgie, you don't mean the things you say during sex.' Harsh times. I am on the point of relating this story to Gary but decide it's too pitiful to share in the early stages of our budding friendship.

'Actually,' Gary continues, 'I learnt from the experience that "I love you" is a very useful tactic to bring out when someone's pissed off at you. Save it for the right moment and you can save your relationship. I once was really broke – really broke, I would never do this now – and stole £50 off some guy I was shagging. He was super-suspicious and angry but after those three magic words – phhf! – all that vanished into thin air and he started apologizing for thinking I would ever do such a thing. Magic!'

'Gary! That's a terrible thing to do! I would never stoop so low. Maybe if I was really desperate, I guess, but really.'

Now I am glad I didn't mention the Anthony thing. Of course, I am years younger than him, so being less worldly is to be expected.

'Hey, I didn't say that I'm proud of it! Just that it works a treat. Lying, cheating, stealing, these things happen, though they happened more frequently when I was in my coke-fiend phase, I admit. But I'm not gonna beat myself up about it on my deathbed, you know? Now get back to work, Ol' Toothless is waiting.' Gary uses a teacloth to whip my arse teasingly and starts to take the order of a couple on the other side of the bar who try not to stare at the gaping hole in Jonny's patient smile.

I turn to Toothless Jonny. Though he could be fifty-something, years of hard living have etched themselves deeply into his face and that, combined with his disregard for dental hygiene, makes him appear far older. The first time I saw him I was a bit shocked they allowed him to drink in the pub, considering that much of their clientele is young and trendy. I suppose that is Scott's kindness again. Though I'm not entirely certain allowing a hardened alky to while away his life at a bar is kind, he is a paying customer. If he wasn't here, he would find a less salubrious watering hole.

''Ello, love. A pint of your finest, cheapest ale if you please,' Jonny lisps, his eyes twinkling beneath their heavy folds.

Though it has become quite cold recently, he is wearing only cut-off jeans and a thin jumper over his wiry frame. It occurs to me that he might come here so often to avoid excessive winter heating bills.

'Only the finest for you, Jonny!'

'Yer a fine young lady, George. Though I take exception to a name like that for such a fine young lady. You can never be too careful in this life. Do you know – I have known six-hundred-and-twenty narcissistic perverts in my lifetime. SIX-HUNDRED-AND-TWENTY! How many have you known?' Jonny's constant smile and general air of near-dementia make it difficult to know when he is having a laugh.

'Wow, six-hundred-and-twenty! What an exact number. Do you know, I'm not sure I know any narcissistic perverts . . . what should I look out for?' I look around desperately for Gary but he has popped out for one of his frequent fag breaks.

'A narcissistic pervert is a vampire. A vampire of the heart. But sexual – wild even! A deviant. Both my parents, they were that. Narcissistic perverts. I was packed off to a school near my gran so they wouldn't have to deal with me and look: just look where I am now. Touched up by the headmaster cause I was so cute. That's the wrong kind of love, what it does to you, my girl. It sucks up your very soul. You find a good man and keep him or you'll be sucked dry.' Toothless Jonny has stopped smiling and is looking off into the distance.

I am not sure how to respond to this confessional advice.

'Well, thanks, Jonny. The next time I run into a narcissistic pervert I'll be sure to tell him where he can get off.'

I shake my head wonderingly as he wanders off with his pint to his habitual corner, sticking out his spindly ankles in front of the fireless fireplace.

'Talking about me again, babe?'

I whirl around. It's Beardy. I haven't seen him since his gig, though he's asked me round for dinner and drinks regularly. I just haven't found the energy to see him with everything else that's been going on, namely my dad's balls, my mum's voodoo, university and work. I should probably put in a bit more effort; normally I would be delighted to have the Illustrious Beard pursuing me. Typically, the moment he senses that I actually can't be bothered rather than my usual faux-indifference he's all over me like a cat in heat. I have unwittingly gamed him. Whenever I play hard to get with people I like too much I never pull it off. The attention is flattering, but it does prompt a niggling worm of a worry – if I fall for him and let him get me, will that be the moment he legs it, uninterested in what I have to offer beyond the chase?

I come round the bar and give him a swift kiss, which he tries unsuccessfully to deepen. I am unwilling to get tongues involved with the watchful presence of his companion, who is familiar, although I can't quite place him.

'Just coming to pay you a visit, seeing as you are clearly too poor to text me back.' Beardy grins in a slightly threatening fashion that is compounded by the dratted glasses, which he's wearing again. He does look very sexy, in a wolfish-dandy way, with his beat-up Acne jacket, one-button-too-many-undone shirt and tattered skinny jeans. I feel a thrill of desire and embarrassment as he pulls me over to bite my neck while groping my arse.

'Oh sorry! Did you text me? I've been having phone trouble. Hi, I'm Georgie.' I push him off me and lean over to kiss his friend on the cheeks.

Tall and gangly in a manner that would have made him a bit of an outcast twenty years ago but is now eminently chic, he has razor-sharp bone structure, big brown eyes, pouty lips and the smooth cheeks of a nymphet. Though too androgynous to be my type, he is undeniably gorgeous. I suspect he knows it, too.

'Tim,' The Pout mumbles as he accepts my greeting with a sardonic air. 'Doing two are we? How Continental.'

'Oh, are you Alice's brother? You look a lot like her.' I could see it as soon as he spoke; they have the same large but perfect teeth with a slight gap breaking up the middle of their smiles. Though he hasn't been rude exactly, there is a coldness to his manner that makes me feel ill-at-ease. I try to compensate for my perceived inadequacy by being extra friendly and grinning at him like a loon, which probably doesn't raise me much higher in his estimation. Although I can be a bit feisty at times, I lack the Teflon shield of disregard for out-side opinion that one needs to be perceived as cool.

'Yeah.' Tim looks less than impressed by my powers of divi-nation.

'How do you know Alice?' Beardy says suspiciously, looking at me as if I have spent the time since I last spoke to him feverishly investigating his private life. Usually I am not immune to some minor stalking but in his case I genuinely haven't. Mostly because he isn't on Facebook, but still.

'Oh, I ran into Scott at your gig and she was there. We talked for a few minutes but I don't know her super-well. You must know Scott, right?' I say casually.

Beardy relaxes; I wonder if he has something to hide.

Alice is so beautiful that I would be shocked if he hadn't tried it on with her at some point and frankly I wouldn't even mind. If he hadn't, it would make me question his het-erosexuality. She's the kind of woman you don't try to fight your man for; it would only be humiliating. It is much less awkward for all concerned to just bow out gracefully. If they have already had a thing in the past that is now over and done with, it works out better for me. Assuming there no longer remains a secret tendresse between them. This thought, as well as the fear that he has compared her naked body to mine, will haunt me later tonight.

'Yeah of course, we've been drinking in Scott's pubs for years, it's where I met my bruvver here.' Beardy punches Tim in the shoulder, who rolls his eyes and winces. 'Alice has been talking about managing our band now that we're getting big. She's in PR but she hates her company, she's been looking for an out and wants to cash in on us!'

'That's exciting! Things must be going well for you if she's willing to risk the day job,' I say, aiming for a jocular tone. My heart sinks at the thought of Alice hanging around him all the time. I do like her, she's too nice not to; my insecurity makes me painfully aware how petty and pathetic I am capable of being. Yet I can't help my desire to shave off her eyebrows.

'In six months' time you're gonna be bragging that you knew us before we were famous, just you wait. Especially with Alice at the helm – she can charm the pants off a priest, so someone like Nick Grimshaw will be a piece of piss. I mean, Radio 1 is commercial shit, but obviously you've gotta hit all the bases on the airwaves.'

There is a too-long pause in which I wonder to what extent this extreme self-confidence is put on. Is he overcompensating for his insecurities? He must have some self-doubt rattling around in that gorgeous skull somewhere, surely. I certainly have enough for both of us.

'You guys were good, I enjoyed your set. Do you have more lined up?' I ask, struggling to think of an interesting conversational gambit.

'Baby, I've always got something lined up! Don't you know

me by now? You should have stayed – I can't believe you ran off like that. We had a wicked after party. Tim had to beat off fifteen-year-old girls with a stick; it was a fucking feeding frenzy.'

'Oh dear! Tim, you don't seem very pleased, is that not your thing?'

'No.'

God, Tim is a bit of a monosyllabic fucktard, I find myself thinking.

'For my part, I hate teenage girls. Disgusting creatures who only want one thing. What a man really wants in life is a sturdy woman who's handy with an iron. Can we have two pints of Grolsch? We'll be over there.'

Beardy and Tim saunter off to a corner, laughing loudly, leaving me to stand with a fake smile by the bar. I feel a coil of anxiety about whether he expects to pay for the drinks. Obviously false orders are done for mates; many's the time that I've scrounged a free pint or two from willing friends, but I've never expected it and feel funny about risking it now.

'Is that your man?' Gary questions me as I come round the bar. He has a talent for appearing at inopportune moments, but at least I now have an excuse not to give them their drinks for free.

'That's Leo, he's not really my man, he's just . . . something I'm trying out for a while, I guess,' I say, pouring their pints.

'I've seen him around quite a lot, never properly met him

though. I seem to remember Scott . . . Well, it's none of my business.'

'What?'

'Oh, nothing major, I've got a terrible memory for gossip. I'll tell you if something comes back to me,' Gary evades, looking at the clock. 'Oh look at that! It's past time for me to fuck off. Where the hell is Joy? She's always late and moody when Scott's not here, it's bloody annoying.'

'Is she ever not moody?' I'm not one to put much stock in auras, but hers is a black cloud spewing shit, let me tell you.

'Sure! You haven't seen? She's fucking schizophrenic. If she's got her eye on someone she can be very, very charming. Intense, but charming. Ah! There's our little ray of sunshine now!'

'Fuck off,' Joy snarls. Taking off a big fake-fur coat, she reveals her perfect body, draped in a flimsy slip-style dress that may actually be straight-up lingerie. She has paired it with woollen thigh high socks, combat boots and a holey cardigan. Her googly-eyed hatchet face is supremely unattractive to me, but her figure never fails to take me aback. I smile at her as I walk towards Beardy and Pout's table; she actually rolls her eyes.

'Here you go, my dears. You should feel special; I don't usually do table service you know. £7.85 please.' I hold out my hand to the boys, feeling schoolmarmish.

'Isn't she a gem? Generous too. Come on babe, you're not

gonna give me a sneaky pint?' Beardy attempts a puppyish expression, failing miserably.

'Ah, I've never done that here before – I'm not sure. Later, when it's just me behind the bar,' I promise. Though the staff have the right to a few cheeky drinks, I feel bad about 'stealing' from Scott, which is stupid, because if I were working for any other person I probably wouldn't care at all. Apparently my moral compass is only activated by men who comfort me in storeroom closets.

Back behind the counter, Joy is staring fixedly at their table, toying with a lock of her hair. I feel a sudden jolt of possessiveness over Beardy. Despite my ambivalence of the past few weeks, I must really like him after all. That or I just really hate her, it's difficult to tell. I don't need to worry, however – her eyes are all for Tim.

The rest of that evening saw one of the strangest changes of character I've ever witnessed. She was coy, flirtatious and downright vivacious towards all the customers that night, though it was clear her focus was targeted, like a laser, to Beardy and Tim's table. Her blue eyes were a-sparkling and a tinny laugh emerged at odd intervals, unrelated to the conversations surrounding her, so jarringly unexpected that it was actually somewhat frightening. The moment they left she did an abrupt volte-face, transforming into her normal surly self. Poor Toothless was quite confused.

Though I generally hate to exaggerate the facts, I implied I know Tim better than is strictly true to make use of her new-found, fake attitude of acceptance towards me. If sacrificing Tim, who I don't know or give a fuck about, on the altar of her magnificent tits and cruel soul means a temporary end to her usual rudeness, I will take it. Joy even deigned to ask me some semi-amiable questions about myself before disposing with pleasantries and demanding outright that I put out some feelers to see if he might be interested. Subtle she ain't, but lots of men are very attracted to unhinged psycho-bitches provided they have nice enough assets. She could be in with a chance. I've never been particularly talented at playing matchmaker, but for the sake of an easy life, I am prepared to give it my best shot.

A Joyfully Inert Slug

The Christmas holidays are a time of year when one should be relaxed and peaceful. Nothing engenders love for one's fellow man like a life of mince pies, mulled wine and the radiant glow born of a roaring fire. However, one is more likely to be found spending this special season in a Bacchanalian extravaganza of conspicuous consumption, avarice, vomit, divorce and death. The sick on the floor may be particular to me, but the rest is no exaggeration – the stress and burden of unmet expectations loom over this most dangerous of months. Mortality and separation rates tend to spike around Christmas Day, Boxing Day and New Year's Day; the *Daily Mail* would never tell a lie.

I have spent a lot of time shopping recently, though the

experience can be hellish. It feels as if the entire population of England has been disgorged on Oxford Street to engage in a buying frenzy. I end up spending far more than I mean to, as I keep seeing lovely things for myself. This selfishness is by accident, not design, I assure you. It would be unnatural to spend hours trying to find something for Dad, whose interests are limited to Formula 1 and spaghetti westerns, and not have a trinket catch my eye. Frankly, presents for men are always doomed to be disappointing unless you have the hard cash to spring for an Audi, or the generosity of spirit to buy them an hour with a stripper. I could just about afford the latter, but something tells me it might be inappropriate. I eventually got him a vintage Hermès tie and a luggage tag set – with mohair mittens, pirate boots, and YSL mascara for me. (These purchases will be more than offset when I eventually give up smoking in a few years' time).

Though my choice of profession might suggest otherwise, I don't enjoy endlessly trawling the shops; the surfeit of products can make me indifferent to them all. Of course, when you do find that one fabulous thing – Ah! The danger lies in looking at so many ridiculously expensive garments that, after a while, a Balenciaga leather jacket starts to seem reasonably priced at £3,000. Especially when you take into account the buttery quality of the leather and a design you are positive you will not tire of for decades to come.

Luckily my overdraft does not extend to such dizzy heights so designer impulse purchases are out of the question.

To kill two birds with one stone, I take photos and notes as inconspicuously as possible for my comparative shopping and trend research. My purposes are innocent; I would never steal a design from someone else, or what would be the point of my degree? However, as many Oriental companies regularly nick ideas in this manner, the shop assistants look out for likely culprits and it can be a stressful endeavour. I waltz into Dover Street Market in my smartest finery in order to try on expensive dresses, while hoping the lurking sales assistant doesn't hear the beeping from my digital camera. Then comes the embarrassing process of handing them all back, pretending they are not quite right for whatever classy function I have invented. It requires acting chops I am not certain I possess.

Though hitting up Selfridges, Harvey Nics, Liberty's and Browns in the space of a few days is a strain, the only time I reach the end of my rope is in Harrods. Not even the puppies in The Pet Kingdom can raise it in my estimation. It is a giant, windowless rat-cage-maze covered in gilt, essentially an upmarket Primark from which the swiftest exit takes twenty minutes in every direction. With the heaving crowds, it can take a full forty to escape. Filled with women who would sooner impale your foot with a Louboutin stiletto than step to the side to let you pass, I quickly realize from the sea of green-and-gold carrier bags that the much-lauded trend for conspicuous abstention after the crisis has not taken off. *Vive la Résistance*!

Despite the stress of all this feverish expenditure, I absolutely love the holiday season. It is the only time of year one can feel truly content with oneself after a gluttonous binge of epic proportions. Instead of being mired in a haze of self-recrimination while blearily taking in the empty bottles, over-spilling ashtrays and ravished trays of confectionery the morning after, I feel that I have accomplished a nearly impossible physical feat of digestive prowess. When faced with the last five truffles in a 650g Charbonnel & Walker box given to Stacy and swiftly donated to me, do I give up, relent and decide to finish them another day? No! They are my Everest!

Ultimately my pagan joy in this Christian holiday outweighs my desire to avoid ballooning by January. I will nobly bear the consequences of everything I cannot say no to (which is everything). With diets, self-restraint and restrictive waistbands pencilled in for sometime next month, I feel I can truly unleash the obese, foul-mouthed trailer-trash whore inside me, who likes nothing better than to sit in front of the telly smoking, drinking and eating, completely orally fixated.

And it's all in the name of the Baby Jesus. By all accounts he became a great man who did some things, but most importantly, at his birth he was brought rare riches from far and wide. We commemorate this today by giving our loved ones cashmere socks, £35 for thirty-two ounce Crème de la Mer lip-balms and other silly luxury items. The things that catch our eye but that we would never normally have the chutzpah to purchase for ourselves. Understanding this is the key to good gift giving and why getting something useful is somehow soul-crushing.

Anyway, this Jesus grew up into a garrulous fellow, fond of symbolic hand gestures and wine-laden dinner parties that would start out as politically minded intellectual soirées but finish with drunken sleight-of-hand magic tricks. For all these reasons I think we would get on rather well. He is particularly dear to my heart for his assertion that carbs and red wine are Godly. One cannot help but admire the enduring power of his trend-setting. The Diana Vreeland of organized religion, his influence can still be felt in the unfettered facial hair and gladiator sandals sported by fashionable people today, all over the world.

It is now Christmas morning and I am lying wrapped in my duvet like a joyfully inert slug. The shenanigans will begin when I travel to Mum's flat – I am tempted not to get out of bed. Someone had the bright idea for us to spend the holiday all together in our reconstituted family unit – Mum, Dad, me and Vitoria. This decision was undertaken while we were aware of the finite nature of our lives.

Now that the reason for this rare sensitivity has been revealed to be a glorified zit, we bitterly rue the consequences of this hasty sentimentality. I've been having horrible flash-backs to the post-Vitoria/pre-divorce period when they were trying to work on their marriage. Every moment of peace was the calm before a storm; every kind gesture seemed heavily weighted with guilt; an undercurrent of recrimination and fury pulled on our spirits. Mum played the martyr and Dad wore our family like a hair shirt.

I wish I could spend the next few days alone at home, rather than sitting at Mum's enduring the awkwardly polite silences interspersed with terrible rows that are bound to follow. For once, I feel utterly free and able to do as I please in the house, as Stacy has gone to visit Tarquin and Cordelia for three glorious weeks. She's staying at their place in the countryside with a few other guests; she assures me it's a very exclusive party. Apparently their house marches alongside some grand National Trust estate and has gorgeous views. I've studiously avoided looking at the *Tatler* Stacy left lying on the kitchen counter folded to a page where she mentioned it is featured. I'm curious to meet Tarquin and Cordelia, just because it would be fascinating to see what kind of people would voluntarily invite Stacy to stay with them for nearly an entire month without having some sort of recompense, sexual or otherwise.

Still, family duty calls. I should ready myself by finding something fashionable enough to assure Mum that I have made an effort and baggy enough to comfortably shield my food-baby from view. After a quick shower, I choose a red woollen Christmas jumper-dress, paired with flat black over-the-knee boots and a full face of sparkly slap for morale. Feeling boosted with my warpaint on, I gather up my gifts and take the bus, on my way back home sweet home.

Mum lives in the lower-ground-floor flat of a Georgian townhouse in Primrose Hill, a chic part of North London just a short walk from Camden. The area became infamous in the nineties as the wife-swapping, cocktail-imbibing, drug-snorting area of choice for a clique of A-list celebrities and their C-list neighbours. This wildness was eventually worn down by the monotony of divorce, rehab and the school run, but I like to think they carry on with the occasional festive spit-roasting, if only for old times' sake.

Tucked into a quiet side road, Mum's place is not a particularly impressive piece of real estate in size or grandeur but has private access to a charming garden that in summer is completely overgrown with grass, flowers, ivy and weeds. Though she hasn't tended it at all in the years since she and Dad sold the old flat to buy separate properties, I like the unruliness of it; it is refreshing, a mysterious enclave of bare, twisted branches in winter and a romantic wilderness of plants and colour in summer.

We are both of the opinion that an overly manicured lawn speaks of the character of its owner as anal and controlling. Ours probably suggests that we are lazy and unhinged but I rather fancy the idea of carrying around an unloaded antique pistolet to wave threateningly at small children, noisy dogs and traffic wardens. Whenever I spend an extended period of time here, we end up either laughing uproariously together over a bottle of wine, or bitterly sniping at each other. This, combined with my frequent forays into her wardrobe to see if any of the old designer togs she's held on to from her youth will fit me (they don't), makes me fear that if I ever need to move back home, we will turn into the second coming of *Grey Gardens*.

Mum is not at her best around the holiday season, or indeed at special occasions of any kind. It brings out in her something that begins as a tremor of nervous energy and eventually builds into a crescendo of full-on hysteria that usually strikes at a moment in which someone else should be shining. This includes but is not limited to: eulogies at funerals, the exchange of vows at weddings, any time 'Happy Birthday' is sung and Easter Mass. If I ever give birth, I will have to bar her from the delivery room so I can hear myself scream.

So, turning the key and letting myself into the flat, I am surprised to hear her singing happily along to Frank Sinatra carols in the oft-unused kitchen, from which strangely delightful smells are emanating.

'Mum? I'm home! Happy Christmas!'

I slam the door, pulling off my boots in the narrow hallway

and searching for a place to put them. Every bit of available floor space is taken up by stilettos and shoeboxes. They wantonly display varying levels of sexiness inappropriate for the firmly middle-aged. I appreciate that she's a good-looking woman still in fine form, but what need does she have for leopard print with silver spiked studs, I think as I pick up a pair enviously, stroking the dyed pony-skin with lust. Unfortunately, we do not share a shoe size.

'Hello, darling! I'm in the kitchen!'

I hang my jacket on the decrepit old radiator which functions as the coat-stand and step into the living room to put my gifts under the tree. The largest room in the flat, it has high ceilings, an incongruously fancy chandelier and inviting leather couches covered in ethnic pillows that she picked up on her travels. The shelves are adorned with ornamental plates, statues, paintings and vases of flowers. It is cluttered and eclectic but cosy and inviting, the result of trying to cram a lifetime's worth of things into a sudden downsize.

This year, rather than getting out the old artificial tree, which is held hostage in the laundry cupboard, she has sprung for a real one. Though it is small, it looks enchanting atop the piles of Turkish rugs that are strewn over each other on the floor. Adding my purchases to the loot spread out beneath it, I try to have a quick look-see through the tags to find out how many are intended for little old undeserving me. I am prevented by the schizoid hissing of Heisei. Originally

Next Door's cat, Mum started secretly feeding him in our garden at night, lured him into the flat and has never let him out. That was eighteen months ago. Misanthropic, inbred, resentful and lazy, it is easy to ignore him as long as you are not in his 'Spot of the Day'. This is usually directly in front of a toilet or vital connecting door and is currently on top of the parcels. I originally wondered when Next Door would clock his new home and request him back; now I realize they know, have always known.

'Wow, it smells amazing. I'm well impressed by whatever you've rustled up!'

I enter the kitchen, leaning against the doorframe as Mum puts the kettle on. We share the habit of always needing to be sipping on a glass of something, going through endless rounds of tea, coffee and, the hour permitting, alcohol. She credits constant hydration for her good skin, though I'm not sure caffeine and booze are known for their collagen-preserving qualities.

'Thank Marks & Spencer, dear, I decided to forgo the stress and disappointment of another burnt turkey.'

More of a takeaway queen than a gourmet chef, she left the plastic packet of giblets in last year, resulting in an extremely peculiar-smelling and overcooked beast. I ate it nonetheless, with the addition of lots of cranberry sauce, alone in front of *Doctor Who* while she cried in the toilet for a good two hours. If I've learnt anything from growing up with dodgy cooking,

ELIZABETH AARON

it's that a hefty dollop of a store-bought condiment can save almost any dish from being consigned to the bin. Except for the time when she tried to flash-fry beef that should have been stewed for two to three hours, which was rather like I'd imagine chewing a pleather handbag to be.

'Good old M&S ready meals, the taste of my childhood. When are Dad and Vitoria coming round? Can I have a coffee? Thanks.'

'You know what I tried the other day, darling? Green tea and vodka with a splash of jasmine liqueur. It was wonderful.' Mum turns around with two steaming mugs and sits with me on the old shabby-chic desk which functions as the dining room table. Wearing a draped jumper with smart dark jeans, an enormous strand of pearls, kittenish black eyeliner and orange French Sole ballet pumps, she looks chic and girlish, somehow less severe than usual.

'Mum, are you a mixologist now? What happened to the *Divorced Lady Solves Your Marital Woes* or whatever you were going to write?'

'Oh, that's still in the works, darling. I've got so many years of material in my head begging to get out, so many experiences to share, but you know, it is hard to find the time to actually put pen to paper. You see, if I could afford a secretary or an assistant it would move along much more quickly but at the moment I have to admit that I've just got the title page and a brief outline.'

She grins wickedly, leaving me to wonder if she hasn't already had a few nips at the cooking sherry. It's 11 a.m., but I wouldn't put it past her. Nor would I blame her, faced with a family Christmas with the ex and her replacement; in Mum's place, I'd have lightly tranquillized myself. Still, I do wonder when all the 'I hate your father' awkwardness will end. Two years from now, five, ten? It's not as if the divorce is recent, although I suppose after more than a quarter of a century together even six years can seem an impossibly short time to move on. Some people never put aside their resentments or desire happiness for their former partner.

'I think it's probably best to have at least the outline of a product before you start hiring an assistant, don't you think? Unless it's some young stud, in which case go for it, he might prove indispensable in other ways! Speaking of which, when are you going to start dating again?' I ask.

I have always been curious about why she has never tried to find someone else to share her life with; as she often declares, she is far better looking than the majority of women her age and she tells me every six months about a fresh batch of divorcés in her social circle. Apparently the propositions from 'happily married men' came on thick and fast when she and Dad separated, but she has very strong feelings about stealing another woman's man, even if he is the one offering to be stolen.

'Oh darling, it's not as simple as all that. Your father, much as I am rude about him . . . I realize I am far more honest with you about my feelings than perhaps I should be, and for that I apologize. But despite the fact that I call him a faithless prick and so on, he was my faithless prick and he was the love of my life. For some reason, I always thought he would be faithful, or that if he did slip up, he'd be rather Continental about it. He might cheat on me, but he would never leave. I should have married an Italian,' Mum sighs, 'like dear Raffaello. He was madly in love with me. He was a total philanderer and slept with my best friend, so I got into a bit of a huff and ended it. But it was the seventies, and I'm quite certain that if I'd chosen him he would have kept married life separate from whomever else he had on the side. Catholics are good at that sort of thing.'

'Mum, this Raffaello guy sounds dreadful, I don't understand why you mention him wistfully every time you talk about Dad leaving.' Finishing my coffee, I stand up to put the kettle back on for round two and try to keep the irritation out of my voice. 'This was decades ago, do you even remember what he was like? He's now probably some balding man with a mahogany tan and giant belly overhanging his Speedos, hitting on teenagers in Capri.'

'No, Raffaello was far too vain to ever get fat. He might well have hair plugs, I grant you that. He was a bit of a con artist, so I imagine he is either very successful or in jail. Still, I was fond of him. Every man who hurts you stays with you, my dear. It's the good ones you forget, unfortunately. I've never quite understood why, but there you are. At any rate, are you prepared for some good news? Vitoria isn't coming.'

I turn around to stare suspiciously at Mum, who looks quite gleeful. I'm shocked she didn't blurt this out the minute I came through the door; she loves nothing more than good gossip.

'Oh really? Did you scare her away? I thought that last dinner we had actually went fairly well, considering. Did you say something horrible to her when you were at the doctor's?'

'No! Well, nothing out of the ordinary. I'm never *that* rude to her and when I am she just stares back at me with the blank eyes of a cow. Either her English is still rudimentary or she really is a stupid little thing. I don't know the details; your father said that she's gone back to Brazil to see her parents for the week. He'll be arriving soon, so it's just us three. I've bought a Scrabble board in case we run out of safe topics to discuss. I know he is not in any immediate trouble with his health – Doctor Chase gave him a full check-up – but these things do make you realize that perhaps you could be more fair about the twists life has taken.' Mum sips her tea, looking thoughtfully into the distance. 'After all, being married to me can hardly have been a piece of piss, could it?'

'Mum! Are you drunk?' I can't help but goggle at her. She is not best known for admitting to her faults without some secret underhand motive that becomes apparent only months later, which of course may still be the case here.

'Darling! It may be Christmas Day but there is nothing so depressing as a champagne breakfast alone. I'll have an aperitif in an hour or two like all reasonable people.'

I say nothing, wondering how long she will be able to contain herself.

'So, do you think there is trouble in paradise? Or do you think she actually is just going back to see her parents now that your father is out of trouble?'

I make that a four-second pause. Not bad!

'God, Mum, I have no idea. I hardly know the girl, do I? I mean, we did a few shopping trips together but it was generally just painful small talk. She's nice and everything but I don't think we ever really progressed beyond the weather.'

Obviously, I wasn't best pleased with Vitoria initially and was furious with my dad. However, when a parent chooses a different life partner, even in unsavoury circumstances, it's better for all concerned to try to swallow your grudges and get on with things for the sake of an easy life (something I relentlessly pursue). While I never welcomed her, I did try to find some common ground between us and, considering the minimal differences in our ages, it should have been relatively easy. I have always been of the opinion that if a man cheats the fault lies squarely with him and not the other woman, but my general ambivalence towards her would be suddenly upended by a rush of disgust whenever she would try to have a girly chat about their relationship.

As for Dad, well, my previous estimation of his character crumbled. However much I try to appreciate the many finer elements of his personality, my overriding sense now is that he is just weak. Having held him on a pedestal as a child, now my greatest, unspoken fear is that if he could not be faithful, no man can. If he had gathered the courage to end his marriage before beginning another, I imagine this might be different. This mistrustfulness has carried over into my personal life ever since, no matter how hard I try to remember that my parents are just people – bumbling along, fucking up and eventually dying just like everybody else.

'Well, I'm sure it's probably nothing, but it is rather sudden, don't you think?' Mum is rabbiting on and my mind drifts back into the conversation. 'What kind of girlfriend jumps ship so soon after such a stressful time? I mean, I know it was just a spot, but your poor father was terribly worried. Oh, there goes the bell; he's here early. Act surprised she's not here.'

Mum presumably wants to seem above such petty concerns as Vitoria's presence or absence. This tactic will reveal itself to be a transparent lie the moment she gets a bit drunk and starts making snide remarks. But, no matter. A woman's got to keep some semblance of pride.

'Daddy! Merry Christmas!' I cry animatedly, getting out

of my chair with my arms wide as Dad comes into the small kitchen still wearing his coat and loaded down with carrier bags. One benefit of having a cheating father: expensive gifts chosen by a young piece with far better taste than his own.

'Georgie, my darling! You look well, look at those cherub cheeks!' Dad sets his parcels on the table and swoops me into a bear hug.

'Oh, God, chipmunk cheeks more like. I've been main-lining carbs like they're going out of style. If I weighed myself I'd probably die of a heart attack.'

Leading up to the Christmas hols, I had my nose well and truly to the grindstone at university, with most of my spare time spent working at the Newt. So, with my week off I have done little but sleep and catch up with friends in a revolving series of pubs, clubs, bars, cafés, restaurants and markets. All my preferred social activities are foody boozefests. It's surprising to what degree you can inflate in the space of eight days.

'Well, I think it charming you still have a bit of baby fat.' Bless Dad.

Mum scoffs loudly.

'She's far too old for it to be baby fat. It's bloat. This time of year you can have wine or pudding but never both. Don't say I didn't warn you.'

'I don't care,' I say, thinking that I could probably get away with wine and pudding if it wasn't also for the spiced cider, winter Pimms, chocolate-covered nuts and cheese plates. I change the subject. 'You're looking way better, Dad! Have you lost weight?'

'I've been working out and paying attention to what I'm eating, I've lost half a stone this week. Vitoria being away has made it easier, without all those cakes she's always baking. She never eats them so I end up scarfing the lot.'

'Half a stone in a week? Why is it that men seem to shed weight as easily as they do their ex-wives? It's so unfair,' Mum says. Dad eyes her warily but she laughs. 'Oh come on, Edward, it was a joke. All in fun and all that!'

'I wouldn't say shedding you was easy, Polly,' Dad says solemnly. 'Quite the opposite in fact.'

There is an awkward pause, as Mum and I look at each other, unsure if his tone is regretful or accusing, before she busies herself tidying away his things and putting the kettle on again.

'So, where's Vitoria at then?' I ask innocently.

'She's gone back to Brazil for a while. It was all a bit much for her recently, she hates hospitals and the whole health situation was difficult. She hasn't been back home for months and hasn't spent a Christmas at home in years so we both decided it would be a good time for her to go.'

'Will she be gone a few weeks, then?'

'I expect so,' Dad says evasively. 'But tell me your news.

How is university? Are you still with that ratty rocker boy you were dating?'

'Oh God, can we not talk about that or boys, I'm sick of them both—'

'Come on Georgie; buck up! I see you once a month at most and you never want to share the details of your life. Which I fund for the most part, let me remind you.' Dad is doing his kind/stern/reasonable thing that I am never quite petulant enough to stand up to.

'Fine. It's all fine. I had my Final Design Selection tutorial with my tutor Zelda, she likes my range plan and we've chosen what to take through for the final show. I've been working pretty dementedly but it's going well with the boy, too. I think. I like him.'

Is it going well? Do I really like him? I've been so busy the last month that though I've been seeing Beardy and he's grown to be a part of my life, I haven't given the relationship my usual neurotic attention. He's more like a comforting routine.

'He isn't quite a boy, is he darling? Didn't you say he was in his thirties? In my generation that would be considered to be a grown man.'

'Yes, Mum, he is nearly thirty. But he still acts like a boy. He's a man-child, but so is everyone these days.'

This is probably not true, but I do meet a far larger preponderance of men well past their late twenties who spend all of their spare cash on Nike trainers, beer and Wii games than those saving it towards a mortgage or kids. Maybe these men do exist and they just go straight from work back to their live-in girlfriends to make low-fat curry from scratch, curl up on the couch and have a half-suffocating, half-comforting argument over what series to watch.

Not being ready for such domesticity yet, I content myself with navigating the confusing limbo between coupled-up and penis pals, trying not to get dickmatized in the process. I find myself hoping that what some people (Sarah) might interpret as the crumbs of affection Beardy flicks me, are mistaken; that they are in fact seeds of affection. Seeds are a point of growth; crumbs decompose. I make him sound awful; it's often more than just crumbs. Seeds!

Amazing how with one parental question a month's worth of anxious self-scrutiny can shoot out from whatever jack-in-the-box it has been repressed into.

'Does he like Van Morrison?' Dad's question is drowned out by Mum who says simultaneously,

'He doesn't live in a squat, does he?'

She is suspicious that all artists and musicians are alcoholic ne'er-do-wells living in a constant state of near-homelessness, unless they are wildly successful, in which case they are of course visionaries.

'No! Christ. Let's open gifts, shall we?'

Retiring to the living room, we settle around the little tree.

When I was a child, opening gifts with the older, conservative family members on my Dad's side, I would pass out everyone's allotted present and we would go around the circle taking individual turns to open them. It was, to me, a torturously slow, painful charade of gratitude before the wrapping was even off. This gratitude would remain determinedly lacquered on, whatever the bitter disappointment of the actual gift. We would outwardly ooh and ahh, inwardly wtf-ing, over things that we mostly didn't want and definitely didn't need.

Now that it is just us three, we quickly dispense with such politeness. Mum immediately re-gifts the fifties-style Roberts radio Dad has given her to me, saying that if her technology isn't modern, guests will think she's just held on to random junk from her childhood. Dad sweetly pretends that the Hermès tie I've given him isn't too slim to suit his girth and that he doesn't already own the Ayrton Senna biography that Mum gave him. I receive a beautiful cashmere jumper, some really strange jewellery and books on fashion and art. Mum declares that as Vitoria would never eat the marrons glacés she bought for her, we should open them now and have a glass of champagne before lunch.

A few hours later we are stuffed to bursting with turkey, Brussels sprouts and Christmas pudding. We have spent the day mostly pleasantly; the BBC holiday specials soothe us to the point where we send forth only an occasional sally of half-hearted criticism. It feels almost like old times. With the only tears and shouting related to a heated Scrabble battle, I start to think that maybe, just maybe, we've turned a corner and a new peaceful era of forgiveness, love and proper grown-up behaviour has begun.

Where I'm Henry

'I've done something bad, Georgie. But I don't feel terrible about it at all. Does that make me a bad person?'

As Sarah and I sit down at a table in The Newt for our traditional Boxing Day hair of the dog, I have a rising sense of déjà vu. Though I usually avoid drinking where I work I am stingy and staff discount has lured me in. Besides which, I love Gary and though Scott hasn't been around much, he always puts a smile on my face.

'I'm sure it can't be that awful, doll. Have you and Henry fought again or something?' I ask.

I have some juicy gossip to share myself, but clearly whatever Sarah has done is so dreadful that it takes precedence; we will dissect whatever drama she has embroiled herself in like a mutilated cadaver in *CSI: Relationships*. The last time she did something 'terrible' was when she drunkenly carved 'I HATE YOU' in giant letters with her keys on the front door of Henry's flat during a particularly embittered row. The marks were so deep that paint couldn't fill them and she ended up having to replace the entire thing. Therefore, this confession could be pretty bad, but my job is to soothe her worried fears, not concur that she can be a total psycho. Loyalty works in strange ways.

'No, we've been getting on better than ever recently. But . . . I'm having an A-F-F-A-I-R!' She spells the word in an exaggerated whisper, looking around her with the paranoid air of the recently institutionalized. It takes me a moment to work out what she means. Then I gasp.

'Whaaat? No way! You've always been so anti-cheating!'

Sarah may be many things: loud, theatrical, brutally honest and disconcertingly direct. But although she is a very sexual person, who talks a big game when it comes to men, she has always said that she has never and would never cheat. However tempting, she considers it an act that it is for cowards and liars, two things she prides herself on not being. Fidelity is arguably a quality that has nothing to do with love. It is a matter of how you view yourself. Internalizing the notion that 'I am not the type of person to cheat, lie or steal' is, after all, the only thing that prevents most people from cheating, lying or stealing.

'I know, I know. The thing is, if you've never done something it's easy to dismiss it out of hand as something you would never do! I mean, I just had never been really tempted before and when I gave in I thought, well, this can just be a one-time-thing, a slip-up I'll never repeat. But I had no idea how I'd react to doing it. I'm like an Amish teen that's suddenly discovered bars, booze and boys. I feel like I'm addicted to him.'

'Wait, wait, wait, who? Someone from work?' I ask, trying to think of a Don Juan alluring enough to overturn her principles.

Sarah is gnawing on her fingernails with a demented air; the manifestation of her nerves chewed onto her bloodied cuticles. But at this, she rolls her eyes.

'Ye gods, no. You've come to one of our after-work dos haven't you? No, no, it's Alistair. Remember the tall Irish guy in the fur coat at Beardy's gig?' I cast my mind back to that night, vaguely recollecting a man fitting this description. He was, though very handsome, camper than a row of tents.

'The lanky one? You're sure he isn't gay?'

Sarah's all-time favourite, alive-or-dead fantastic famous dream-fuck is Tim Curry circa *The Rocky Horror Picture Show*; she likes a high-kicking edge to her masculinity. So if this Alistair is indeed a skirt-chaser, I can see how she was overpowered by lust.

'Er, trust me, I think I have firmly established by now

that he is definitely, definitively, one-hundred-percent straight.'

Sarah manages to look guilty, lovelorn, pleased and tormented all at once. I notice that she is wearing sky-high fuck-me heels and a low-cut, clingy jersey dress that showcases her perky tits to perfection. I begin to wonder if she is going to ditch me later tonight or if she is now just dressing the part of an adulteress.

'How did this start? You barely spoke to him that night.' She also barely mentioned him the next morning after she stayed at my house. She had ample opportunity, as we went for a late brunch of sausage and mash at the aptly named S&M Café the next day. Not best known for her subtlety, she must not have been so taken with him at the time.

'He found me on Facebook a few days later and we started messaging each other. We had always had a spark between us, but, I don't know, it was one of those stupid things where I met him when I was younger and I didn't really realize how rare it is to have that kind of electricity with someone. I just let it fizzle, for pastures new, not yet knowing that those pastures would be by-and-large the sort of non-arable bits of land the American government palmed off on the Native Americans.'

'You're comparing Henry to non-arable land? Harsh, dude.' I sip my wine and wonder what unflattering analogies ex-boyfriends may have made about me to their friends. After all, even Tony Curtis said kissing Marilyn Monroe was like kissing Hitler.

'Not Henry, no, but I was single and dating for a good two years between the two of them and yeah, it was a drought-stricken desert. I speak in terms of quality, not quantity, of course. It was never serious between Alistair and me, so I thought why not meet up, just as friends, you know?'

'Ah. The old non-date date, I see. That rarely works out for anyone concerned, especially the clueless boyfriend. Is this guy seeing someone as well?' I purse my lips in mild disapproval.

It's not that I'm above cheating – when I am in love I have no interest in it. You can't really congratulate yourself on good behaviour that requires no effort. Maybe I have never sustained a relationship long enough to want to. I don't think I would, though – after my dad I can't help but find these situations a bit tawdry.

'No, Alistair's single, he broke up with his ex a year ago and hasn't met anyone special since, apparently. I've been totally upfront and honest with him about my situation.' Sarah is getting defensive. I wipe any lingering judgement from my face.

'Oh, poor boy! He's probably going to fall in love with you; a year after his last girlfriend is a ripe time for it.'

'Whatever, Alistair knows what he's getting into, it's Henry I'm worried about. I mean, I feel terrible, but ever since I've started seeing Alistair it's like all our problems have resolved themselves. It's like old times. I can't explain it. I used to get so angry with him about little things, like leaving the toilet seat up. Now I don't really care.'

I've never understood the big deal about toilet seats. Up or down, down or up. When was it decided and by whom, that the toilet seat should be left permanently down for the benefit of women, when it is men who are doing us a favour, going out of their way not to whizz all over the porcelain that we will then grace with our delicate arses? It seems an incredibly petty thing. Much like the stereotype of women eating a pint of Ben & Jerry's when our boyfriends leave (vodka, a gram and a rant is both more satisfying and less fattening), it is a cliché that has arisen from the ashes of chick-lit laziness to become self-fulfilling. I've not yet reached the stage of living with a man but I imagine that 'He always leaves the toilet seat up' is not-very-enigmatic code for 'Our love has been replaced by tedium and urine. I hate him'. It is the only feasible explanation.

'Well, I imagine a little something-something elsewhere makes you treat him with a bit more affection in some weird way, or maybe it's just the magnanimity of guilt,' I hazard a guess. 'Though I thought you said you didn't feel terrible?'

'Well, if I'm totally honest, I don't. I feel great, not a bit guilty and the knowledge that I must be such an awful, selfish person makes me feel terrible intellectually, though I don't care emotionally. Do you see what I mean?' Sarah takes a large sip of her cider and tugs worriedly at her hair. 'This is totally off topic, but do you think shoulder-length is too long for me? I haven't been for a trim in a while and I feel like it makes my jaw look fat.'

'What? No, it looks fine. Don't change the topic, woman, there are more important things to talk about here! How often have you been seeing him?'

'A few times a week. Henry's been off with his mates a bit more than usual, we sort of talked about taking some time to do our own things separately to give us time to miss each other. Which has worked, I did and do miss him when I don't see him every day. I've just—'

'Been getting some dick on the side?'

'In a nutshell. Georgie, Alistair is so great, so everything that Henry isn't, you know? He's fun and always joking, things are an adventure with him. We've . . . well, I've . . . been kind of paranoid about running into someone I know so we've taken day trips to Brighton, then we stayed in a country hotel . . . basically we've been doing random things. It's all so thrillingly spontaneous.'

I feel a pang for Henry. Perhaps if she had tried some thrillingly spontaneous escapades with him, she wouldn't have reached the point of no return. Or maybe they would have spent the entire time locked together in a cottage, arguing about the low-count bed sheets and the weather.

'And the sex,' she carried on. 'Oh my God – just incredible. Fantastic. I-forgot-it-could-be-like-that kind of sex. With Henry, it's always me making me come, you know? I have to really work at it and sometimes if he tries and fails, I get superangry but repress it. He barely ever goes down on me. With Alistair, the first night we spent together, I came four times like that.' Sarah clicks her fingers, the skin on her cheeks flushed with colour and a gleam in her eye. 'It was just so good.'

'Why don't you just break up with Henry before he finds out and carry on seeing Alistair then? It sounds like you're really into him and from what you've said in the past, things haven't been right with Henry for a while now.'

Poor Henry. I feel disloyal and almost guilty myself for talking about him in this way, but it is what it is; Sarah is more important to me than him. I suspect she will come to regret this affair, only realizing what she's had when it is gone, but she has been unconsciously set on messing things up, in one way or another, for months now. She seems fairly relaxed about the situation, but then cheating is like shoplifting. You only get caught when you get comfortable and therefore, complacent. Or so I've heard.

'I can't break up with him, yet. I'm not ready to let go. I still love him. He's good to me and he's good for me, I think. We complement each other. He's so kind, Georgie, kind in ways we have firmly established that I am not. I respect him. He

224

frustrates me but he also can make my heart melt, you know? And isn't that just what being in a long-term relationship is about? Boredom and frustration intermixed with moments that pain you with their sweetness, so you hold on, hoping the next surge of affection will come along sooner? I do really love him. I just feel trapped with him.'

'Well, you can't just have your cake and eat it, Sarah. At some point you're going to have to choose and if it isn't sooner, your choice will probably be taken from you. Can you imagine how devastated Henry would be, if he found out?'

'I know. It's so selfish. I would kill him if he did this to me, but the thing is that I genuinely think he never would. But you never know, do you – if someone asked him right now, I'm pretty sure he would swear down that I would never cheat on him. One month ago I would have said I would never behave like this. But I'm quickly realizing the only moment I'm likely to feel guilt is when I'm caught. If I'm caught. God I hope I'm not caught.'

Sarah fiddles with a long, stylized hangman's noose necklace made from woven gold, staring at it sadly. She had lusted after it for months and every time she passed by the jeweller's window display in which it had pride of place, she would give a little squeal. Henry gave it to her this Christmas.

'Christ, Sarah. I don't know what to say.'

'This is a stupid question, but I feel I have to ask it because it seems so glaringly odd to me, now. Why can't I have my cake and eat it? Surely it's the most natural thing ever to want to do, to fulfil all parts of myself with different people. No one can truly find perfect happiness in one other person, so why not share ourselves? Where, really, is the harm? We've been conditioned to accept monogamy as the answer, but maybe it's far more natural to have multiple loves that sometimes cross over, don't you think? I mean, it happens all the time.' Sarah purses her lips, deep in thought – her mood temporarily buoyed.

'Ah, man, I have no idea, you're asking the wrong person. I need to hold down one successful long-term relationship before I can think about taking on anyone else. But generally speaking, I thought they tried and failed with all that free love stuff in the sixties. Then the seventies put a seedy, avocado-hued nail in that coffin.'

'True. But I was thinking more along the lines of a bohemian, thirties Henry Miller, Anaïs Nin and his wife June open relationship I guess. Where I'm Henry.'

'I've seen that film and though I can't remember the ending, I'm pretty sure it wasn't idyllic. Plus, what you're proposing seems unlikely to sit well with Henry or Alistair. But hey, you're not married, you don't have kids; sometimes these things happen and you obviously haven't made a choice one way or another, so you just need to do that. Don't make any hasty decisions and whatever you do, don't tell Henry if you suddenly get the guilts. There's no point hurting him unduly over this. Ending it would break his heart as it is, I think.'

'Ha. Getting the guilts, I like that, like getting the shits. If only guilt could be prevented with Imodium. The pharma corporations should get on that, it would sell like hot cakes, besides being the obvious progression from Viagra. But no, I won't tell him anything, I couldn't bear to see the look in his eyes.'

There is a pause, as we both think of poor cuckolded Henry.

'Do you believe in karma? Or reincarnation, that sort of thing?' Her hand shooting out to grab my wrist as she leans over the table, Sarah holds my gaze with a sudden intensity. Never having previously shown an iota of interest in the after-life, maybe the double life she's been leading for the past month has got to her more than she's been letting on.

'Well, I haven't seen a hell of a lot of evidence for it. Although I guess many people find the thought comforting, seeing as there isn't a hell of a lot of natural justice playing out within our lifetimes,' I say as an afterthought.

'I'm afraid I'm going to have some sort of cosmic, karmic comeuppance. Like being reincarnated as one of those abused donkeys in the aid appeals on telly.'

'Seriously? You're joking. The first time I saw that advert I thought it was satire, something to show up the difference between what the RSPCA and Childline make from donations.

What a fucking waste of money that could go towards actual people in need. Christ. I know exactly what to do with the bloody donkeys. Skin them, tin them and send them to the needy! I should throw my hat into the political ring. Vote for me and I promise to wear revealing tops during Prime Minister's Questions and do my level best to shag Boris Johnson.'

Sarah is laughing and shaking her head at me, torn between hilarity and horror. This is a frequent reaction to what I think of as eminently practical schemes to better our prospects on God's Good Earth. I do love animals, by the way, whether they are at the end of my lead or the end of my fork. I just don't feel that love and hunger need be mutually exclusive.

'If you're that concerned why not do something to offset the karmic balance? Volunteer for Save The Donkeys since you fear they're your future brethren. Get involved with some charity.'

'Oh please, I'm not that scared.'

Confession made, penance ignored, Sarah gets out her phone and scrolls through her messages for a moment, before remembering me:

'So, what's your news?'

'I thought you would never ask! Well, I told you I had an unexpectedly easy Christmas, right? Not quite easy-peasy-lemon-squeezy but close enough, considering how dreadful the last few were. Vitoria didn't come, we all got on quite well and it was perfectly civil and everything. I didn't check my emails until after Boxing Day and it turns out Vitoria sent me a message Christmas Eve, asking me to look after Dad as they've broken up!'

It is Sarah's turn to squeal, 'Whaat?'

'Yes! So out of the blue! Basically, he didn't mention it at the time and I don't really know how to bring it up now, considering he clearly doesn't want to talk about it. But she chucked him! I don't even know if she's coming back to the UK. For all I know she's gone back to Brazil for good.'

Why does it seem that everyone's relationships are falling apart? Maybe it's just that time of year; people are casting off their better halves with a seasonal shrug, like a snake sheds its skin.

'You're joking! What a bitch! Not that I can talk. Though I do feel that if you are self-aware enough to know you're a bitch, the sin is mitigated somewhat. Why did she do it?'

'It's quite sad really, I kind of feel for her. In a strange way, I even respect that she ended it. I've always thought she was lacking in gumption. Though you must have a degree of that to get with a married man in the first place. Basically it came down to the age difference. His health scare put her off; she doesn't want to be caring for some old, decrepit man for the rest of her life. She wants kids, a real family life of her own, not this half-life they've been living pretending all is well to justify some initial passion – ugh – or loneliness or whatever it was that brought them together. I mean, she didn't say any of that, but I read between the lines. "We want different things, your father doesn't feel he could look after young children again", that sort of thing. But he didn't say a word about it!'

'It would be rather humiliating to admit to your mum, I guess. Being left is always hard, especially if you've thrown someone over for that person. It smacks of failure.' I can tell from the scrunched lines on Sarah's forehead that she is considering the potential parallels to her own situation.

'Yeah, Mum's not very good at hiding the gloat, either. Still, I have a feeling from little things he said that he thinks she'll come round. I definitely didn't get that impression from her email, though. I think she made the decision a while ago but his infected testicle spot was what gave her the push to move on.'

'Amen, sister. An oozy ballsack is enough to give any woman pause for thought.'

We share a cackle. I hope no one ever speaks of my future health problems in this way, but there you go.

'You don't think your mum would take him back, do you?'

'I dunno, man. She's got a lot of pride. It's probably what drove them apart in the first place. I kind of hope not, as she seems like she's been happier recently and I'm afraid it might send her into a tailspin. I think too much has happened between them, but God knows. Whoo can saay?' I enunciate oddly in a very poor impression of Bubble from *Absolutely Fabulous*.

'Christ. Well, I hope your Dad's all right. It must be rough being dumped like that. Quite emasculating, really.'

'Yeah. I feel bad for him, I do, but my pity only extends so far. The reasons Vitoria has given for ending it are pretty damn sound. I respect that she knows what she wants and that it isn't him, you know? To be honest, I think once he gets over it he'll be relieved. Novelty and soft flesh only goes so far once you're past a certain age. Surely you want someone with some shared history, or at least some sort of generational understanding of your references as you bitch about the quality of the news while reading the *Sunday Times* in tweed slippers.'

Reaching the dregs of my drink, I swivel my chair towards the bar to find that Craig, a recent addition to the bar staff, has been replaced by Joy.

'Oh fuck, it's Joy. I haven't seen her in a few weeks; the last time we spoke I promised to set her up with Beardy's bandmate – you know, Tim? You were salivating over him at the gig. I haven't seen her since and have made no efforts whatsoever so I fear our *entente cordiale* may come to a swift end.'

'What the hell is an *entente cordiale*?'

'Oh, like, the intention of cordiality. Basically it was a Franco-English agreement not to keep infringing on each other's territory back in the day. Don't ask me what century, whenever Bonaparte was living, I assume.'

I stopped taking History after GCSE and as a result my general knowledge of the subject is a patchy reconstruction from literature, ranting friends, snippets gleaned from book reviews and half-forgotten HBO miniseries. I may not be able to tell you the exact year or date of just about anything important that happened ever, but I could quote from B-films at a competitive level. The problem with this skill is that unless your conversational partner 'gets it' you just sounds unhinged. Also, the moment you decide to say in a slightly-louder-than-normal voice, 'I have a problem with pussy!' I guarantee the entire room will fall silent.

'Well, she's giving some serious bitch-face in this direction, so I think you may be right.' Sarah peeps over her shoulder before looking back at me with a grimace. 'She is quite intimidating. I don't say that about a lot of people, being a scary bitch myself.'

'I'll sort out our drinks and have a chat with her. Wine time? I thought so. How do I bring this up? I'm not really sure how to go about these delicate matters. I also have no idea if Tim would be interested. What do you think of her?'

'She looks terrifying but she has great tits. Who can say?' She mimics my previous impression as I head to the bar, feigning enthusiasm.

'Joy! All right? Have you had a merry crimbo and all that jazz?'

My fear of her makes me express myself with an unnaturally jovial edge. I try to keep the wince off my face as she stares at me blankly and then shrugs in reply.

'Right . . . can I have a bottle of Sauvignon? Please?'

Joy says nothing, giving me a look as if to say, 'That's why I'm behind the bar, you twat.' She is very articulate in her mute dismissal. She should consider an alternative career as an angry mime. Her silence makes me nervous and impels me to do something I am sure to regret.

'You know, I'm sorry about that whole Tim thing, I should have made more of an effort but you know, I lose track of things around the holidays . . . but Be— Leo's band is playing New Year's Eve down the road, you should come along! The after party will be here afterwards, Alice has organized a lock-in.'

'I know. Scott wants me there. That's £16.'

'Right. Well, great! If we don't share a shift beforehand, I'll see you then.'

'You'll see me in thirty minutes when you want another bottle.'

Laughing nervously in agreement, I hand her the money. I do not remind her that I should have a discount as I am too cowed by her unblinking stare. It's like she has two eyes of Sauron. What is wrong with me? I need to grow some balls.

And possibly start going to AA. All you need is the desire to stop drinking, after all, not the wherewithal to actually do it.

'Well, I'm pretty sure she still hates me but I did get a sentence out of her so it wasn't all in vain. I mentioned Beardy's thing and the after party but it turns out Scott already invited her. I don't get it – she's such a cow! I mean, not to him, I think she fancies him. She sort of brightens when there's a hot man around. Like a two-faced light bulb. I would have thought Scott would be wise to her ways but maybe not.'

I say all this fretfully, as I pour Sarah a very large glass of vino before filling my own, stopping about five millimetres higher. I feel that roller's rights should be extended to all shared recreational substances, illegal or not. This includes cake. I am greedy.

'Maybe she just wants to keep her job? There are plenty of people like that where I work, they act like complete tossers to anyone slightly below them and rim the big bosses, and it is totally repulsive. Me, I may be upfront – okay, possibly even a bit rude – but at least I'm consistent. If you're confident in yourself and your worth there's no need to suck balls. Generally the higher a position someone holds, the more genuine they are.'

'Nah, man, it's more than that. Gary's the manager and she doesn't bother with him. The limited reservoir of her charm is just for the men she has an eye on. It annoys me that no one seems to cotton on to it. I mean, she even said he wanted her there, not that he invited her. What does that mean? He wants her? I refuse to believe that.'

'Look at you; you're like a petulant child! Why is this upsetting you? Do you fancy Scott or something?'

'What? No.'

Sarah looks at me shrewdly, before poking me in the chest with her long tapered manicure.

'You lurrrve him—'

'Oh, fuck off! Why would you even say that?'

'I don't know, why wouldn't you? I totally would. I mean, I know you have Beardy and all but Scott seems more your style. Less hirsute but also less of a prick.'

'Scott is my boss. We are friendly, I like and respect him and I admit that he is not monstrous to look at. However. That would cross the line into Shitting—'

'Yes, yes; you don't shit where you eat, I know.'

'I was going to say shitting on my own doorstep, but yes, same principle.'

'You do know that means you exclude everyone vetted by friends and family as decent human beings before you even start looking for a dude? Ideally you should have at least two positive recommendations before you let someone into your bed.'

'There should be an app for that.'

'Definitely! Rose told me a bit about Beardy and that

sticking it in business, I'm starting to think he is a massive weirdo.'

I cringe into my wine glass. I knew I would regret mentioning this, as my initial indifference towards Beardy has shifted dramatically. I would say now that I am mildly (completely) obsessed with him. Maybe it is because what little free time I have between uni and The Newt, I spend with him, but the tables seemed to switch alarmingly fast. One day he was the one insisting that we must meet, the next I would be fantasizing about him all morning while pattern cutting. Fashion is dangerous for ill-advised daydreaming, as there are many time-consuming tasks to be completed that only require half your attention.

It's easy to develop disproportionate feelings for someone when everything else in your life is a constant, thrumming source of stress. I have begun analysing all our interactions based on who has retained the most power, which I know is unhealthy. Ultimately, no matter how Rico fucking Sauve I've been, the winner is automatically him as I doubt he is making the same mental calculations. The 'sticking it in business' she's talking about, though, is another story.

'Oh God, that. Rose has such a big mouth! To be fair to him though, he didn't actually stick it in without my permission.'

'I believe that is a perfect articulation of what is known as "damning with faint praise".'

'Let's go for a fag, I don't want to talk about this inside.'

Beating On Tiny Tim

We leave our bottle of wine to reserve our table and automatically throw our coats over our arms to disguise our glasses, which are technically not allowed outside. Exiting the pub, we shiver alongside the other exiled addicts sheltering in the tiled doorway. The English are made of strong stuff; frigid winds will not turn us into quitters. Taking a seat on a cold wooden bench that has seen better days, I roll up a cigarette between wind-bitten fingers as we stare out at the council block opposite us, resplendent in its faux-Corbusier cement glory. I reflect, not for the first time, what a different city London would have been, had it not been blitzed. France may have rapidly capitulated, but at least they preserved their skyline.

'Go on; tell me. I've already decided he's odious based on what Rose told me, so there's no point sugar-coating it.'

Sarah holds my gaze steadily, sucking on her Marlboro with gusto.

'I know, it's a bit awful, I think. Though it's hard to judge what is normal behaviour these days, I've dated so many strange men. Basically, there was an incident quite early on where he was suggesting we dispense with condoms cause I needed the morning after pill anyway. He was quite insistent but I wasn't into it, he used one, I considered the matter dropped. Then, a few weeks ago, we were about to have morning sex from behind and it was only when I reached back and held his cock to guide it in that I realized he wasn't wearing one. He said he was sleepy and forgot.'

'What. The. Actual. Fuck. "Forgetting" to put on a condom is like "forgetting" to put on a bra – it only happens in the minds of horny teenage boys.'

'I know! He said he was half asleep, but who knows. So, the other night, we are messing around and he looks into my eyes and spreads my legs – it was forceful, hot – but all without going for the johnny. I ask him if he has any left; he says no. I sort of play-struggle and say, "Stop it" and remind him I'm not on the Pill and he's like, "Don't you want to do it natural, baby? I've done this with lots of girls and nothing's ever happened." I tell him no, that I don't want to take the risk and then we're kissing again – the whole thing is this confusing push-me-pull-you, cause I want it too, just not like this. Things are getting heated. He pins my arms above my head and says, "You wouldn't be able to stop me, you know". And though his tone is light and he has a smile on his face, I have a moment of doubt where I don't know if he's joking.'

'Fucking hell, Georgie, this is way worse than Rose said. I feel like you're telling me a date-rape story!'

'I know, but the thing is, I like dominance, so aside from this vital component, it would have been great.' I worry my lip between my teeth. I did tell Beardy that I like a man with throwdown, after all.

'Consent should be the only vital component. I love a bit of throwdown too but this sounds fucked up, darling—'

'I know, I know. At this point I was just kind of looking into his face, hurt and bewildered, thinking, "Is this the kind of man you are?"'

'Jesus, what a cunt. And I don't say that lightly.' Sarah hands me one of her cigs as she sees me struggling to roll my second. Though we are sat on a bench underneath heaters, I can no longer feel the tips of my fingers.

'Yeah, well, he just stopped really suddenly, pulled away completely and as he walks to the other side of the room he reaches into a drawer and brandishes some Trojans at me. He laughs and goes, "Just kidding, I have a whole pack!"'

Sarah looks at me, disbelievingly.

'I know. Then came the weirdest explanation ever. He said that it was all a test to see how I would react, that so many girls were easy these days and with a bit of pressure they'd do whatever a guy asked them to. He wanted to see if I was like that.'

'Georgie, that is some really fucked up women-hating bullshit. You should dump him immediately.'

I know this. Rationally, I know this. Emotionally, I know this. Spiritually, I know this. But a twisted part of me keeps making up justifications for his behaviour. Yes, it was totally inappropriate but in the end it was a joke. So he says. A joke in extremely poor taste. I am guilty of that myself from time to time. Clearly, he should know better than to pressurize me, but he also knows that I like things a little bit rough. Should I have been clear about boundaries I was uncomfortable with before we ever slept together, on the off-chance that he would think acceptable what I think is clearly unacceptable? Do people really have a State-of-the-Union-style talk before they get down and dirty? I had never considered it necessary before, but maybe I should start.

'Is it really a dumpable offence? I don't know. He clearly thought he wasn't doing anything wrong. He hasn't done anything like it before. It makes me wonder if I am over-reacting,' I muse. This all went down a week ago and no longer upsets me, though I have started to look at him in a different light.

'You're definitely not overreacting. I hope you gave him a right telling off!'

'Yeah, I did. I totally did.' I totally didn't. I was too confused as to how I felt about it. Now it seems a bit late to bring it up. 'Have you ever been in a situation like that?'

'Fuck, no. Well actually, there was this one time. It was a different circumstance but equally manipulative. I was on a date with this guy years ago and we went to see some anniversary screening of *Titanic*. His choice, not mine. Anyway I noticed that he was crying during the end credits—'

'He was crying! That's sweet but not exactly your cup of tea.' Sarah likes men in touch with their emotions, but weepers are a step too far.

'It's true; I took the piss a little bit. He got defensive and started talking about how he used to watch this film with his father and that they had bonded over it. I assumed his dad had died and asked him if he had passed away recently but he didn't answer. I thought he was too upset to talk about it. I wasn't so attracted to him and we hadn't slept together yet. But by the time we ended up back at his, he was still acting so traumatized that I basically gave in to a pity fuck.'

'That's so unlike you!'

'I am capable of sentimentality from time to time! But when it was over, the first thing he did after rolling off me was to say, very casually, "You know, my dad isn't dead."'

'Whaat!' I burst out laughing.

'Bastard made up some line about how his relationship with his father had changed and in some ways it was "As if" he was dead. As if! It's hardly the same thing. "As if" doesn't even merit a handjob.'

'What the fuck.'

'No shit. I haven't given in to a nurturing impulse since. It's rarely worth it. The more you give, the more you're taken. More women should know this.' Sarah lights up another cigarette. 'Seriously, Georgie. Look out for yourself first.'

'Wow. Maybe I should count myself lucky Beardy didn't bring any dead relatives into his condom-avoidance speech.'

'All right, ladies? You must be dedicated smokers to bear this cold,' a familiar voice calls out. Scott has come round the corner of the pub to the left of our bench. He pauses in front of us, taking out a packet of Camels and lighting up, before raising it in a smoker's salute.

'Scott! What a surprise!' Reddening, I pray he heard none of our conversation. My Joker-esque grimace can hardly be termed a smile; I wave a maniacal greeting from my seat.

'It can hardly be such an unexpected encounter, considering that my bedroom is upstairs.'

Though the statement is completely innocuous, his eyes are dancing in a way that makes my stomach flip. A brief, unbidden fantasy of being in his room, pressed up against the wall rushes at me. Must stop fantasizing about off-limits men. I arrange my face into a semblance of normality. Prettiness is too tall an order, but I can do better than the contorted buffoonery that overtakes my features in his presence.

'An unexpected encounter is always the sweetest. That's why I'm on Craigslist!' Sarah can always be counted on to shamelessly chortle at her own bad jokes.

'Craigslist, really? Surely things aren't as bad as all that,' Scott says, his eyebrows disappearing underneath the scruff of his messy hair, the colour of ginger biscuits in the light of the streetlamps.

'No, not quite yet. But it gives me a thrill to read the encounters section at work in my lunch break. Far more entertaining than flipping through *Grazia* in Pret, not to mention free!'

'Not a bad idea. Free is my favourite number,' I say feebly. Sarah once told me that, from time to time, she masturbates in the toilets at work. I had hoped that she was joking. Now, I have a frightfully clear idea of what it is she's been thinking about and it involves bad grammar, loneliness and dick pics.

'Luckily your work doesn't involve any computers, or I dread to think what you would be wasting your time with,' says Scott, touching me lightly on the shoulder.

I bark out a laugh. My level of hilarity is completely disproportionate. What is wrong with me? Please God, if you exist, ignore the starving orphan's prayers and grant me the power to behave normally!

'With the *Daily Mail*, if I know Georgie!'

Back-stabber. Why is it that supposed friends always bring

up your embarrassing pastimes in front of men? Sure, he's not a love interest (I suspect he must be dating Alice or someone equally fabulous) but he is my boss. I invited Sarah to join me at the Saatchi Gallery last week which she turned down as 'Too far, too much, can't be arsed', so I went alone. This she obviously does not mention, preferring to tar me with the grandstanding newspaper favoured by those who are, publicly, barely the right side of the BNP. Privately, I suspect that anyone who actually buys the broadsheet probably has a poster of Nick Griffin on their bedroom wall and eyeholes cut into half their linens.

'You read the *Daily Mail*?' Scott's disbelieving tone suggests he is torn between disgust and disgust. Alice probably alternates between Tolstoy and Dostoyevsky when she wants a light break from Foucault. Damn her sparkly eyes.

'Just the shitty celebrity section,' I say defensively. 'It's an amusingly terrible rage-read! Plus, it's updated constantly, which is the key to solid procrastination. You should try it sometime.'

It's the best defence I can muster for this most guilty of pleasures. I would like to pretend that I fritter away hours on the *Guardian* or *It's Nice That* while waiting for the debut of something truly worthy, like 'Mensa V. Design Weekly' or whatever the hipster cognoscenti has up its sleeve. Obviously, this would only be deemed suitably avant-garde for a few months and I would discover it long after it had ceased to be cool. I just don't have the patience for things with any political or artistic import online. At three in the morning, deadline looming, a super-bland piece about our dry-as-dust Princess Waity Katie's blander outfit, quoting the blandest of all her bland statements, seems far more pressing.

Maybe I am doing Kate a grave injustice. Perhaps she has just been slowly weaned off personality in her capacity as a future head of state. Underneath it all she may be an off-beat, wacky nymphomaniac who thinks that Jesus was an alien-human crossbreed that will carry the lucky few off to the thirteenth dimension in 2017. Though a royal wedding would involve too many uneaten dinners and other bother for those anticipating transcendental teleportation to the next realm within a few years.

Still, she could be so much cooler if only she put in a little bit of effort; imagine a revamped 'Culty Katie' in Martian warrior gear designed by Nicolas Ghesquière. I live in hope that Prince George is a martian half-breed. For fear of being thought a weirdo with an enormous over-interest in the secret lives of celebrities, I say none of this and bring my mind back to the conversation at hand.

'You'd be amazed by how many people read it. There are quite a few undercover *DM* lovers amongst our sex, myself included.' Sarah is defending me against what may have been a tirade from Scott.

Scott reprimands me in a manner I fear is only half joking.

'Christ. That might be true, but there's no need to advertise it, hey, Georgie? Keep that stuff on the down-low so we can remain friends.'

'I'm not ashamed. I'm a modern, multi-faceted, independent woman,' I say, unsure why I added the independent bit, considering it won't be true until I stop depending on my parents for tragic handouts in addition to rent. Katy Perry must have subconsciously infected my vocabulary with the meaningless pinkwash 'empowerment' she refuses to call feminism.

'I read trash and I read proper novels, too, when I have time to fully enjoy them,' I say haughtily.

'Oh? What was the last one you read you really loved, then?' Scott has a habit of lightly touching me when he speaks. It is very unnerving.

'Erm,' I say eloquently.

The last book I read was *Tiger, Tiger*, the memoir of a woman who was manipulated into a long, psychologically damaging affair aged eight with a very sick father/lover figure; my favourite book is *Lolita*. Both suggest an unhealthy interest in paedophiles. When put on the spot with these sorts of things, the most dubious answers always spring to mind.

Once upon a time, in a land far, far away, I was actually very well read, though wallowing in a misanthropic, pseudo depressive phase that at the time I attributed to existential angst. It was really just the inevitable insecurity resulting from acne, bacne, and rackne.

Makeup can act as a temporary mask for these things. But my denial wasn't so deep that I could convince myself the spongy, uniform application of a yellow-beige shade with the underlying texture and consistency of asphalt fooled anyone. The colour of my foundation at that time may have been called 'Sunny Porcelain' but it was closer in tone to Lisa Simpson. Later, the addition of powder and bronzer to my arsenal led to bizarre orange stripes. Basically, throughout most of my adolescence I felt only shakily confident when standing in pitch darkness with a five-foot radius of empty space surrounding me.

Then, the face-plague cleared. I found the joys of friendships and lost weekends replete with alcohol; my remaining years have been spent living as a happy philistine. Though it saddens me to think that I reached my scholarly apex at fifteen, I justify the superficiality of my current interests by thinking that most people cultivate their minds in order to pontificate at dinner parties.

Anyway, I can take up stimulating my grey matter again when I eventually retire. One of the lesser-known benefits of smoking, after all, is that it staves off Alzheimer's. While it is a more expensive method than Sudoku, it is also more social. Those of us still heartily puffing away will be having rousing intellectual debates around our emphysema tanks. The more prudent residents will be stationed in front of the telly: drooling, abandoned husks forced to submit to *Everybody*

Loves Raymond on a loop, trapped in the solitary confinement of their own minds.

I roll up another cigarette and bring my wandering attention back to Scott.

'*Erm*? Never heard of it. Did it win a Pulitzer?'

He lights up another fag, shivering. He is standing too far away from the tiny heater to benefit from its warmth. I feel pleased at the thought that he is enjoying our company enough to chain-smoke beside us on this chilly evening. Though maybe he is just a heavier smoker than I had thought.

'I can never think of my favourite anything when someone asks me directly,' I say in childish protest, 'I get stage fright. Also, with knowledge, I am like a sponge. In the literal sense – anything I absorb is immediately ejected under pressure, leaving a holey lump of foam. I've been trying to get through *Great Expectations*, but it's a bit frustrating the way he describes every little thing in fifteen different ways. But I admit I am basing my entire opinion on the first three chapters.'

'Hmm, you should probably stick to decorating the female form and leave the literary criticism to others, dear,' Sarah says rather condescendingly, considering I don't think she's read anything longer than a press release since leaving university.

'What's so wrong with decorating the world? There's this Protestant undercurrent in our society that shuns beauty as frippery, but when so much of our sensory input from the world is visual, it's so important that that information has value. I mean,' I am drawn back to the concrete monolith across the road offending my eye, 'look at that butchered Bauhaus monstrosity. Le Corbusier's vision for social housing elevating the living standards of the poor became warped into this idea that if you give people an ugly tower block to live in, all their bodily desires will be met and they should be satisfied with their lot. Consequently, the middle and upper classes feel owed a certain standard of behaviour from the inhabitants.'

I am on a roll now. I add feistily, 'A certain basic need in our souls connects beauty and worth, beauty and intellect, beauty and goodness. It's not politically correct, but it is true. If you give people a pile of shit to live in, they will feel like shit and treat it like shit. I think our basic needs extend beyond food, water and shelter. Our outer shell is an extension of our creative expression. Has Gok Wan taught you nothing?' I finish my rant in a mock-indignant squeak.

'I wish I could feign manly ignorance of Gok Wan, but unfortunately Channel 4 does the best hangover telly. You may have a point there, though amidst the tangents I'm not entirely sure what it is.' Scott says with an air of faux-perplexity, a smile playing on his lips.

'Just that decoration is as natural and worthy a human impulse as anything else, I suppose,' I finish lamely.

'Well, what a speech! I've never heard you defend your chosen industry like that. Usually you're complaining about the amount of energy and stress you put into finding the right button, saying it's all ridiculous,' Sarah says.

'Can't I hate and love something at the same time? I think beauty has a high value but the process of creating it can be a massive ball-ache. It just annoys me when people act as if it's an entirely worthless, shallow endeavour.'

'People don't think it's worthless, just that it's not rocket science.'

'Rocket science is easier! It's formulas. Trying to predict whether a pleated skort can make a global comeback is a gamble based on trends in Shinjuku and raw intuition.'

'Running a pub is hardly rocket science,' Sarah adds dryly.

'Ah, but as a purveyor of alcohol in this fine and thirsty nation, I am and always shall be afforded immense respect. Everyone and their gran are fond of me. Whereas to the average Joe, fashion is full of preposterous snobs or heartless profiteers, or both,' Scott says.

The same people who deride the fashion industry as a self-indulgent effusion of ego would never deny the beauty of tribal markings, masks, ceremonial robes and headdresses. Anyone who has seen the exquisite intricacy of traditional costumes can see that even in eras of relative scarcity and hardship, presentation is important. The explosion of consumer society is an extension of this urge.

Fashion simply fulfils demand. We generally choose not to think about the provenance of our clothing. Though it could be wilful delusion that makes people believe a £6 cashmere jumper is not just a bargain but humanely produced, it is more likely the human cost doesn't even occur to them.

Saturated with novelty, there is a thrum urging us to buy more, not better, constantly. Terribly overt messages that whatever we purchase will somehow alter or disguise our flaws are so all-encompassing that we do not notice them any more. High fashion may be hated as elitist but it has the workmanship and craft to be considered an art in its own right. Those skills should be preserved.

I open my mouth to voice some of these thoughts but a wave of fatigue overtakes me and I shut it again abruptly. I've been on my soapbox enough for one evening. Mum has always advised that it's best to reveal only the top ten percent of your true thoughts, the more light-hearted the better. The remainder should be kept on lockdown, saved for the ears of your future husband. It goes without saying that your real opinions will only be revealed after the ceremony. 'Men don't want bolshy wives', was how I believe she succinctly phrased it. Dad must have been in for a terrible shock on their honeymoon.

'Heartless profiteers is a bit harsh! But of course a stiff drink will always trump a frock,' I say with a Gallic shrug. 'Though if all people really want is for their addictions to be fed, why is more respect not afforded to drug dealers?'

'Cause you have to pretend to be friends with them and they never fuck off when you want them to. I don't go round insisting on sharing a drink with all the punters, do I?'

'Georgie, can we go back in? I'm freezing my tits off.' Sarah opens her jacket to flash us her breasts; her nipples are indeed protruding beneath the silky weight of her dress. I shake my head and laugh. Scott is looking around in every direction but hers, ineffectually trying to pretend he didn't get an eyeful. I think of Beardy and wonder if he would have leered in response. Sighing, I reflect that I've started to hate him a little. Why do men have to make you hate them? Why can't they just not fuck up?

'Let's. Do you want to join us for a drink, Scott?' I ask.

'Are you asking because you want the pleasure of my company or just to ensure I pick up the tab?'

'Can't I have it both ways?' I murmur.

'You can have it all the ways you like,' he grins in response.

I raise my eyebrows at Sarah as we stand up and follow him through the door.

'I can tell,' Sarah says to me, cryptically.

'You can tell what?' Scott answers.

'That Georgie is happy to spend some more time with you.'

I feel myself reddening and have to resist a strong urge to pinch and kick her.

'Oh really? And what would you ladies like to drink?' Scott sounds surprised, but pleased. As he goes round the bar to get two G&Ts to add to the queue (we still have half a bottle of white left) I turn to Sarah with alarm.

'Why did you say that? Oh God, he's going to think I'm totally infatuated with him. This is so embarrassing.'

'Aren't you happy to spend time with him? Ok, I know I am totally interfering but Beardy is a cock and Scott is handsome and at the very least seems like an asker-before-he-sticks-it-in-her. You're too timid with these things and have your stupid "Shitting Rule". So what if he thinks you fancy him! Everyone loves being loved. I think he likes you and I don't want to see you languishing through a horrible relationship with someone who treats you like a blow-up sex toy. Well, more truthfully, I don't want to hear about it for the next however many months.'

'I see your point, but I still kind of hate you for it. Also, Beardy isn't that bad.'

And I intend on seeing him tonight, directly after the pub closes.

'You'll love me at the wedding.'

'Shut up!' I whisper as Scott returns, deftly wielding the two doubles and a pint of beer for himself.

'I see you girls haven't even finished your wine . . . you are terrible opportunists.'

'Get when the getting's good, is what I always say,' says Sarah, with a significant wink in my direction. This time I do kick her under the table and at least she has the good grace not to flinch.

Half a bottle of wine, four G&Ts, two beers and a shot of tequila each later, we are all really very intoxicated and having a grand old time. Scott has been regaling us with tales of his misspent youth travelling the world. He was kicked out in his first year at university for accidentally urinating on the Dean of his course (Geography! Horrors!) out the top-floor window of a particularly raucous house party. He probably would never have been caught had a clever friend not scrawled 'I pissed on Smeagly' in black marker pen on his forehead while he was passed out. Scott, mirror unseen, lurched his way to class after a few hours' sleep and waved cheerfully at said man in the corridor. For some reason, the poor fellow felt he was being unjustly mocked. Scott feels that as urine is sterile and the Dean was never in the way of any real harm, he should have been given a slap on the wrist, but no matter.

After a few years in Southeast Asia, he returned to Europe and by an extraordinarily lucky twist of fate aided by cheating, won a large sum of money. Annoyingly, he refuses to divulge the details of this con, in which he was helped by a charming but shady card-shark friend in Monte Carlo – this character has since been put in jail for bigamy and fraud. Scott loyally insists that 'He is, or was, at heart, a good man,' but I have my doubts about anyone named Juan who preys on greying, bejewelled beauties to earn his keep. While his friend pissed away the winnings in a matter of weeks, Scott used the cash to return to London and fund his first business venture, a bar with the (hopefully) ironic title of 'The Shithole of Shepherd's Bush'. Due to the dearth of good nightlife in West London, it became an instant success in the mystifying way that a dive-bar with good music and hot clientele can. This he credits, in no small part, to Alice frequenting it regularly with all her beautiful friends.

Alice, Alice, Alice, it always comes back down to Alice. Scott's casual observation that her crazysexycool was key to his success leads me to note for the first time how little separates 'Alice' from 'A lice'. I find myself wishing she had some sort of (non-life-threatening) grave hidden flaw. Something like an unbreakable hymen that prevents her from ever having sex. Though with a bit of luck he wouldn't know about that through personal experience. I honestly don't really fancy him; she just makes me deeply insecure.

Clearly, I am an awful person. I try to rid myself of such evil thoughts but they crack open and emerge with a force of their own. Don't we meanies deserve a happy ending too? Surely everyone indulges in cruel fantasies from time to time? The important thing is not to voice them, or at least, only to a well-chosen audience.

Scott is waxing lyrical about the fun he and Alice, as well as some dude named Jason, used to have in their teens. He is a very good storyteller, speaking in a deep Scottish burr, with a crooked smile that appears when he is being self-deprecating. He is quite captivating; I probably resemble an entranced goldfish by now, in my drunken state.

After his family moved to London when he was thirteen, these Three Stooges (his words) bonded in the mews by their local comp over a stolen pack of fags. The truants ran around smoking weed and mucking about so much their parents feared it would lead to their ruin. He is reminiscing about the havoc they used to wreak, the rambunctious mischief of adolescents refusing to submit to staid adulthood, when Sarah interrupts him.

'Have you and Alice ever been a couple?'

My stomach muscles, such as they are, clench tightly in response. I am disgusted with myself. Anything to do with Alice makes me immediately anxious, especially now that she is managing Beardy's band. I am torn between badly wanting to hear and never wanting to know.

Obviously the ideal answer to this question would be, 'No, I've never been remotely attracted to her. Raving beauties repel me.'

Failing that, a no would suffice, though I would still always wonder if he carries a torch for her. If he says yes, I will also always wonder if he still carries a torch for her. Alice is the kind of girl you can imagine dozens of men reflecting on fondly in their dotage as the one who got away. At best, I fear

I'm more of the funny-story footnote: 'The Girl Who Set Her Hair On Fire', 'The Girl Who Spat Phlegm In My Pint', 'The Girl Who Left A Tampon In The Toilet Cistern'. A trifecta of humiliation that will probably be etched on my tombstone by embittered grandchildren. At this rate, I am likely to leave them only a mountain of debt and thirty cats sporting hand-knitted turbans.

'No, no. She and Jason were made for each other,' Scott says, a shadow crossing his face before his smile returns and he adds, 'I was just third-wheeling it.'

Gah. What could that glimmer of sadness mean but that he has been secretly in love with her for years? She is a man-magnet, enticing men everywhere she goes. I stand no chance, particularly as she no longer seems to be with this Jason, whoever the hell he is. Fuck!

'Oh, young love sort of thing? Were they together a long time?' Sarah continues her unwanted sleuthing on my behalf as I look about, pretending I am not interested.

'Ten years . . . quite a while.' Scott is taciturn, but I decide to doggedly pursue him for information while I have the chance.

'Why did they break up?'

'He died,' Scott states shortly, hurriedly swallowing a gulp from his pint as Sarah and I stare at each other in cringing horror.

Oh God. A wave of guilt hits me. Poor, poor Alice. I am a

terrible person. I make the appropriate tragic noises, trying to quell my morbid curiosity over the circumstances of Jason's death. I am reminded of other moments in which my evil nature has by accident or design, though more likely through total self-absorption, missed a point and sailed on mercilessly past the point of no return. The time I kept talking about having 'fingers in lots of pies', a phrase I almost never use, to a man missing most of his fingers. Another time I got into a drunken debate with an irritatingly devout young Christian about the unlikelihood of God or an afterlife, later finding out that he had just been diagnosed with ME. With the benefit of hindsight, it was like beating on Tiny Tim with his own crutch.

'Wow, that's . . . so, so sad. And so young.'

'It was crushing. And Alice was . . . in a bad way, for a long time. But, you know, life eventually goes on, trite as the saying is. Jason was a part of my life I'm hugely grateful for and now I just try to keep his memory alive by living it as best I can with the opportunities that are given to me, you know? Well, in my better moments that's what I try to do. But it's not something I like to talk about too much,' Scott says quietly, in the manner of someone who has given similar speeches before and does not want to be drawn further.

An uncomfortable silence descends. I reach over to pat him on the hand awkwardly, muttering something unintelligible

ELIZABETH AARON

in tones of sympathy. The gesture seems to both rankle and
exhaust him.

'It's getting late, I'm going upstairs to get some kip. But
it's been a pleasure. I'll be seeing you both for New Year's,
right?' Scott abruptly stands up, taking his leave as we nod
our assent.

'See you in a few days, then,' I say softly.

'Hey, don't give me those doe-eyes, Georgie. I'm fine. I've
just had a long day.' Scott's warm gaze locks on mine and he
gives a pained grin, before walking across the room to speak
to Joy for a moment. As I stare at his receding figure, I catch
her baleful glare.

'Well, aside from the dead-friend bit, that went well! If it
had ended differently, I reckon you would be upstairs for a
nightcap right now,' Sarah says after a long silence, the most
callous would-be matchmaker since Cinderella's stepmother.

'Sarah,' I reprimand, somewhat weakly. Despite my best
intentions at purity and selflessness (and my semi-boyfriend)
I had been thinking along the same lines.

My Friendly Local Dealer-man

On the morning of New Year's Eve, I'm thinking about a different kind of line. For the most part, my drug-taking days are behind me, barring special occasions. They have become another phase in my short life, like acne and science fiction, which I have managed to grow out of unscathed. This is in part due to my memory erasing the more shameful lows that pop, unbidden, now and again into my mind, but they are easy to ignore. Anyway, why is it that horrible experiences that are inflicted on you by a fit of cosmic bad luck, like cancer, are character-building battles to be won while horrible experiences that you inflict on yourself are a source of disgrace and regret? Experience should be honoured in all its forms, once endured. And special occasions are special occasions, New Year's Eve being the most special of them all.

Sarah is spending all day with Henry as he has other plans tonight, Beardy is more into drink than drugs and Rose is completely terrified of being on public transport when carrying. Thus, it has fallen to me to source the goods for this evening. There are sure to be bags of MDMA and ket going round that we can dab off of for a few quid or a smile, but for old times' sake, we are getting six grams of coke. One is usually fine for me, but as Sarah is a fiend, Rose will probably spill or misplace half her share and as I am uncharacteristically generous with near strangers when high, we've decided to err on the safe side.

My parents would be horrified and it's all terribly immoral of course, but the thing about morality is it's not very enticing when weighed up against a good time. The best argument for not doing drugs, to me, is not their illegality, health issues or the rate of addiction. They are consequences that you accept as part of the risk (safe in the secret conviction that they will never, ever happen to you). What is far worse is the unseen effect on the lives of other humans – those faceless people who bear the real cost of our casual, consumer involvement.

But of course, none of the unfun stuff is ever at the forefront of my mind when calling Dwayne, my friendly local dealer-man. His charming bedside manner, tight Fred Perry shirt encasing ripped arm muscles, gang-related tattoos and gold teeth combined make a rather seductive whole. I've always fancied him, despite the atrocious spelling and grammar of his text messages.

As per usual, I'm chilling in a dodgy car park in Elephant & Castle, trying to look inconspicuous. Though I've streeted myself up in a hoody and combat boots, I feel that I stick out like a sore thumb. I while away the first fifteen minutes day-dreaming about him forcefully taking me behind the council bins and throwing the drugs at my feet in payment when he finishes. As the hour drags on, with still no sign of Dwayne, my fantasies turn to laying into him for always keeping me waiting.

Unfortunately, when someone has a product of limited availability they are aware you really, really want, they can do pretty well what they please. He knows I will still smile with bourgeois supplication, hand him £50 a gram for something half cut with speed or drone and still come back for more. Finding a good dealer is something of a connoisseur's task in London. At any rate, I don't know how to go about it – the best stuff I've had has always been through the most arsehole-ish of people, who fiercely guard their contacts.

Finally, a red Smart Car whizzes in, chosen presumably for ease and discretion. I admit the first time I saw it I was terribly disappointed it wasn't a seventies pimp-mobile. They parallel park at a dangerous speed with élan.

ELIZABETH AARON

Dwayne hops out, looking fit as usual, his smile glittering gold in the winter sun. He kisses me on both cheeks and gives me an appreciative once-over. I melt. We do the dreadfully obvious handshake exchange of money and goods. Pleasantries made, he tips his hat at me like a Victorian gent and leaps back into the car as his driver, a man always wearing a cap pulled down low over his face and whom I have never properly seen or spoken to, takes off.

Now for the long bus journey home. The most irritating thing about picking up is, if you are out of your way, you are limited to the slowest and shittest forms of public transportation for fear of sniffer dogs on the tube. I've seen a fair few people caught before (most wearing an expression that roughly translates to 'Aw shit, man' but none, surprisingly, too upset) and though I haven't carried regularly in years, whenever I pass a police officer my heart still seizes up in fear. I endure the long slow chug of the 133 bus towards Liverpool Street Station, where I will have to change again. A taxi is obviously preferable, but having already spent £100 on the night to come and it not yet being one in the afternoon, this feels rather extravagant. Much better to sweat in paranoid fear, abnormally still, listening to the beat of my heart in my ears, irrationally convinced that something is going to go wrong, until I finally arrive at my stop. Murphy's Law has bypassed me and nothing has gone wrong, like usual, silly me.

Several hours later finds me drowning in a mound of discarded clothes, all of which I hate, all of which make me look fat. The Christmas gorge-athon has taken its toll and though I don't weigh myself on principle (the principle being ignorance is bliss) I reckon I might well have put on a stone in under two weeks. I finally manage to winch myself into a leather skirt that has corset-like properties and from which I may never escape. I team it with sucky-in black tights, a button down shirt knotted at the waist and six-inch black heels (the numbing properties of cocaine will make them bearable). I look at myself in the mirror and think, 'You look as good as you can. Your clothes aren't making you look fat – your body is making you look fat. You may resemble a prostitute but this is the best you can do for the moment.'

I have never been able to master the hyperbole necessary to transform a straight-talk into a pep-talk. Like many women, if I try to tell myself I am beautiful, fabulous and worthy, it rings impossibly hollow much of the time. Still, I am satisfied, or least calmly resigned, having done what I can with what I have (cleavage). I pile on the slap with a trowel and make my hair as big as possible to balance out my chins. A white rabbit-fur coat, giant gold earrings and a gold-teeth mafia necklace complete the ensemble (if you're going to choose a theme, mine being Dallas Hooker In A New York Winter Circa 1987, you might as well adhere to it fully). I grab my clutch, armed with all the essentials and am good to go.

Tin Can Bang are playing tonight in a warehouse in Bow. It will have all the trappings of an illegal rave: geographically undesirable, limited alcoholic options, airy and freezing and equipped with only two sporadically flushing skanky toilets complete with festival-sized queues on the verge of pissing themselves. It is in fact legal and costs £35. I had hoped that my association with Beardy – as Pseudo-Girlfriend? Favoured Fuckbuddy? Preferred Penis-Pal? – might gain me free entry or at least some sort of discount. Either I have overrated the nature of our association or he is telling the truth and the large number of bands and DJs playing have scuppered my chances for the guestlist.

Rose, Sarah and I meet later than is planned and end up shouting along to the countdown on a street corner ten minutes away from the rave with a ragtag group of tramps who are sharing a bottle of JD. This is the fourth year running I've managed to miss being in an actual venue when the ball drops, but it adds to a rare feeling of London-all-together-ness that warms the cockles of the heart, particularly when shared with people you would normally avoid eye contact with at all costs.

When we finally arrive in front of the huge redbrick building, formerly an electricity factory, we are greeted with a queue in which we must shiver for forty-five minutes. To pass the time, we take nips of life's sweet nectar: a litre of vodka. Wisely, Rose suggests we decant a third into a flask for later. We may be in our mid-twenties, but we still drink with the stinginess and enthusiasm we had at sixteen.

Though we are getting through the bottle at an alarming rate, the Charlie should take the edge off of our indulgence. To be honest, I've put myself in the way of physical harm far more often binge drinking than doing drugs. Being paranoid and loved-up but hyper-aware after a pill or a line makes you look after yourself far better than when half-blind with booze. In my teens I was a stumbling, horny wreck likely to eye up the unwashed denizens of the night bus for potential talent. The night wasn't over till I reached my front door.

Rose at least has benefited from the interminable wait. She is flirting outrageously with a tall Swede named Sven who is sporting a handlebar moustache, furry Russian hat and a neon-green Lycra catsuit under a Puffa jacket. We pass the bouncers without any problems and are finally greeted with what we've paid for – loud techno and swarms of bright-eyed clubkids chewing their faces off, illuminated by flashes of blue strobe through the smoky dimness.

It is far more practical to take pills or dab when you have the luxury of a quiet space with a flat surface to cut lines, but tonight we are equipped with pre-cut and decanted bullets. These handy little gram-sized glass jars have a screw top attached to a small spoon, so all we need is a minute in a toilet or a private corner to take a bump. Sarah, the most avid cokehead amongst my friends, is nonetheless the most controlling and obsessive when it comes to how, when and where we can take it. She feels there is a delicate ratio of drunkness to highness that needs to be respected, otherwise one becomes either too out of it or too manic. She informs us, with the seriousness of an officer laying out military strategy, that we need precisely two more doubles to add to the vodka before we will be properly primed.

Sarah hadn't pissed in three hours in an attempt not to break the seal but even her well-trained bladder is not super-human; she has given in to the queue. So, we are taking advantage of the illegal element of the rave by chain-smoking in a filthy staircase nearby. Rose is otherwise occupied – Sven's huge blond moustache is consuming her milkmaid face.

Though I notice my words slurring alarmingly, I shout con-versation at a random for whom I feel no sexual attraction whatsoever. Nonetheless, I allow him to touch up my arse as he pretends to care about whatever shit I'm talking. A little light gropage, I've decided, is a small price to pay for avoiding standing around like a mug next to the happy couple. Unfor-tunately, being across from them means I also have a very clear view of Sven's tightly showcased, shiny green erection.

'It's like if a ninja turtle had a penis!' I say, pointing, as Sarah comes up the stairs.

'It's time to sober you up with some hard drugs, doll. Rose? Let's go back out, yeah?'

With the casual cruelty of the uninterested female at the

beginning of a night that promises many more opportunities, Rose and I wordlessly break off from our respective beaux. They try to stop us, but we ignore them and are swallowed back into the heaving bosom of the warehouse, where our bodies reverberate with the bassline. We take shelter sitting cross-legged on a dirty table in a corner and take a few bumps. We needn't have worried about finding a subtle place to snort – it is busy, dark and none of the staff give a fuck – but Sarah is concerned about attracting hangers-on.

'How many have you had?' Sarah asks me earnestly, her hand shooting out to grab my wrist.

'Um . . . two on each side?' Actually, I took four on each side, but I need to be plucked out of my bleariness back into sharp, chemically induced reality.

'Good. Me too.'

'I wish I hadn't left Sven. He had a huge willy,' Rose says sadly.

'His English wasn't very strong, though, was it?'

'No. But the language of love is universal.'

'More men should wear spandex trousers. It would save so much time and effort if you could see who was packing what. I once slept with a guy with a micro-penis and even though I didn't really like him that much, I felt obligated to shag him again so he wouldn't think it was due to his size.' Sarah sticks out her pinky finger, waggling it, before declaring shortly, 'That would be a generous assessment.'

'Sarah, that's so thoughtful of you,' Rose says gravely as she grips Sarah's upper arm.

'I have hidden depths of altruism, what can I say.'

'Doesn't surprise me,' I joke, humming the opening notes to 'My Heart Will Go On', though she doesn't hear me over the music.

'My first boyfriend had a tiny willy. I really thought we would be together for ever and sometimes when I thought about only ever experiencing his penis, I cried.' Rose shakes her head with rueful nostalgia.

'This is why you have to ask men to send you dick pics beforehand! So useful.'

'What, you just ask them to send one out of the blue?' I ask. It's hard for me to envision the appropriate conversational build-up that might precede such a request. But then, I am a terrible flirt. Really, really bad.

'It only works when you've been sending saucy texts but most guys are very willing. The male ego is such that they really think it turns you on and they don't realize that you are just doing research.'

'What do you send them in response?'

'Nothing,' Sarah says with some surprise.

'Guys, are we ever going to move? It's nearly two! Beardy should be on soon and I should make some sort of appearance, even if I doubt we'll ever find each other.'

Generally, when we buy coke, it is with the intention of

dancing, but we end up maniacally chatting in a huddle complaining about how difficult it is to hear each other and viewing anyone who approaches us as an intrusive line-snatcher. Why it is considered a social drug is a bit of a mystery. Still, I am feeling sharper, shinier, happier – buzzing and now capable of walking in a straight line. Or close enough, now that the fault lies with the height of my stilettos and not my level of inebriation.

'I still don't approve. He plays mind-games. Men like that are scared of women and fuck them over to keep them in their place. To be perfectly frank, Georgie, since you've started seeing him you seem diminished. If he wasn't handsome and hairy would you even want to spend thirty minutes in his presence?' Sarah's direct summation of all my doubts takes me aback. I stop in my tracks, wounded.

'You think I seem diminished?' It goes without saying that if he weren't handsome and hairy I would not have been drawn in by his personality. I guess being made to feel small is the price you pay for being so superficial.

'You have been a bit down on yourself lately,' Rose says. 'Let's go back to the smoking room, I want to smoke and do more coke and talk about what an arse Beardy is.'

'Look, guys, thanks for your concern,' I say as we totter back to the stairwell. I knew that one way or another we would end up spending the majority of the night here. 'I know he's not ideal – but it's not serious between us. And recently I've been kind of having second thoughts – well, I think I'm interested in someone else.'

'Scott?' Sarah shrewdly deduces.

'I knew it!' Rose says. 'You mention him constantly and you are insanely jealous of Alice and Joy, which is not like you at all. Plus, every time I see you two talking to each other you look just like a smitten kitten.'

'Jesus Christ, a smitten kitten? But, yes, I think I've got a wee, itty-bitty, miniscule infatuation with him. I hate it, it's such a cliché to fancy your boss!'

It has recently become undeniable to me that I am labouring under a hideous crush of epic proportions. I was working a lot leading up to NYE and Scott was, unusually, in the pub almost constantly. I'm not sure I've been able to hide my secret love for him very convincingly. Though I am well practised in the subtle art of staring-while-not-staring, I have started behaving strangely, alternating between outrageous drunk-uncle flirting and sulky bouts of awkward silence. Basically I spend half my time acting like an over-enthusiastic reject from a *Carry On* film and the other half like Harold before Maude. It's not an attractive combination.

'I doubt my ardour is returned.'

'You don't know that!'

'Bless you, Rose, but you have never met Alice and therefore have no idea what my competition looks like. At this point I'm grateful to have Beardy as a distraction, even if he is a consolation prize. The likelihood of anything happening between me and Scott is painfully slim.'

'Oh, fuck off, you're obsessed with Alice! He said the other day she was with his dead best mate, I think she's off limits.' Sarah is rolling her eyes and openly racking a line on a filthy windowsill, all pretence at subtlety and hygiene abandoned.

'That doesn't mean he doesn't love her, just that he might feel he doesn't have the right, which makes it even more tragic. Fuck, I'd fall for her. She's gorgeous. And nice. They've known each other since they were kids, they have this shared pain – I'm sure it's one of those things where it's just a matter of time,' I conclude glumly.

'You're crazy. I don't deny that she is beautiful – she's like Vanessa Paradis in her jailbait years. But if it hasn't happened already I doubt it will. Not everyone goes for the most beautiful, you know! They're childhood friends, so maybe they're like brother and sister and sexual relations are repulsive.'

'Do you think?' I say eagerly, 'That could be true. Though I feel pathetic clinging to the notion that the only way he could conceivably prefer me over her is that their love would be tinged by incest.'

'You're hardly an ogre, Georgie. Plus there's more to it than looks, chemistry counts for a lot. You two really seem to spark off each other, I seriously don't understand why you are so pathologically insecure,' Rose accuses.

'Much as I'd like to believe you, what you probably saw was

a sparkle in my eyes and friendliness on his part. We're sort of flirty in a really lame ho-ho-ho matey double-entendre way, usually when Gary is around, but recently when we've been alone together I totally bottle it and start talking about the weather.'

'The weather? Seriously?'

'If I talk at all.'

'What? Usually you're like a one-woman bad pun machine with an encyclopaedic knowledge of dick jokes,' Sarah says.

'Then maybe it's for the best I've been shocked into silence.'

'How well do you really know him, at this point?' Rose asks.

'Well enough to fuel the flames of love unrequited, not well enough to reeeally know him, see his faults and get over it.' At this moment, whether due to love or drugs, I do not see a single flaw in him.

'That is a dangerous combination. Intimate knowledge of character is the enemy of passion.' Rose always gets all intellectual on us when she's fucked.

'So, what, you're just going to carry on with Beardy regardless? A guy who tells you that you would be beautiful if only you were a size eight?' I forgot he even said that, but Sarah's mind is a steel trap when it comes to slights against her or her friends.

'I don't know. You know me; I have no balls! It's a matter of availability. Scott's never tried anything with me, ever. Beardy has, to some degree, chosen me and he's not that bad. We have some good times and I could do, have done, worse. For the moment I've made my choice,' I say with finality.

'God, that's depressing. I may be cheating on my boyfriend but at least I know I love him, too.'

'That's awful, Sarah! You're cheating on Henry?' Rose is shocked.

'Shit. You don't know? I thought Georgie would have told you.'

'You swore me to secrecy!' I protest.

'I didn't expect you to adhere to it. It's a long story, but in short, I've been shagging an old flame and he's coming to the after party . . .'

Sarah and Rose dissect the sordid details of her lover as I cut some lines for us to take before we leave the stairwell. We are all in agreement that if we don't go now, we never will and will essentially have paid £35 for an evening sat on some squalid steps, avoiding everyone.

Rose leads the way as we push our way through the main room, which features DJs, into a smaller one with the stage set up for bands. I sway to the music of the current group, whose electro-rockabilly via Morrissey-style crooning is working for me. I feel perfect – drunk and high, but not to the point of fatigue or mania. Just great, present, alive. The erratic beat of my heart and my body feel in tune. The music momentarily transports me, though in the back of my mind the awareness of the transience of this feeling lurks, constantly assessing my level. Feeling so excellent now spells the beginning of the end; I will never quite sustain this cloud of charged contentment, I will be grasping after it increasingly desperately through the night to come, never quite to my satisfaction. Still, whatever happens, I am pretty sure I will not reach the desperate lows of last New Year's Eve, which saw me spilling half a gram on the floor of a foul public toilet and racking grubby lines off it with the residue. I may even have rubbed some on my gums.

The crowd around us thins as the set ends. The sound of balloons being filled in a corner perks up Rose, who runs off to find the source. I can see Beardy and Co. setting up on stage and feel a burst of affection for him, though I'm not sure if this is due to genuine fondness or my chemical rush. Sarah pulls out the extra flask she had hidden between the back of her skinny jeans and her pants, waving it with a mischievous smile. As the first thrums sound from Beardy's guitar, Rose returns with three balloons, ends clutched carefully between her fingers. Reaching us, she turns towards Tin Can Bang, stops and gasps. Thudding her hand on her chest dramatically, she lets half the precious air escape from a yellow balloon, now tragically half-deflated. She appears not to notice, which is highly unusual.

'What a hunk of absolute burning love!'

'Rose, I know we were just listening to rockabilly but "hunk of burning love"?' Sarah takes a sip from the flask and nary a twitch betrays the fact that it is straight vodka. When she passes it to me, I take a glug and gag.

'I know but . . . but . . . he is seriously dreamy. I want to wear his pin.'

I look towards the stage. Beardy is looking in fine fettle tonight, his curly black hair, longer than usual, tied up in a little bun on his head; he has trimmed his beard to reveal more of his handsome face. I hate his jacket – an aggressively eighties brown leather monstrosity, with absurdly huge shoulders, lapels and fringing. Still, paired with a white wife-beater, ragged jeans and Cuban heels, it is passable. Tim is looking very handsome, too, as well as surprisingly ripped – he is shirtless, in black jeans and desert boots.

'Do you know him? The lanky one with the soulful eyes on drums? God, look at those arms. I bet he has throwdown in droves.'

'That's Tim, Alice's brother! Beautiful but a bit of a dick, I find. Or at any rate he doesn't seem to care for me, so it makes me not care for him, if you know what I mean. You know what I mean? Still, look at those guns; I was not expecting that. Can I have one of those balloons, or are they all for you,' I babble, gesticulating wildly. I am more coked up than I thought.

'He will be mine. Oh yes, he will be mine,' Rose says with a frightening gleam in her eye, her stare unwavering from the object of her desire as she hands me the balloon.

Laughing, I see Beardy looking in my direction and blow him a kiss. He half-smiles in response, before the too-cool-for-school mask he has been wearing reasserts itself.

'God, I have to say, that is one hell of an ugly jacket.'

I nod, but am prevented from answering as we all suck in the laughing gas, careful to inhale and exhale directly into the plastic. Sarah and Rose look transported, but I fuck mine up when a sudden coughing fit hits me. I content myself with watching them go cross-eyed and blissed-out with exertion, their heads bobbing as if neckless before their faces break into jack-o'-lanterns split with silent hilarity.

They slowly come back to reality, shaking their heads at themselves, trying to explain what they saw – the beat – the vibrations – you were doing that! – it all made perfect sense – I can't explain it! – then are silent for a minute.

'More Charlie?' I pipe up, as they return to normal.

'Yes!'

'God, that is one hell of an ugly jacket.'

'Sarah, you just said that.'

'Did I? Clearly it bears repeating. I think I tripped out over it.'

'I know, every time I go to meet him I pray he won't be wearing it. He seems to have gone off it recently, thank God. Hopefully this will be its last chance to dance before it is interred into the pit of his wardrobe. Part of me is tempted to say something but why relieve him of the women repeller? It's so bad that it functions as a groupie-shield.'

My jaw is feeling a bit achy and I am overcome with the familiar moreishness of cocaine, an urgent restlessness in my chest. As Tin Can Bang start up, opening with what I now assume is their calling card and not, as I hoped, a one off – 'Ladies, this is for you! Everyone else can fuck off!' – I take several bumps, my eyes scanning the crowd for security, like an over-stimulated owl.

'Hey, isn't that—'

'Alistair!' Sarah cries gleefully, her eyes brilliant, one reddish nostril proudly displaying a lump of congealed powder.

'My dearest heart,' Alistair murmurs, bowing low over her hand with an aristocratic elegance. 'You look ravishing even with a rock hanging out of your nose.'

Sarah laughs without embarrassment and brushes the offending article away, then twirls kittenishly before him. Her slim waist and small perky breasts are cupped by a fifties-style brassiere-top in black silk, her dark brown curls set off by a flash of blood-red lipstick. Though she has paired this with silver foil-printed jeans and orange platform boots, Alistair is even more of a draw to the eye. He is decked out in skin-tight leather trousers, velvet brocade slippers and a transparent chiffon blouse open to the navel. A rather fantastic mink stole is draped on his shoulders. With his slicked back blond hair, he is channelling a 'Modern Love' meets *Labyrinth* Bowie, with a dash of Clara Bow. On anyone else it would be absurd, but outré suits him.

'Ladies, what a pleasure to meet you. I deduce from your russet locks that you, the Rossetti, must be Rose.' Alistair's voice projects well over the din. He has the perfect articulation and well-practised flattery of the failed-actor-turned-hair-dresser I know him to be.

Rose, her expression disapproving, still pinks with pleasure at the compliment.

'Georgie, you look every bit the vixen tonight,' Alistair manages to purr while simultaneously shouting over the sound-system. Irish accents really are delicious, though his foppish airs are a bit disingenuous.

'Oh gosh, I knew this outfit was too much. I've got so fat over the holidays that my only choices were burka or whore. I chose whore,' I say with embarrassment, tugging down the leather of my skirt. It normally fits like a glove but now is riding up my chubby thighs.

'As I hope you continue to. Sarah, my dove? Drink?'

When the happy, illicit couple return, any pretence of dis-cretion that Sarah had been making goes out the window. Seemingly welded together in homage to The Kiss, they embrace with myopic passion. Meanwhile, Rose and I ride the light fantastic. Inhibitions shattered to smithereens, we dance like loons, twirling each other around and feverishly masticating chewing gum. We flirt with the boys next to us

– from their enraptured smiles and rapidly chomping jaws, it is obvious that they too are riding the wave. We persuade them to give us some dabs of MDMA. Licking my little finger, I stick it into the baggie; it emerges with much more than intended. My default setting when confronted with a questionable idea being: 'fuck it', I roll the thick layer underneath my tongue, trying not to make a face as a battery-acid flavour floods my mouth.

Seconds, minutes that feel like hours elapse; we are gripped in the strange time-suspension of the really very fucked, interrupted only by sudden intense desires that must, absolutely must, be fulfilled at that instant – to drink, to go stand over there, to urgently explain an epiphany, to smoke and of course, to piss. It is the one urge we resist, knowing that once in the toilet after a forty-five minute wait we will produce an absolutely piddling amount of wee as our dehydrated bodies desperately retain whatever water they can.

Eventually the siren's song of the grotty johns becomes too much for me to bear; I turn to leave and see someone standing a few feet away from our group. A strange figure, stock still amidst the arrhythmic spasms that now pass as dancing. Staring fixedly at Sarah, face void of all expression.

It is Henry.

An Oesophageal Slinky Of Pain

Lying in the foetal position in my darkened room sixteen sleepless hours later, I am trying not to obsess over four horrible things that have now come to pass. Luckily, I had some emergency Valium left over in my room, bulk-bought from Annabelle when she got back from India. The emotional trauma I would otherwise be experiencing has been mitigated by a Zen-like distance; the full impact will hit me sometime tomorrow, along with the full comedown.

My despondence is not helped by the shuffle on my iTunes, which chooses songs specifically designed to elicit existential angst. Surely the random sequence of 'Piggies', 'Meat is Murder', 'Happiness Is A Warm Gun' and 'Strange Fruit' is a sign from a long-abandoned God, calling on me to readmit him into my withered heart and give up the self-destructive behaviour that has led me into this mess.

I think about doing volunteer work for a charity, quite seriously, for five minutes; preferably one working with addicts, prostitutes, or similar lost souls, with whom I currently feel a spiritual kinship. This would have the dual advantages of doing good for once in my life while also hearing horror-stories of lives derailed that would make me feel better about the comparatively trivial misery of my own. Which isn't terribly altruistic, but my transformation into Mother Teresa will have to be baby steps. Rome wasn't built in a day.

The first disaster of the night was the Henry affair. I could only watch with stunned horror as Sarah, sensing something, broke off the passionate embrace she had been sharing with Alistair. Turning with her hands still clasped around his neck, she met Henry's eyes. The immobile blankness that had settled on his features changed into implacable fury. Henry, who I have always known as even-tempered, grabbed Sarah by the shoulders and pushed her into the wall where she fell like a crumpled packet of crisps. He then launched himself at a stunned Alistair, tackling him to the ground and proceeding to beat the living daylights out of him. Rose ran to help Sarah as I ineffectually tried to pull off Henry, whose wildly flying fists caught me in the face once or twice.

On a normal night in an English pub or club, other drunken spectators would have got involved, roused by half a dozen pints of Stella and bloodlust. However, everyone being drugged up, the crowd just parted like the Red Sea for the giant bouncers scuttling out from the woodwork, trying not to let it ruin their buzz. Though the whole episode probably happened in the space of ten seconds, by this point Alistair's nose had been broken and one eye was beginning to swell shut. Blood was streaming from his nostrils and a cut on his head; he half sat up, looking at his shaking hands in a daze as if perplexed by what had actually happened. Henry, with a strength I didn't think he possessed, threw off the fourteen stone of pure muscle restraining him and legged it, though not before shooting Sarah a glance that truly chilled me.

We were swiftly chucked out of the warehouse. Police were not called, nor was an ambulance, which was a relief to Sarah but possibly not to Alistair. A guy whom I was chatting with years ago who worked security told me that the only concern bouncers have is to get you out on the pavement as quickly as possible, whether you've been in a fight or OD'd. If you die inside a club, the management is held liable. What happens to you once you are on the street is none of their business.

So, summarily abandoned, Sarah was left to cry as she mopped the blood off of Alistair's face with his blouse. Alistair tried to soothe her, acting manfully unaffected by his trouncing. This performance was ruined rather when it suddenly hit him that his mink had been lost in the fray. He shouted, 'Fack! I've lost my favourite stole!' in the tones of anguished frustration a thespian would reserve for 'Will no one rid me of this turbulent priest?'

Rose and I had been trying to console Sarah with lies to the effect that everything would be all right, but at this, both of us burst out into the kind of nervous, unstoppable laughter that inevitably strikes at moments of total inappropriateness. For a moment, Sarah barked a hoarse laugh, before breaking into miserable sobs yet again; Alistair saw no fun in it. Huffily, he took his lover by the arm and marched her down the road with what little force he had left.

We scurried after them, supplicating – 'No, come back! We're sorry! It was a beautiful stole! Call us if you need us! We're here for you, Sarah!' – but they jumped in a minicab before we had a chance to offer to accompany them. We took a rest stop for morale (racking a few lines on a windowsill) on the way to The Newt, reliving the whole sorry palaver in scandalized tones. Our loud gossiping must have disturbed the occupant; just as we finished snorting the curtains twitched open. We legged it; I lost a shoe in the process.

The second terrible thing to happen was almost a wonderful thing. Thinking back on it now, on the moments just before it all went wrong, constricts my chest with miserable pleasure. It's that or an incipient stroke.

When we arrived, it was just gone four – a bit early for the after party, but with celebrations in full swing. The people there were the odd sort that gather for New Year's Eve at a pub: friends of staff members, some regulars and random locals who couldn't be arsed to fork out for a proper party. Donna Summers was playing loudly. I guessed, correctly, that Gary had taken over DJ duties briefly but the power had corrupted him.

'Lover! I adore your disco tunes. Happy New Year!'

'Georgie! My darling, you look like such a slag tonight. I love it! Why are you here so early?'

Though I had been sworn to secrecy over Sarah's infidelity, even keeping it from Rose, Gary already knew everything. Being one step removed, it felt safe enough and as a gay man, he inevitably acted as a modern Roman Catholic confessional. Now that the cat was well and truly out of the bag I felt free to fill him in on the violent denouement to the rave, all the while casting around for Scott. I saw no sign of him and inwardly scolded myself for this pathetic mooning. The conversation segued into altercations involving ex-lovers (Rose's ex once stabbed someone in the arse; Gary has been chased around with a butcher's knife). Having nothing to add myself (I have always gone for lovers, not fighters; the problems arise when they start loving someone else) I make my excuses to go to the loo for a top up, catching Joy's sneering eye along the way.

'Joy! Cheer up, love, it might never happen,' I said by way of greeting, temporarily transformed through my buzz into a Cockney cab driver. She was slinking around in an oversized

T-shirt with a faded Andy Warhol print of Marilyn Monroe and very little else. I always feel it is a mistake to wear women who are more beautiful than you. It invites comparison.

Coming out of the toilet, freshly invigorated, I spied Scott emerging from the stockroom, gripping two bottles of whiskey with an unlit cigarette hanging from the corner of his mouth. A bubble of pure happiness burst inside of me and I thought to myself, 'God, I am totally in love with this man.' So I did the only rational thing in the circumstances. I nodded casually when he smiled at me, walked back to Rose and proceeded to ignore him entirely for the next half-hour, wishing all the while he would come over and strike up a conversation.

At 4.30 a.m., the lights came up, off, then on again and gradually all but a select few were ushered out of the pub. Cigarettes were lit inside and in a surprisingly short amount of time the fumes of ten people made a bluish haze through which the old-fashioned lamps on the tables glowed. The bar became a boozy free-for-all; Gary and I engaged in a bad-cocktail contest, a game I invariably win as my knowledge of fine liqueurs is limited and I am unafraid of ruining them with Tabasco. The loser is required to down all of the offending concoction and thus really is the winner. After some particularly raucous rounds of this game, only my frequent forays to the toilet were keeping me on my feet.

I tried to get Scott involved, flirtatiously asking if he could help me find another bottle of Cointreau in the storeroom after I finished it (cocktail: The Ivory Coast. Equal parts Cointreau, Malibu and Absinthe. Verdict: Awful). He gamely led me away and I managed to keep my face composed, but felt myself dying a little bit inside with want. Completely off my tits and far more indiscreet than I would normally have been, I couldn't keep myself from mouthing 'I love him!' with a sort of pleasant anguish to Rose behind his back. When inside, however, he merely picked up a bottle on a shelf directly facing the door at eye level and shook his head at me with a little smile, before looking down and asking me why I had no shoes on. I couldn't remember.

Back in the bar, delusions of seducing Scott shattered, but with a new, obsessive question to ask myself ('Why do I have no shoes?'), it was starting to get rowdy. More people had filtered in and Someone-Not-Gary took over the iPod playlist and put on 'Killing in the Name'. For those of us who were around when indie-rock was cool, this is like throwing a lit match into a barrel of gasoline. A mosh pit formed and I happened to be in the centre of it. Normally I love a mosh pit (manic pogo-ing while stranded somewhere between a group-hug and a brawl is exhilarating) but it resulted in the third accidental punch to the face I'd taken that night (a well-timed elbow during the 'Motherfuckeeers' scream). This time the injured party was my nose, which began to bleed profusely.

'Muuuuck!' I gurgled, the 'F' becoming strangely contorted under the pressure from my squashed sinuses.

'Georgie! Are you all right?' Scott appeared, as if from nowhere (even moshing I had managed to peripherally track his whereabouts; he had been talking for a distressingly long time with bloody Joy). He clasped my shoulders and peered into my face with concern.

I tried to nod while tilting my head back, blood recoiling back into my nostrils. I felt, to my horror, my eyes start to brim with tears.

'Ah, you poor thing! Come upstairs with me and we'll get you sorted out.'

Thinking that it was almost worth a bloodied nose just to have his hands on my shoulders, I let him lead me upstairs. Through my watery eyes, I spied around his apartment. There were a large number of books piled willy-nilly on antique table tops and around the giant leather couches. I sat down on one and waited as he returned from the bathroom bearing loo roll, cotton balls, scissors, a glass of water and a hand-held mirror.

'Let me take a look at this. It doesn't seem to be broken. But you are bleeding a hell of a lot.'

'Ids da coke,' I mumbled, as Scott gently wiped at my face.

'Ah. That will do it. I thought you seemed a bit . . . high-spirited tonight. Aren't you getting a bit old for carrying on with that stuff?'

'Almodst twedny-five.'

'Ah, you've got a few years on you yet for hell-raising then. Do you have a tampon?'

Being alone, us two, in his flat, my hopes had risen. My treacherous mind had already leapt to fantastic and unlikely conclusions. Tampons were not the turn I had hoped things might take.

'Hab you god your period?'

'No, it's for your nose, you cut it in half and stick it in . . . for absorbency.' Scott looks embarrassed, 'As in the usual fashion, I guess. I saw it once in a film. It's okay, I'll just twist some loo roll – like this – tilt your head back. Okay, next one – good. Does that hurt? Sorry, I'm not very good at this stuff.'

'Yer gread,' I said, and burst into tears.

As Scott sat on the couch next to me and folded my body against his broad chest, I desperately tried to stop crying, but his soothing hands stroking my hair produced only mild hysteria. As I hiccupped and tried to catch my breath, one snotty, blood-soaked cone of bog roll shot out with the force of my exhalation and lodged itself in the armpit of his white T-shirt. I stared at it in horror and disbelief, wondering how it is that these things happen to me.

Looking up at Scott from my crumpled position, one nostril trickling blood and the other stuffed with stained paper, mascara trails down my cheeks, our eyes met. We looked at the bloody cone. Our eyes met again. We both burst into convulsive laughter. When it had subsided, my body was practically lying on top of his. Our faces were inches away from each other; the green flecks in his eyes seemed to glow. His hands had wandered to the sides of my cheeks, his thumbs caressing my skin. His lips parted and he drew me in for what, I am quite sure, would have been the most passionate, loving, sensual and tender kiss of my shortish life, had we not been interrupted by the door swinging forcefully open, revealing Joy.

'Scott! Alice is downstairs, she's very upset. She wants to see you.' Throwing me a filthy look, Joy whipped around and stomped down the stairs.

'I . . . I need to find Alice. Wait here – I'll be back in a minute,' Scott said huskily, after a pause.

Cursing Joy to a merciless circle of hell, I tried to at least make use of this opportunity to fix my face. Luckily I had all of the makeup essentials that might be required after an unexpected bout of heavy rain or passionate sex, but equally applicable to a nosebleed.

After ten minutes of careful removal and reapplication and then a further ten minutes spent sitting on Scott's couch in what I hoped was a nonchalantly sexy pose, I tired of waiting and went downstairs to investigate. Joy was leaning against the wall at the entrance as if waiting for me and looked me up and down with a cool and cruel amusement.

'Hey . . . have you seen Scott?'

'Yeah. He's outside kissing Alice.'

For a moment I felt a deep pain, as if someone had pierced my spleen with a long needle, before a degree of coke-delusion reasserted itself and I flatly stated that I didn't believe her. In response, Joy lifted one long finger and flicked it towards the window on the opposite wall. In a trance, I walked forward, pressing my face against the glass to witness what I had always been convinced would happen. Though Scott's back was to me, it was clear they were locked in a passionate embrace. After a moment the handsome couple broke apart. Alice's beautiful face bathed in moonlight, she murmured something to him; he tenderly kissed her forehead. Numb, unable to watch any more, I walked back towards Joy.

'He's always loved her, you know,' Joy said matter-of-factly.

Her sneer was gone. Seeing me vanquished, she appeared almost bored. With one quick jerk of the hand, a single cigarette emerged from Joy's pack of Marlboro Reds.

'I know,' I said as I took it. As peace offerings went, it was as toxic as Joy herself.

From then on in, the night became wilder and worse. Disguising my pain with abandon in case Scott should see me (he didn't; they had fucked off somewhere), I ate a pill, took a dab, danced on tables, attempted to stuff my nose further despite the dry rust encrusting it and when that failed, settled on rubbing the next gram on my gums. Rose being otherwise occupied in a flirtatious tête-à-tête with an ugly-sexy artist type, this terrible waste was noted by two girls who insisted on helping me out with my surplus drugs.

I was easily persuaded, once I realized that in return they would listen to my inchoate misery-guts rambling about how there was a girl (me) who would never love nor be loved in return, and had the decency to feign intense interest in my mutterings in between lines. These intimacies were shared with all three of us crouched over a toilet basin for forty-five minutes, though the entire point of a lock-in is that there is no need to hide. Habits, and cold tiles on which to lean, are comforting in times of stress. Once finished, we all exited the toilet and like pool-balls, immediately ricocheted to opposite sides of the room without a word to each other. I was having a gripping conversation around 7 a.m. about the probable exist-ence of aliens with Toothless, when Beardy finally arrived.

'Babe! I called you a billion fucking times. What the fuck happened to your face? I saw you all being dragged out by security. Very rock and roll.'

Beardy looked more annoyed that we might have stolen some of the Tin Can Bang thunder than concerned for my wellbeing. However, he was handsome, present and, crucially, not snogging Alice. I threw myself at him with drugged-up abandon, stroking and cooing at his face in a manner most unlike me. For some reason, I even extravagantly compli-mented his heinous leather jacket, which will now probably be a constant feature. I also, in an act of untrue neediness, told him I love him. Don't do drugs; they lead you to make choices that, in retrospect, are poor.

Staring at me as if for the first time, he smiled in a twisted sort of way and then pushed me up against the wall, kissing me passionately.

'I've been waiting for you to say that,' he bit out when he finally released me. 'You're my woman now.' I briefly thought this was kind of a weird response. Perhaps due to subconscious conditioning from reading one too many erotic novels as a teenager that featured violent (but secretly tender) Vikings, I went with it.

'So, you mean – we're a couple?' I cringe to remember that these words actually left my mouth, in a pathetically clingy tone, but they definitely did.

'Yes, my little idiot.' Beardy kissed me again, savagely, before looking around shiftily and growling, 'Let's get out of here. I had an argument with Tim; Alice made a scene over some stupid misunderstanding.'

Being fit to do nothing but follow commands at this point, I made hurried goodbyes to Rose and grabbed my coat as Beardy stalked out to wait for me on the pavement. As I was opening the door to leave, I felt a hand grab the back of my fur collar and jerk me back. The night had been full of man-handling one way or another and it belatedly infuriated me. Slapping the hand away, my eyes spitting fire, I reeled around to meet Scott's stricken glare.

'What are you doing, leaving with that fucking scum?' He spat out the words. I had never seen him discomposed, let alone in a rage. Rather than cowing me, it fuelled my own.

'W-what do you mean, what am *I* doing? I'm leaving with my boyfriend. What were *you* doing? After that display of . . . of – whatever, you ran off to be with Alice!'

'Have you any idea how upset she was? That bastard—'

'He explained everything to me. I love him. You love her. Let's just leave it at that and be happy for each other,' I said in a fit of hurt pride, not entirely sure what had happened between Alice and Beardy. I was quite certain in my ego-cloud of resentment that it couldn't possibly be worse than the crushing of my idiotic hopes hours before.

'You are a *fool*, Georgie.' I hadn't thought that the word 'fool' could possibly be articulated with such a mixture of disgust and anger, or that it could cut me so deeply.

'Just-Fuck-Off!' I shouted, rushing to open the door before my throat could constrict in bands of gnarled sobs, an oesophageal slinky of pain. I slammed it on my way out. I presume at this point he doesn't expect or want me to turn up for my shift the day after tomorrow.

By the time Beardy and I made it back to his, I was already experiencing a splitting headache, burning nose and the general wretchedness of the first stages of a sleepless comedown. After a half-hearted attempt to get into my pants, Beardy had passed out fully clothed on the bed, with the corpse-like peace of the wasted. Silently contemplating him for fifteen minutes, chain-smoking and hating myself, I left him a cheery note devoid of the true state of my emotions and called a minicab to take me home.

So there you have it. Sarah's broken Henry's heart and possibly her own; I've lost my job and gained a boyfriend I don't actually want; the only man I've ever loved is with another woman. The only upside of this whole thing is that I genuinely believe that Scott and Alice will be happy together. I really want him to be happy. Her too, I decide, after a moment's consideration, too long to actually be gracious. They deserve each other; I am too polluted to deserve that kind of love. Or any love. I deserve the callous possession of a Beardy, who now that he has been led to think he has me, will probably lose interest, cheat and give me an STI.

After what seems like hours, I fall asleep with a brilliant idea in mind for an invention that will make me a multi-millionaire before I turn thirty. It is – dun dun dun – The Ice Balaclava. Basically, it is an ice-pack in the shape of a balaclava, which you can pull on after particularly rough nights to bring down facial swelling. It may even (based on my research of freezing procedures for fat reduction) be beneficial for those like me who suffer from chipmunk cheeks, engorged lower eyelids, overhanging wattle and the like.

An American-style voiceover will introduce it on telly – 'Do YOU suffer from Fat Face? Do you drink too much? Did you forget your gum at a rave and chew your cheeks off? We have the solution for you! The Ice Balaclava is here! Just slip it in the freezer before a night out, wear it as you sleep and wake up refreshed, with skin as tight as Joan Rivers'! Left at room temperature, it can also function as a form-fitting, post-modern paper bag when you are feeling especially ugly. Buy now or regret for ever! At only £24, including postage and packaging, it is truly a steal!'

A small kink to work through is the potential skin necrosis that could result from repeatedly freezing your face, but nonetheless I dream of high-ceilinged vaults full of money, which I finger on a hard gold throne, naked and alone.

Fuck You Very Much, See You Never

I once read, without fully understanding, an article on how quantum physics was a possible gateway into proving the existence of God. Something about subatomic particles reacting in ways beyond our current comprehension – thought seems to will them into being. Apparently consciousness reacting with matter suggests some sort of larger connective life force within the universe.

I tried to use this information to shape my destiny in the days following New Year's Eve by willing Scott into calling me, before giving up the ghost and accepting my lot. Maybe it didn't work because I was sending out mixed messages – 'He will call me and beg for forgiveness' versus 'He will call me and forgive me', alongside 'Fuck, what the hell have I done, this is all my fault' just to confuse matters. Eventually, my denial lifted. Resigned to the consequences of events (the event being, I've fucked up, the consequence being, I've fucked myself over) I called up the Newt with my heart in my throat, spoke to Gary and quit. He sounded incredibly off with me on the phone, but unsurprised.

The upside of being unemployed is that it's left me with far more time to focus on my degree. I spent the first few weeks of January dementedly working on my final collection. My range plan was finalized, with technical specification drawings alongside coloured illustrations and tacked-on swatches of the fabrics for the seventeen looks in my collection. Of these, six will be made up as garments. Zelda and I will choose in my final design selection to best display the aesthetic of my range, my tailoring capabilities and that all-important fashion-forwardness.

We decided to include two showpieces – the extreme styles that are created to draw the eye and promote the brand's craftsmanship, luxury and creativity but are less likely to be worn outside of a photoshoot or red carpet event. Balancing the range between design stories that hang together cohesively but are not repetitive, with price points suited to the individual clothes, the quality of their fabric and the time it takes to sew them is difficult. Without drifting into ludicrous mark-up territory, at any rate. If you create a stunning party dress that will be sold at £5,000 by the time it gets to the shop

ELIZABETH AARON

floor, you had better have an established brand owned by the Gucci Group, a trust fund or a raft of Arabian princesses as customers.

Drafting patterns is no easy thing; it is the transformation of a visual idea imprecisely drawn, into a functional, wearable, flattering garment, perfectly fitted to the body. Changes are often made in the process, as it is a vital time to experiment with a product so it is better adapted to a woman's shape when it falls flat – or worse, fat. Thus far, the six toiles – the first drafts, so to speak – are in various states of readiness, but are going smoothly enough to leave me one step away from a gibbering wreck.

I tempered the relentlessness of my schedule by spending the occasional night with Beardy, with whom I felt little emotional satisfaction but who filled a hole, as it were. He distracted me from my depression at an incredibly stressful time. Bringing a creative vision into physical being is much like giving birth. After conception, gestation and nourishment you force it into the world through blood, sweat and tears. In moments of exhilarated hope, you are convinced your creation is the most perfect specimen ever to grace the planet. In other moments (vortexes of despair), you are convinced it is wretchedly deformed, unlovable, best left to the wolves. Clearly, my ideas of motherhood are so warped that I should never procreate.

Insurmountable though my workload appeared to be

at times, Julian managed to persuade me to help out at Schrödinger for the week leading up to the show. One of their key interns had most inconveniently been in a cycling accident and ended up in A&E with a broken pelvis. Despite her enforced bed rest, they equipped her with a computer to work on prints from the hospital; still, qualified manpower was required on the front lines.

Trigger is nervous about this collection, hoping that it is well received enough to launch him to Paris Fashion Week. Technically, anyone with enough cash can show; but like all rich people, he wants to feel that he has made it purely on the strength of his genius. It is the step-up he has been striving for the past two seasons, which leaves no room for fuck-ups. He wants someone he trusts, with previous experience in the studio, knowledge of his process and crucially, someone who also doesn't expect to be paid. Enter me.

Normally, the first day on the job at a fashion house would find me waking up an hour earlier than usual to try to dress myself in a way that is at once cool, practical, flattering and not try-hard. This is nearly impossible. Having a woman's body, with tits and arse as well as all the other bits no one cites when promoting their 'curves' (wobbly thighs, small pot, disproportionately fat band of armpit flab) anything that is nonchalant, effortless or cool generally looks shit on me. I sometimes try to wear these things anyway and end up in the on-trend but unbecoming zone of the lumpy-sack wearer.

Vintage is flattering for hourglass girls, but can look like a pastiche if you wear too much of it.

This morning, I don't care about any of that. I throw on some baggy jeans, craggy old boots, a fisherman's jumper nicked off my dad and a sheepskin coat that has seen better days, my unwashed hair in a ponytail. Note: this could look cool if I was very thin but as things stand I am one cardboard sign away from looking like a homeless person of dubious gender. It is very cold and miserable out, but even if it were summer I would have not bothered too much with my clothing, as I know most of the team already. There is no particular need to impress them and I will actually fit in better looking slightly hellish.

You are far more likely to bond with your co-workers in the weeks leading up to a show arguing over whose eye-bags, Haribo-addiction and stress-related acne is worse, than in a love-in over platform boots. If you want money, success, fame, glamour, or at least to look like you have these things, do not go into fashion design. Do PR or fashion journalism instead. The entire studio, save the front-of-house press girls, are bound to look like zombies, having worked solidly for the past two months. They survive on crisps, fags, Pret à Manger sandwiches, diet Coke, adrenalin, cuticle skin and the occasional late night booze-up for morale, bitterly rued the next morning.

I arrive on Monday morning at 10 a.m., as requested. The

studio is tucked away on a side street in Bethnal Green that from the outside looks like any anonymous, dilapidated East End building. Only a subtle gold plaque beside the steel entrance with the name, logo and address emblazoned on it distinguishes it from the other blocks. Once inside, the difference is striking. The interior rooms have all been gutted and renovated into three floors of large, light studio space. The first-floor reception, front office and showroom have managed to retain the original goal of airy minimalism, with black and burnished steel tables displaying rows of shiny MacBooks. Angular leather chairs support thin and polished young marketing girls and the walls display a projection of the last show on a continuous loop. It is Spring/Summer 2013, the one I had been working on – overexposure makes me eye the video now with a curious mixture of pride, anxiety and hatred.

As I take the stairs up to Julian's open-plan office on the second floor I can see that the usual chaos has asserted itself. Rails of toiles and rolls of fabric are lined up on the far side of the room, with inspirational images tacked up on every inch of the wall behind them. On the left side of the room the drawings for the collection are grouped in stories – i.e. cohesive styles – arranged in order of outerwear, dresses, tops and bottoms. Two long tables have rows of interns sitting at them, hunched over their laptops with the beady focus of drug-stimulated research chimpanzees. Every available surface is covered in research material, abandoned fabric swatches, large plastic bags full of patterns and paper with specification sheets in various states of finality.

Though it looks completely disorganized, I'm sure there is an underlying method to the madness, which it will behove me to discover as quickly as possible. I am to help Trigger with the model fittings; I feel a frisson of fear. I will need to familiarize myself with the collection in a matter of days, with no prior knowledge of the little details that make fittings run smoothly. What fabrics are being used and from what mill? What is each garment named? What colourways are currently being finalized? These are the things that everyone else has lived and breathed for months.

Julian is by the window, gulping down a grande Starbucks (a sugarless, milkless Americano, if I remember correctly – he is one of the few to maintain a rigid pre-show diet), smoking furiously and screaming down the phone at someone in broken French. It is clearly not a good time. I decide to make the rounds, taking orders of tea or coffee as I go, always a good method to re-ingratiate myself with the harried staff. I haven't seen most of them in several months and they look at me with blank incomprehension, before crying – 'Darling! It's so good to see you! Let's talk later; I'm swamped. God, I'd love a cup of tea, thanks'. Standing around like a log is always a poor plan, as is acting like any job is beneath you.

'Georgie, God, sorry, I've been on the phone trying to get a last-minute stretch georgette addition through before Friday and those bloody frogs are so pedantic about getting an out-standing payment through before I do. Christ, they know we're good for it, eventually, we've used them for five seasons. Let me take you through things.'

As Julian runs me through the mood boards, designs and completed garments for Autumn/Winter 2014 I try desperately to remember the references he is making. Which fabrics are aligned with what styles, what might change and go in, what needs to be completed . . . the list is endless and confusing but not such a departure from last season that I feel incapable of getting a handle on it. The usual astrological points of inspiration have been changed this season in order to get closer to what Julian describes as, 'Our original source material – human cells and DNA. But, like, with an edge, so it's about darkness, death, entropy. Imagine the Bloomsbury Group with HIV. That's obviously not going into the press packet, but do you know what I mean?'

This has manifested itself in images of platelets and diseased organisms (heavily derivative of a Gilbert & George exhibition I saw a few years ago; I suspect Trigger did as well) that have been reworked with portraits of decaying flowers. The illustrations are disturbing and delicate. The colour boards have been drawn from an obscure Finnish film from the forties; cool, muted oyster neutrals and deep greyish blues juxtaposed with rich Bordeaux, soft violet and accents of sunflower orange.

About three-quarters of the collection has been finished and it looks beautiful. Soft, sleek coats in lambskin and nappa with a loose tailoring recalling nineties grunge are hanging alongside high-waisted jacquard hobble skirts, sheer blouses, deconstructed jumpers and Marlene Dietrich trousers. It has a *Blonde Venus* meets Poirot vibe, yet somehow minimalist – stripped down to the bare bone and then topped with fur. Luxe feminine pieces are contrasted with those that have an androgynous, off-duty-model chic. The shoes, which apparently arrived yesterday to a collective squeal of joy, add the weird factor with their foot-binding style in futuristic matte metallic leather. It's impossible to describe a collection without sounding somewhat idiotic, so suffice to say that it looks 'Ah-mah-zing!'

Trigger has gone AWOL today in a cloud of nervous stress (much preferable, I remember, to him staying when in a fit of nervous stress) so the fitting has been abruptly cancelled. I send the fit model, Katinka, home with a tin of Waitrose biscuits by way of apology. They are sure to remain uneaten; her job depends upon retaining the exact sample size measurements to the millimetre. She is expendable in a way the catwalk models who are pencilled in for castings tomorrow are not. Once the models are selected, all the finished garments will be grouped into one to two looks per girl for the show by the superstylist, Paloma Stone. Afterwards, the absolute final fitting will take place. Needless to say, they are extremely petite, with the exception of their feet, which run to the freakishly huge at size forty-three.

With no design work they can set me at the moment, I am given the sort of dogsbody tasks that are the bane of any intern's life but are also the supporting skeleton necessary to keep a business up and running. I am relieved to have a chance to spend time familiarizing myself with the collection, helping out in the pattern cutting room cutting last-minute garments for the seamstresses and later, printing and organizing the latest specs – technical specification sheets, the ideally idiot-proof, completely clear images of garments that are sent to factories and are worlds away from the glossy, artistic fashion illustrations you see in magazines.

At half past eight in the evening, Julian wearily trudges up to me as I sit on the floor organizing a huge box of zips. Someone had dumped all the smaller boxes together so it is a mess of different colours, sizes and manufacturers. He runs his hand through limp hair.

'I give up. I need fags, food, more fags, a bitch and a break. How does a greasy Chinese takeaway sound to you?'

'Super!' I say manically, feeling like a mechanical toy suddenly wound back up.

As we wait for our food, Julian explains with animated irritation everything that has gone wrong this season, which is, it seems, a lot. The problem with being a perfectionist, an idealist and genuinely good at your job, is that you will rarely find satisfaction in it, being too consumed with endlessly finding flaws. Julian is of this temperament, but has a sense of humour. Trigger does not and has been using him as a scapegoat and verbal punching bag.

'Basically, I think Marco told him something about that dick pic business and now he resents me. Trigger's not the warmest of guys but about a month ago – poof! – it was like I'd gone from teacher's pet to gum on his shoe overnight. Fucking Marco! If I am fired just before we start showing in Paris, shit will go down, man!' Julian's attempts to sound gangster rarely succeed and this failure is compounded when he adds camply, 'Hell hath no fury like a designer scorned!'

'Whatever happened with that? I thought you were worried Theo might find out,' I say a bit guiltily, realizing that I've been so self-consumed over the past month that I haven't bothered to enquire.

'Do you know, I actually did the thing I least expected myself ever to do. After I'd acted like a defensive, jumpy spastic for about five days, Theo confronted me and I told him the truth! The complete truth! Can you believe it?'

I can't. In the long history of emotional fuck-ups within my friendship circle, I don't think that this simple solution has ever actually been tried. Half-truths, white lies, omissions, yes – but confessions? Those have always been considered as something best left to deathbed agnostics.

'That's so brave! How did he take it?'

'My fear was that he wouldn't believe me, but he did, immediately! Apparently when I lie my eyes go flat like a shark and he can always tell. I mean, he was upset of course, but he said that I'd been acting so strangely all week he thought it could be something far worse. He went to his mum's for tea and sympathy for a few days. I had to endure a hideous seventy-two hour period convinced he wouldn't return. We had a beautiful heart-to-heart when he came back and he claims to have completely forgiven me, though I haven't had a Sunday morning breakfast-in-bed since, so I think he's still holding out on me a little bit.'

'You got weekly breakfasts-in-bed? Christ, you're spoiled. Marry that man!'

'Well, I did propose,' Julian says lightly as he grabs his take-away baggie of Kung Po Chicken and rice from the counter, a warm sparkle in his eyes belying the archness of his manner.

'No way! Oh my God! Did he say yes?' I jump up and down in a ridiculously clichéd display of feminine excitement.

'He said he'll think about it. I'm going to do it again, properly, sometime after the show, I'll plan something really extravagant to win him over. I gave a pretty little speech but I didn't have a ring or anything. So I am going to do it properly next time'

We walk back to the studio talking about what the ideal proposal and wedding might be. Julian favours the ostentatious; a hot-air balloon ride in the countryside, passing over a field that has 'Will you marry me?' picked out on it through flattened stalks of wheat (this idea is dismissed as having creepy crop-circle, matchmaking-alien connotations). He has also looked into hiring a band to perform as he serenades Theo under the windows of his Golborne Road workshop with their song, 'That's How Strong My Love Is' by Otis Redding. I must admit to some surprise that it is not either an impossibly hip electro track or, alternatively, Madonna.

Personally, I would prefer something less public but nonetheless dashing, like a spontaneous elopement to a random destination with only the clothes on your back and your passports. Holes are picked in this otherwise brilliant idea due to the vacuum of romance that are airports, the inevitable frustration that would result from having wedding pictures featuring hastily bought, local tourist-monstrosity clothes, the practical issues with finding an English-speaking pro-gay-marriage priest to officiate, anger of friends and family at being excluded and the possibility that the only tickets available might be to Albania via Ryanair. Not that there is anything wrong with Albania, but there are sexy countries and there are countries that may be perfectly wonderful but nonetheless conjure visions of underage sex trafficking.

Julian finally admits that due to financial constraints and Theo's hatred of scenes he will have to tone it down, but wants to do something very special and do it soon. As he is completely overworked for the next few weeks (after the show he has forty-eight hours off then sales and production begin, a whole new circle of hell), he doubts he will find a solution straight away.

Back in the studio, we wolf down our meals and then are back to work until midnight, as Schrödinger is obliged to reimburse taxi fares if we miss the last train home. While stingy, this also works out fairly well as the only true all-nighters are likely to be the two days before the show next Monday afternoon.

When I get home, I trudge into the kitchen with grand plans to make myself a second dinner to eat out of nervous stress. However, Stacy's presence guilts me into putting the kettle on for a pot of camomile tea, possibly the most prudent beverage in the history of the world and as such one I usually despise.

'All right, Stacy? I haven't seen you about much recently.'

Stacy is sitting on the kitchen countertop opposite the sink, her head leaning back against the cupboards, her crossed leg swinging jauntily as she nurses an organic cider. Wearing only a worn-in grey Ralph Lauren polo shirt that comes down practically to her knees and I presume (hope) pants; her hair is mussed and her eyes are bright.

'Fantastic, darling! Super!' Stacy smiles brightly. 'How are your projects going?'

'Oh, you know, fine, I'm back at Schrödinger for a week to help out and then it's back to the grindstone.'

ELIZABETH AARON

'How exciting! That's nice that they thought of you to help them out. How much are they paying you?'

I am so unused to her girlish tone that I say, 'Nothing,' my shoulders flinching in anticipation of some cruel jibe.

'No! Really? After taking time off in your final year to help them? Surely you must at least be gifted something for your time. A dress or a handbag?' she insists with wide, innocent eyes.

'I doubt it. They have lots of interns you know, if they did that for everyone it would be kind of unsustainable.' I think back to the time when, feeling dissatisfied with some of his earlier samples in the archive, Trigger had instructed us to throw them all away, chopping them up first so that no one would be able to fish them out of the bins to wear or sell them. Many of the garments still had swing tags on them with their wholesale prices. It's an odd feeling, taking shears to something worth upwards of £2,000, but it was judged necessary to protect the brand identity.

'Well, that's a shame. You deserve more. Still, I suppose you know when all the sample sales are . . .' She trails off, as we both reflect that even at discounted rates, all this really means is that you are paying your own, hard-earned-elsewhere money back into the company for which you toil for free.

'That I do. So, things are going well with Cosmo, I take it?' The kettle whistles its readiness and I pour the hot water slowly over my tea bag.

311

'Yes.' Stacy smiles happily and I am once again shocked by the transformative powers of love. This is how one should feel in a relationship. Not bored, tethered and resigned. 'He's upstairs, out like a light. I couldn't sleep. He told me he loved me on New Year's Eve, you know.'

'That's wonderful! I'm not at all surprised.'

'I wasn't so sure about him at first. Well, I liked him of course, but not so much more than all the others. But when I was away over Christmas I realized that I actually really do care for him. I haven't said I love you back, got to keep him on his toes a little. But he's taking me to Paris next weekend and I've planned to show him my favourite little spot in Parc Monceau and tell him how I feel as the sun sets.'

The words are uttered in such a totally unexpected tone of wistful romance that I choke and sputter out my gulp of tea, which sprays all over Cosmo's shirt.

'Oh shit! Sorry, sorry! That sounds lovely, Stace, really romantic. Shit, sorry about the shirt, I hope it doesn't stain,' I apologize.

'Oh, that's all right, I'm not terribly fond of this. I'm just wearing it because it smells like him. Tell me, fashion girl, why is it that these brands find it necessary to scale up the size of their logos times ten? So vulgar.' She picks at the giant Man On Horse Swinging Stick, which is about three times the size of her dainty left breast.

'Arabs and Russians, I suppose.'

We both stare into the distance contemplatively, sipping our respective drinks. I am knackered but Stacy looks like she wants to continue this rare little chat and I feel obliged to respect the rapprochement in our relationship.

'So, things are going well with Leo, then?' she asks. It's weird to hear him called by his real name.

'Oh, I don't know. "Well" is such a strong word . . .'

'Oh, dear. That doesn't sound promising. I thought you said that what he lacks in character he makes up for in lust?'

'Did I?'

I can imagine myself saying this, just not to Stacy. Maybe we had a conversation when I was pissed and then I forgot about it. Who knows, maybe we have an entirely different, really close connection that I've blanked out. Maybe these midnight chats are a weekly occurrence. Maybe we're best friends.

'He does have a good beard. I was sure that looks and sexual chemistry were enough for me, but I've recently had doubts about my staunch superficiality and it's kind of thrown me,' I muse.

'That's good! That's progress, right? You can't just keep falling into bed with people hoping that their facial hair will satisfy you emotionally. So who is the other man?'

'The other man?' I start guiltily. Perhaps Stacy is psychic. How can I have lived with her for so long while knowing so little about her?

'If there wasn't another man, you would be in love with Leo, wouldn't you? Nothing turns a woman's head so much as a lack of other contenders and regular sex. You'd see his flaws in a different light and magnify his good qualities until he fit some romantic idyll.' Stacy is very matter-of-fact. I wonder if this is because she has fallen into this trap herself or just judged other people for doing so.

'That . . . could be true.' I have definitely experienced that in the past. I thought I had grown up a bit since then, but the passage of time does not necessarily denote progress if you remain the same.

'I knew I was right,' Stacy chirps with a hint of her old smugness.

'Honestly, I'm still hung up on my old boss. But there was a cock-up of epic proportions.' I proceed to fill her in on the whole sorry drama that was New Year's Eve.

'So why was Scott so angry at Leo?' Good question. One I've had niggling doubts about myself.

'Some stupid argument. I asked Beardy about it; apparently he and Tim, Alice's brother, got into a domestic over something Alice said. Beardy said she's oversensitive and blows things out of proportion. He got really annoyed when I pressed him about specifics so I let it go, but whatever it was it was enough to cause a massive rift between them. They broke up Tin Can Bang – the world will be missing out on some quality tunes there. Beardy's since joined a new band.

They don't have a name, just an icon of a square with a sort of squiggly thing in the middle.'

I sigh and wish I didn't have a boyfriend whose taste prompted me to voice such a sentence aloud.

'Wow. This might sound harsh, but you have really low standards. I mean, you're all about women's rights, aren't you?' I am startled. While I am a feminist, I don't think I have ever said anything strident to Stacy and can only assume she is making this judgement on the infrequency with which I wash my hair. She continues, 'The sexual revolution is all very well. You have the freedom to sleep with some handsome guy who doesn't seem to care about you that much and that you don't care about that much, without any social or emotional repercussions. But don't you want more than that?'

Stacy says this not unkindly, but nonetheless my eyes and mouth are round like saucers as I digest her appraisal of my first real boyfriend in almost a year. Of course, one of the reasons I wanted to pin him down, as it were, was just to have some sort of social stamp of approval – 'Not Rejected!' – rather than feeling that he is a man I could fall in love with. Isn't that perfectly natural when the majority of my dating attempts have ended in disaster? The initial shagging stage is exciting and fun; later you realize it took only two weeks to know them well enough to satisfy your curiosity for ever.

And that there is a humiliatingly good chance they stole

£50 from your purse, as well as the last muffin from the bread basket. Fuck you very much, see you never.

'What about you!' I say defensively. 'You might be loved up with Cosmo right now but you treated your men like cash-points and holiday funds. You manipulated them and disrespected them and they were too blinded by your face to care that you were using them.'

At this, Stacy shrugs her slim shoulders with a Gallic insouciance. She is unoffended, supremely confident in all her choices as usual.

'At least I was getting something. Money for beauty; that's a fair exchange. I knew they didn't care about my personality, my wants or needs, so I didn't care about theirs. I didn't respect them, I did use them, but I respected myself and didn't let myself be used. I can't say that I feel the same way about the way you've behaved. Did you even ask Scott about what happened? You ran away. You took the easy way out, by settling for someone who you won't care if you lose. I was looking out for myself. You're lying to yourself about what you want because you're afraid you won't be able to get it.'

I try to spark some anger within myself in reaction to this assessment, but find that I can't. Maybe I am too tired, maybe I don't care, maybe she is right. It's always seemed to me that finding someone who loved me the most, who I also loved the most, would be an impossible task. So why bother?

Anna Karenina? Is she a Model?

'Paloma, you've sent me another anorexic dwarf. Seriously, where are all the two-metre girls this season? I get that she's just turned fifteen but surely we haven't rinsed Eastern Europe for all the gangly freaks already? I need endless legs this season – you've seen the hem-lengths. It needs to evoke repressed, smouldering sexuality.'

Trigger is standing facing the left wall of the showroom, biting at a manicured thumbnail, perfectly threaded brows knitted in deep concern. It is covered in the models' profile cards, stuck on with Blu-Tack with a perfect inch of empty space bordering them. Trigger cannot bear it when they are uneven. Paloma Stone, stylist supreme, is sprawled on a rotating chair, her next-season spiked Balmain ankle boots jutting into the air above the table they rest on like shiny, malevolent scarabs.

'Darling, I know she's a midget but those cheekbones! They're so gloriously swollen it's as if she's eaten a dumb-bell. Besides which she's booked for the next Prada campaign and already has major buzz online. You can't think she's too thin? Her proportions are beautiful, darling, so elegant.'

'No, no, her body is perfect; it's her height I'm concerned about. Amazons are what I'm going for, except, you know, not strong-looking. I want super-willowy. I have a vision for the new nineties waif, but less street urchin and more frail and ethereal. Like Ophelia dragged out of a lake. Sexy but consumptive. Do you know what I mean?'

'Ophelias-on-smack, of course I know what you mean, darling!' Paloma laughs throatily, throwing back her head. Her mountain of candyfloss bleach-blonde hair bobs up and down, pinned and braided around her head in an impossibly chic birdsnest.

'Like that Karen Elson image by Roversi. Except no red hair, I feel like that has had its moment. But pale, very pale. I want real dishwater blondes and minky-browns. Very natural, a bit wild. The silhouettes are prim so I need lots of long shins and nipples and just-fucked hair, you know?' Trigger is pacing back and forth with the concentration of a major general strategizing his next attack.

'Darling, I feel you; I can see it exactly. Vanessa Bell taken roughly in a hedge and then throwing a dinner party not realizing her blouse is ripped and her red lippy is smeared.'

'Yes! Exactly. Thank God you're here, Paloma.'

They both cackle wildly, their pre-show nerves asserting themselves. Trigger calms down first and abruptly slumps his head into his hands. He is a very attractive man in that particularly English, fine-boned aristocratic fashion. He looks like he emerged from the womb in a vintage tweed suit, shotgun in hand, fully prepared to deliver pheasants and foxes into the afterlife. Nonetheless, stress has taken a toll on him – his face is wan and tight, his hair greasy, his thin shoulders hunched.

'Did you see the calves on Bin Shu? She's looking almost sturdy. She'll definitely have to wear trousers. When will all this BMI bullshit go away?' he despairs.

'It will, it will. These things always have their moment and then pass. Fashion isn't for fat people. Look at Ruby. She was the poster girl for plus size and she got her hipbones back in no time.'

Though I know, intellectually, that it is completely fucked up to view someone whose waist is over twenty-four inches as tipping the scales, in photos one's eye quickly adapts to what seems absurdly thin in real life. At the moment, I am organizing the assembled preliminary looks together on a rail, each girl's shoes and accessories placed in Ziploc bags with their names on, as quietly and efficiently as possible.

They both seem to have forgotten that I am here, or they don't care to censor themselves.

This sort of conversation may be very non-P.C. but is typical amongst many people in the industry. I am complicit in it as well. I laugh along to the jokes, while inwardly reflecting that if these girls are heavy, one more cupcake will tip me into morbid obesity. I secretly admire women with visible ribcages and if I read an article in *Heat* captioned along the lines of 'Wasting Away! Heartache And Mental Illness Take Their Toll On Troubled Starlet' I wonder where I can get myself some of that.

Most of the time, I view my body fat as smothering my potential for a better, more glamorous life rather than completely normal and healthy. It's hard to adhere to feminist principles of self-acceptance and love when constantly surrounded by reminders of an ideal that is impossible for most to achieve. Even if I'd studied Biochemistry and went on to work in a lab searching for answers to worthy scientific questions, far removed from deep and meaningful contemplation of the legs of a lucky one percent, the female urge to self-annihilate by comparison is so strong that I don't think I would feel any different.

As each girl enters the room for the casting, they are fussed over like princesses; the moment they've left they inspire either enraptured appreciation or a cruel dissection of miniscule flaws. The common complaint is that they are expanding. At first, when issues over the life-threateningly low weights of models began to get media attention, the British Fashion Council tried to encourage healthy standards. The girls retained their tiny measurements, clearly afraid of losing campaigns. Then, gradually, some of them started to fill out. Not in such a way that they would be deemed over-weight in real life. Enough that a few centimetres' difference here and there could be discerned by distressed designers.

Of course, some of the girls are naturally tiny. You can always tell the ones that aren't by the protruding spines, jutting pelvises and downy hair covering their bodies. That isn't to say that the naturally thin ones are eating in a way that one might deem 'typical', though who knows – it is impossible to monitor someone's eating habits and if they say cheeseburgers and pizza are a daily staple, who am I to cry bullshit? Bizarre diets and sporadic starvation seem to be the norm whether or not our jobs depend on them; for many women it is a weird badge of honour to self-efface. Models are just paid for it. I would certainly be thinner if I had thousands of pounds hanging in the balance. Although I should say that most of them barely eke out a living, living in cramped shared apartments, their initial fees going straight back to their agencies to cover the cost.

'Who's next?'

'Gaia,' I say after a pause, not immediately realizing that this was directed at me. Trigger's habit of only looking his equals or right-hand man in the eye can make it difficult to know when he is actually addressing you. As is his inability to remember names. We are all interchangeable, shadowy 'You there's, bearing dresses, fabric, scissors, coffee.

'At least Gaia's always been fat,' Trigger sighs. 'No surprises there. We'll probably have to put her in a toile again.'

Last season, all the garments had been so tightly fitted that they had to pull out a dropped stretch-crepe evening gown for her to wear. Even then, the fabric rippled, too tight along her slightly rounded stomach and shapely hips. As it was in the show, it then needed to be put into production. It didn't sell particularly well in spite of Trigger's hope that it would attract what he dubbed the 'Big Girl At A Wedding' customer.

'You've got to have some occasional bosoms, my darling, and the press love her. Besides, she's so nice. And since she got out of rehab her face has lost that puffy look, she's really never looked better.' Paloma admires her long tapered manicure in the air, a bubble-gum Barbie pink so tacky that it comes all the way back to the realm of cool.

'I'm not saying I don't love her, I do, she's fantastic. I just wish she'd get a bout of dysentery twice yearly. Is that so much to ask?'

They are still laughing as Gaia comes in, all dirty-blonde hair, long legs, swollen breasts and bee-stung lips. She is a walking Bardot-esque wet dream and at a standard, consistent size eight, the token 'voluptuous' girl. I've always admired her. It takes balls to always be the largest in a room full of girls paid for their ability to be small and not to change. Now she is a big enough name not to have to warp her body to fit the dresses, but that wasn't always the case. Though I would kill for her figure, after dressing girls with limbs like gazelles all morning, their size has been normalized to me. In comparison, Gaia does carry notable heft.

'Gaia! You look fantastic. Love agrees with you! How is darling Steve?' Paloma gushes, her long legs swinging off the table in one graceful movement as she stands up to air-kiss.

'He's wonderful, wonderful. So sweet to me. I'm going on tour with him next month,' Gaia whispers in breathy, little-girlish German-accented English.

From what I've gathered, she is referring to Stephen Biche, a slightly cheesy but very sexy singer whose messy separation from his wife (also a model, but a late-thirties brunette so, clearly, he has broader taste than some of his ilk) has only just begun to die down in the papers.

'How fabulous! I know his ex-wife a little socially, total bitch. Dresses like a WAG as well, I bet you she'll end up with a washed-up footballer, if she manages to land another ring. You two are a much better match,' Paloma assures her.

Gaia has the grace to look uncomfortable at this, but smiles politely.

'So, let's get started, I'm thinking one of these transparent loose-knit jumpers, we want to showcase those fantastic bosoms, darling.'

Gaia strips down to a tiny, flesh-coloured thong, shoving her size forty-one feet into a pair of dangerously high and cripplingly tight size thirty-nine stilettos. I pull out the garments they had previously cordoned off as having enough stretch to fit her. I manhandle her smooth legs into a pair of trousers that barely zip up at the back, thinking about how many men would kill to be a fly on the wall right now. The sight of such physical feminine perfection is wasted on Trigger and Paloma. Myself, I am trying to be professional and not stare, but cannot help marvelling at the gravity-defying, cream-coloured, peachy-nippled breasts hovering directly in front of me. I slip a deconstructed loose-knit mohair jumper covered in holes over Gaia's obediently raised arms. I am in awe of her jackpot beauty, not even slightly jealous. You might as well curse a sunset for its brilliance.

'Right. Love the jumper but literally the whole of your left tit is hanging out. We want sex but this looks like assault, and after Lee, no one can do rape-y without looking derivative. You know what I mean? But those trousers are so conservative . . . let's take it all off,' Paloma states bluntly.

'You think the trousers are too conservative? I wanted to overprint them, but the shape is quite accessible,' Trigger says defensively. Accessible is code for 'able to be worn by someone over eight stone'. He continues, 'And I don't know if the woman who would wear an accessible trouser would wear a printed trouser.'

Trigger drops to his knees in front of Gaia and makes a twirling motion with his finger, sighing with concern. The reality of being a designer who owns his own company is not, as you might think, greater creative freedom. Being bought by an LVMH or Gucci Group will allow you to scale heights of creative freedom that will be guzzled up by a select quota of celebrities, oligarchs' wives and Saudi princesses. This is funded through the expansion into the real money-makers of the industry: the extravagantly marked-up perfume, cosmetic and accessory sales that are affordable enough to enable the average woman to buy into the dream.

'I don't know darling, does the Schrödinger girl wear accessible trousers? Is she an accessible woman? Or is she an aspirational woman? Aspiration is press, accessible is filler.'

Paloma is far from an accessible woman. Though not especially thin herself, every wildly tailored designer item on her over-accessorized body screams 'aspirational'. Even her eyeliner is intimidating.

'You think it's accessible?' The word pushes Trigger close to tears. Paloma rapidly backtracks.

'Darling, I'm talking about one pair of trousers! Not the whole collection! They are beautifully sharp and we need a few minimal things but we need to put them with something else to ratchet up the weird factor. Here, you, get her out of this and into something like – this.'

Paloma pulls out a dove-grey jersey dress with a plunging neckline and complicated loops of beading accenting a spidery black-and-acid-yellow print. It is just stretchy enough to fit Gaia, encasing her like a supremely indecent glove. She then pulls out what Trigger has dubbed the 'Clochard Cape', a beautiful distressed lambskin inspired by a Parisian tramp. She skews it to the side so it swings open rakishly.

'That is fantastic. So beautiful. Can you walk?'

Gaia marches up and down the showroom, scowling in impossibly hip mock-fury doubtless aided by her too-small six-inch heels. It is quite remarkable.

'Fur. Do you have any fur hats? I love these stoles but I think one or two Anna Karenina hats would just perfect this. Don't you think?' Paloma purrs.

'Go find Julian! Tell him we need fur hats! Pronto! Fox, orange and fluffy!' Trigger barks in my direction.

I run up the stairs to find Julian and say breathlessly, 'Anna Karenina hats! Fox, orange, fluffy!' He whips around to the nearest intern and instructs her to search all the nearest vintage shops. As I run back down the stairs, I can hear her asking in confusion, 'Anna Karenina? Is she a model?' The Chinese whispers that function as commands are a hazard in an intern-heavy industry dependent upon delegation. Who knows what she might return with.

At a quarter to midnight, I have just about finished mounting the Polaroids of the looks on the wall. What was a few hours ago an insurmountable chaos in the fitting room, has now been carefully arranged on labelled groups of hangers. Quite a few pieces have yet to be finished, but by the time the girls return to be fitted before the show all the toiles will be replaced by completed garments. We hope.

There may be one or two final additions, the result of creative doubt and panic, hastily sewn up and then drawn up on Illustrator as tech specs, ready to be put into the online ordering system should they make it into the show. More likely, these will be scrapped, the all-night work of exhausted Polish seamstresses ultimately fruitless. It might appear to be a waste of money, fabric, energy and time but is a necessary part of the process. Many people don't realize when they buy a designer frock how much hair-tearing thought has gone into every aspect of it. A few centimetres' difference here and there in the hem, the painstaking consideration of the colour and fabric, the changes that have gone into the prints or embroidery, how many versions have bitten the dust, how much work is abandoned.

Truly, though spending an exorbitant amount of money on a piece of clothing might seem absurd to some, you get what you pay for. Whether or not the final product is a revelation or a hideous blot on the face of design (for these do frequently appear), rest assured, a hell of a lot of work has gone into it. Work that is paid for with a living wage to the designers, seamstresses, suppliers and factories involved in the supply chain in a way that a dress from the high street might not be.

Excepting, of course, the interns. In an industry where payday arrives months after all your budget has been spent, how would they survive without a free, infinitely replaceable workforce desperate for experience? We can learn only so much at university and we are unlikely to land a job without considerable previous experience, thus interning is indispensable.

The morning of the show, 9 a.m. and running on two hours' sleep, Julian and I share a sneaky, shaky fag break outside the building. We are both clutching coffees and gabbling about what still needs to be done. Technically, at this moment, nothing needs to be done, by us at least. Everything has slowly come together to the point where all the garments have all their hardware and correct finishings with labels and swing-tags in place. With the looks lined up neatly in runway order ready to be transported to the show, hung with OCD levels of care in assembled Schrödinger garment bags, the essential work is over.

A board divides each look on the rail – an A1 card with the model's headshot, name, a Polaroid with her looks and notes on the styling to make everything idiot-proof for the team of professional dressers who will expertly guide them in and out of their catwalk changes. Taxis are scheduled to arrive in thirty minutes and we have nothing to do, but feel that we should be running around like headless chickens, having done so all week. Though it is not unusual for stressful last-minute changes to be made the night before the show, this time around little was dramatically altered. Whether through foresight, exhaustion or prioritizing looking good for the cameras over tailoring at 3 a.m., Trigger burst into the studio at 11 p.m. and said to Marco ominously: 'I leave this in your hands'. He then swept out majestically in his wool Margiela jumper-coat.

The only major adjustment to do on Sunday was over-printing on a jacket, dress and skirt when Trigger suddenly decided he hated the underlying motifs. One of the first final-ized prints of the collection, it was probably a matter of him having seen it one too many times and its having lost its allure rather than through any inherent ugliness. However, this print being something that Julian worked on start to finish, he is worried.

'He's dropped practically everything I had a hand in, Georgie. Things he loved a month ago. What the fuck? I don't care about everything I do getting in the show but I'm starting to worry about my job. I feel like maybe he's edging me out – that he's going to replace me with Marco. Fucking Marco!'

Nervous tension often manifests itself as paranoid

bitchiness, I find. At this stage in the game, everyone is either chatting shit about someone, running their mouths in a continuous stream of nonsense or acting as the silent recipient of this hyper-fatigued prattle. I reassure Julian for ten minutes, though in his place I would share the same concerns. Even if he can't be outright fired, things can be made so miserable for him that he can be pushed out if Trigger so wishes it.

The show is being held at 1 Terrance Place, a gorgeous mansion in Mayfair that normally functions as an exclusive members' club but can be hired out for events. Its exorbitant expense has been offset by Premiere Vodka, who are in the midst of a rebranding attempt and hope to get an in with the fashion crowd through sponsoring the show and after party.

The girls will walk out through a side door into the enormous indoor greenhouse garden, down a cobbled pathway that winds around a fountain before pausing in front of an enormous banquet. Here they are instructed to pose for the photographers cordoned into the far left corner before cutting a swath through the centre of the garden, entering the main door and marching up the spiral staircase in the main hall to hurry into their next look.

The seating plan for the guests has been arranged in order of importance and fame, with top editors, journalists, buyers and celebrities nabbing upholstered William Morris couches and vintage rocking chairs scattered at key viewing points.

The rest of the *invités* will have to be content with standing space in the hallway. An effusion of imported exotic plants has made the garden savage.

The best view can be had from the wicker swing hanging from a tree near the banquet, but the front of house girls have been put under strict instruction not to seat anyone there. This is because it is a feast with a difference. Continuing the themes of life, death, sex and decay, the food (specially commissioned from a Michelin-starred chef) was cooked ten days ago and is now swarming with flies and maggots. The hothouse flowers surrounding it had been chosen for drama, not scent, but their odour rises up and mixes with the smell of putrid flesh. The glass atrium is oppressively heady.

Trigger had debated whether or not to go ahead with this concept, as it is so clearly derivative of Hirst. The important thing, Paloma assured him, is that the right mood is evoked, not whether it is an original idea. What is original these days? The blooming flowers contrasting with the rotting meat against the gloriously decadent clothing is a powerful image for the press.

All the garments have been unloaded and organized, the model boards spread out and the hair and makeup teams set up in the upstairs dining rooms. The girls start to wander in and disrobe, having their hair backcombed and crimped into shagged-in-a-bush abandon with long gold-plated twigs art-fully arranged in their knotted locks. Lipstick in deep blood red and plum is perfectly applied and then roughly smeared across one cheek, as if they had just been passionately kissed. Those of us backstage are left hanging around. We receive an occasional command along the lines of 'Find Tit-Tape!' (said with the urgency of a First World War doctor shouting for a saw and morphine) but otherwise we have no further responsibilities. We eat the sandwiches provided for the models, wander around, gossip and pretend to be busy as we wait for things to start.

Finally, the guests trickle in at a quarter past one and we help put on the finishing touches to the girls – straightening a skirt here, tucking in a blouse there. We keep up a soothing stream of mild chat as the girls are obediently lifted, tweaked and adjusted, ethereal rag-dolls. Trigger is occupied with interviews downstairs, so Julian and Marco run around making sure no fuck-ups are being made. They shout encouragement and tips to the models – 'Fantastic! You look beautiful! Now remember we want a strong walk but limp wrists. A knackered feel. Pretend you're dying of consumption. Have you seen *Moulin Rouge*? You are Satine!' – which elicit laughter from the English-speakers and blank confusion from the rest. As they are all clearly exhausted from a non-stop week of travelling, walking, standing, waiting around and parties, looking elegant and near-death isn't much of a stretch.

As melancholic strains of contemporary orchestral-electro are struck up, everything begins to go very quickly. I peek outside at the hushed crowd below as they watch the runway. Their expressions behind raised handkerchiefs (silk, hand-embroidered with a monogrammed SC, both gift and vital protection against the potent smell of decomposition) vary from the excited to the blasé. The girls languidly march forward, beautiful faces sensuously wan. The collection is magnificent, decadent and replete with a buttoned-up volupté. The bass reverberating, the intoxication of smell, sight and sound overwhelm the guests, some of who are physically overcome. This is what Trigger intended. People love nothing so much as to be shocked into feeling again after so many similar presentations.

The show seems to last mere seconds, rather than minutes. After all the build-up – the sleepless nights, the stress, the hysterical laughter, the escaped tears, the inflated and injured feelings, all to lead up to this moment – the actual event is a brilliant but rapid climax. Fifteen minutes to sell this vision to the world, six months in the making. As the girls all line up in a row and Trigger comes out to bashfully take a bow, there is a standing ovation from the crowd. He has arrived. The guests start to leave, already late for the next show. We are left behind – congratulations are made – the girls are stripped – garments are carefully rehung – makeup wipes are distributed – we clear up. We sleepwalk through the motions, dreaming of a long afternoon nap before the after party tonight.

We Are All Of Us Prats, At Times

I step out of the taxi, wobbling on my Marant rip-off heels. I am already a little bit tipsy from the bottle of champers that Julian, Theo and I had downed before throwing out of the window in giggling abandon (we were severely reprimanded by our driver, yet unrepentant). Somehow, on a diet of stress, cigarettes and Hobnobs, I have managed to lose the majority of my Christmas coating. I just about fit back into a body-con dress that is admittedly both a bit tacky and slightly Essex Girl, but fuck it, flattering. Sometimes you only want to feel sexy, especially after being cooped up with girls, gays and lank, greasy locks for an endless week. So – tits, arse, heels and hair are the order of the day.

'Fucking hell, look at this joint all done up,' Julian says, a cigarette rakishly hanging out of the corner of his mouth. He has been smoking like a fiend, though he is always threatening to quit as it goes against his obsessive skin-care regime.

'Not bad, not bad at all.'

The after party is in the same venue as the show – a large expense but the extra cash was the only way Terrance Place would agree to keep a slowly rotting table of gourmet food cordoned off in the greenhouse for the better part of a week. The white eighteenth-century façade has been lit up with spotlights, and intricately drawn illustrations of flora and fauna are projected on to the walls, slowly decaying in stop-frame. Though it is past midnight, a long queue still snakes its way up to the clipboard-clutching guardian of the door, who looks appropriately sphinx-like, her bitch-face set to petrify.

Fashion parties can go one of two ways. Either they are uptight, pretentious, cold affairs where people stick to gossiping with a handful of intimates, or they are the most riotous, silly, disco-heavy, smile-at-the-ready, drug-fuelled fun ever. Luckily, this looks as if it will fall into the latter category.

Inside, the light is dim enough to flatter but bright enough to admire, with giant yellowing antique-lace handkerchiefs recalling *A Streetcar Named Desire* swamping the lamps. We perfunctorily admire walls covered in bouquets of dried flowers before leaving our extra layers at the cloakroom and heading straight to the bar. An array of sponsored vodka cocktails are being made by gorgeous mixologists who dispense eye-fucks along with drinks. Flamboyantly dressed guests smother each other in kisses, smiling with manic magnanimity as they twitch with tell-tale tics, rubbing their nostrils, sniffing and chomping enthusiastically on gum. As for me, after the New Year's debacle I have sworn off drugs for ever, with the vague willpower of one who has not yet had the opportunity to turn them down. The techno beat makes me itch with desire for a little pick-me-up, but as Julian and Theo think that drugs are common, I figure I will be safe enough in their company.

We get silly drunk with the clear buzz that comes from imbibing only high-quality spirits, quite unlike my usual beer-haze or wine-bubble, or toxic mixture of the two. We have arrived at just the right time – the music is getting progressively cheesier. I expected to feel some am-I-inside-or-outside-the-group awkwardness due to my short tenure this season, but the dual social lubrications of alcohol and Rihanna are impossible to deny.

If I am not on a natural high, I am at least on a legal one when I run into Gary in the mixed-sex loos. I am trying to blow-dry the perspiration rings under my armpits with as much nonchalance as I can muster. Catching sight of his shaven head emerging from a toilet, I lower my arms with the swiftness of a ninja and stick my hands under the dryer like a normal person.

'Gary! Oh my gosh! What are you doing here?' I lean in to give him a hug.

Taken by surprise, Gary responds warmly with 'I'm shagging a famous makeup artist!' before realizing who I am and pulling back with a narrow-eyed once-over.

'Georgie, all right?' he says guardedly.

A naturally convivial person, this greeting is, for him, cuttingly glacial. I nod in response, laughing at nothing with a strained rictus grin. It is one of my Life Goals Before Thirty to be able to present myself with a cool, collected veneer of confidence in such situations. When that is accomplished, I can focus on other things, like marriage and kids.

'How are things? With – how is – The Newt?' I blurt out, as he turns to leave.

'Fine. How is Leo?' he says with contempt.

'Oh, I'm so glad. I don't know. I imagine he's fine, we broke up.'

'Did you now? What happened there?' A glimmer of renewed interest sparks Gary's eyes and as his handsome friend makes impatient moves towards the dance floor, Gary waves him off with promises to join him.

'Oh, it was nothing dramatic, not like New Year's . . . I just kind of realized one day – well, last week – that he's a bit of a dick and always will be.' The words stumble out in a rush. 'And what does that make me if I'm girl-willing-to-put-up-with-a-dick? Either someone with really low self-esteem, or, you know, also a dick. So I broke up with him. To which his response was, "Then just go. Go home, have a nice life, or not, I don't care". So, no regrets there.'

My unspoken regret is the Scottish elephant in the room. A smothering feeling of dread still creeps up on me on the rare occasions I allow myself to think of how I behaved. The hollow victory I chose, a poor decision based on fear. I reassure myself that he probably wasn't that interested and that this current, mild heartbreak is better than the crippling heartbreak that would have eventually ensued if I had actually dated him. It's a small comfort.

'Just a bit of a dick? Jesus, Georgie, the man was a giant fucking cock. I couldn't believe that you took his side when he assaulted Alice,' Gary says with some disgust.

This time my only response is to hang my mouth open in utter shock. I try to shout 'Whaaaaaaat?' but the only sound to escape my throat is a choked whistle of shock.

'You don't know? Clearly you don't know. Thank God, I hoped you weren't that much of a bitch. Fuck me. Let's get a drink.'

I numbly follow Gary, who dances nimbly through the crowd to where the vodka sings its siren song. He grabs four long cocktails from a tray behind the bar and shouts to follow him. We wind through the kitchens, scramble through the service door and sneak up a back stairwell that has been cordoned off. A series of smallish rooms hold couples sharing

intense conversations and passionate embraces. I don't recognize anyone from Schrödinger. Typically, the random,
least deserving guests are having the best of secret times.
Gary leads me to a quiet corner near an open window. He
sets our drinks down on the floor, reaches into his blazer
and smoothly pulls a deck of Marlboros, a pack of Golden
Virginia and an electronic cigarette from various hidden
pockets.

'Pick your poison,'

Taking a cigarette, I take a deep gulp from my glass and
say solemnly,

'Tell me what happened.'

Gary, a natural storyteller, takes a bit more delight in the
gruesomeness of the encounter than I would have liked, but
being The-One-Who-Sided-With-A-Sexual-Assailant, for me to
bring this up now would be quibbling.

'This is the culmination of a drama that had been going
on for years,' he begins. 'Starting at one of Scott's house parties, 2011. Tim and Leo had just become close and Alice was
passed out in the spare bedroom. She went through a long
phase of caning it on the weekends. When I first met her she
was still a bit of a mess to be honest, it's only quite recently
that she has been more together. Soo, Scott walks in to check
on her and finds Leo lying next to her, clearly awake, drunk
and acting shifty when the lights come on. Her top is off.
Alice is still passed out. Scott yells at him, wakes her up and

she laughs off the incident, saying it was nothing. I think she just didn't want to rock the boat.

'So, Leo acts totally outraged, said he came in and she had taken her shirt off and he was trying to cover her up with a blanket, rah rah rah, super-dodgy story. For whatever reason, Alice backs him up and then Tim does as well and Scott's the only one with serious concerns. As you can imagine, he's always been suspicious of him. And he had massive doubts about Alice managing their band.'

'He never seemed that concerned to me, why didn't he say anything?' I ask, puffing away in a fever of angst.

'He had his concerns, but Alice is a big girl. Sometimes supporting someone silently and being there for them when things inevitably fuck up is more helpful than being a loud voice of dissent from the beginning, you know? People always see through their worst mistakes with the most determination, I've noticed.'

I sigh deeply in agreement, wishing Scott hadn't been so discreet in this case, whatever his motives.

'But this time, things were really grim. After the gig on New Year's Eve, Alice was helping Leo to load their equipment in Tim's van – Tim was off drinking with the promoter – in this empty car park behind the warehouse. She's knackered; Leo offers to give her a backrub, starts kissing her neck. At first I think she was probably sort of into it as they'd all been drinking, but then he pushes her on the floor of the van and starts getting rough with her. She hasn't been very detailed about what happened, it didn't get too far, but apparently she was trying to fight him off and he wouldn't stop.'

'Fucking hell.' I take a huge gulp of my cocktail, hoping to calm the bilious roiling of my stomach. This is so much worse than expected. I feel sick to my soul.

'I know. Luckily, Tim came back earlier than expected and heard scuffling noises coming from the van. The doors were shut and locked. He bangs on the door; he can hear Alice shouting – he starts screaming that he'll smash a window to get in. Alice finally opens it and spills out sobbing, her skirt up around her waist and bruises on her arms. Leo scrambles out, Tim tries to tackle him to the ground but Leo is way bigger and stronger than him. He pushes Tim off and just runs away without saying a word. No explanation, no apology, nothing.'

Runs off to The Newt, to me. To the one who never questions, never demands; the one least likely to investigate and most likely to take his explanations at face value. The blind faith of the permanently disappointed wishing to remain ignorant.

My eyes fill up with tears. I have to wait a few minutes for them to subside, for the lump in my throat to clear, before I am able to speak. Gary gives me time, putting a sympathetic hand on my shoulder.

'Jesus Christ. I feel terrible for Alice; I can't believe it.

Actually, I can totally picture it, isn't that fucked up, that I am not that shocked? God, that's so fucked up. I am so appalled . . . that I ever let him touch me. Poor Alice, God, how is she now?'

'She's okay, it's been a while. She's carrying on managing Tim, he wrote most of the songs, you know. So it's not like she quit her PR job for nothing. She doesn't seem to be dwelling on it but she just needed to cut him out of her life, totally. I can't believe she didn't press charges, but these things are so difficult to prove and so emotionally draining, she didn't think she could cope.' Gary shakes his head sadly. 'It's only on Alice's account that Scott didn't track Leo down and beat him to a pulp. She just wanted to forget it ever happened.'

'How could you all . . . think that I knew all this? And that I still chose to be with him?' I ask, heart in my throat. It is far and away the most depressing assessment of my character, ever. And I'm pretty sure not everyone of my acquaintance thinks highly of me.

Gary looks a bit guilty, then shrugs.

'Scott was very angry with you. I wanted to think you wouldn't be so stupid but we were all furious, it was easier to just shut out anyone associated with him. It didn't seem so impossible – I wanted to think the best of you – but in these situations women are often blind. You have to know how it looked.'

'I do. God, I need to apologize. I need to apologize now. They must be so disgusted with me.'

My veins boil with a sudden urgency, to find Scott, now, wherever he is, find him and explain. I hold no hopes for anything between us, beyond him not remembering me in such a horrible light, even if my behaviour was awful and selfish and this is probably no more than I deserve.

I stand up abruptly, my knees wobbling. Necking the rest of my first drink, then swiftly downing the other – if ever there is a time for ill-conceived Dutch courage, I rationalize that it is now – I set down both glasses with a firmness of resolve that nearly shatters them and declare that I am going to find him.

'What, Scott? Now? Georgie, it's half past two in the morning. The pub is closed, he'll be in bed. Wait until tomorrow, when you've sobered up a bit.'

'No, I need to find him now,' I say as I sling my bag over my shoulder, slurring slightly. 'I need to explain. I can't bear that he thinks—'

'Georgie . . . this is really not the time. It's been two months, what's the difference of a few hours? Harassing a man in the middle of the night is never a good idea.'

'It's not harassment! If he doesn't answer the door I'll go home. I just – this is killing me – I feel like every second that passes that I can't explain . . .'

Gary rolls his eyes, clearly disapproving, but finally raises his hands and says,

'Fine, but darling, sort out your makeup before you do, you've got mascara all down your face.'

I hadn't even realized that I had started crying. I know I am in no fit state to find Scott, but once I am drunkenly determined to do something, there is no stopping me. Luckily, I still have enough presence of mind to know that reapplying my makeup wasted in a taxi is not the look one wants to sport when begging forgiveness of a man.

Back in the toilets, Gary blots away the trails of greyish misery that pigment my cheeks with damp bog roll, as I sip a glass of water he insisted I take. He finishes wiping it off and asks for my makeup bag, fixing the trainwreck that is my face with a deft, surprisingly motherly hand.

'What a transformation, eh?'

He spins my shoulders towards the mirror. It is indeed impressive. I have gone from looking like inebriated hell to passably normal, the best I could have hoped for.

'I used to live with a drag queen,' he says modestly by way of explanation. 'Don't worry, I'm not sure you can see straight enough to notice but I held back on the eyeliner.'

'Gary, you're a star. Why are you so nice to me when I've been a total prat?' I whisper pathetically.

'Doll, we are all of us prats, at times. The important thing is, you've got your heart in the right place. You're a good egg even if you have horrible judgement. And you make me laugh,

I guess. I still think you should wait till tomorrow, but if you insist on disturbing him tonight, go get him, tiger!'

The pulsating feeling of urgency returns as I realize it is nearly three in the morning. The sensible part of my brain – always tiny and now drowning in booze – emits a little wail, vainly signalling that nothing will change in the next ten hours. That I should wait, be refreshed, showered, clean and sober and call him beforehand to warn him I'm coming and possibly bring him some sort of peace offering, like Beardy's head on a platter or, failing that, a really, really good sandwich. But I feel time pressing on me, a horrible feeling that somehow action, now, is pivotal to my success. I kiss Gary on the cheek and make a dash for it, trying not to knock anyone over as I stumble through the dance floor on my increasingly unsteady heels.

'Georgie! Where the fuck have you been? I haven't seen you for ages. Have you been getting off with someone?'

Julian has spotted me just as I finally retrieve my coat from the cloakroom. The queue was packed with fashion people of both sexes drunkenly swaying on all manner of absurd platform heels. I had waited a good fifteen minutes, barely preventing myself from loudly declaring a state of emergency in order to be served first, but my English reticence is stronger than even my most extreme desperation. I groan, leaning against the wall with no energy to explain my absence.

'Julian, it's a long, long story, a terrible story . . . I need to go. I have an awful story to tell, so awful this story. I will tell you when next I see you, I need to find Scott—'

'Darling, you look really, really pissed. I can barely understand you. Go home to bed. Let me help you find a black cab, there are loads of dodgy minicabs outside.' In spite of my nonsensical protestations, Julian forcefully takes me by the arm and leads me outside. I am really very, very woozy, increasingly bone-tired.

'Miss? Ma'am. Hello? Excuse me. Hello! Wake up!'

I groggily come to, slumped diagonally over the seats of a taxi, my legs splayed in a way that reminds me of the Wicked Witch of the West's striped socks when she is found flattened by a house.

'Er . . . Wha—? Where . . . where am I?'

'Your home, I hope to God. Your friend gave me your address and promised you wouldn't puke. This is your house, right?' The driver seems concerned. When late-shift taxi drivers, who arguably have to deal with the messiest, darkest sides of humanity on a nightly basis, appear to be worried about you, it is not a good sign.

'Yes,' I say blearily, before I look out the window to make sure that it is, in fact, my house. 'Yes, this is me . . .' I struggle to put myself aright, fumbling through my purse.

'Ah . . . Your friend left you some cab fare. It's . . . in your shirt.'

I look down. Indeed it is. There is a crisp, folded £20 note slotted into my cleavage. Bless Julian's cotton socks.

I manage to open the front door after about five minutes. I was beginning to freak out, thinking that I had broken or irreparably bent my key, before realizing I was using the set to my mum's flat. I didn't think I would be so affected by only four or five cocktails. Maybe it was six. Oh, and that bottle of champagne we shared on the way over. And the cider I had while putting on my makeup. All on an empty stomach. It's for the best I haven't found Scott tonight.

I crawl into bed, hating myself. My laptop, resting against the pillow next to me, is still playing my getting-ready-to-go-out playlist; it is horribly jarring. I search for something soothing. Something I haven't listened to before. Mum gave me a meditation disk once. I select Paul McKenna's *Change Your Life In Seven Days*, 'A mind-programming technique that will help you to feel happier in yourself, focus on success, release your true potential and create more abundance in your life'. I fall asleep, lulled by a soothing voice telling me that when I awake, it will be with an inner sense of calm.

The Guilt Gremlin

DO NOT LISTEN TO THIS EYES-CLOSED PROCESS WHILE DRIVING OR OPERATING MACHINERY; ONLY LISTEN WHEN YOU CAN SAFELY RELAX COMPLETELY.

Urgggh. My iTunes has been set to Repeat. The calming meditation was sporadically interrupted all night by a violently shouted beginning set to tinny A-I-robot music. Even in my passed-out state, I have had very strange dreams. I can't remember the particulars, but the lingering image I have when I awake is of the Michelin Man operating on my uterus, which in my dreamscape world is made up of automobile tubing.

I hastily mute my computer, noting bitterly that it is only 10 a.m. After a night like last night, this is ridiculous-o'clock.

Still, maybe it was worth it, perhaps McKenna has started to subconsciously heal the self-directed bile I can feel rising up inside me now. Wait. That is not emotional bile, but actual bile. Running to the toilet, I manage to lift the lid just in time before I gag, a thin trickle of acidic liquid emerging from my mouth to pool, disconsolately orange, in the watery basin. I barely ate yesterday and my body is so dehydrated that I can't muster up the essential fluid to eject the ethanol I poisoned myself with last night. I am twenty-five years old in six weeks and I can't even puke properly.

Back in bed, the full horror of this mess I have got myself into hits me again. I have been such an enormous dick. I don't even know where to start reprimanding myself. It's a new low.

I seem to be using that expression a lot recently.

The thought of finding Scott and opening up to him, sober, terrifies me. But I also start to think that really, he is not the person I owe an apology to, or at least he is not the first in line. Beardy is awful. I saw the signs and ignored them; low self-esteem and an appreciation for superficial characteristics created a bubble around him I dared not penetrate. I placed more value on a beard than on myself and others. Not that there was anything I could have done, exactly, to prevent what he attempted with Alice. But at least I wouldn't have blindly, unquestioningly followed him, dashing other loyalties in the process.

I take a long bath, retch again, get dressed and feel ready to eat something. I breakfast on runny poached eggs with wholemeal toast spread with horseradish, cottage cheese and a dash of Tabasco. It sounds disgusting but is my hangover cure-all (particularly when combined with a Bloody Mary, but I am swearing off alcohol for the next eight hours). It is early afternoon, an acceptable time to ring Gary and hope that he will pick up. He does, on the third try. The guilt gremlin pressing on my chest outweighs my normal concerns about phone-harassment protocol.

'Georgie? God, how did it go?' he says groggily.

'Gary. I want to thank you for telling me last night and helping me, you could have just blanked me, I couldn't have even blamed you for it—'

'What happened? Give me the edited version; I have company.'

'The edited version is that nothing happened. I was too drunk and ended up going home. The thing is . . . I've been thinking this morning about talking to Alice first. I don't know if she will want to hear it, but she is the real victim here and I want to see that she is all right and just say how terrible I feel about . . .'

There is a long pause. I can hear Gary sitting up and lighting a cigarette.

'Love, I dunno about that. You don't even really know her. Is this for your benefit or for hers?'

I had been mulling that one over. In much the same way that a well-meant AA apology might come as an unwanted intrusion in someone else's life, stirring up shit they prefer to ignore, I don't know if it is appropriate to infringe. Is what I am after forgiveness? A pat on the back for finally opening my eyes? Not really. If she hates me for ever, I will understand. I just want the chance to extend my sympathy and explain. I say all this to Gary, brokenly.

'Bloody hell. I don't know what to say. I do know that she's been working part-time in a café on Upper Street while she waits for Tim's solo career to take off. The Violet Bakery, or something. If you go, don't say I sent you. I have enough of a reputation as a gossip as it is.'

'Thanks so much. I appreciate this—' Gary hangs up before I can finish the heartfelt speech I had prepared. I steel myself for a similar reaction from Alice.

There is no Violet Bakery, but having walked down the whole of Upper Street to Angel, I pass The Orchid Bakery, which is a likely bet. Entering, I immediately see Alice behind the counter, preparing a bag of goodies for a mother pushing a pram. Weirdly, I am floored, not expecting to actually find her there. I hesitate in the doorway. She finishes serving her customer and turns around with a friendly smile in my direction. It vanishes when she recognizes me.

'Alice—'

'Georgie. What would you like?' A fake, professional smile is set on her full lips.

'I . . . can I talk to you, for a minute?'

'I'm working. You need to order, to talk to me.' The café is almost entirely empty. If I am going to do this, now is the time.

'Ok . . . I'll have this,' I set a bottle of orange juice on the counter. I could really do with a strong coffee, but don't want to speak to her back as she prepares it. 'Alice, I just want to say that I am so, so sorry. I just recently found out what happened with Leo – what Leo did. I feel awful about it. I know that stalking you where you work is not the way to go about things, but I just wanted to say that it's terrible and I didn't know and that I am disgusted with myself for having sided with him. And I hope you are all right.'

She rings up my purchase, stony-faced.

'That's £3.50.'

'Right . . . here you go. I'm so sorry . . .' Silence. 'I'll just go then. I . . . I wish you the best.'

I walk out the door, feeling her eyes boring into my back. I mindlessly follow my footsteps eastwards in the biting winter air, absorbing the reception of my apology. I leadenly prepare myself for the likelihood that Scott's reaction will be exactly the same, if not worse. I'm not sure if I have the strength to do it all over again immediately. And yet, if she mentions this to him, it will be even stranger if I turn up at The Newt with a cowardly time-lapse of several days.

Better to get it all over with in one fell swoop. The forty-minute walk that brings me to the door of the pub has cleared my head; I am determined.

Swinging open the door, I march straight up to the till. Joy appears from the other side of the bar, exactly the last person in the world I want to see. By the expression on her face, the feeling is mutual.

'What do you want?' Joy leans aggressively on the counter-top, eyes flashing. I cringe, before reasserting myself. After all, if it wasn't for her manipulation, I might have missed the entire Alice/Scott embrace, which I have since come to realize was not what I had thought I'd seen.

'Is Scott here? I need to speak to him.'

'He isn't here,' Joy says coldly. 'And he isn't available for you, ever.'

Crushing, but not unexpected. Short of camping out outside the pub, there is nothing I can do but go home.

My reputation as a hardened stalker probably already beyond my control, after going back to mine, making dinner and drinking a few stiff whiskeys I decide that the only option available to me is to stake out the pub. This isn't quite as creepy as it sounds – it being too cold to wait outside for hours, I rang an increasingly reluctant Gary to ask him to do some sleuthing on my behalf as to when Scott will be home. Actually, that may be creepier, but nevertheless, I receive a text around 11 p.m. with the brief missive, 'Between 12.30 and 1 a.m. You owe me big.'

I arrive at 12.15, hiding in the bushes down the road until I see Joy and Craig close up and leave. When they are out of sight, I emerge from my spy-hole, walk over and resolutely stand in front of the door, not wanting to startle him by lurking in the darkness. I practise my little speech, becoming more of a nervous wreck with every passing minute. The reservations that would have prevented any rational person from attempting this in the first place surface with a vengeance.

What the hell am I doing? What will I say? Will he really appreciate being accosted in the early hours by a girl he hasn't even kissed, who he hasn't seen for weeks and moreover thinks of, quite rightly, as an emotionally retarded fool at best, immoral bitch at worst? Will Alice have warned him I might turn up? Did Joy? What might they have said? What do I think could possibly happen?

If this was a rom-com, he would accept the pathetic explanations from the quirky girl misguided by her insecurities, take her upstairs and make mad, passionate love to her by way of happily-ever-after. In reality, if I even succeed in making him take the time to hear me out, he will probably nod, tell me to leave, open the door of the pub and walk directly upstairs to bed. I am an idiot.

I've been outside for an hour now. Shivering madly, I sit down on the pavement to light a fag and decide to give myself five minutes to think this over logically and then do something socially appropriate, in the daylight hours, like call him. As I take a few deep, desperate puffs, a coughing fit strikes me. I try to smother it in the armpit of my coat with some success before putting my head in my hands and growling a low, gravelly groan of repentance.

'Eh, excuse me? Are you all right?'

My head whips up. Wrapped up in my tortured navel-gazing, I had not heard footsteps approaching; in the dimness, Scott hasn't recognized me and probably thinks I am just some wasted girl who has chosen his doorstep to recover. He is standing still, a metre away from me, his messy barnet the colour of Stroopwafel in the weak light. His hair has always reminded me of my favourite carbs. I should have known it was love from the start.

'Scott! I . . . um . . . it's Georgie,' I say, scrambling up.

Scott's expression of mildly disapproving concern shifts to one I hesitate to analyse, but which definitely holds no trace of concern.

'Who are you?' a second voice calls out assertively in cut-glass tones.

There is a petite, pretty redheaded girl just behind him, looking none too pleased to find a female interloper crouched in front of what is possibly, probably her lover's home. How could the risk of interrupting him on a date not even have occurred to me?

'Er . . .' The unexpected addition completely throws me for a loop. They are both staring at me as I fail to add to this brilliant opener, my mouth hanging open in a panic. I am such a fool. Obviously, a grovelling apology is still in order, but this manner of going about it reeks of desperation.

'This is Georgie, a former employee. I'm not sure what she's doing here.'

I wince.

'Scott, can I . . . speak with you? Privately.'

Silence, but for the barely muffled laughter of his companion.

'Please?'

Though I've tried to contain myself, my voice cracks and I fight back tears, with little success. This show of feminine weakness, however pathetic, does have the effect of loosening the expression of rigid displeasure from Scott's face. He turns to the girl, whispers something in her ear and curtly declares that I have five minutes. He unlocks the door, letting her pass through before shutting it behind him. He turns towards me, leaning against his pub, arms folded. Evidently this conversation is to take place outside in the cold. I had noticed the girl, whoever she is, had walked assuredly over to the stairs that lead to his bedroom. Clearly this is not just some one-night stand. I have never felt so small in my life.

'I . . . just w-wanted to say . . .'

I lapse into silence, filled with the horrible conviction that if I utter another word I will be carried away in a flood of self-indulgent sobs.

'Well? Georgie, what the hell are you doing here? If you're so upset about – whatever it is that's bothering you, you should really be leaning on your boyfriend,' Scott spits out.

Weirdly, his bitter mention of Leo gives me a surge of optimism. If he really didn't care for me at all, surely the thought of Leo as my boyfriend wouldn't upset him? It is also possible that he just really, really hates the man who attacked his best friend and consequently all those associated with him. I place all my hopes in the former interpretation and pull myself together.

'Scott . . . I just want to apologize. I found out from Gary last night what really happened between Leo and Alice. I didn't know. When I came downstairs, after we . . .'

Silence.

'After you helped me with my nose and I maybe, probably wrongly, expected something to – and I saw you and Alice together and Joy said you were in love with her, that you were kissing her – I just sort of lost it. Not that that excuses my behaviour; I didn't ask, or look hard enough or think beyond my own pride. Basically I've just behaved like a complete and utter twat and I want to say sorry for being a coward. I apologized to Alice. Maybe it was the wrong thing to do, but I felt

357

so awful about everything and that it was the very, very least I could do because I really hope that she's all right. I feel like such a tosser. I just – wanted you to know that.'

'Okay.'

I had relayed this un-pretty speech to his feet and now, looking into his eyes, am unable to read them. His shoes again capture my attention. Good, solid, brown leather workman's boots, worn-in and masculine. Comforting. Even his footwear is breaking my heart.

'That's it, really . . .' I don't recognize the soft, broken whisper coming out of my mouth. 'Except to say that I hope, I hope that whatever, however little you think of me, it isn't as little as that. I hope you might think of me fondly someday, unrelated to all this . . . horrible mess . . . because I think of you. Fondly. A lot.'

Gulping, I find the courage to look at his face again. I search for some sign, some micro-expression of sympathy or compassion that might relieve me from this hell of my own making. He just looks tired.

'Thanks for letting me know. Go home, Georgie.'

It is the second time in less than two weeks that I have heard those words coming from a man, but the first time that it really hurts.

Turbans Aren't Deranged

April 15th, London Fields

Birthdays are a weird time. Either you enforce a celebration of your own existence on your mates or you choose to be anti-social and go it alone. The latter option may seem eminently sensible when considering the pressure to have a Great Night but will lead to a spiral of depression if no one picks up on your secret desire for a surprise party. (They won't. This only ever happens in sitcoms.)

Birthdays are a barometer for how well you are succeeding in life combined with an annual reminder of how little time remains to catch up on your inevitable failures. When I was twelve, the thought of turning twenty-five was thrilling. At that point I would no doubt have completed my transformation from Ugly Duckling to Glorious Swan and be travelling the world as an International Woman Of Mystery, collecting as many ex-husbands and diamonds as Elizabeth Taylor. Here I am, a quarter of a century old, a student with no fine jewellery to speak of, living in the same city I always have, without even one divorce under my belt. Yet, somehow, I am serene in the face of my future, strangely assured that things will be all right in the end.

Maybe it is because I am working towards a goal, my creative energies put to good use without the emotional distractions of a relationship. I am thinking of myself, doing what I want to do, caring for my future. The liberating thing about losing something you think you need is that you realize how little you really need at all. That want can be left unsatisfied yet you can still be at peace. That the bittersweet pleasure of life lies not in the having but in the trying. In the words of Churchill, you Keep Buggering On.

The past few weeks have been a maddening tussle between conflicting emotions as my final collection took shape. When things were going smoothly, I felt more zen than I ever have in my life, happily working until 3 a.m. Of course, when mistakes made at 3 a.m. required 6 a.m. unpicking sessions, I was stuck in an exhausted hell. Painful treks to obscure boroughs were necessary to source hardware that had not arrived on schedule and miscommunication with printers resulted in off-tone dye-jobs. I made peace with the conclusion that to get the results that I really wanted in the time that remained, I had to do almost everything myself.

At times, I was left holding my face metaphorically (sometimes literally) in the manner of Munch's *Scream*. Averaging four hours' sleep a night, with everything taking twice as long as anticipated, the days passed in strained concentration broken up with many, many coffee and cigarette breaks. This led to a brand-new lightning-bolt stain on my front teeth (marking me for magical greatness?) as well as a tubercular cough. I somehow avoided a nervous breakdown. In fact, I felt weirdly invigorated.

Days before my final six looks were due, on the phone to my mother during one of my harried pauses, I outlined the fuck-ups that had already occurred and those I knew were to come. It was a moment of particularly shattered morale and Mum asked me a question that in times of stress and self-doubt, I had been asking myself.

'Darling, if you hate it so much, why are you doing this for your career?'

'I don't hate it. I'm just tired.'

'You sound like you hate it.'

'It's not that I hate the work, I love it, I just hate doing anything for sixteen hours a day,' I said, leaving out that I was averaging twenty hours a day due to my poor organization. Mum is not sympathetic to what she has dubbed for years my 'chronic unmanageability', though she spent her own youth partying with one crafty eye out for a husband. I add defensively, 'Besides, I can't think of anything I would prefer doing. I just needed to vent to someone.'

'Well, at least you have that Leo fellow as your boyfriend. You are so modest. I had no idea he was doing so well. Pin him down and then you won't have to bother working after your degree,' Mum said, sounding gleeful for the first time in what may have been years.

As I didn't want to prove her theory about my dire taste in men right, I had elected not to tell her about any change in my love life. I knew it would eventually come back to bite me in the arse. Why was she suddenly a struggling musician's greatest fan? Something was not right with this situation.

Mum misinterpreted the quiet on my end of the line as qualms about being a kept woman and added generously,

'Or carry on working, if you really want to! Leo will be a great source for contacts now that he's on television and you'll have some financial and emotional support from someone other than me. That's all I've ever hoped for you.'

I had no idea what she was on about and had never heard her sound so pleased with me. Typically, when she is happy with my performance as her only child, it is a happiness based on omissions and white lies spun to avoid further lecturing. This time was to be no different; her pride misplaced in a falsehood. I had to burst her bubble in case she was already designing wedding invitations.

'What are you talking about? Leo was on telly? How do you even know what he looks like?'

'Your generation isn't the only one gifted with the ability of online stalking, darling. You shut me out so often, at times it's the only way I can feel close to you. I've had a burner Facebook account for years. And what do you mean? He's on that new talent show, *Rock Rebel* or whatever it's called.'

'Whaaaat?

'You don't know?'

A judgemental silence bore down on me as I tried to think of a way to explain the situation without getting caught in my web of lies. I never suspected that Beardy would have enough success, or tabloid infamy, that my bourgeois mother would hear of him and approve of our now fictitious relationship.

'Either you have not made him engage in a real relationship with you, Georgie, or the television production company is making him hide you for ratings.'

I tried not to laugh at this, still reeling from Beardy's blatant fame-whoring. Signing up for a reality contest, when I was with him, would have been the last thing I ever imagined him doing. He was far too pretentious, too willing to declare himself an 'artist', too concerned with being 'real', whatever the hell that even means. Clearly, the squiggle in a rectangle band he joined didn't work out. Knowing now that he never wrote any of Tin Can Bang's repertoire, I guess it didn't take long before doing the rounds as a simple guitarist-for-hire made him hungry enough to sell out. On this *Rock Rebel* show, no less, which is exactly the sort of thing he used to deride.

'He's doing super-well,' Mum said, adding with an edge, 'Such a handsome boy.'

'I broke up with him, Mum, months ago. I just didn't tell you because I thought you would be less concerned about me if you thought I had "pinned down a man", to use your charming expression.'

I held my mobile an arm's length away from my ear but could still hear her shouting down the phone. After giving her two minutes to rant, I interrupted her protestations.

'I don't want a man I have to pin down, I want a partnership of equals with someone who thinks I'm fantastic. Someone who I think is fantastic. I don't need some big swinging dick around to be happy. I am happy. Things will work out for me just fine.'

'Georgie, you know I just want you to be happy and supported! But why did you have to end it just before his career took off? That's such bad timing. Maybe you should give him a friendly call to say hello—'

'No, Mum, no. I didn't want to tell you this, but I found out after we'd broken up that he had sexually assaulted someone I know.'

A reflective pause ensued.

'Well, we all have our flaws. Maybe he just has too much testosterone?'

As justifications went, it was a doozy. Unbelievable.

'I'm hanging up now, Mum!'

'Good luck with your deadline, darling! Give some thought to what I said!'

The thought of ever speaking to Beardy again made my stomach turn. I concentrated on the essentials, i.e. my final collection, and managed to hand in everything on time. It is now the Easter holidays. I don't know yet if I will make it into the final show, but I am satisfied that I did my best and have got a head start on the portfolio work that will make up the last term's project.

'Georgie! It's been ages, how are you?' Sarah calls out.

'Happy birthday, so sorry we're late!' Rose says.

They saunter across the park to where I am sitting on a picnic blanket with a cake and a bottle of wine. I have decided to keep the celebrations simple: food on a sunshiny day, followed by drinks with Julian and Theo and maybe a little dance somewhere afterwards.

'Thank you! But what are you guys wearing, the theme is *Sunset Boulevard*! Crazy old diva women who refuse to let go of youth!' I squawk. Just because I am having a chilled birthday doesn't mean I can't take the opportunity to wear a costume.

They are wearing stylish, flattering outfits. The dress code

I had chosen: 'We Didn't Need Dialogue. We Had Faces!' was apparently too vague a visual reference. I am wearing a floor-length, mega-shoulder-padded zebra-stripe dress with mad-art-teacher necklaces, cat-eye sunglasses and an orange turban. They are in tight jeans, Swedish Hasbeens and leather jackets.

'I'm so sorry, Georgie! I'm staying at Tim's tonight and we're having dinner with the fam tomorrow, I can't turn up looking deranged,' Rose apologizes. In a weird twist of fate abetted by stalking, she ignored my pleading and managed to track down and seduce Tim, Alice's brother. I am pretty sure she has kept me on the D-low. I am her secret friend. It is like being seven years old all over again.

'Turbans aren't deranged, they're fabulous!' I swish my head, unconcerned. 'What's your excuse, Sarah?'

'Dude, I am single and ready to mingle! Mad Old Woman is not the look I am going for. But I did bring you champagne!' She whips a bottle out of her bag. Excellent.

'Amazing! Let's crack that baby open.'

'You look great, Georgie, really healthy,' says Rose, handing me her gift.

'Thanks! After my lifelong exercise hiatus I started running.'

Though I have been going four times a week for the past few months, the thing about exercise is you really need to diet alongside it to lose weight. I've toned up but if anything I am a little bigger than before as my musculature has expanded. I feel fit, healthy and energetic. The breaks outside, away from the studio, have been essential for my mental state. I have even given some thought to giving up smoking. Just thought, mind.

'Aww, Rose! *The Big Penis Book* from Taschen. Just what I have always wanted!' We flip through the pages as Sarah pours three glasses of champagne. 'Good Lord, look at that!'

'It's a bit objectifying, but to hell with it,' Rose says.

'Oh, let them be objectified for once. The Male Gaze isn't so bad as long as there is a Female Gaze to counteract it. That's the annoying thing – men make no effort! Now that Alistair and I have broken up I really notice it. I walk around and think, "Look at you! I don't want to fuck any of you!" And yet men still get manage to get laid.'

'I know what you mean. I definitely objectify men, I just have so little opportunity to do so that I forget how pleasurable it is,' I say, eyeing up a particularly extraordinary phallus.

'Sarah! You can't really think objectification is the answer,' Rose protests, conveniently forgetting that her gift started this discussion.

'Sure I do! We need something to get the juices going. No one ever came thinking, "Oh God! I – I respect your thoughtful . . . yet hard-line attitude to corporate tax evasion! So! Much! Right! Now!"' Sarah giggles uproariously. One of the things I love about her is that she is never afraid to laugh at her own jokes.

'Well, obviously no one ever comes thinking about taxes.'

'You know what I mean – it doesn't need to be about love though, either. Taking pleasure in a body doesn't mean that it is degrading. With hindsight, I realize things with Alistair were all about sex. If I hadn't thought it meant more, maybe I would have made different decisions.'

I give Sarah a sympathetic squeeze on the shoulder. The showdown with Henry was bitter and brutal. Sarah tried to make it work with Alistair afterwards, but too much heart-ache had tainted it. In the end, she decided what she really wanted was to be alone for a while.

'It's fine, Georgie! I needed to go through that. It's still hard, sometimes, but I'm glad to be free.' Sarah flips the page of the book and raises an eyebrow, impressed. 'But back to my argument. Look, you can't help taking pleasure in an image. If I were a man, I might be called misogynist. I mean, if I look at a delightfully turned out cake, I'll fantasize about consuming it, devour it ravenously and afterwards feel a bit disgusted with myself.'

'Women are not cake!' Rose is getting upset.

'I know that! I am not saying women are! What I am saying is that if cake had feelings, a mother, a painful childhood and complex body-image issues, in a fit of gluttony I'd still want to come on cake's face.'

Sarah takes a glug of her champagne and smiles like a Cheshire Cat.

I personally think that sexual objectification is impossible to avoid. As long as there is sex, there will be objectification. Unless humans evolve to a point where we start self–propagating. Even then, if we still have a libido, the situation will just turn into a frenzy of narcissistic masturbation. No one will ever leave the house and the welfare state will be overwhelmed.

'Ridiculous.' Rose cuts herself a slice of cake and takes a bite. 'Mmm, delicious.'

'We will be equal when everyone can look at a naked photo of a woman and enjoy it, even sexually, but not make assumptions about her qualities or essential value as a human being. As we do with men.' Sarah finishes, reaching for the champagne bottle.

'Look, guys, let's just all agree that we like eating cake while looking at dicks. I propose a birthday toast,' I say, 'to a wonderful year, spent objectifying, or not, the ones we love, depending on how we define the term. And lots of cake!'

'Hear, hear!' Sarah raises her glass.

'To cake!' Rose declares.

We all tuck in, bathed in spring sunshine.

Epilogue

It is the 30th of May, the day of the show – and I am oddly calm. Though I still have niggling doubts over decisions most consumers would never notice – the finishing on a hemline, the wrong bloody buttons for a dress – I have emotionally exhausted myself with the collection to the extent that I no longer care how it will be received. Like a message in a bottle, addressed to no one in particular, I want to rid myself of it, fling it out into the world. I am 'detached with love', to use an expression my mother uses when defending a lack of feeling in situations that would suggest she is sociopathic. Even the thought of my parents and friends in the audience leaves me strangely unaffected. Maybe this preternatural calm is actually nerves.

Backstage the mood is buoyant or hysterical, depending

on how prepared the other students feel they are. We congratulate each other, oohing and ahing over the collections of those in our cliques; the less subtle of us sniff or raise an eyebrow at the aesthetic of the unfavoured, murmuring a cruel 'My gosh, what a brave choice in cut!' or 'I always feel duchesse satin is too bridesmaid, but she nearly gets away with it' *sotto voce*. Personally, though I genuinely like the majority of my classmates, I have always tried to keep out of these dramas. I get on with things politely, head down, dressing my models with care.

My work is a luxurious swirl of draped silks and embroidered crêpe de Chine contrasted with tailored leather pieces in muted Gothic tones, recalling the dramas of Theda Bara. Vintage elegance with a minimalist edge, the strong silhouettes have a touch of nineties Calvin Klein. I am satisfied that I have created a collection with the powerful, modern femininity that I had envisioned.

I take a deep breath and move to the side of the catwalk entrance as my girls line up, ready to stride out. From this angle, I can see a few faces in the audience, but the majority of the guests are hidden from view. Between the beat of my heart and the beat of the music, it is impossible to judge an initial response, good or bad. The models strut elegantly to fast-paced electronic music; my long year's work unleashed into the world for four whole minutes that pass in the blink of an eye. I duck my head out afterwards, give a wave, seeing nothing but bright lights; come back in, shaking. I am afraid that I might burst into tears with the weight of this off my shoulders. I am not so impervious to the emotion of the day after all.

After thanking the girls, I undress them and make a start on repacking my collection. Heartfelt congratulations and cheap red wine are shared with the other students. I succumb to the large table of sandwiches. I am halfway through stuffing a second roast chicken, avocado and salsa wrap into my mouth when I feel a tap on my shoulder. I turn around, one cheek bulging.

'Hello,' Scott smiles lopsidedly.

My eyes widen in shock. I nearly splutter bits of poultry all over his shirt. Chewing my mouthful as rapidly as I can without choking, I swallow, throat dry as a bone. After an excruciatingly slow thirty seconds during which I lose the ability to speak, I am finally able to reply with a weak, 'Hey'.

Scott says nothing, shuffling from side to side, looking from my face to the floor and back again. My chest constricts with confusion, hope and anxiety. What the hell is he doing here, I think. My heart is leapfrogging in the prolonged silence. He must be here for me. Why else would he be here?

As the silence and shuffling continues, I start to doubt myself. Oh God, maybe it's something to do with that little redheaded girl he was with when I cornered him at his pub. Maybe she works here. If that is the case, I hope she's doing something menial.

Scott clears his throat. I want to reach out and brush back a lock of his tumbling hair but stop myself. The awkwardness between us is palpable, painful. This is not at all how I had envisioned a grand reunion.

'Your collection was beautiful. I want to congratulate you.'

I forgot how his accent makes me melt.

'Thank you very much. That's very kind. I appreciate that,' I say formally before blurting out, 'What are you doing here?'

'I took the ticket you gave to Gary. I hope you don't mind. You see, I want to tell you something.'

'You want to tell me what?'

I am shocked by the calmness of my voice. This is it. I am sure of it. Come on, man! Speak! I stare intensely at him. His eyes draw me in like a magnet but his own gaze keeps slipping away. I feel every particle in my body buzzing with longing and panic; I fear that I might spontaneously combust from impatience, fear and delight. Like in *Repo Man*. It happens sometimes. People just explode. Natural causes.

'I just want to say congratulations.' Scott clears his throat again.

I continue to stare at him expectantly, waiting for him to continue, ideally to declare his love. He looks down at the floor again.

Seriously? Is this it? He just wants to say hi and fuck off out of my life again? I think with irrational anger. At least when I thought that he hated me, I could convince myself that it was because he still cared. This is bullshit.

'Oh . . . You already said that. But thanks.'

Silence. He looks up searchingly; our eyes connect. He opens his mouth to say something; shuts it again. I try to wipe the disappointment off my face; nothing more appears to be forthcoming.

'Well, it was nice to see you again.' I can't believe this is it. My voice wobbles.

Scott clears his throat for the third time.

'I also want to say . . . that I think of you. Fondly. A lot.'

The remains of my chicken wrap drop to the floor. I smile brilliantly.

'You do?'

'I do.'

Taking my beaming smile as the encouragement it is, Scott takes me by the shoulders and pulls me towards him. His eyes are laughing in that way of his that never fails to touch my heart; his smell is both familiar and intoxicating. A bubble of relief, exhilaration and pure happiness bursts inside of me. Moving his hands to stroke my hair and cradle my face, he slowly leans in to kiss me. I have to stop myself from grinning so widely. At first it is soft, uncertain, with a hesitant tenderness. As his strong arms clasp me closer to him, the kiss deepens and an electric shock goes through all the nerves in my body. I melt into him, suspended in a timeless urgency.

Acknowledgements

I would like to thank:

My most brilliant of mothers and kindest of fathers, who have always been a source of endless love and support.

My amazing grandparents, who are so interesting and interested in the world. I hope I am always so curious. Sadly, this is the only page you are allowed to read.

My darling sisters Anna and Leila, who make me laugh everyday I am with them.

My agent Becky Thomas, for seeing potential in me. Without her hard work this exciting new chapter in my life would not have been possible.

My editor Katie Gordon, who has cleverly cut the worst of my humorous excesses and ensured there was always enough heart in *Low Expectations*.

The lovely and talented Golan, Fyodor, Natalie, Gabby and Basil, for helping with the promotion process and just being all-around excellent company.

And last but not least the fun, funny and fabulous women whose lives I have shamelessly pilfered for material. Hanako, Iz, Maggie, Ollie, Deeba, Jane, Kat, Eve, Josephine and Marie-Anna, I love you girls!